Shore

The
Property
of a Lady

ELIZABETH ADLER

**Delacorte
Press**

Published by
Delacorte Press
Bantam Doubleday Dell Publishing Group, Inc.
666 Fifth Avenue
New York, New York 10103

This book was first published in Great Britain by
Hodder & Stoughton Ltd.

The trademark Delacorte Press® is registered in the U.S. Patent
and Trademark Office.

Library of Congress Cataloging-in-Publication Data

Adler, Elizabeth (Elizabeth A.)
     The property of a lady / Elizabeth Adler.
          p.   cm.
     ISBN 0-385-30123-5 : $19.95 ($24.95 Can)
     I. Title.
PR6051.D56P76   1991
823'.914—dc20   90-19578
                                                     CIP

Manufactured in the United States of America
February 1991

10 9 8 7 6 5 4 3 2 1

*For my husband Richard and
my daughter Anabelle
with love*

PART
1

Prologue

Bangkok

The girl stepping from the air-conditioned taxi outside the Oriental Hotel was tall, with long, polished brown legs, glossy black hair that swung around her shoulders, and a face that was an elegant mix of the East and the West. Despite the blazing heat and humidity, she looked cool in an expensive linen dress and broad-brimmed hat.

She sauntered past the sparkling fountain and the quartet playing chamber music in the lobby toward the arcade of shops at the back of the hotel.

"My sister left a parcel here," she explained to the assistant in the antique shop. "She asked me to pick it up for her."

Carrying the bag emblazoned with the name Jim Thompson Silk Shop, she strolled back along the arcade to the beautiful orchid-laden terrace overlooking the Chao Phraya River, where she ordered tea. With the bag on the floor beside her she sipped the tea unhurriedly, watching the busy floating traffic. Half an hour later she left the terrace, descended the steps to the river, and took a water taxi to the downtown area.

She walked quickly now, away from the river. After hailing another taxi, she asked to be taken to the Hotel Dusit Thanai.

In the ladies' powder room, she changed into a plain white T-shirt and jeans, folded her smart black linen dress carefully, and placed it in the bag. She pulled her smooth hair into a ponytail, secured it with a white elastic band, and added a brighter lipstick. As she left the hotel by the back door, she covered her eyes with an expensive pair of Ray-Bans—not the cheap copies sold at every street corner in Bangkok—and took another cab to the Patpong Road.

The cab driver grinned slyly at her through his mirror. He knew all about Patpong, the honky-tonk area of red-light bars, seedy clubs, massage parlors, and sex shops, and he figured he knew what her trade was. After ignoring his attempts at conversation, she paid him off with a modest tip and threaded her way expertly through the maze of littered alleys. She paused outside a narrow gray building squashed among a hundred others on a side street, checking the name on a small, stained business card pinned to a board with a tack. Satisfied, she hurried past the clinic offering treatment for VD and other sexual "malaises" to the second floor, where she pressed the entry phone, waited for a reply, and then gave her name quietly. The door opened to her touch and she slid inside, closing it firmly behind her.

She was in a dark, narrow passageway smelling faintly of urine and chemicals, at the end of which was a second door. Unhesitatingly she walked the long corridor and pushed it open.

A small, high-intensity lamp blazed onto the surface of a shabby desk, leaving the man sitting behind it in half shadow, but she could see that he was immense, a grotesque caricature of a human shape. He lifted his head from the small pile of glittering stones he was studying and the light caught his face suddenly. "Come in, take a seat," he said.

Her lips curled in revulsion as she sat opposite him. His features were porcine. The small eyes, lost in their folds of flesh, rippled over her like sunken gray pebbles. His accent was guttural and his tone rough as he said to her, "I already told you: You are wasting your time."

She pulled a small twist of black tissue paper from the folds of bright Thai silk in the bag she was carrying and held it out to him. "I think not, Mr. Abyss," she replied, watching as he unwrapped it quickly, noting his sharp intake of breath as he saw what it contained.

He shot a speculative glance in her direction, then pulled the high-intensity lamp closer. Holding the jeweler's loupe to his right eye, he turned the gem in his fat, hairy fingers like a spider clutching a pretty butterfly. After a few minutes he removed the loupe and placed the stone on the square of black velvet in front of him. He leaned back in his battered leather armchair, folding his hands across his immense stomach. Her blue, almond-shaped eyes met his in the silence.

Finally he spoke. "There is only one emerald of this size and quality anywhere in the world. And that has been missing for more than seventy years. May I ask how it came into your possession?"

She shrugged. "You may not. Let us just say I am not working alone. My partners are very interested in your decision."

Silence fell again as he surveyed first her and then the giant emerald lying between them.

"This is an exquisitely cut stone," he said at last. "There is nothing I can do to improve on the artistry of the original cutter. So? What exactly do you want from me?"

Leaning forward, she touched the stone with a long red-enameled nail and said, "I want you to cut it into two equal pieces. Two emeralds instead of one."

She thought she saw a glimpse of something like emotion in his leaden eyes: She had caught him off guard, touched a responsive chord in him somewhere.

"Cut a stone like this? Are you crazy?" He reached into a drawer and pulled out a bottle of whiskey and a small, stained glass. He lifted the bottle inquiringly and she shook her head, watching as he filled his glass to the brim and tossed it back. He refilled it quickly and this time she noticed that his hand trembled as he drained the glass. That tremor was the reason Abyss, the master gem cutter, now occupied a single room in a sleazy back street in Bangkok instead of the grand suite of offices in Paris that had been his twenty years ago. A gem cutter with an unsure hand was worthless. And yet there was no one else who could do what she asked. It was a risk that had been discussed at length and one they were prepared to take.

"I know this emerald," he said, turning the gem again in his fat fingers. "It has not been seen in Europe since the great tiara was sent to Cartier in Paris for redesigning eighty years ago. An emerald of ninety carats, of such perfection . . . it is unique."

"Exactly. It is unique and therefore easily identifiable. We are asking you to give us *two* emeralds, Mr. Abyss, so that it will be impossible for it to be identified positively. And yet the value of each stone will still be in the millions."

A flicker of greed darted through his pebble eyes. He turned the stone this way and that under the light, examining it intently through the magnifying loupe.

She watched, tense as a coiled spring. It meant a lot to her; she was there because he was still the best in the world, the only one who could do the job. "We will pay well," she said softly. "Seven percent."

Their eyes met. "I can guarantee nothing," he told her. "You are aware that emeralds are the most fragile of all the stones. One tap and this valuable jewel might be just crumbs for cheap rings. And after all, the emerald as a whole is worth far more than two halves would ever be."

She smoothed back her already smooth hair, dabbing with a tissue at the rim of sweat along her hairline. There was no air-conditioning and the heat and sour smell of the room were beginning to get to her. She said crisply, "How soon can it be done?"

His eyes disappeared into the fat folds of his face as he smiled at her. "Fifteen percent," he suggested softly.

A chuckle rose from his throat, bubbling into a cough as she stared at him. They had already considered the man in Israel and the other in Amsterdam. Abyss was the only one, their only chance. "Ten percent," she said, pulling the T-shirt from her sticky shoulder blades as she stood up. She stared hard at the trembling hand holding the emerald. "I don't know," she added doubtfully. "Maybe Amsterdam would be better after all. . . ."

"Ten," he agreed quickly.

"You have one month," she told him, picking up her bag.

He gasped. "A month? Impossible. I need to handle the stone, to study it, to consider every point . . . it could take a year. . . ."

"One month and ten percent. That is the deal. Can you do it or not?"

Her red-lacquered nails drummed impatiently on the desk as he stared at her, shocked. Then his eyes disappeared again in a mirthless smile. "Let us just say it will be a challenge," he replied.

She nodded, then turned with her hand on the door. "We are being very generous, Mr. Abyss. There is more where this came from. You could be a very rich man—if you don't get too greedy." Her beautiful almond eyes raked the sweating folds of his face contemptuously. "And if you should—then my partners will know what to do."

Leaving the threat hanging in the air, she closed the door softly behind her. She slid through the dank hallway and down the stairs, and disappeared like a shadow into the milling crowds as Bangkok's nightlife got into full, raucous swing.

Moscow

The gray hair of the man occupying the large office within the Kremlin signified not only his longevity but also his importance within the Politburo. Marshal Sergei Solovsky's ZIL limousine had cruised the central lane reserved for the elite in Moscow's traffic for many years now. Apart, that is, from a long spell in Siberia under Stalin's regime, and two years of banishment to the provinces when Bulganin, mad with lecherous power, had made a play for his wife, a young pretty dancer who had refused his advances. Solovsky had preferred Siberia: The provinces were a bleaker kind of wilderness, reminding him of a childhood he would rather forget.

A catalog advertising a sale of fine jewels to be held by Christie's in Geneva lay on his desk. Alongside it was a note from his brother and enemy, Major-General Boris Solovsky, the head of the KGB. It drew his attention to the item on page fifteen, a large unset emerald of flawless quality. He read the note again.

"Although this stone is slightly less than half the weight of the Ivanoff emerald, there is little doubt that it is part of the same jewel. There is only one in the world of this quality. It is our belief that the emerald has been cut and is now being disposed of in separate lots, though the other half will probably not appear until some time has elapsed. In view of the diamond that came on to the market last year, which was also thought to have come from the same source, we believe that the Ivanoff treasure is being unloaded. At last."

He glanced at the catalog again, checking the provenance. No name was given. The emerald was described only as "The Property of a Lady." Sergei sat back, considering. He knew what his brother was after. It was something more valuable than emeralds and more powerful than the Ivanoff billions amassed in Swiss banks and awaiting a claim of ownership. The KGB wanted whoever was selling those jewels to be found and brought to Russia before someone else got to them first. And Boris Solovsky had a personal interest in the matter.

He ran his hands wearily through his iron-gray hair. The Ivanoff story was etched indelibly into his brain. The past had finally caught up with him, and now, ironically, he was to be the one to set the wheels in motion.

After pressing the intercom switch, he told his secretary to summon his son Valentin Solovsky, the diplomat.

Washington

There were half a dozen men at the confidential meeting in the White House: The President himself, his secretary of state, the secretary of defense, the representative of the Arms Control and Disarmament Agency, the head of the CIA, and the representative of the National Security Council. Copies of the Christie's catalog lay on the oval table in front of them. The President glanced at his secretary of state as they listened carefully to Cal Warrender, a bright, rugged-looking man of thirty-eight and already a power in the National Security Council. Cal trod the delicate path between the White House and the State Department and was well thought of by both. He was considered one of Washington's up-and-coming young men.

Cal was saying that he had been to Christie's in Geneva in the guise of a potential buyer and had taken along an expert from Cartier. He had inspected the emerald and was sure it was part of the Ivanoff treasure.

"Emeralds are notoriously fragile," Cal said, "and to attempt to cut a stone like the Ivanoff emerald was a great risk. They could have ended up with a million shards of worthless green glass. It was cut by a master, and we know there are only three in the world skilled—and confident—enough to do the job. One in Amsterdam, one in Israel, and one in Bangkok. I believe that if you trace that gem cutter, you will find your mysterious seller, the anonymous 'Lady.' "

He handed the President a reproduction of a faded sepia photograph taken in 1909 in St. Petersburg, Russia, pointing out the diamond court tiara centered with the great emerald, telling him that the unsmiling woman wearing the tiara was the beautiful Princess Anouska Ivanoff on the occasion of her wedding.

"The fact remains," the President said crisply, "that whoever the anonymous woman selling the jewel really is, she holds the answer to an issue we have been trying to resolve for over seventy years. And if Russia finds her first, the balance of world power will tilt sharply in their direction. The race is on, gentlemen. Whatever it takes, wherever it leads you . . . find that 'Lady.' "

Düsseldorf

A tall, gaunt, blond-haired man paced the floor of his luxurious office at the Arnhaldt Group of Companies, whose worldwide trade encompassed iron, steel, armaments, mining, and construction. The Arnhaldts had supplied armaments to every war since Napoleon's time, always reemerging, regardless of who won or lost, with even greater wealth and power. Among the world's leading corporations, they were a powerhouse.

Ferdie Arnhaldt stopped his pacing and stared out of the window of his solidly grand office, but he didn't see the traffic snarled thirty storeys below. His mind was on the catalog on his desk, open at page fifteen. He knew that the possessor of that emerald threatened the security and stability of the Arnhaldt empire. And he also knew that if he found "the Lady," his company would be the richest and most powerful in the world. It was all—or nothing. He must find her and deal with her, before the other interested parties got there first.

Geneva

Genie Reese paced the Hotel Richemond's front steps moodily. She was twenty-eight years old, blond, and what her mother had once termed laughingly "almost gorgeous. If only your nose were a little smaller," she used to tease, "and your hair three shades blonder, you would be a movie star." Of course her mother had only been laughing and vivacious on her good days; most of the time she didn't speak to Genie at all. Her mother had died some years ago, but Genie thought maybe now she would have been pleased with the way she had turned out.

As she had grown up, somehow her features had placed themselves in the right proportions: Her pretty nose no longer looked too big for her delicate face and, thanks to the magician at the hairdressing salon, her hair was now the required three shades lighter.

She was tall with great legs and she had "style." But she wasn't the movie star of her mother's dreams; instead Genie was a reporter on American network television.

She usually covered the political beat in Washington. As she waited for her crew to set up, she reflected angrily on the fact that she had been sent to Geneva to report on a trivial event. She had been planning on covering the crucial speech the President was to make to the oil industry in Texas, she had done her research, got her angle . . . and then her producer had told her that because she was a woman, jewels would be right up her alley. He'd sent her rival, Mick Longworth, to Texas and Genie to Geneva, and for once her long-assumed cool had almost cracked and she had fought back tears of anger.

"Who cares what jewels rich women are selling and buying?" she had demanded furiously.

"That's just it," he'd replied with an irritating grin that just made her want to kick him. "The rumor is that Washington is interested, and so is Russia." He had forestalled her next question, saying he didn't know why, but she should get moving and find out.

And so, three days on, there she was in Geneva at Christie's jewelry sale at the Hotel Richemond. Her crew had filmed the customers arriving: discreet, tight-lipped men in business suits studying their catalogs and smart socialites in Chanel suits checking their profiles in the long mirrors and gossiping wickedly.

Now it was all over and they were filming her outside the hotel. The wind blowing fresh from the lake caught her blond hair and she tossed her head impatiently, squinting her blue eyes in the glare of the lights.

"So," she began, "in a surprise move, the emerald—'the Property of a Lady'—was withdrawn from the sale only moments before the auction was to begin. Rumor has it that it was expected to sell for at least seven million, but so much more was offered in a private bid that the seller decided to accept. The sum is said to be over nine million dollars. But why so much? The experts tell us that the stone is flawless, and that itself is unique. But the rumors around town say that it may be one half of the Ivanoff emerald, last seen in the court tiara of Princess Anouska, wife of one of the richest princes in tsarist Russia . . . and let me tell you, there were more than two hundred of those princely families and all of them *seriously* rich. But Prince Michael—*Misha* Ivanoff—was reputed to be even richer than the tsar himself. The story was often told in St. Petersburg that because of the upkeep of the tsar's great estates, his dozens of palaces and his many servants and retainers—as well as all their families—there were times when the tsar was short of a ruble or two. But not Misha Ivanoff. *And* he had a beautiful wife who spent money like water. Anouska Ivanoff was an acquisitive magpie: Anything that glittered she had to have. In her time, she was known as Cartier's biggest customer.

"The story of the emerald in question is that it was given to an earlier Ivanoff prince by a maharaja when he was traveling through India. The prince had taken a dinner service of pure gold to present to his host, from whom he was negotiating the purchase of tracts of land thought to contain valuable minerals and ores. Not wanting to be outdone by his guest, the maharaja plucked an immense emerald from the jeweled headdress of his favorite and most adored"—she paused, laughing—"his favorite and most adored *elephant!* It seems the maharaja loved the creature more than all his many wives, and it was to Prince Ivanoff's credit that he recognized the value of the gift; not merely the precious stone, but the esteem in which the elephant was held. Apparently he was a shrewd businessman and managed to add even more millions to the Ivanoff coffers. There was so much that not even a generation or two of gamblers and wastrel Ivanoffs could dissipate it. However lavishly they spent, there was always more.

"Later, the great emerald was set by Cartier in Paris into the princess's court tiara, a sunburst of twenty-one rays of large diamonds that was so heavy it gave her a headache on the official occasions she had to wear it.

"Did the Ivanoffs live too ostentatiously? It would seem so, because when the day of the revolution dawned, their flamboyant lifestyle and extravagant possessions earmarked the family for a tragic end. The prince was reported burned to death in his country estate. The princess fled with her mother-in-law and two children, six-year-old Alexei and three-year-old Xenia, but they were overtaken in the frozen winter forest. All were reported slain and their bodies left to the wolves. The princess's famous collection of jewels disappeared, among them the great court tiara—and the maharaja's emerald.

"So, was this a little bit of history that was sold at Christie's here in Geneva today? Is the rumor true that several governments were after it? And if so, why? All we know is that the jewel was sold privately, but was it to Russia? Or the U.S.A.? The anonymous seller, indentifiable only as 'a Lady' in this catalog and protected by the secrecy that shrouds the Swiss banking system, is the only person who might be able to unlock the secret to the Ivanoff fortune—a fortune that rumor now says has been safely locked away in the bank vaults, gaining interest each year until it amounts to one of the richest in the world. Billions and billions of dollars, we are told. But whoever knows the answer is not telling. The 'Lady,' who is today reputedly more than nine million dollars richer, is as elusive as the ghost of Princess Anouska Ivanoff. May she rest in peace."

Genie put down her mike wearily. "That's it, guys," she told her crew. "I'll edit it back at the station, but right now I'm going to buy you all a drink. Because I'm tired, and I'm bored with these goddamned jewels and rumors, and I'd rather be anywhere else in the world than right here, right now."

Maryland

The old lady imprisoned in her large chair by the window reached a fragile, blue-veined hand to the table beside her. She pressed the remote button to switch off the television set and leaned back wearily. So, she thought, it had finally happened. All the years of hiding, all the years of fighting to keep her promise—in one day they had come to nothing. She had warned them but this time her warnings had gone unheeded. And she knew it had been done to keep her, a tired old lady, in luxury. The sale of the Ivanoff emerald was an act of love, but it was one that she no longer needed.

She coughed, gasping air into her failing lungs, an act so habitual now she scarcely heeded it. She thought of the girl she had just seen on television, talking of the Ivanoffs as impersonally as if they had been pawns in a Russian chess game. But it hadn't been like that at all. She knew because she had been there. And she knew what it was, besides the billions of dollars and the ransom in jewels, that great nations wanted. They were on the trail of a secret to which only she, Missie O'Bryan, knew the answer, she and a Russian gypsy who had prophesied many years ago that a great responsibility would fall on her shoulders. A responsibility that could change the world.

After pulling open a drawer in the little table beside her, she took out an elaborate silver frame bordered in rich enamels. At the top was the Ivanoff crest of a wolf's head and five diamond plumes banded with rubies on a sapphire ground. In tiny gold Russian lettering was the family's motto, "Upholders of Truth and Honor."

She peered closely at the fading sepia photograph of Prince Michael Alexandrovich Ivanoff, whose forebears had served at all the Russian Imperial courts since Peter the Great, remembering the first time she had seen him in the vast hall of the St. Petersburg mansion. She had hesitated by the door, awed by its grandeur. Her eyes had been drawn like a magnet to the tall, blond, handsome man standing at the top of the marble stairs, his hand resting on the collar of a great amber-colored dog. And she was to wonder ever after if time really did stand still as their eyes met.

With a sigh she replaced the photograph in the drawer. She had never, in all her long, eventful life, been free to display it. Misha's face, along with her secrets, had been locked away for over seventy years.

Then, of course, she had still been Verity Byron, but the prince had always called her "Missie," with that special touch of tenderness in his deep voice that had sent a thrill down her spine. She had loved him then, and she loved him now, more than any other man in her tangled life. And one day soon, if heaven was the reality she believed it to be, they would be together again and they would both be young and beautiful and their love would last for ever. Only then, of course, she would have to explain to him what had happened. She would have to tell him that she had tried to keep her promise.

But before she died she knew she would be called upon to explain the true story to the last person left who really loved her. The one who had sold the jewels and so innocently caused an international crisis.

Missie sighed as she remembered the night her old life had ended and her new life began. It was branded into her brain so clearly that even time had been unable to dim the memory of horror and a guilt so deep that she had wished she too could die and bury her memories with her.

If she closed her eyes now, she knew the scene would unfold again, perfect in every small terrible detail, just the way it always had every night of her long life.

$$===2===$$

Russia, 1917

The night was the blackest Missie ever remembered. The old wooden troika sped noiselessly along an invisible path that wound its way through thickets of birch toward the forest. After a while her eyes became accustomed to the darkness, and she could make out the rim of white frost edging each tree and the ice crystals forming on the fur rug pulled over her mouth to stop her breath from freezing. And then the birch trees merged into evergreens and they were in the forest and she could see nothing but blackness, as thick and tangible as frozen velvet.

The enormous borzoi, Viktor, was Prince Misha's favorite dog, with the massive head and thick shaggy coat of a true old-fashioned Russian hound, bred not merely to course foxes but to hunt wolves. Viktor rarely left his master's side, but now he loped along in front of the sled, guiding the team of dogs through the forest along an icy track only he could see.

No one spoke. There was only the hiss of the metal runners cutting through the ice and the labored breathing of the dogs. And the blackness.

Missie thought about her eighteenth birthday celebration yesterday. Varishnya, the Ivanoffs' beautiful country estate, had been under a cloud of fear and gloom, and despite the champagne and Misha's brave smile, she had known what he was thinking. That this would be the last celebration at his lovely home. It might even be the last time they were together. They might never see Varishnya —or each other—again.

Most of the servants had already disappeared; only the chef and Princess Anouska's maid, who were French and considered themselves above a "peasant revolt," had remained. But yesterday they too, at Misha's command, had taken the train to the Baltic port of

Tallinn where they would find a berth on a ship bound for Europe. Missie had refused to go with them. She had no real home in England, now that her father was dead, and besides, she was hopelessly in love with Misha Ivanoff. And now she was running for her life, away from the Bolshevik revolutionaries who were storming the country, murdering and pillaging without mercy.

Xenia's head drooped against her shoulder and Missie thanked heaven she was sleeping. Lost in her dreams, she would not feel their fear. Still, it was uncomfortable with the child's weight pressing the great tiara against her ribs.

Princess Anouska had been determined not to leave her jewels behind. Her beautiful bedroom had been in chaos. Her fabulous Paris dresses were tossed carelessly across the bed and her sumptuous furs thrown impatiently onto the floor. All the gray suede drawers had been pulled from the jewel cupboard as Nyanya, the children's old Russian nanny, hurriedly sewed the ruby rings and sapphire brooches, the diamond necklaces and ropes of pearls, into hems and bodices. Even the hem of Xenia's little woolen pinafore had been stitched with diamonds. But it was Anouska herself who had prised apart the ends of the great tiara so that it fitted snugly against Missie's small waist. It had been reset by Cartier years ago. Misha had ignored the jeweler's advice to use platinum and insisted that they use the almost pure gold of the original setting. He had never realized that the gold's softness would be so useful.

Anouska had tied the ends with ribbon around Missie's back, "like a jeweled cummerbund," she had exclaimed, laughing. Her beautiful eyes had glittered as brightly as the jewels and her corngold hair tumbled about her shoulders in disarray, but Missie knew that Anouska Ivanoff walked a strange tightrope suspended between elation and despair. She glanced at her in the darkness, wondering what her thoughts were now.

Anouska was sitting quietly, her six-year-old son Alexei snuggled inside the soft sable cape she had insisted on wearing despite Misha's protests that for safety, they must dress as peasant women and servants.

"Nonsense, Misha," she had retorted, taking the bunch of the fragrant violets grown specially for her in Varishnya's great greenhouses and pinning them at her shoulder. Tilting her chin arrogantly, she had stared at him with that strange, beautiful half smile that always seemed to Missie to be edged with steel. "After all," she had said, "who would dare harm the wife of the greatest of the Russian princes?"

Wrapping her arms tighter around little Xenia, Missie prayed she was right.

Misha's mother, the Dowager Princess Sofia, sighed as the ancient troika jolted over an icy rut. Missie glanced at her anxiously, but in the falling snow she could barely make out her face.

Sofia was seventy-five years old but no one ever thought of her as an old lady. Of course her thick black hair was streaked with white, but the beautiful bone structure was still the same. Her skin was still smooth and her luminous dark eyes, inherited from a gypsy ancestor, missed nothing. She had begged her son to let her stay at Varishnya, the beautiful country estate to which she had first come as a bride fifty-five years before, or in St. Petersburg where her beloved husband had been buried in the great cathedral of St. Peter and St. Paul.

"I'm too old to leave now, Misha," she had pleaded, admitting to her age for the first time. "Let me stay here with you and face whatever is to come." But he had refused to listen, telling her that he was staying simply to see that Varishnya was not destroyed. He said there was no danger and that he would join them in the Crimea, in the far south of Russia, within a few weeks. Both of them had known he was lying, but she had obeyed her son's wishes.

The snow was getting heavier, changing the dense blackness to swirling white, but Viktor plunged onward, his long bushy tail waving an arc through the blizzard.

"We must have been traveling for over half an hour," Sofia said at last. "We can't be far from the railway at Ivanovsk now."

Her voice changed to a gasp as a volley of shots suddenly crashed through the night and the sled dogs lunged upward, screaming in agony as the heavy troika slid out of control across the icy track. Missie glimpsed the dogs' gaping mouths and lolling tongues and then the troika slammed into a tree and she was hurtled into a bank of snow with Xenia beneath her.

Fear filled her mouth with its bitter taste, choking her as she waited for the next volley of shots that would finish them as surely as they had finished the dogs. But there was no sound. Trembling, she raised her head the merest fraction and peered into the blizzard. Anouska lay twenty yards away, and even through the heavily falling snow she could see the blood matting her hair and staining the icy white carpet beneath her head. There was no sign of Alexei and Sofia.

From the forest came the sound of raucous voices raised in argument and the crunch of booted feet on the snow. And then the sudden flare of burning torches held aloft.

A shiver of terror ran the length of Missie's spine as she peeked at them. They were not soldiers, but half a dozen bearded peasants in rough, stained clothing and thick felt boots. They carried bottles as well as rifles and some wore expensive fur hats. They had obviously been looting and were now very drunk on the stolen potato vodka, whose pungent smell penetrated even the clean forest odor of pine. She shut her eyes tightly as they staggered toward her, hiding her face and praying they would not notice her trembling.

"A peasant woman," one said scornfully in Russian, lifting her shabby padded servant's coat in his grimy fingers, "you can tell from the smell of her."

The others laughed raucously. "Dead too, I'll bet," said another. "There's blood all over her . . . still, just to make sure . . ."

Missie's ribs exploded into pain as his kick landed, but fear froze the scream in her throat.

Their footsteps crunched on the frozen snow as they walked away. Holding their blazing torches aloft, they crowded around Anouska. Her blond hair tumbled across the dark sable cape and huge pearls gleamed in her pretty ears and at her neck. Suddenly her eyes flew open and she stared at the half-dozen men surrounding her, her gold-brown velvet gaze taking in their rough looks and peasant attire.

"I recognize you," Missie heard her say weakly, "you are foresters from the Ivanoff estate. You, Mikoyan, you came to Varishnya with your children for the Easter festivities . . . and you, Rubakoff, and your brother. . . ."

"Enough!" the man Mikoyan cried. "There will be no more Easter festivals at the Ivanoff estate. It belongs to us now, to the people, the revolutionaries." He grabbed her silken hair in his filthy calloused hand. "And women like you will be for our heroes to enjoy!"

Missie caught the look of pain on Anouska's face as Mikoyan lifted her head and put his coarse, bearded face close to hers.

"But not before we find out for ourselves what the prince has been enjoying all these years, eh, comrades?"

They laughed as they passed him another bottle, and he let

Anouska's head drop cruelly back into the snow, straddling her, gulping back the fiery liquor until it was finished. After throwing back his head, he hawked the phlegm from his throat and spat it out. Anouska groaned, turning away her bloodied head. Mikoyan flung back her cape and her lovely eyes widened with fear as he slowly fitted the bayonet onto his rifle.

A thin high scream pierced the night as Alexei ran from the trees toward his mother. "No . . . no . . . no . . ." he screamed. "That's Princess Maman, leave her alone, go away. . . ."

They swung around, training their rifles on the small figure stumbling on the ice as he ran to his mother. Hot tears burned Missie's eyes and she wished she dared move so she could cover her ears against their cruel laughter as they grabbed Alexei by the collar, holding him aloft like a squirming puppy while he pleaded frantically with them to leave his mother alone.

Mikoyan butted the end of his bayonet against the boy's chest and Alexei's slate-gray eyes grew black with fear.

"So, here's the young princeling himself, shouting for his mama!"

"Leave my son alone," Anouska commanded weakly, summoning her most regal voice, "or I swear to God my husband will have you horsewhipped. You will hang from the highest tree at Varishnya . . . all of you. . . ."

Mikoyan flung back his head in a great roar of laughter. "Watch, Prince," he yelled, thrusting Alexei closer to his mother. "You are going to learn something they would never teach you at home in your grand palaces! A lesson of the *real* world! A lesson about the world of men with a thousand years of anger in their hearts!"

Alexei trembled as Mikoyan lunged at Anouska with his bayonet and slit her pretty woolen dress swiftly from neck to hem.

Mikoyan fell silent, staring at her. He had never seen a woman like this, all smooth golden flesh clad in delicate silk and lace.

Anouska closed her eyes, shuddering as he stretched out his filthy hand and ran it the length of her body. The stink of him was in her nostrils as his hand closed cruelly over her breast and then, suddenly, he gave an angry roar.

"What do we have here?" he cried with a growl, ripping her silken camisole with his bayonet so that the hidden diamond rings and brooches tumbled onto to the snow. There was silence for a second, and then they fell on their glittering prizes with loud obscenities of delight.

"Riches, riches . . ." they caroled, thrusting their trophies into their pockets and taking great swallows of vodka. They glanced craftily at each other again as they realized there must be more where this came from.

Laughing, they tore off the rest of Anouska's clothing, snatching the pearls from her throat and ears, ripping the lining from the sable cape and scooping up handfuls of jewels. When they had finished, she lay on the remains of her sumptuous fur, naked and trembling with cold and fear and the pain of her wounds.

"Bring the boy closer," Mikoyan commanded as they crowded around her, lust burning in their eyes. Tears coursed down Alexei's tight little face as he stood silently, head down, in the grip of his captors. And then Mikoyan began to unfasten his clothing, and the hot tears burned Missie's own eyelids as she shut out the horror of what was taking place. But she couldn't shut out the sounds, the jeering laughter, the bestial grunts, and Anouska's agonized cries. And the endless sound of the little boy screaming *"Princess Maman, oh, Maman, Maman . . ."* Missie knew that if she lived through this night, she would remember those sounds forever.

There were six of them, and before each had had his turn Anouska fell silent. Then suddenly she began to laugh, wild, frenzied insane laughter.

Missie knew that laughter. She had heard it before, many times. But this time she was glad, because she knew it meant that Anouska had retreated to her own private world where no one could reach her and no one could harm her.

"Stop it, you bitch!" the man astride her shouted, staring at her, puzzled, but still she laughed.

After lifting his rifle, Mikoyan aimed it between her lovely pansy-brown eyes. *"Stop it, I say,"* he said with a drunken snarl. But Anouska never heard him, and she didn't hear the crack of the bullet as it split open her forehead, obliterating her beauty in a mass of splintered bone and remnants of bloody flesh.

Silence fell as the men looked first at Anouska and then back at Mikoyan, still holding the smoking rifle. The man holding Alexei released his grip, but the boy did not run away. He just stood there, staring numbly at what was left of his mother's face.

"So?" Mikoyan demanded with a shrug. "Whose turn is it now? She's still warm—and you don't need a face for what you are going to do." And with a burst of callous laughter, the next one fell on her.

Missie hid her eyes and prayed. She prayed for Anouska's soul and for the safety of the small boy, though she wondered if he might not be better off dead than seeing what he was seeing now.

The men were drinking and laughing noisily and didn't hear the horses approaching, but Missie did and she peered hopefully into the forest. Was Misha coming to save her after all?

The captain in the People's Revolutionary Army was about thirty years old, clean-shaven and smart in a long blue-gray overcoat and fur cap. The two young men with him wore Cossack uniforms, and their horses were prime, tough combat animals, obviously captured from one of the tsar's own crack cavalry regiments.

"My God," the officer whispered, forgetting for a moment that he no longer believed in Him and that his loyalty was only to the new regime and its leader Lenin. Drawing his pistol and keeping his voice low, he commanded his men to dismount and take aim and then suddenly he noticed Alexei. "Wait," he whispered urgently. "Hold your fire, there is a child."

Mikoyan and the other peasants were still sprawled on the snow, shouting obscenities and laughing drunkenly as they watched the next man mount Anouska.

Suddenly the captain ran forward, kicking the nearest lumpen body savagely. "Get up," he roared. "Hands over your heads." They staggered to their feet, astonished, as he kicked away the man astride Anouska and the young lieutenants leveled their rifles and took aim.

As if released from a spell, Alexei suddenly took to his heels and ran toward Missie. He flung himself on the ground beside her and took her icy hand in both of his. "Missie, Missie," he begged, "help me, please help me, Missie, I'm so frightened. . . ."

She shut her eyes tighter, yearning with all her being to take Alexei in her arms, to hold him and comfort him, to try to restore some sanity to the nightmare he was enduring, but she knew these new men were enemies too. They were a different sort, but still enemies. They already had Alexei, and if she tried it meant they would find Xenia too. And she knew only too well what both children's fate would ultimately be as prisoners of the new regime. She steeled herself, telling herself she could not help him, she *must not* do it. She must at least save Xenia. Alexei's tears scalded her hands and she prayed silently for strength to ignore him.

"You drunken filthy cretins! You belong in the piggery with the rest of the swine," the captain roared. "Line them up," he told his men as they butted the peasants into a straggling line with their rifles.

Then, "Bring the boy here to me," he commanded.

They brought Alexei to stand in front of him. His face was ashen and his beautiful eyes were still filled with horror as the captain looked him up and down.

"I knew your father," he said at last. "If I could, I would have spared you what happened tonight. But what is done is done and you must face it like a man. Now I want you to watch something, little boy. I am going to show you how the Army of the People will avenge your mother." He glanced dispassionately at the straggling line of cowardly peasants, the very people the revolution was supposed to be for. Then he commanded, "Fire."

Alexei put his hands over his ears to shut out the terrible screams and curses, but he didn't shut his eyes. He watched their bodies spin and jerk as the bullets raked them, waiting until the final spasms had finished. Then he lifted his head and looked the captain silently in the eye.

"Come," the captain said, holding out his hand, "we must leave now." But instead, Alexei ran to his mother's side. Kneeling, he wrapped the beautiful dark sable cape tenderly across her bloody, naked body. After taking her poor, icy hand in both his, he smothered it with kisses. Then he hurled himself to the ground, burying his head in the softness of the fur at her breast, breathing in the familiar scent of the violets she always wore. By her side, like a droplet of fresh blood on the snow, lay a ruby ring. His hand closed over it instinctively.

From the distance came the sound of a huge explosion, and the sky above the tall fir trees filled with an orange glow. "They've dynamited Varishnya!" the young lieutenant shouted.

"The fools!" Captain Solovsky exclaimed angrily. "There is no control over these peasant rabbles. They must be stopped now, if we are ever to achieve our aims."

Alexei stared silently at the glowing sky. His face was expressionless, closed to all emotion. He put his hand in his pocket and dropped the ring in there.

"Come," Captain Solovsky said again. "You must forget all this." Alexei met his eyes. "There is a new life ahead of you," he said more harshly, "and who knows, maybe *you* will help to make the new Russia the great country it will become." He laughed at the irony. "Yes, maybe *you* will be a new breed of revolutionary."

Alexei followed obediently as they walked to the horses, and Captain Solovsky lifted him onto the saddle in front of him. "Leave the bodies to the wolves," he told his men carelessly as they rode off into the forest. "I doubt they will last the night."

3

Grigori Konstantinov Solovsky held the boy safely in front of him on the long slow ride through the storm, all the way to Dvorsk, thirty kilometers to the south. He took the treacherous, almost invisible road past the halt at Ivanovsk where the railway lines were buried beneath the snow and only the signalbox and smoke from the railwayman's hut marked the Ivanoff family's tiny private station. And every step of the way, he told himself he was a fool.

Solovsky was an officer in the newly formed "Red" Army. He was a hard man brought up in a hard way, and there was no room in his life for finer feelings. Another life lost, whether it was his own or a child's, was not important. What mattered to him was the Bolshevik cause, and in his mind that meant the Russian people. Yet the boy's helpless, terrified face had struck a chord in him. It was the same look he had seen reflected in his own face when he had watched his three young sons die of typhus in the epidemic four years earlier. He, who had been the proud father of four strong boys, who he planned should be part of the new Russia, had been left with only one son. And just now, in that forest, he had simply not been able to leave another boy to die.

The idea had come to him suddenly. He knew it was a risk and that it might cast doubts on his devotion to the revolutionary cause if his secret were ever discovered, but he had studied the workings of the human mind long enough to know the risk was minimal. Solovsky had been in charge of frontline soldiers returning from the horrors of the war with Germany, he had studied prisoners who had suffered severe torture; he knew that these people spoke little and asked no questions. The ones who survived were those who kept their private vision of horror and tragedy locked away in a special vault deep in the brain, never to be opened. Those who remembered went mad.

The next few weeks would decide Prince Alexei Ivanoff's future. The boy would forget the scene in the forest, forget who he was and his short past life. He would become an orphan of the revolution and the adopted son of Grigori and Natalya Solovsky. Or he would retreat into madness. So be it.

Solovsky was from Siberia where the people were tough and hardy. If they were not, they did not survive. Now his home was in the small provincial town of Polotsk in his wife's home province of Byelorussia, where life was softer and greener. But on the rare occasions he was home relaxing with his friends over a meal and endless glasses of vodka, he would always remind them of his superiority as a "Siberiusk." As the potent spirit took hold of him he would haul himself to his feet and repeat an old saying. *"In Siberia,"* he would thunder, his deep bass voice commanding silence. *"In Siberia, forty degrees below is not a frost."* He would pause, glancing around his audience, gathering their attention. *"A hundred kilometers is not a distance, a half liter of vodka is not a drink."* He would raise his glass to be filled again before adding with a grin, *"And forty years is not a woman."* Then he would toss back the vodka in a single gulp to great roars of appreciation and laughter, but Solovsky believed what he said was the truth.

He remembered the saying now as his tough old cavalry horse struggled through the blizzard. The snow was freezing even as it fell and the animal slid and stumbled, whinnying and rolling its eyes in fright. Solovsky glanced sideways at his men; they were barely recognizable under a layer of snow. Only their eyes, fringed with frozen white lashes, peered ahead into the storm. Solovsky shrugged. He had weathered worse storms than this in his youth. They would press on to Dvorsk.

He wrapped the skirt of his greatcoat tighter around the motionless boy, unsure whether he was alive or dead. And as they rode slowly through the icy night, he thought of his own childhood, and how strange life was that he, the son of generations of peasants, now held the destiny of the son of one of Russia's greatest princes in his hands.

Grigori had been born just before the turn of the century, the fifteenth child of a peasant whose family had lived in the same village for as long as any of them could remember. The Solovskys were related through intermarriage over many years to everyone else in their village, and his father had married his second—or maybe it was his third—cousin. He had fathered sixteen children in all, five of whom survived childhood, but Grigori's mother never lived long enough to become a *babushka,* a grandmother. She was married at sixteen and dead at only thirty-five, though she had looked like an old woman.

The family lived in a hut built by his father for his bride and made of logs floated down the river from the lumber camps in the vast, endless forests of the north. The nearest town, Novosibirsk, consisted of a huddle of wooden huts on the banks of the river Ob, and the only reason for its existence was that the newly completed Trans-Siberian Railway bridged the river at that point.

One of Grigori's first memories was of being taken by his father to the railway halt to watch a slender, bearded man as he stepped from the train. The man's pallor had matched the gray skies as he surveyed the bleak landscape and the few poor peasants watching him. His glance fell on the young boy and they stared at each other somberly for a moment. A sad smile lighted the man's face and he said, "You, boy, are the future of Russia. Never forget that." As he climbed back on board and the train pulled away, his father told him that the man was Vladimir Ilyich Lenin on his way to exile in the depths of Siberia. Many years later, when he was a student, Grigori had read what Lenin had written about Siberia that day. "It is," he had said, "a barren wilderness with no habitations and no towns." And Grigori knew he was right because the desolate landscape seemed to merge with eternity and nothingness.

Grigori's elder sisters both married loggers and went off to live in the far north. He never saw them again. His two brothers married their cousins and settled in the growing town of Novosibirsk, working on the railway, and as far as eight-year-old Grigori could see, they were no better off than his father had been.

Although he had no chance to observe a life any different from his own, something told him that there was more than just this same peasant existence. Sometimes he would stand by the great railway bridge spanning the Ob, wondering how it was built and who had the knowledge to construct such an edifice without it falling down and how they came by that knowledge. He would watch the rare train as it wound its way across the river on its slow journey from Moscow, waving until it faded into oblivion, leaving him wondering about the passengers whose faces he had glimpsed briefly before they disappeared into another world. Those people came from places he had barely heard of, they rode on trains that came from great cities. Grigori didn't even know what "a city" looked like. He would lie awake at night, listening to the distant hoot of the train whistle sounding mournfully across the flat Siberian plains, and, when he finally slept, it haunted his dreams. The train and its passengers were a mystery, and it was one a poor boy like him could never solve because he was as ignorant and illiterate as his peasant forebears.

As was the tradition, at the age of six he had already been sent to mind the cows along with the other young boys in the village, and at eight he had advanced to looking after the horses. When he attained the age of sixteen, he would be admitted to the *skhod,* the assembly of the heads of the families, and considered an adult. It was different for the girls of the village. They were given the more menial domestic tasks, fetching water from the river and collecting wood, and generally helping their mothers about the house. There had never been a school in his remote village, but one had been built in Novosibirsk for the children of the local railway administrators and supervisors.

One winter morning Grigori walked the twenty kilometers into the ramshackle town and presented himself at the door of the little wooden schoolhouse. The *klassnaya dama* stared at him in astonishment. He was small for his age with a peasant's stocky body and strong legs, and he was bundled up in layers of rough homespun garments, the traditional high-necked shirt and baggy pants topped with a makeshift cloak. He wore rough *velenki,* felt winter boots bound to his legs with birch bark, and his bushy black eyebrows sparkled with a coating of early-morning frost. But there was no mistaking the intensity of his purpose as he stared at her with deep dark eyes and told her he wanted "to learn."

"But what do you want to learn, little son?" she had asked, smiling as the warmth of the old tiled stove defrosted his eyebrows, sending a shower of droplets down his face.

Grigori didn't even notice. "Everything," he had answered simply.

The teacher had sighed with satisfaction. A year of tutoring a reluctant brood of young students who would far rather be out sledging and throwing snowballs at each other in winter, or dipping themselves in the river in the softer days of summer, had left her frustrated in her chosen career. At last she had someone who wanted only "to learn."

Arrangements were made for Grigori to lodge in the teacher's tiny house, where he slept on a narrow wooden shelf over the tiled stove that warmed the house in winter and on the tiny porch in summer. The *klassnaya dama* taught him to read and write, and when he had mastered that, she opened up the entire world to him through geography and history, sharpening his mind even further on mathematics and scientific matters. In return he brought her water and wood, ignoring the scorn of the other children because he was doing "girls' work." And every now and then his father left precious little parcels of fresh eggs and butter on her doorstep.

When Grigori was almost thirteen she knew she had taught him all she could, but he was ready for more. A scholarship was applied for and won to a school in Moscow, and the *klassnaya dama* herself accompanied her prize pupil to the city. But first she took him to the local tailor, an enterprising Jewish man who, with Novosibirsk's tenuous new prosperity, had set himself up in business there. The man made Grigori his first proper pair of trousers and a coat, for which the teacher paid. Blushing with pride, Grigori vowed that somehow, some day he would repay her.

Feeling strange in his new city clothes, Grigori had finally ridden the train that had bypassed his life for so many years. The teacher deposited him at the school, and under the curious gaze of its middle-class pupils, she kissed him good-bye affectionately before leaving to visit her family in St. Petersburg. Grigori was alone and terrified of his new environment.

His new clothes were exchanged for a blue-gray military-style uniform and his terror was hidden under a mask of aggressiveness. But it still didn't stop him from blushing angrily when he heard the girls, demure in brown dresses and black aprons, giggling behind their hands about the new "wild boy from the sticks."

A month later his beloved *klassnaya dama* was killed in a train accident near Moscow, on her way back to Siberia, and for a while Grigori wanted to die too. She was his only link between his past and his new life, and alone, he didn't know how to cope with either. It was his steely core of ambition that came to his rescue. That and the magic of his classes.

He survived the school by keeping to himself, ignoring the baiting of the smart city children until eventually they left him alone. At the age of eighteen, and still a loner, he entered the St. Petersburg Politeknik College on another scholarship. The students were mostly the sons of nobility or the military and professional classes, with very few from the working class and even fewer from the peasantry. Grigori had no affinity with any of them, but he acquired a bitter grudging envy for the noble sons who treated their studies with such carefree contempt and who spent more money every night on drink and gypsy girls than Grigori had ever conceived of having in his pocket. One part of him longed to be like them and the other part hated them, because he knew it was impossible. It was then that he realized that he, and others like him—for by now they were growing in numbers—formed a new class, and he knew that one day it would be a force to be reckoned with.

Young Grigori was a willing victim of the new ideology. He absorbed the teachings of Marx and Engels, Trotsky and Lenin, eagerly, because they struck a chord in his heart. *He* was the man they were talking to, the peasant who had pulled himself up by his bootstraps through hard work and education. *His* were the brains and skills the new Socialist Democratic Labor Party would need when the time of revolution came, as it surely would. Grigori joined the Party and the secret meetings were the highlights of his week. He was soon given minor administrative jobs to do, and by his diligence and dedication earned the respect of the area leaders.

When he graduated from the Politeknik with a degree in engineering, he got a job with the railway company in Moscow. At last he knew how to build the bridges he had dreamed about as a boy. But that dream was already fading into one of the new Russia owned by the people, for the people, a utopia where ultimately all social categories would be eliminated. Grigori truly believed in his heart that with this accomplished, all men would be equal and would share in their country's prosperity.

He became more and more active in the Party, touring the regions, recruiting members, and encouraging the local workers' committees, or "Soviets," to strike for their rights. The Bolshevist leader, Lenin, the man glimpsed on the bleak station platform in Siberia twenty years before, remained his idol.

It was on one of these trips that he met Natalya. She was sixteen years old, the age his own mother had been when she married his father, and she had the cool white skin, rosy cheeks, and bright blond hair typical of the region of Byelorussia. Natalya became his only other obsession. It didn't matter that she was uneducated. The stocky dark peasant was sensually in love with her plump milky fairness. It was enough just to touch her smooth, flawless skin, to kiss her cherry-red lips that were as innocent as his own and run his hands through her coarse yellow hair. Her family knew he was a catch for Natalya, and the couple were married within a month.

Grigori took his new bride back to the dismal room that was his "home" in Moscow, and the country girl struggled her best to cope with life in the big city. She kept the old-fashioned samovar bubbling so that she could serve tea to his "friends" when they came for meetings and was secretly shocked when all they drank was vodka. But she had no idea of what their talk of "anarchy" meant, and Grigori traveled so much she was often alone.

He knew she was unhappy, and after a few months, when she was pregnant with their first child, he took her back to her family in Byelorussia, visiting her as often as he could. Four sons were born in quick succession. He was happy and over the years his prestige with the Party increased. And then tragedy struck with the typhus epidemic that wiped out many thousands of people, including three of his boys. Only Boris, the youngest, was spared.

In 1914 Russia went to war against the Germans and Grigori was inducted into the army. Because of his degree and his riding skills, he was made a noncommissioned officer in a cavalry unit of the tsar's army, but the war quickly took its toll with great losses for Russia, and suddenly he found himself promoted to full captain. He was sickened with the futile waste of life he saw every day at the front. Passage over Russia's narrow muddy roads was slowed to a crawl by supply wagons that never got through, and his men were being mown down by an inexorable enemy. The frozen, hungry soldiers were being slaughtered or were dying of dysentery, and he was helpless to do anything about it.

The revolution he had worked toward for so long began with riots in St. Petersburg in February 1917 over shortages of bread and coal. After returning from the front, Grigori helped to form the new militant Soviet of Works. Soon Tsar Nicholas was forced to abdicate. But as the months passed it became obvious that the new government was incapable of dealing with the food shortages. Lenin arrived back in Russia and under his leadership the October Revolution began.

Grigori's finest hour had been when he was presented to his hero. Lenin had looked just as he remembered him, pale-faced, bearded, and frail, with an intense gaze that seemed to see into Grigori's soul. He had known then that he would give his life for this man if necessary, because he was convinced that only Lenin could save Russia. He had never wavered from that decision.

He glanced at the boy, huddled beneath his greatcoat. Now he was going to prove to himself that he could make a revolutionary from the class they were overthrowing.

The town of Dvorsk was a mere cluster of dark wooden houses spread in a straggling line alongside the railway. Grigori was billeted above the bakery, and even though the baker had only a meager supply of flour to make his bread, at least the place was warm and there was always a bowl of steaming hot potato soup and a crust of bitter dark rye bread to eat and a glass or two of home-brewed vodka to wash it down. His men would sleep on the floor of the bakery. After telling them to get warm and to eat, Grigori rode on to the station. The train to St. Petersburg had been due at seven that evening, but the hour had come and gone and there was still no sign of it. The stationmaster had had no communication, and no one knew when it might be expected—it could be hours, days, weeks even. . . .

After telling the stationmaster to inform him immediately when he had news, Grigori rode back to the bakery and carried Alexei upstairs to his room, where he put him on the small iron cot that served as his own bed. The boy's face was chalk-white and his hands icy, but his eyes were wide open, and still transfixed with the memory of horror.

Grigori sat beside him on the bed, talking to him quietly in English, the first language of all good Russian families and one he had acquired at the Politeknik. "So, young man," he began, "for after tonight you can no longer be considered a mere boy; we must look to your future now and not the past." He spoke sharply. "I want you to put what you saw from your mind. Your father and mother are dead. You are no longer the son of Misha Ivanoff. Now you are my son and your name is Sergei . . . Sergei Solovsky. Do you understand?"

Alexei nodded, staring at Grigori with wide, fathomless gray eyes. His father's eyes.

In fact, Alexei looked so like Prince Misha Ivanoff, whom Solovsky had seen many times at the meetings of the *Duma,* the Parliament, that he was afraid he might be recognized. He wondered again if he had done the right thing, but with a shrug he told himself it was too late now to turn back; he would just have to keep the boy out of sight for a while. Besides, his experiment excited him. He was going to reverse the natural order of things. He was a common man who because of his education had become part of the new elite. Now he would turn this elite young princeling into a common man—and then he would see what he could make of him.

After telling the boy to go to sleep, Grigori blew out the candle. He wrapped himself in his coat, stretched out on the floor beside him, and was asleep in minutes.

4

Cal Warrender stared into his champagne glass thinking that it had seemed like a good idea at the time. The bar of the Hotel Beau Rivage was softly lighted and luxurious, but outside the windows flurries of snow swirled in the wind before settling in soft white drifts. The sudden storm had closed Geneva airport, and he faced a lonely dinner and the worrying knowledge that he had failed to secure the Ivanoff emerald. He had been beaten to it by a smarter adversary.

Valentin Solovsky was sitting at the bar silently drinking vodka with two other Russians. They looked as glum as Cal felt, and he wondered if that meant that Valentin too had failed to buy the emerald and, like him, was no farther along the trail that led to the "Lady." Yet if it wasn't the Russians, then *who* had bought the Ivanoff jewel?

He knew Valentin was there for the same reason he was: He had been delegated to find the "Lady." And both he and Valentin knew it wasn't just for the money, it was for the mines.

When Prince Ivanoff had met the maharaja all those years ago, they had traded their gifts in celebration of the prince's purchase of certain lands in the state of Rajasthan. The prince had discovered that the lands contained valuable deposits of tungsten, an element used to harden steel, and had realized their value to a newly mechanized world. But after the revolution the Russians had claimed ownership of the mines, saying they had the legal documents signed by Prince Misha Ivanoff making them over to the new Soviet Republic. They stated that in any case, as all property was now owned by the state, the mines rightfully belonged to Russia. The authenticity of the documents was questioned at the time, but as no member of the Ivanoff family had ever come forward to dispute their claim, nothing had ever been done about it. Though the mines were valuable, they had never seemed of great importance to the rest of the world. However, they had recently been found to contain vast quantities of certain strategic elements essential to modern industry— especially defense. *Or war.* And now the entire world was prepared to dispute Russia's ownership.

Cal knew that the Russians desperately needed an Ivanoff signature on the title deeds as indisputable proof of their claim. If they found the "Lady" first, they would get that signature. And they would again become the world's most intimidating power.

He sipped the champagne that had been meant to cheer him up— and maybe bluff the Russians into believing he was celebrating the purchase of the emerald—thinking about the events of the last few weeks. He had asked for and been given carte blanche to conduct his own investigation into the search for the mysterious owner of the Ivanoff jewel. He had requested no CIA heavies, no elaborate FBI investigations . . . he had wanted this one for himself. He realized its importance and knew it would boost him up the political ladder. Besides, he was already onto a lead. "It's a simple enough matter," he had told them easily at the meeting. "All I have to do is find these top gem cutters. They will know who the owner is."

It had started out like a game. First he had gone to Amsterdam, where he had met Peter van Stalte, the doyen of gem cutters and an honest man. Van Stalte had said the emerald had not been seen in that city and that he personally would not have liked the job. "Too risky," he'd said, frowning and pulling on his short pointed beard. "The surest hand in Amsterdam could not have guaranteed success."

In Jerusalem the Israelis had told him that not only had they not seen the emerald, but they too would never have attempted to cut it. They said there was only one man who could have attempted such a cut with any chance of success: Gerome Abyss. But Abyss had disappeared from Paris and the gem-cutting world years ago after a series of disasters involving large and expensive diamonds. Lifting a cupped hand to his mouth, Stein had said, "Scotch whisky, that's what ruined Gerome Abyss. Rumor had it he went to Hong Kong, or was it Singapore? Or maybe Bangkok?"

Cal had followed Interpol information that Abyss had last been seen in Bangkok, one of the major gem centers of the Far East, but his search had ground to a halt in a seedy back street in Patpong. He had found himself staring at a stained business card tacked to a peeling door. There was no answer to his ring, and the people at the Therapeutic Sex Clinic on the first floor had told him Abyss had not been seen in weeks. It had taken two days of inquiring from bar to bar along the malodorous network of neighboring streets to find the owner of the building, and when he finally encountered him, he wished he hadn't.

They met in the man's office in back of a glitzy neon "massage parlor" and bar. Disco music was blaring from enormous speakers as half-naked Thai girls gyrated lethargically on a small stage while the bored customers lewdly assessed their merits. When Cal inquired for the owner, two muscular guards emerged suddenly from the shadows and, without a word, grabbed his arms. They hurried him along a corridor at the back of the bar, past "massage girls" lounging in front of flimsy-curtained cubicles, smoking and gossiping, waiting to apply their "skills" to a continuously passing trade. One called out to him, running her hands provocatively across her naked charms. "Try me, Mister, I make you feel good," she said with a giggle as the two henchmen pushed him into a room at the rear of the building. The girls' heavy perfume failed to disguise the sickening odors of sweat, ammonia, and strong disinfectant, and he thankfully inhaled a breath of the merely stale air of the office, staring at the little man behind the enormous desk.

The man he had come to see was not Thai. He was Laotian, and he seemed ageless, with an unlined yellowish skin and eyes so narrow it was impossible to tell their color or read their expression. He was tiny, his childlike hands fiddled continually with a string of amber beads, and his immense carved teakwood chair only made him look smaller. Another menacing pair of bodyguards flanked his chair, and Cal's throat suddenly felt dry. He was aware of the criminal underworld in Bangkok, but he hadn't expected to stumble on it quite like this. These men meant business and it was a good bet it wasn't the sort of business he was involved in: They were drug pushers, pimps, loan sharks. . . .

"My request is simple, sir," he had said, carefully polite. "I am searching for a gem cutter by the name of Abyss."

The Laotian eyed him silently for a minute, then asked in a high, squeaky voice, "Why?"

"Why?" Cal repeated uncertainly.

"Why you seek Abyss? Perhaps he owe you money?"

"No, oh, no. Abyss does not owe me money. I—I have a job for him."

"Show me the stone you want him to cut."

"The stone?" Cal felt the sweat rise along the back of his neck and he wondered how he had managed to get himself into this. "I left it in Amsterdam. It's a special stone. They told me only Abyss could cut it."

There was a long silence and he had forced himself to stare into the Laotian's face, wishing he could see his eyes, cursing himself for getting into this dumb situation.

"You are lying," the Laotian said finally in his thin voice. "Abyss is a drunkard. His gem-cutting days are over, destroyed in Paris many years ago. He has been making just enough to finance his drinking by cutting and polishing minor commercial stones for the cheap end of the market. But not enough to pay me. Mr. Gerome Abyss disappeared two months ago, owing me for certain services. This was an . . . an oversight. You understand?" His smile was as narrow and expressionless as his eyes as he added, "My collector was remiss; he allowed Abyss to stall him for the money—something that is against my rules. Of course, the collector has now been dealt with. But Mr. Abyss . . . well, he owes me a total of one thousand dollars. Not a great deal of money, of course . . . but no one, *no one* ever owes my organization money and gets away with it. So, Mr. . . . Warrender, since Abyss is a friend of yours, what do you say you pay his debts? Let's call it a fine, shall we? And in return, I shall tell you what I know."

The crocodile smile disappeared as Cal stared at him, surprised. What could the Laotian tell him? That for a thousand dollars they had killed Abyss? He wouldn't put anything past these bastards . . . death was probably one of their sweeter options. "A thousand dollars?" he said, reaching in his jacket for his wallet.

The thug next to him grabbed him and he felt the smooth, cold steel of a knife against his neck.

"Shall we say—with interest—fifteen hundred?" the Laotian suggested with another smile.

Cal nodded, and with a quick gesture of his tiny hand the Laotian indicated the thug should set him free.

Breathing a sigh of relief that he wasn't going to end up as another anonymous statistic fished from the deep Chao Phraya River, Cal said nervously, "You guys take travelers' checks? Just joking, just joking," he added hastily as the Laotian's eyes disappeared into angry slits and his thin mouth tightened. "Fifteen hundred dollars, right?" He took the fifteen bills from his wallet and placed them on the table. "And now you will tell me where Abyss is?"

Waving to one of his henchmen to remove the money, the Laotian said, "Mr. Abyss had been traced from Kuala Lumpur to Singapore, and then to Jakarta, where, I understand from my contacts, he was seeking passage on a freighter heading for Istanbul. My research has gone no further than this. And since the debt has now been repaid, it will no longer be necessary. Good-bye, Mr. Warrender."

As the guards grabbed his arms and marched him back along the corridor, Cal wondered how he had known his name. He must have heard he was making inquiries and made it his business to find out about him. The Laotian was not the kind of man to let anything pass him by.

The massage girls lurking behind their curtains eyed him silently as they hurried past, and then he was back in the red-and-blue neon glare and heavy disco beat of the bar. A thrust on his back propelled him suddenly into the street and he was breathing Patpong Road's moist, fetid air as if it was the breath of life itself.

He took the next flight out to Istanbul, the ancient city that was formerly Constantinople and before that Byzantium. It was raining and the beautiful domes and minarets were hidden under a bank of low gray cloud. Even the famous Bosphorus was a depressing gray.

The harbor was surrounded by an area of peeling industrial squalor, filled with Russian freighters and rusting Turkish ships looking ready for the junkyard. Land and sea merged together in the ghostly gray mist and a fine rain soaked him as he walked along the docks, searching for the minor immigration official Interpol had told him might help—for a certain sum, of course. When he finally reached him it took him two more grim, gray rainy days of searching through papers until he found what he wanted.

He compared the picture of the man on the immigration documents with the one in the photograph given him by Interpol. There was no mistaking the round face stretched tight over layers of fat, shining with a film of sweat under the hot photographic lamps, nor the small eyes and fleshy lips. Abyss's sparse hair was now dyed a strange reddish color and the mustache was a new addition, but it was the name that confirmed the identity. Gerome Abyss was obviously not very inventive. He had renamed himself simply "Mr. Gerome" . . . Georges Gerome, clothing manufacturer from Nîmes in

France. He had stated his business in Istanbul as seeking manufacturers of Turkish cotton goods for sale in Europe. And the address given was a small downtown hotel.

Cal had copied down the information, pocketed the photograph of Abyss, laid an extra fifty bucks on the nervous official who accompanied him thankfully to the door, and headed for the hotel.

A word with the clerk on Reception and another fifty got him permission to search the guest lists for the past two months, but no Mr. Gerome had registered there. A few discreet questions confirmed that no one of his description had set foot through the hotel's portals, and Cal knew he was back where he started.

Behind the tree-lined boulevards of modern Istanbul a labyrinth of narrow, medieval alleys crisscrossed the city's hills, filled with tumbling wooden houses and dark mysterious courtyards. It was a city where, if he wished, a man could simply disappear from the face of the earth. Cal knew one thing was certain: Abyss would not be pursuing his trade. He would have been paid lavishly for cutting the Ivanoff emerald and the odds were he was now busy spending it on the best scotch whisky and happily drinking himself to death. He shrugged. Whichever, he had drawn a blank.

Now he was stuck in snowbound Geneva, and without either the emerald or a clue to its owner—old or new. His brooding gaze shifted to Solovsky, still drinking at the bar with his fellow Russians. There was definitely something different about Solovsky. It wasn't just that he stood head and shoulders above his countrymen physically; there was a sort of old-Russian quality in his bearing and his manner. Confidence combined with courtesy, he decided—the essence of a diplomat. Solovsky turned suddenly and met his gaze. He nodded, unsmilingly acknowledging Cal's presence, then turned back to the bar and ordered another round of vodka. They knew each other only slightly, though Cal figured he probably knew more about Solovsky than Solovsky knew about him.

Valentin Solovsky had been schooled all his life toward high political office and at the age of thirty-six had already begun to make a name for himself in the foreign service. He had held posts as press attaché at his country's embassy in Paris, as military attaché in London, and his latest post was as cultural attaché in Washington. Paris, London, Washington, Cal mused, finishing his glass of champagne. Nothing but the best for the son of top Politburo member Marshal Sergei Solovsky and the nephew of the KGB's feared Boris Solovsky. Nepotism lived, even in the People's Republic.

Valentin swung around, staring toward the door. Cal followed his gaze. Genie Reese stood hesitantly at the entrance to the bar. She looked beautiful, but moody and unsmiling.

Cal had met Genie Reese several times at White House press conferences and Washington parties. He knew she was a damned good reporter. She was bright, always well researched and un-manipulative with a story. And she was absolutely straight-arrow honest. She was also one of the most attractive members of the Washington press corps—a detail that he noticed had not escaped Valentin Solovsky.

He called out to her as she walked by on her way to a table by the snowy window. "Not thinking of drinking alone, are you, Genie?" He waved at the champagne in the ice bucket by his table. "Why don't you join me?"

She hesitated, her blue eyes undecided, then she said curtly, "Sorry, I need to be on my own for a bit. I've got some thinking to do."

"Haven't we all," Cal murmured, sinking back into his chair, watching as she took a seat at an empty table, shook back her mane of blond hair, and asked the waiter for a glass of fresh orange juice with ice. No booze? he thought, surprised. The work day was over and most other press persons would be hitting the bottle as if it were likely to dry up tomorrow—celebrating, like kids out of school. Genie Reese must have some *really serious* thinking to do.

He sighed as he poured another glass of champagne, wishing she had said yes, noticing that Solovsky had turned back to the bar and was listening intently to something one of his companions was say-ing. Cal glanced at his watch. Eight-thirty wasn't too soon for din-ner in this city, was it? Well, damn it, even if it was, he was hungry. With a nod to Genie and to Solovsky, he made his way to the restaurant.

5

Genie watched from beneath her lashes as Cal strode from the bar. He looked fit, she thought; no Washington paunch from too many expensive business lunches and political dinner parties.

She knew Cal Warrender was considered a "catch" in the Washington social and marriage market. He was the right age, unattached, good-looking, and straight. He was tall, with steady reddish-brown eyes, springy dark hair, and the kind of tight, well-muscled body women liked to touch. And he was a man reputed to be very much on his way up. What more could any conniving society hostess want for her party? Or any woman for a husband? But Genie had a sneaky feeling that work was first in Cal's priorities. Like her, he loved his job.

She assessed the company in the bar, recognizing the stringer for Spain's *Holá* magazine and a couple of very chic Frenchwomen she had noticed at the auction, as well as a few other half-familiar faces of the kind that didn't interest her because they were merely social. Let's face it, she told herself with a sigh, you too are a political animal—and just as ambitious as Cal Warrender.

Her eyes narrowed as she studied the back view of the tall blond man sitting at the bar. *Valentin Solovsky.* What was *he* doing here? She hadn't noticed him at the auction—and yet what other reason would he have for being in Geneva? No UN committees were in session, and she would have known if there were any meetings important enough for his presence. Besides, there was plenty going on in Washington to keep Russia's cultural attaché busy. Today, for instance, the Kirov Ballet was to perform at the Kennedy Center. The President himself was to attend and the Russian embassy was throwing an elaborate party to which the entire diplomatic corps had been invited. It was one of the highlights of the cultural calendar. *So if Solovsky was in Geneva instead of Washington, he had a very important reason. And so did Cal Warrender!*

Her shaking hand sent the ice tinkling as she put down her glass. My God, she thought, then the rumors *are* true. Russia and America *are* fighting for possession of the Ivanoff emerald—at any price. But *why?* And *why* had they let someone else beat them to it? Could there really be billions in the Swiss banks? Was that what they were after? Then what about the other whispers, that there was something else they all wanted? Smoothing her black skirt, she stood up. There was only one way to find out. As she walked from the bar and across the hall to the restaurant, she was uncomfortably aware of Valentin Solovsky's speculative dark eyes following her.

"Hi." She flashed Cal a suddenly friendly smile as she stopped by his table. "Mind if I take you up on that offer to join you? It's kind of lonesome being stranded in a snowstorm. All alone in a foreign country . . . you know what I mean?"

"I sure do." He leapt to his feet as the maître d' pulled back the table and she slid into the banquette next to him.

The waiter filled Genie's glass with champagne. She picked it up and raised it in a mock toast. "Celebrating?" she asked innocently.

Cal grinned. "Now that *you* are here, I am."

She propped her elbows on the table and leaned toward him. "Oh, come clean, Cal," she whispered seriously. "*You* bought that emerald today, didn't you?"

He clasped his hand to his chest in mock-horror. "Why would I do a thing like that? Anyway, I couldn't afford it on a White House salary. I'm only a poor kid from New Jersey."

Their eyes locked and she said, "You bought it on behalf of the U.S. government. The rumors are true after all."

He shrugged nonchalantly. "You've got the wrong guy, Genie, and the wrong rumor."

"Oh, let's talk about it later," she said, pushing her hair from her face with a nervous gesture. "I've had a hard day and I'm starving." She looked at the elaborate menu and sighed. "I'm incapable of making any more decisions. What I'd really like is comfort food, ribs and fries—at Monty's."

The waiter looked pained and Cal laughed. "Why don't you let me order for you?" He spoke to the waiter quickly, then turned back to her on the banquette. Their eyes met. Nice eyes, she told herself, like a red setter's—no, the comparison was unfair. Sure, they were the same color, but his were shrewd. *And* she'd bet they could be hard when he wanted. She shivered suddenly. There was something about Cal Warrender that warned her he could be a tough adversary.

"I think you'll find the food comforting enough," he said lightly, "but I promise you I'll take you to Monty's when we get back to Washington."

"Monty's is in L.A. It used to be my favorite place when I was a kid." She sighed. "It's a pity our expectations of pleasure have to change when we grow up . . . from ribs and fries to oysters and truffles, milk shakes to champagne."

"Oh, I don't know, it's not a bad swap. . . ."

They laughed and he patted her hand encouragingly. "I'll tell you a secret. You look more upset than I do, and I'm the guy who didn't get the emerald."

"You're kidding!" Her eyes widened with astonishment as she stared at him. "Then who did?"

Cal shrugged, nodding in the direction of the door. "Maybe our friend Solovsky?" he suggested.

"Then it is true," she murmured, watching as the Russian made his way through the restaurant to a table opposite them, in direct view but too far away to overhear. Solovsky bowed to them before taking his seat.

"I don't know about true, but I'll tell you something else strange," Cal said. "Solovsky is alone." Her eyebrows rose in a question and he explained, "Important Russians are never alone, there's always someone hovering behind them to make sure they don't pass on any secrets or defect to the West—and someone else behind the watcher to make sure *he* doesn't defect. For a man of Valentin Solovsky's prominence, to be alone is very strange indeed. I wonder how he got rid of the two guys in the bar."

"Probably told them he was having a sandwich from room service and then sneaked in here alone for a feast," she replied with a grin. "I'll bet he couldn't stand the sight of them any longer."

Cal laughed, watching as she slid an oyster down her throat, closing her eyes with pleasure.

"I don't know about Valentin," she said, "but now *I'm* happy." She glanced at the Russian. "I thought in the bar he looked a bit gloomy, but then Russians are, aren't they? It's a characteristic of their race."

Her glance lingered on Solovsky as he studied his menu. He had a fascinating face, so romantic-looking, all planes and angles with deep-set gray eyes and thick, smooth, dark-blond hair. And that passionate-looking mouth. . . . He glanced up suddenly, catching her eye, and she felt herself blush, as if he could read her thoughts.

"I'll tell you something," she said quickly to Cal. "He looks like a movie star. I'd expect to see him starring with Garbo in *Ninotchka.* Put him up for President of Russia and *glasnost* will flourish! At least, it will among the female population of the U.S."

The waiter poured more champagne and Cal said interestedly, "So you're a California girl? The kind the Beach Boys had us all dreaming about?"

She shrugged. "California is lousy with tall, tanned, great-looking blondes. That's why I left," she added with a grin. "The competition was too tough. Yes, I'm Los Angeles born and bred. No, I wasn't a cheerleader. Yes, I do play a good game of tennis. And no, I do not want to go back."

Cal took a bite of delicious walnut bread. "Your family still out there?"

"My parents were divorced, I never knew my father. Mom died a few years ago." She shrugged again. "There's no real reason to go back. Home, you might say, is now the place I hang my hat—and that seems to be Washington."

Her face had softened with sadness as she talked of her mother. Cal thought she must have been a very pretty little girl, every mother's dream child, blond, blue-eyed, beautiful, and bright. "No eyes for New York?" he asked, "Big-time anchorperson, six o'clock news, top interviews, Barbara Walters . . . ?"

She laughed. "I'm like you, politics is my game. I'm hooked on the White House and diplomatic missions and cover-ups in high places—sex and scandal in the seat of power. To me, Washington is as glamorous and exciting as Paris. Besides, I've got this great little house on N Street in Georgetown, right next door to one of Washington's ritziest society hostesses. Of course she has eight bedrooms and a butler to take her tiny poodle for a walk and I only have one bedroom and a very large dog I have to pay a walker to exercise, but I live vicariously. I get to watch her guests arriving and I notice who leaves with whom. I'm no dummy," she added with a wicked grin. "I'm the first to know if a scandal is brewing. It usually begins right on my doorstep."

"Your family have money?" he asked, sampling the salmon approvingly.

She shook her head. "No money, at least not all the time. Mom worked every now and again. She was an actress. Sometimes there was a lot—sometimes nothing."

They paused, forks in hand, looking at each other, liking what they saw. "And you?" she prompted. "What about your life?"

"Born in the Bronx, parents sold the house for a parking lot and made enough to move out to Fort Lee, New Jersey—their decision, not mine! I was a bright kid, I worked hard and got myself into Bronx High—one of the best schools on the East Coast. From there to Harvard—Political Science, and then the Kennedy School of Government. The rest you probably know."

She nodded. "Okay. And now will the real Cal Warrender please stand up?" He stared at her with surprised red-setter eyes.

"I mean, now I've heard your résumé . . . *but who are you?* Where do you live? What do you do when you are not at the White House? What do you like? What do you hate? What is the most important thing in your life—apart from politics, that is?" She waited for a moment and then added softly, "Is there a special woman?"

Cal looked at her in silence. "Oh, come on," she murmured, "imagine we are in a Somerset Maugham novel, two strangers, stranded together in a storm, the only thing to keep them amused their life stories. . . ." He was smiling now and she breathed a little sigh of relief; she wouldn't want him to think that she was just a nosy TV reporter, snooping for a story.

"No *special* woman," he said, "I just don't have the time. Not that I would say no if someone 'special' ever came my way."

His grin was engaging and she laughed. "That's called 'having your cake and eating it.' I know, because I'm like you, just too busy."

"I heard you were an honest woman," he said, raising his glass in a toast. "To the special people who never come our way."

"What motivates you, Cal?" she asked, sipping her champagne. "What makes a politician? Are you born to the role, like an artist or a musician? Or is it an acquired talent?"

He looked at her for a moment, deciding he liked her style. He said, "Now I see what makes you a good reporter. You know the right questions to ask to make your subject open up—and you put them in such a charming and flattering way, they can't refuse to answer. I can't claim to have 'talent,' but I guess I've always been a political animal. I came from a family where politics were always discussed—usually heatedly—over supper, and maybe breakfast and lunch too.

"But I made my decision early in life—I was just a kid, seven years old when my parents took me on a visit to Washington. They wanted me to see the capital, 'to feel the seat of power,' my dad said, and I remember how dazzled I was by the wide avenues and stately columned buildings. I thought it must be as grand a city as Paris. I've never changed my mind. It still gives me a buzz to remember that kid from the Bronx touring the White House with his mom and dad, remembering the first stirrings of political ambition. I just knew I wanted to be part of it. I wanted to be there, in the White House where the decisions were made, I wanted to help—even on the lowest level. I would have been a mail boy—anything, to get through those doors. Me and a million others, I guess," he added with a grin. "Only I did something about it and for me, politics still beats selling junk bonds or making movies as the most exciting business in the world."

"I envy your single-mindedness," she said admiringly. "Everyone says you are destined for the top."

He shrugged. "Maybe. There's a lot of game-playing in that town. I'm not too happy about it, but it seems to go along with the job."

"They say you're one of that rare breed—an honest politician," she said provocatively.

"I hope so," he replied seriously. "And now, what motivates *you,* Genie Reese?"

She thought for a moment, then said, "I'm not sure. Maybe to prove myself to my mom, even though she's dead. She had such a hard time, just never seemed to get it right. . . . I guess I want to make it for both of us."

He looked at her sympathetically, thinking it seemed a very sad reason for success. "Atonement for your mother's sins?" he asked.

She smiled ruefully. "Nothing as grand as that." They looked at each other in silence until she said briskly, "And you? What *else* motivates your famous ambition?"

"*Famous* ambition?"

She laughed at his surprise, "Surely you know that you are 'a man dedicated to his job—a true political animal, possible future presidential material'? Don't you read your own press cuttings, Mr. Warrender?"

She pushed a hand through her long hair and said with a laugh, "Tell me, where do you live? No, let me guess . . . Watergate."

"How did you know?"

"Easy. A political bachelor needs a place with easy access to government offices and the White House, *and* somewhere where he is looked after. Watergate fits the bill—maid service, laundry service, restaurants on the premises for the odd meal alone, smart shops for a quick purchase of a new shirt or tie. . . ."

"And not too far from your place," he countered, laughing. "Maybe you'll ask me in for a home-cooked meal sometime. That's one thing a Washington bachelor never gets—all the dinner parties are catered."

"I'll bet you think I can't cook," she said indignantly. "I'll have you know I learned at my grandmother's knee."

"And was *she* a good cook?"

"The best—though I must admit, not quite as good as this." She tasted the ethereally light chocolate praline mousse. "I never eat dessert, so it just goes to show what being stranded in a storm can do. It takes away all your control."

"You look as if you live on moonbeams and champagne," he said, glancing at her admiringly.

She laughed. "That's exactly the way it's meant to look."

"I'd say your charms are not lost on our Russian friend," Cal said quietly. "He's scarcely taken his eyes off you all night."

Blushing, Genie reached for her glass and knocked it over. As the waiter hurried to mop up the spilled champagne, Cal said, surprised, "I didn't expect Valentin to have quite such a drastic effect on you."

"Sorry, sorry . . . I guess I'm just tired." She ran her hand nervously through her hair again. "Let's have coffee in the lounge. I think I hear someone playing a piano."

Solovsky stood up as she slid from the banquette, their eyes met across the room, then, with a smile, he bowed to her. And again she was aware of his gaze following her as she walked, a little too quickly, from the restaurant.

Snow was still piling in great drifts outside, but inside the Hotel Beau Rivage all was calm and luxury. The lounge was welcoming, with soft lights, silken curtains, and the scent of flowers. A fire blazed in the huge grate and the young man playing the piano slid easily between Cole Porter and Debussy.

Genie glanced at Cal, sitting beside her on the pink-striped sofa.

She just had to get him to tell her what was going on, but how? The only way was to speak the language he understood. Leaning forward, she touched his hand. "Cal," she said hesitantly, "I'm at a crossroads in my life, in my career." His eyes acknowledged what she had said and she hurried on. "I was sent here to do a job I didn't want to do. I had planned to cover the President's visit to Houston, but the station sent me to the jewelry sale instead. Because I was a woman."

Cal took a sip of his brandy. "Genie," he said thoughtfully, "there's no denying you are a woman, and women talk to other women about jewelry."

"Exactly!" she retorted triumphantly. "And therefore I should exploit being a woman—to the hilt. Agreed?"

He nodded. "I guess, careerwise, it's legitimate to use everything you've got."

"I need your help, Cal," she whispered. "I know I'm sitting on the brink of a great story, but nobody is letting me in on it. Cal, if I could have an exclusive on this Ivanoff business, it would *make me* as a national reporter. I thought we might be able to help each other. You tell me something I want to know and I'll tell you something you want to know."

"Like what?" he asked, carefully spooning sugar into his coffee.

"Like who bought the emerald," she said softly.

Cal's red-setter eyes hardened. *"You know?"*

"It was after the auction," she said quickly. "I'd bought my crew a drink in the bar at the Richemond. I was on my way to the powder room when I noticed the door to the auction room was slightly open, so of course I peeked in. It was empty, but there on the dais was the red ledger in which I had seen the auctioneer enter every bid. I thought there was just a chance that he might also have entered the bid for the emerald—after all, it was only withdrawn from sale moments before the auction began. I didn't stop to think about the ethics of the situation," she admitted, glancing guiltily at him. "That red ledger just beckoned me the way the apple must have done Eve. I can tell you my heart was pounding so hard I felt sure someone would hear it and come running in and catch me and I would end up in a Swiss jail. But anyway, I tiptoed to the dais and stole a look. . . . It was there, all right, on the first page: Lot Fifteen, a large fine emerald of forty carats, the property of a Lady . . . sold for $9.26 million."

"That was extremely careless of the auctioneer," Cal said quietly.

She shrugged. "His mistake—my lucky break."

Her heart sank as he stared silently down at his untouched coffee. Oh, God, he wasn't going to go for it . . . she had blown it. . . .

"I'm just trying to figure out what *else* I'd get in return for my information," he said at last.

Her eyes widened in shock. It wasn't the first time she had been propositioned, but she hadn't expected it from a man like Cal.

"Don't get me wrong," he said with a smile. "I meant how we might mutually help each other. *Careerwise.*"

"Anything," she agreed breathlessly, "anything I can do to help you. . . ."

Cal realized he was being handed a golden opportunity on a plate. Solovsky was interested in Genie, and *he* needed to know where the Russians were at. She surely knew how to use those beautiful blue eyes, and it wouldn't be the first time a woman had been used to find out information.

"Okay, Genie Reese," he said finally. "You tell me who bought the emerald, and I promise you the scoop."

"How do I know I can trust you?" she asked cautiously.

He held up his hand, "Scout's honor," he said with a grin.

"The emerald was bought by a dealer in Düsseldorf. His name is Markheim."

"Did the ledger say who he was acting for?"

She shook her head. "Just Markheim."

Cal frowned. It wasn't the name he needed but it was a lead, and he hoped that was more than the Russian had.

He said, "Okay, Reese, put away your notebook and pen, and you'd better not have a tape recorder either, because what I'm going to tell you is for your ears only—until the White House gives the word." Her eyes widened in astonishment as he added, "This is a matter of *national security.* And I'm warning you now that I'm only telling you because I'm going to ask for your help."

"Of course, anything," she agreed eagerly.

"After the revolution," he said, "Russia was broke. The great nations disapproved of the new regime and its actions and refused financial aid. The new Soviet Union had no money to fund agriculture so people were starving, they had no money to finance industry so there were no products to sell. The revolutionaries had confiscated all the bank accounts and property of the noble classes they had just eliminated, and were busy selling off Russia's priceless heritage of paintings, jewels, and antiquities for a fraction of their real worth. They knew about the Ivanoff billions sitting in the Swiss banks, and they did everything they could to get their hands on them, but of course, without a document signed by an Ivanoff giving them the right, they came up against the brick wall of the Swiss banking system. No Ivanoff signature—no billions.

"The Secret Police, the forerunner of the KGB, were known as the Cheka. They still believed that some members of the Ivanoff family had escaped. Only one body had ever been found, that of Princess Anouska, though eyewitness reports also confirmed the death of Prince Misha. They searched Russia for the missing Ivanoffs, the grandmother, the six-year-old boy and his little sister, and then combed Europe, the U.S., even South America. Though they never found them, the KGB have never closed that file.

"All these years the Ivanoffs have been like a thorn in Russia's side. The family represented everything they hated, and they couldn't even get their hands on their money. They think that whoever is now selling the emerald—and we are pretty sure it is the *Ivanoff* emerald—must be a member of the Ivanoff family. They mean to find that 'Lady'—the last Ivanoff—and get her signature to the document. And then the money is finally theirs."

Genie said, awed, "Then it is true. There really are *billions* of dollars."

"*Billions.* But whoever the 'Lady' is, she has never tried to claim them because she was too frightened. She still believed the old threats that if the Russians ever traced her, they would kill her. I can only assume she thought that because the emerald had been cut, it would go unnoticed. Maybe she thought the jewels had been forgotten by now, that it was only the money they were after. But you can't disguise historical gems like that just by cutting them."

Genie glanced shrewdly at him. "There's something else, isn't there?" she said.

He looked innocently at her. "Something else?"

"You know," she replied with an impatient wave of her hand, "what *else* is it the Russians are after? What is it that *America* wants?"

He shook his head. "I can't tell you that. At least not now. Later, when it's all over, I promise you will have the exclusive. But first we have to find out from Markheim who bought the emerald and who the seller was. *We have to find the 'Lady' before Russia does.*"

She looked away, staring thoughtfully into the blazing fire. Cal watched her for a few moments, then he said, "I mentioned that I needed your help, but it's not just for *me,* Genie Reese. *It's for your country.* I am asking you to find out from Valentin Solovsky if he bought the emerald through this dealer, Markheim. And if not, who did."

She looked frightened as she said, "Why me? . . . I thought they *trained* people to be spies."

"Not a *spy,* Genie," he said gently. "You are just asking a few innocent questions. There's no danger. All you have to do is be as good a reporter when you're talking to Solovsky as you have been with me. After all, you got the information you wanted from me, didn't you?"

He nodded in the direction of Solovsky, who was now sitting by the window staring out into the snowy night. "Why don't I leave you to think it over? Meet me in my suite for breakfast tomorrow and let me know what happened. Nine o'clock okay with you?"

She nodded but her eyes were still scared and he relented a little. "There's really nothing to be afraid of," he said. "It's the Ivanoff woman they are after, not you." After taking her limp hand in his, he kissed her fingers lightly, adding with a grin, "Besides, you're no Mata Hari. You're just a damned good reporter sitting on a hell of a story. *An exclusive story.* Remember?"

With a casual wave he strolled to the door. As if drawn by an irresistible force, she turned her head to look at the man by the window. As her eyes met Valentin Solovsky's, Genie faced her choices, and she knew what she had to do.

6

Valentin Solovsky had sat for a long time alone at his table in the deserted restaurant. A solitary waiter stood by the door, a white linen napkin folded over his clasped hands, waiting patiently for the distinguished guest to finish the last of his bottle of Château Margaux.

He had swiveled around in his chair and was gazing at the blizzard raging outside the window. As a Russian, it was a sight he was used to although not one he had expected tonight, and he had certainly not expected the airport to close. He took another sip of the excellent claret, savoring the soft dark flavor on his tongue, but his mind was thousands of miles away, back in Moscow with his father.

The day that had changed his life had started out as any other day. He had risen early in the small but elegant apartment in the mansion on the Kutuzovskiy Prospekt. It was an old building with high ceilings and carved marble fireplaces that had somehow survived the revolution intact, and some years ago it had been divided into apartments suitable for party members earmarked for the top. Thanks to his foreign postings, Valentin's three rooms were furnished with Russian antiques brought back from London and Paris and his kitchen had the latest gadgets from New York City, though the only one that looked used was the coffeemaker. Floor-to-ceiling shelves held books on many subjects and in several languages, for he spoke French, English, German, and Italian as well as Russian and some of its dialects.

Surprisingly for such a dedicated Party member, there were no gaudy Soviet paintings of the revolution, no propaganda posters of agricultural workers standing proudly beside a tractor or factory workers in front of shining modern machinery. But there was a picture of Lenin.

The only other pictures were four framed photographs displayed on a table in his small sitting room. One was of his grandfather, Grigori Solovsky, taken at the age of sixty, dark-haired and swarthy, standing solidly on his short peasant legs, one arm flung around his wife. Her yellow-blond hair had faded early to white, but her blue eyes were as innocent and twinkling as a young girl's. They had died within weeks of each other ten years before, he of a brain tumor and she of a broken heart.

Next to them was an official portrait of his uncle, Boris Solovsky, stern and unsmiling, his head as naked as a billiard ball, with bitter lines running from nose to mouth and a perpetual frown between his paranoid dark eyes. Boris had never married, though rumors of his affairs were whispered throughout Moscow, none of them salubrious. His uncle was said to be a sadistic man not only in his love life but in his control of the KGB, of which he had been head for seven years.

The largest photograph was of Valentin's father, Sergei Solovsky, and his mother, Irina, taken on their wedding day. Both were smiling into the camera and it was Valentin's favorite photograph because he had never, in all his life, seen his father look as happy as he did in that picture. Irina looked young enough to be his daughter, but there was no denying the glow of love on her sweet face. They made a beautiful couple: Sergei tall, blond, strong-jawed, and hawk-eyed, and Irina a petite, slender ballerina, her dark silken hair worn pulled back in the classical style of dancers. Valentin could never remember his mother making an ungraceful move, whether floating lightly across the stage of the Bolshoi Theater or digging in the garden of their country *dacha* in Zhukova. The last photograph was of her alone on stage. Irina, daughter of a village carpenter and his illiterate wife, looked like a princess in the spangled tutu of Aurora in *The Sleeping Beauty*.

The apartment had been Valentin's home for ten years except when he was away on foreign assignments, and he hoped the only reason he would ever have to leave it would be because of a move to the top of the power ladder. And that was what he wanted more than anything in the world.

Like all young Russian boys, Valentin had joined the Pioneers organization and, later, when he was fourteen, the Komsomol—the Communist League of Youth. Religion and God had never entered his life because the children were taught to devote themselves only to the Communist Party, and very few ever disobeyed. Valentin remembered how his schoolmates had taunted two boys whose parents still attended church, baiting them until their lives became unbearable and the family had suddenly been "relocated" from Moscow to a remote, frozen territory on the North Cape. He also knew that anyone who did not join the Komsomol would not be able to continue his education at a university. Of course in his case —the son of an important Party member—these questions had never arisen. He was automatically enrolled in everything suitable for the education and grooming of a clever boy toward high political position.

He had completed his studies at Moscow University, reading international politics and law, followed by a year as an officer cadet at the infamous *Spetsnaz* training camp at Ryazan, in Byelorussia. His regiment's motto was "Prepare to Sacrifice Yourself in the Name of Your Socialist Motherland," and the unit lived up to that promise, training their ranks to obey their officers' commands without hesitation, no matter how extreme. They soon became experts in murder, assassination, and terrorism. A hundred soldiers were crammed into each small cramped barracks, and they worked day and night. They marched everywhere: to p.e. after reveille then on to six hours of unarmed combat training. Then they marched to their noontime meal and afterward marched out for more exercise and more training. Later they marched to supper and to roll call before marching back to their quarters and bed. Every Sunday a few men were given leave to visit the local town, but the only time they were permitted home leave was if a family member died. They earned just enough to buy themselves toilet articles and cigarettes, but alcohol in any form was forbidden.

Valentin never understood why young men joined the tough *Spetsnaz* regiment, though as an officer-cadet his lot was a very different one. He enjoyed the hard physical work but loathed the violence as well as the regimentation of his year's training, and he hated even more the six months that followed it on active duty on the borders of Afghanistan. But he knew he was paying his dues.

His goal had been clear even as a boy. All his life he had been surrounded by men of great political power—his grandfather, his father, his uncle, and their friends. And like his father, his only other interest was music. When he was a boy his father had often taken him to the ballet to watch his mother dance, or to the opera and symphony concerts. They would sit side by side in the worn red-velvet seats of Moscow's concert halls, lost in the music, and Valentin never felt closer to his father than he did at those times.

Afterward, Sergei would treat him to supper at his favorite restaurant. It was run by an old gypsy family, and, to Valentin's surprise, his father knew all their songs and sometimes he would sing along as the gypsies played their guitars and balalaikas.

But Sergei Solovsky had worried about his son. When Valentin was offered his first important post as an assistant in the Foreign Service Department, he warned him about the single-mindedness of his ambitions.

"Do not leave love out of your life, Valentin," he had said as they walked together in the gardens of their *dacha,* after the special dinner to celebrate Valentin's new job. "It's one of the last real human emotions still free to us Russians, and it is the most valuable."

"Of course not, Father," he had replied, surprised. But even then he had known that his goal, to be Russia's leader, would always come first. Life had stretched before him with every step toward that goal marked out, and he vowed he would let nothing stand in his way because he knew he wanted to unite the turbulent regions that formed the Soviet Union in a way they had not been united since Lenin and the first days of revolution. And from there, he promised himself he would make his nation the leader of the world powers.

Everything had gone as he had planned. Promotion had followed rapidly on promotion, and he secured the important foreign postings he needed to allow him to study the weaknesses and strengths of other nations at first hand, learning all the time and storing that knowledge for his future use.

He had been surprised when his father had called three months ago, requesting his return from Washington on urgent business, and even more surprised when the nature of the problem had been explained to him. The Ivanoff jewels were finally appearing on the market. Russia wanted the person selling them found and brought back to Russia at once. His Uncle Boris was in charge and had "requested" Valentin for the job.

"But why me?" he had protested, pacing the red carpet in his father's large Kremlin office angrily. "Why doesn't he just put the KGB on to it?"

There was a strange look in his father's eyes as he replied, "This is a matter of extreme 'delicacy.' America knows why we want the person selling the jewels. You are to be our front man, Valentin. As a diplomat you travel the world without attracting attention, you can attend the auction and bid for the jewel . . . but behind you, the KGB will be searching for this mysterious 'Lady.'

"You will discuss the matter with Boris tomorrow," his father concluded, holding up his hand to silence any further protest. "And now I am on my way to the TV station at Ostankino. They are televising a concert by the winners of the National Youth Orchestra Competition. Why don't you join me?"

Valentin had known better than to bring up the subject of the Ivanoff emerald on the ride to the TV station in his father's black bullet-nosed chauffeur-driven ZIL; if Sergei was not talking, there must be a reason, and besides he knew that even the cars of top executives were bugged. "Trust" was not a widely used word in the Kremlin. When they finally arrived Sergei dismissed the limousine, telling the chauffeur to return in two hours.

After the television program was over he suggested they take a stroll, and they crossed the road into Dzerzhinsky Park, walking silently through the Botanic Gardens, past the beautiful grove of hundred-year-old oak trees, toward the arboretum.

"What I have to tell you is extremely difficult," Sergei said at last. "I thought that my secret would die with me, as it did with your grandfather."

Valentin glanced at him in surprise.

"I know sometimes you have wondered at the difference between your Uncle Boris and myself," Sergei began. "Now I can tell you. It is because I was adopted by Grigori Solovsky when I was six years old."

"Adopted?" Valentin cried, stopping dead in his tracks and star- ing, shocked, at his father. "It is not important," he added hur- riedly. "It doesn't matter to me who you *were.* You are Grigori Solovsky's son. You are my father."

"It matters to Boris," his father replied calmly. "He was a slow, clumsy boy and he always knew I was different. Even at six I spoke French and English like the aristocrats, not just a Russian dialect like him. I was clever and a better horseman. I learned quickly and did well in school. He was jealous—and I was terrified of him. Boris was cruel, insane with jealousy. Today he would be called a psycho- path." He turned to face Valentin. "I want you to understand that Boris is your enemy as well as mine." Sergei shrugged. "Black is black and white is white to a man like that. There is no middle road of gray. Those he wants removed, he kills."

They walked on in silence for a while and then Sergei said, "The thing that most disturbed Boris was that Grigori never told his family *who* I was. He simply told them that I was an orphan of the revolution. But Boris always suspected I was an aristocrat and as soon as he was able, he set about trying to discover who I really was. When he found out, he intended to destroy me." He sighed wearily. "All my life I've been walking a tightrope between two identities—the person I knew I was and the person I had become. And two loyalties; the one I had adopted, and the one I belonged to by birth. And always there, waiting to trap me, was Boris. For that reason I decided to live my life alone. I decided it wasn't fair to marry because any day my true identity might be found out and I would be arrested and killed. But then, many years later, I met your mother and fell in love. I was older; I told myself selfishly that if Boris hadn't found out by then, he never would.

"Boris was all smiles the day he came to my wedding. He kissed the bride and laughed and joked. I had never seen him so happy. As we were leaving for our honeymoon, he handed me an envelope.

" 'A little surprise for you, Sergei,' he said with the same malevolent gleam in his eyes I remembered as a boy. And then he added, 'Or should I say Alexei?'

"I'll never forget his laugh as he drove off. He sounded like the madman I *knew* he was." Sergei's voice shook as he said, "Inside the envelope was a photograph of my real father."

Sergei fell silent and as they strode through the park Valentin wondered, puzzled, why his real father's photograph should be so important.

"Of course I realized Boris knew the truth," Sergei said at last, "and on my honeymoon I waited for him to act. I waited for days, for weeks, then months. I was like a man on the scaffold waiting for the ax to fall. Until I realized that though Boris *knew,* he had no real proof. The fact that I resembled the man in the photograph, as you do, Valentin, was not enough to convince the powers that one of their top men was not who he claimed to be. It could be a mere coincidence, and in accusing me Boris would risk his own career. *He still needs that proof.* But all these years he has carried a duplicate of that photograph in his wallet. He knows that I know and that he has not forgotten."

"Surely it can't matter anymore who your father was?" Valentin said hopefully.

"It matters," Sergei replied quietly, taking the ring he had carried with him all these years from an inner pocket. It was a large star ruby in an elaborate gold setting. Handing it to Valentin, he said, "This is all I have left of our inheritance. My real family was one of the richest in Russia. They were so important they were next after the tsar on the Cheka's death list. My father—your grandfather— was Prince Misha Ivanoff. Our family owned those billions and those mines. And it is your own cousin—*your own blood*—you are being asked to track down and bring back to Russia. To Boris and certain death."

And then, as they walked slowly through the park, Sergei had told him the story of what happened on the long, dark night in the forest so many years ago. And Valentin saw his whole life crashing in ruins in front of his eyes.

Valentin drained the last of the wonderful claret and, after pressing a lavish tip into the patient waiter's hand, walked slowly from the restaurant.

He strode into the lounge and took a seat by the window. Cal Warrender was sitting by the fire talking earnestly to the American TV reporter, Genie Reese. He envied him his peace of mind—and the girl. She was the American Beauty rose foreigners like him always dreamed about, long-stemmed, beautiful, and fragile.

He sipped his coffee, wondering what they were saying, they were so absorbed in each other. But all the time, at the back of his mind, lay his father's words: "It is your own cousin—*your own blood*— you are being sent to bring back to Russia . . . and certain death." He had understood at once that Boris wanted the "Lady" not just for Russia, but because then he would be able to confirm the truth about Sergei. *Boris wanted his father dead.*

Valentin had realized early in his career that no one could achieve political power without personal sacrifice; a public figure could be called upon at any time to account for his actions and was expected to be an example to those beneath him. He had thought over his options for a long time. First, there was his duty to his country. The balance of power was at stake. If he found the Ivanoff "Lady" and brought her back to Russia, not only would his country finally get the money it rightfully believed belonged to the state, but even more important, it would finally have indisputable power over the Indian mines. There was only one way to save his father's life as well as his own, and also protect the Russia he believed in. *And gain everything he had ever worked for.* He had to find the "Lady" before the Americans did. *And then kill her before Boris got to her.* He reflected bitterly that his training at Ryazan would finally come in useful, but he knew the "Lady" would find him a more merciful executioner than his uncle, whose favorite punishment was death by torture.

The race was on, he thought wearily. No matter how he did it, whom he had to use, he had to find the "Lady" first.

He turned from the window and met Genie Reese's eyes across the room. Cal Warrender had gone and she was alone. After picking up his brandy, he walked toward her. "Miss Reese," he said, gesturing to the window, "I see we are both orphans of the storm. I wonder if you would take pity on my loneliness and join me in a drink?"

Taking a deep breath, Genie looked him squarely in the eye. "I would be delighted, Mr. Solovsky," she said.

7

Maryland

"Fairlawns" was truly what it claimed: smooth acres of velvet green leading to a silvery lake where, from her window, Missie could watch the mallards busy building their nests in the banks. The sudden cold spell had failed to kill the early cherry blossoms, and the willows drooping over the water were already sheathed in their film of spring green.

"It's a beautiful day," Nurse Sara Milgrim told her with a jolly smile. "Perhaps we can go out for a walk later. How d'you feel about that? See the ducks nests, we can."

"Not ducks, mallards," Missie said firmly. "You can tell by the green head. And I've told you a thousand times, Sara, not to talk to me like a child—or a senile old woman. There's nothing wrong with my brain." Nurse Milgrim was brushing her hair and she winced. "Except when you pull my hair like that."

Nurse Milgrim grinned. Missie was in one of her sharp moods this morning. You couldn't put anything over on her: She always knew when the jolly smile covered up the fact that she'd had a fight with her boyfriend or that she had been on night duty for two weeks and was worn to a frazzle. "You've got such beautiful hair, Missie," she remarked, stroking the brush lovingly through the long silken strands. "The silver surely brings out the color of your eyes. They look like violets."

"Violets?" Missie said dreamily. "Oh, no, it was Anouska who wore the violets. If I close my eyes I can smell them now. . . ."

"Anouska, mmm? Well, I bet her hair wasn't as pretty as yours. You must have been quite something when you were a girl. I'll bet all the boys were after you."

"No boys," Missie said. "They were all men . . . four of them."

She sighed. "And the only one I didn't marry was the one I really loved. My first love."

"They say first love is the truest," Nurse Milgrim said, staring curiously at her in the mirror. "It's a pity, then, you didn't marry him?"

Missie closed her eyes and said, "He died. It happened too long ago to really matter anymore."

Nurse Milgrim glanced at her as she fastened her hair into her usual chignon. Her eyes were still closed and despite what Missie had just said, she could tell by her face it really did still matter.

"I'm sorry, Missie," she said quickly. "I'll tell you what, why don't I just go and fix you a nice cup of Earl Grey tea? That's the kind you like, isn't it? I'll be right back now."

Missie heard the door close and once again she was alone with her thoughts. But what was she thinking of, rambling on about Anouska like that? Was she losing her brains after all? She supposed it was just because it was on her mind. She must be more careful, especially after what she had just seen on television. Milgrim might have remembered the name Anouska and put two and two together. And now she was so afraid for Anna. Where was she? Why didn't she telephone? She sighed deeply. When all this had begun she had not realized it would never end. If Yeventlov had not found them in the forest, she wouldn't be here today and the Ivanoff treasure would simply have disappeared, just like so many others.

Russia

She had awoken to find herself wallowing in the warm depths of a soft goosedown quilt. She was wearing a clean pink flannel nightgown, and her feet and hands were tingling with fiery pins and needles as blood and life returned to them. Firelight flickered on the wooden walls and there was the soft murmur of voices close by. She stared around her bewilderedly. Sofia was sitting at the table in the center of the room, straight-backed as ever, sipping hot tea from a glass. Viktor was drying off in front of the blazing stove, his long fur smelling like a flock of wet sheep, and little Xenia was chatting gaily in English to five small, sallow children who were staring at her as if she were the ninth wonder of the world. She realized that this must be the stationmaster's house, and the memories suddenly flooded back. She began to tremble and tears trickled down her cheeks.

"Stay where you are," Madame Yeventlov said quietly. "You are

safe for the moment. My husband found you in the forest and
brought you here. I will make you some tea and then later, when
you feel better, you shall have some of my good soup." Her brown
eyes held a depth of sympathy and Missie understood she knew
what had happened.

She sipped the tea, concentrating on each sweet scalding sip as it
slid down her throat without melting the ice that still gripped her
heart. She remembered lying in the snow and wanting to die as the
captain had ridden off with Alexei. *Solovsky, Solovsky,* she thought,
anguished, his name burning itself into her brain. She supposed that
shock must have slowed her heartbeat. Her limbs had grown heavy
and she had been filled with a deadly lethargy. Her blood was like
ice water in her veins, and she remembered little by little relaxing
into the stupor that she had known would bring death. She remembered hearing the soft padding sound of the first wolf approaching
her and the fetid smell of its breath as it sniffed her hair, and then
she had known she was not to be allowed to die peacefully in the
snow: She was to be devoured by wolves.

As the beast had danced uncertainly around her, prodding her
with its paw, she dimly recalled Misha telling her that wolves
preyed only on dead human flesh and rarely attacked the living, but
she could hear more of them, a pack running from the forest toward
her. Suddenly there was a terrible screaming and snarling, and she
had looked up to see Viktor tear the throat from the first wolf and
then turn and rout the pack already feasting on Anouska's body.
Then he had returned, whimpering, to her side. His liquid-brown
eyes had gazed beseechingly at her and blood dripped from a torn
ear.

The urge to survive had surged through her like a burst of life-
giving heat; she was just eighteen, and despite all the horrors the
power of youth made her long for life. And besides, she had a
responsibility. She had to save Misha's daughter. She had tried to
sit up then but her legs refused to obey and her heart pounded so
fiercely she could scarcely breathe. Then suddenly everything had
gone black and she knew no more until she woke and found herself
here, in Yeventlov's house at Ivanovsk.

Sofia came to sit beside her. Taking her hand, she said, "Thank
God you are all right, Missie. If it weren't for you, my granddaughter would have perished along with the others. My only consolation
from this dreadful night is that Misha did not live to find out how
his wife and his son died."

Missie's heart felt as if it were being wrenched from her body. She stared at Sofia, and the old lady nodded sadly. "Oh, yes," she whispered, "I am sure Misha is dead. I feel it here." She struck her heart with a clenched fist. "Why? I ask. My son was a good man. Like his father and his grandfather before him, he was an exemplary landowner. He cared for his people with proper fatherly Russian tenderness. He fought for their rights in the *Duma,* the Parliament. So why, Missie? *Why* did they kill such a good man? Who else will care for them as Misha did?" Her dark eyes were filled with anguish as she whispered, "And how could they do what they did to Anouska?"

She turned away, staring tearlessly into the blazing stove. "Yeventlov could not find Alexei's body," she said at last. "He said the wolves must have already devoured it."

"Oh, but—" Missie began, then she stopped herself suddenly. There was no point in hurting Sofia even more by telling her about Alexei. She had enough to bear. And anyhow, she knew there was no hope for him. Turning her face to the wall, she drifted into unconsciousness. When she awoke again, the shutters were still tightly closed and only Madame Yeventlov was awake, busy kneading a coarse black rye dough at the table. Sofia lay on a straw mattress by the stove with Xenia in the crook of her outflung arm. The dog lay close by them, but there was no sign of the others and Missie guessed they were sleeping in the other room.

Madame Yeventlov nodded to her, smiling. "So, you are awake at last," she said quietly. "Now you will be ready for that soup. Oh, yes," she added, stifling Missie's protests with an uplifted hand, "God knows you will need your strength as well as your wits about you if you are to survive."

Sitting in a hard wooden chair at a pine table scrubbed to whiteness from years of Madame Yeventlov's good housewifely attentions, Missie listened as she told her their plan.

Yeventlov said the trains were unpredictable. The only thing that was certain was that everything was running late. The depots had run out of coal for the steam engines and were now using pine logs that burned at a great rate, often leaving the trains stranded without fuel in the middle of the snowbound countryside. Yeventlov had to wait until he got a signal from the big station north of Ivanovsk telling him that a train had left and then wait again for it to arrive.

"How long will it be?" she asked.

Madame Yeventlov shrugged. Nobody knew. A journey that took

four hours in normal times might now take four days, or even more. She told her they must disguise themselves well. The soldiers would be sure to be on the lookout for traitors like herself.

Missie stared at the bowl of soup, wondering how she, the daughter of an eminent Oxford professor, had come to be regarded as a traitor to a country that was not even her own.

It had all started out so gaily a little more than a year ago, just she and her father setting out on another of his jaunts around the world, this time to inspect the latest archaeological excavations in Turkey.

Professor Marcus Octavius Byron had been over fifty years old when he had married lovely young long-legged Alice Lee James, and he was astonished when, three years later, she had presented him with a baby girl they named Verity, but somehow, she had always been called just "Missie." Alice Lee had died tragically of a chill that turned into pneumonia when Missie was only eight, and after that she and her father had become very close. There were no other living relatives. He was all the family she had left, and he adored her. He took her everywhere with him. By the time she was fourteen she had been on archaeological digs in Greece, inspected excavations in India, and helped uncover ancient tombs in Egypt. But home had always been the tall, shabby house on the quiet tree-lined street just around the corner from Trinity College in Oxford.

Her father always told her she was pretty, but she thought he was biased because she looked like her mother. She had Alice Lee's deep violet-blue eyes, pale creamy skin, and sleek seal-brown hair, but Missie had always thought herself unfashionably skinny. Her cheekbones stuck out, her nose, though straight, was positive, and her mouth too generous. Besides, her long legs made her taller than most of the boys she knew.

In the Yeventlov's hut the soup lay untouched on the table as she closed her eyes, conjuring up her father's familiar, comforting image. He was a tall, thin man, stooped from too many years hunched over the fine print of old history books. He had a gray beard and faded blue eyes, and he wore a tweed jacket, turning green with age, that when she snuggled close to him gave off a faint aroma of good cigars and fine old port.

Missie fought back the tears as she remembered how she would tap on his study door, listening for his usual grunted Latin *"Intra."* He always smiled and put down his book to give her his full attention, but sometimes she would come bounding in from school to find him lost in the past and he would stare at her with such astonishment that she could swear he had forgotten all about her.

But the professor didn't forget her schooling. After telling her she would be as well educated as any boy, he sent her off to a famous Oxford prep school where she was the only girl. It was only because of her father's eminence as a scholar that she had been accepted, but she was used to a masculine environment and fitted in as easily as if she really were "one of the boys." When she arrived home one day and announced that she intended to play rugger, even the professor had realized that perhaps it was time to send her to a school for young ladies. But he liked the fact that the boys' school had given her "spirit." She was afraid of nothing.

She sighed, opening her eyes and staring bewilderedly at the tiny shuttered room and the Russian woman baking bread. Suddenly childhood and Oxford seemed so very far away.

The professor had been planning their summer trip to Turkey for a whole year; there were important excavations taking place north of Ephesus with exciting new discoveries dating back to the fifth millennium. Despite her protests that in summer it would be searingly hot, that the mosquitoes would be swarming, that water would be scarce and their rations, so far from any town, would be basic, her father had acted like a child promised a new toy—nothing would prevent him from having it *now.*

In the end, though, he had agreed to compromise. They would go to Turkey for the months of May and June, avoiding the worst of the heat, and return later in the autumn. In between they would take up Prince Misha Ivanoff's long-standing invitation to visit St. Petersburg. When the prince had been reading ancient history at Oxford, the professor had become both his mentor and his friend, and the two had corresponded ever since.

But in Turkey he had sat up night after night, excitedly writing his notes by the light of a flickering oil lamp with never a thought for the marauding mosquitoes. After only three weeks he had been stricken with the severe chills and fevers of malaria. The dig was in a remote area, a hundred miles from the nearest village, and there was no doctor. The quinine and patent medicines Missie had brought along did little to help, and he quickly became dehydrated from the fever. She nursed him anxiously for a week, and then, quite suddenly, he seemed to pick up again. He had told her eagerly that he wanted to get back to his work, but she had thought his eyes looked a little more tired, and his hands had trembled. He had suddenly looked, she remembered with a pang, like an old man.

How she wished she had insisted they return to England, but again she had compromised; they would go to Russia, where her father would recuperate at the palatial Ivanoff villa on the Crimean coast.

The villa had turned out to be more like a marble palace, spacious and cool and with every luxury, including dozens of servants to cater to her every whim. But she barely noticed because the professor immediately fell ill again. Despite the best medical care, Marcus Octavius Byron had died two days later. His last words were "Take care of yourself, Missie. There are big changes ahead of you now." He had pressed her hand lightly and, without even a sigh, he was gone. Missie had no other living relatives. Without her father, she was alone in the world.

He was buried the next day in the immaculate little Orthodox churchyard on a hill overlooking the indigo-blue sea far below. There was no time for Prince Misha to travel the thousands of miles from St. Petersburg to mourn his old colleague, but when Missie followed her father's coffin into the cool domed white church, she found it filled with the prince's own friends who were holidaying at their villas.

They had murmured words of comfort and encouragement as they accompanied her back to the Ivanoff villa, sipping endless glasses of tea and watching her with troubled eyes. "Why does she not cry?" they had whispered to each other worriedly, because they were used to the great outpourings of emotion that were so Russian. "She is so young . . . only sixteen . . . and all alone in the world now, Misha Ivanoff says. . . ."

The tears had come the next day, alone in the cushioned comfort of the Ivanoff private train as it took her to St. Petersburg to stay with the prince and his family. And then when she finally got there and met Misha, her whole life had changed, just as her father had said it would.

The big Ivanoff houses were filled with a mixture of relations, ancient maiden aunts and widowed second cousins, who all lived happily amid a flurry of knitting needles, spicy gossip, and a faint odor of peppermint and cologne. An extra person here and there only added to the expansive Russian family hospitality. But Verity Byron was special; the hearts of all the Ivanoffs went out to her in her loneliness and grief, and with no family of her own to go back to, she soon became one of them. And of course, she was hopelessly in love with Misha.

Looking back now, Missie thought the time seemed to have passed too quickly and she longed with all her heart to be able to turn back the clock. If only they hadn't gone to Turkey her father would still be here . . . if only she hadn't fallen in love with Misha Ivanoff and had gone home to Oxford . . . if only there had been no revolution and things had stayed as they were . . . she wouldn't be running for her life, with the double responsibility of an old woman and a small child to look after.

It was two days before the train finally made its way through the snowdrifts into Dvorsk, and in all that time Alexei had said not a word. His huge frightened eyes had followed Grigori as he paced the bakery, raging at the railway's inefficiency. Only if Grigori was there would Alexei eat the bowls of thin soup and the bitter black rye bread, still warm from the baker's oven. And whenever Grigori put on his coat and went to the door he would find Alexei at his side, staring at him silently, a forlorn little figure following at his heels like a dog faithful to his new master.

The ancient steam engine, fueled with small mountains of logs, spat smoke and sparks into the foggy, freezing early-morning air. Suddenly a great crowd converged on the small station, pushing and shouting as they fought their way onto the already-crowded train. Their carriage had at one time been the luxurious private coach of an official of the railway company, but now it was reserved exclusively for Grigori and his entourage. There was no heat or light, but the velvet seats were cushioned, and two young officers carried a milk churn filled with soup, some loaves of bread, and candles. Compared with the other passengers, crammed onto slatted wooden seats or on the bare floors and corridors, and even lying on the overhead luggage racks, they were traveling in comfort.

Every so often the train would stop and Grigori would jump from the carriage and stride along the track, conferring angrily with the engine driver. But the engine was old and the fuel not enough, so that even when it started again, it merely crawled along.

Soldiers in tattered makeshift uniforms patrolled the length of the train, demanding identification papers and travel permits. Every so often, as the senior officer on board, Grigori would be called upon to arbitrate over some infringement of the rules. Although he was a hard man, he still felt a kinship for those of peasant background. He knew most were only trying to rejoin their scattered families and he dealt leniently with them. The case of the English girl was different.

She was standing in the corridor in the grip of a pair of dirty, unkempt soldiers, and Grigori noticed two things about her: She was very beautiful in a cool, European way, and she was very angry. Her violet eyes flashed sparks of contempt at her captors.

"Tell them to take their hands off me, *at once,*" Missie commanded in excellent Russian. "They have no right to treat an Englishwoman this way."

She turned to look at him, catching her breath as she recognized him, almost blurting out the question that burned in her brain day and night: "Where is Alexei?" But instead she stared down at Solovsky's boots, biting her lip. She and Sofia had come to a decision in the long wait at the Yeventlovs' hut. Everything that was past had to be pushed from their minds, buried with their dead. If they were to survive they could only look forward. And Missie desperately wanted to survive.

At a word from Grigori, the soldiers let go her arms. She rubbed her bruises, avoiding his eyes, wondering nervously if he recognized her. Her mouth felt dry with fear and she thrust her hands behind her back so he would not see them trembling. Solovsky continued to stare at her silently. Her head ached with strain and weariness. They had been on the train for over twelve hours; there was no heat and even though they were bundled in padded coats with babushkas, the traditional headscarves, tied under their chins so they looked like ordinary peasant women, only the crowded animal heat of too many bodies had kept them from freezing. Madame Yeventlov had prepared a small package of food for them, but they had not dared take it out during daylight for fear it would be torn from their grasp by the starving peasants, many of whom were drunk on homemade potato vodka. They ate only under cover of darkness. Not knowing how long the journey might take, they were forced to ration the bread and piroshkis, the little pasties filled with potatoes and vegetables. There were no lights on the train and they dared not sleep, afraid for their lives in the pitch-dark night.

They had told themselves it could all be endured; that eventually the train would get to St. Petersburg. Then they would take a train to Yalta on the Crimean coast where the people were still loyal to the "White" Russian cause, and they would be safe. They had no papers and no luggage and very little money, but somehow they would do it. Only now she was about to be interrogated by Solovsky, and all their lives depended on what she said. And as she looked at Solovsky, she knew her story had better be a good one because this man's eyes told her he had seen and heard it all before.

Solovsky allowed the silence to lengthen as he studied her. Was that a flicker of fear he had seen in her eyes? He shrugged. She had a right to be frightened, being manhandled by those two beasts. And yet what was she doing, a young foreign woman alone on this train in such dangerous times? "Who are you?" he asked finally. "And where are your papers?"

Missie took a deep breath and said, "I am the widow of Morris O'Bryan, an engineer with the American Westinghouse Company, in St. Petersburg. My husband was killed three weeks ago when a bomb destroyed part of the plant. I am with my mother-in-law and my young daughter. We were trying to get home through Finland but there were no more trains. We waited over a week; I thought the only solution was to return to St. Petersburg and see what happens. . . ."

Grigori let her stumble through her story in silence. He had long ago perfected an unblinking stare that destroyed the lies and half truths frightened men wove around themselves. But this girl merely stuck her chin in the air and said haughtily, "Would you please tell your men to allow us to continue our journey in peace!"

Solovsky barked a sudden command and the soldiers hurried back down the corridor, returning moments later with Sofia and Xenia. Viktor padded beside them, showing his fangs in a snarl as they waited nervously for what might happen next.

Grigori inspected them carefully. The old woman was dressed poorly but there was a certain air about her. Despite himself, Grigori felt that old, deep-rooted peasant instinct to doff his cap. Thrusting his hands into his pockets, he turned to the child. He knew children always spoke the truth.

"What is your name, little girl?" he asked in English.

"Her name is Alice Lee O'Bryan," Missie intercepted hurriedly. Alice Lee was the name of her own dead mother. She held her breath, staring at Xenia; all their lives depended on the next words of a child not yet three years old.

Her palms were slippery with sweat and she dared not look at Sofia as Solovsky asked again, "What is your name, little girl?"

Xenia stared back at him with that blank, dreamy look Missie knew so well. Suddenly her face lighted up and her pansy-gold eyes sparkled with amusement. Twirling a flaxen curl around her plump baby finger, she smiled trustingly at Solovsky. "Azaylee," she told him. "My name is Azaylee O'Bryan!"

Instinct told Grigori something was wrong and he stared hard at the child, but she just smiled back at him, twisting the curl around her finger. He knew he should question her again, but then he might look like an ignorant peasant fool in front of these foreigners. "Did you inspect their luggage?" he asked the soldiers instead.

"Our luggage was stolen," Missie said quickly, "and all our papers. We have only what we are wearing."

"I apologize for the behavior of my countrymen," Grigori said formally. "I shall be pleased to give you a document that will ensure your safe travel without further molestation."

Sending one of the men to fetch the forms from his carriage, he added, "A word of advice. The Crimea is the only gateway left from Russia. But do not linger in St. Petersburg. Go straight to Kursk Station and take the first train south, or it will be too late."

Missie could hardly believe it as he filled out a form and stamped it with the official seal of authorization. "I wish you a safe journey, madame," he said, signing it with a flourish.

Their eyes met as she took it from him and whispered, "Thank you." And then she hurried back along the corridor, urging the others along in front of her, aware of Grigori Solovsky's speculative glance following them every inch of the way.

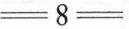

8

Paris

Leyla Kazahn was enjoying the rare luxury of a day alone at her Paris home on the Ile St-Louis. It was cold and gray with a threat of snow but she welcomed the chance to breathe clean fresh air after the stuffy overcrowded salons and hot, smoky photographic studios where she spent most of her time. She was wearing a violet shearling jacket, jeans, and boots, and with her long dark hair pulled back and no makeup, she looked like a different girl from the sleek model of the Paris catwalks and fashion magazines. Only her extraordinary eyes, almond-shaped and a blazing blue, betrayed her identity.

When she was just seventeen, she had been discovered by an agent browsing in Barney's. He had whisked her to the city's grandest photographer, who had insisted on taking pictures of her there and then, a simple unadorned schoolgirl in a T-shirt and jeans. He had emphasized her delicate mixture of the East and the West, and before she knew it *Vogue* was commissioning pictures. Instead of going on to study at the Sorbonne, Leyla had a calender booked a year ahead with modeling assignments. Of course now she had to live in Europe, but right from the beginning she had insisted on keeping two months free every year, because even though she was happy in her spacious Paris apartment, the place that held her heart, her home, and her family, with all its timeless traditions, was Istanbul.

She had chosen to live on the Ile St-Louis because it was just like a tiny moated village in the very heart of Paris; it was exactly eight hundred yards long, it had only eight streets, and everybody knew everybody else. And even though her face was a famous one, nobody bothered her. To her neighbors and the other *insulaires,* or islanders, she was just "Leyla."

As she walked along the Quai de Béthune, the watery light from the Seine softened the façades of the seventeenth-century mansions to pale blue-gray; seabirds wheeled overhead and a barge slid silently under the graceful arch of the Pont-Marie, but Leyla didn't notice the beauty around her. Normally she could not resist Bertillon's wild strawberry ice cream, but today she passed by without even a second glance; she picked up some yogurt from Lecomte's *crèmerie* without a word and dropped off her fine linen sheets at old Madame Parraud's hand laundry on Rue la Regrettier, with only a quick *"bonjour."* The assistant at Monsieur Turpins' Fruits de France shook his head resignedly as he noticed her worried frown; Mademoiselle Leyla's mind was obviously on more important matters than merely passing the time of day.

Leyla hurried back along the Quai de Béthune still thinking about the news report she had seen on television last night. They had said it was like an international convention at the Hotel Richemond with reporters from all over the world, and she had sat frozen with fear while they described the history of the jewel, the rumors surrounding the mysterious "Lady," and the speculation as to the identity of the secret buyer. They had shown glimpses of a handsome young Soviet diplomat and a stern-eyed American from the State Department in Washington, hurrying unsmiling from the sale room. "No jewel in history has ever caused such a furor," they said, and Leyla's heart had sunk.

"Who would have thought it?" she had whispered to herself. "Who would ever have imagined that this would happen?"

Of course she and Anna had known the old reason for secrecy, but they had treated it lightly. It was just an old story, so much time had passed, so much water under the bridge, things were different now. . . . How could there possibly be any real danger? When they had sold the diamond at auction without any fuss or scandal, they had congratulated themselves on their cleverness. Only now it seemed they had been *too* clever, *too* confident. They had allowed their success to lull them into recklessness. Even cut, the Ivanoff emerald had been too easily recognizable.

She hurried up the steps into her apartment building, glancing nervously behind her as she stepped into the tiny cage lift, quickly pressing the button to take her to the top floor. She could hear her telephone ringing but it stopped before she could reach it and she stamped her foot angrily. A red light blinked on her answering machine. She pushed the message playback button and a familiar voice said, "Leyla, it's Anna. We are in big trouble. I don't know exactly what happened but suddenly the whole world wants the emerald. I must talk to you. Meet me tomorrow morning at ten-thirty by the pyramid entrance at the Louvre. Oh, Leyla, what have we done? I know you're probably busy, flying off to Milan or somewhere, but I have to talk to you. Please, please don't let me down. . . ."

The machine clicked off, leaving the sound of the woman's voice still hanging in the air, and Leyla slumped despairingly into a chair.

"Oh, Great-grandfather Tariq Pasha," she whispered, tears trickling down her cheeks, "it's all your fault. All your talk of the Kazahns' old bond of loyalty to the Ivanoffs, making all your children and your grandchildren promise to keep your vow. Now look what you've got me into." She had a strange feeling that somehow Tariq knew what she was thinking and he was telling her to remember *why*, besides love, they owed their loyalty to the Ivanoffs . . . even after all these years.

Russia, 1917

Sofia paced the small room that had been her prison for more than a month, thinking of what to do, where they might go.

The long train journey south had been another nightmare, best forgotten. She had thought everything would be all right once they got to Yalta; they would go to the Ivanoff villa, where friends would organize a passage for them on a boat to Constantinople, and from there to Europe. But she knew the Ivanoffs could not simply run away to their Paris apartment or their villa at Deauville and seek help from old friends. Misha had warned her that the Cheka would hunt them down like animals, and if they were captured they would be tortured until they gave the Bolsheviks the Ivanoff fortune. And once the Bolsheviks had it, they would all be killed.

It had been nighttime when they finally reached Yalta, and they breathed the sweet sea air gratefully. Unlike the arctic north, the air still held a hint of summer and smelled fresh and clean, like the air of a free country. They smiled at each other as they followed the crowd out of the station, and even Azaylee skipped a little as they walked along.

"Madame, madame!" Sofia had swung around at the sound of a familiar voice. It was the stationmaster, who was almost as old as she was and who had known her all her married life. But until now he had never called her anything but "Your Highness."

"Ma'am," he whispered urgently, his gray beard wiggling with agitation, "I'm sorry to greet you with such lack of respect, but now even the walls have ears. Everything has changed, ma'am, there are spies and danger everywhere. Your villa . . ." He paused, shaking his head sadly. "It has already been requisitioned and now it's filled with Cheka, though they are pretending to be something else. If they see you they will arrest you. Oh, ma'am." He shook his head sorrowfully. "Where will you go now?"

Sofia could think of only one place. As it was dangerous to take a taxi, they trudged for two hours up the switchback roads into the hills to the cottage she had given her old coachman and his wife on their retirement fifteen years ago.

She had knocked on the door, waiting apprehensively for a reply. After fifty years in the Ivanoff household, she would never doubt her old servant's devotion, but she also knew that fear can be a stronger master than loyalty. Her doubts melted into relief as the door was flung open and they were welcomed instantly.

Still, she knew their days at the cottage were numbered because, faithful though he was, the old coachman was afraid. She saw it in his eyes every time he brought them food and the latest reports on the war now raging in the Crimea. Only this morning he had told her nervously that the navy had mutinied and gone over to the Bolsheviks. Time was running out fast and, along with it, their options.

Sofia Ivanoff stopped her pacing and stared out of the window across the wide blue curve of the bay to the green hills beyond. She could not see the Ivanoff villa because of the trees, but she could remember it as clearly as if she were there: its white columned porticos and green tiled domes, its immaculate gardens and the marble terraces dotted with urns of brightly blooming flowers, the fountains and pools and the sprawling parklike grounds, thick with blossoming trees and shrubs and teeming with every kind of beautiful wild bird and animal. It was so close, just over there in the hills, and yet it might as well have been a thousand miles away. Closing her eyes, she imagined herself back there, happy again with her family. She could hear their carefree laughter mingling with the bird calls and the faint whisper of the sea; she could smell the springtime orange blossoms and the summer roses and oleanders, the autumn scents of mint and wild thyme. . . . Sighing, she opened her eyes again to reality. She would never enter the Ivanoff villa again.

A crackle of gunfire echoed suddenly across the quiet bay and she peered anxiously from the window. She never left the cottage, but Missie and Azaylee ventured out every now and again, in their new roles as the foreign widow Mrs. O'Bryan and her daughter. She jumped as the gunfire started again. It was coming from the hills near the old domed church where Missie had taken the child for a walk. Sofia's hands flew to her face in horror. "Oh, no," she prayed. "Not my little granddaughter, not Missie. Spare them please, God, they are so young. I beg you, take me instead." And sinking to her knees, for the first time she wept.

The soft ripeness of the long Crimean autumn had faded, but the early December days were still balmy. Missie was sitting on an old marble headstone chewing on a blade of grass and watching Azaylee darting through the pretty little churchyard, kicking up her heels like a spring lamb in the warm sunshine with Viktor bounding at her side, barking with delight at his freedom.

She hoped that if any spirits still lingered in this peaceful place, the sight of the two enjoying themselves would gladden their souls. Yet though her father's grave was here, somehow she knew his spirit was not, and she knew she would always think of him at home in England, working at his desk, waiting for her. . . .

Yalta lay far below, a crescent of white buildings bordering the palm-fringed ink-blue sea. Sandy roads led steeply back into the green hills and the sumptuous holiday villas of the nobility, and here and there among the umbrella pines and acacias, tall cypress trees pointed like dark exclamation marks at the pale-blue sky.

The crackle of gunfire ripped suddenly across the peaceful scene and Viktor stopped his leaping; a tremor ran through his body as another burst shattered the silence. After grabbing Azaylee, Missie hurled her to the ground behind a large pink marble headstone. There was more gunfire and this time she heard a voice shouting orders, coming from the trees at the top of the hill only a couple of hundred yards from where they were hiding.

There was a burst of answering fire and suddenly she saw them. There were three men, Tartars in their traditional wrapped head-dresses, wide-sleeved blouses and sheepskin vests, manning a machine gun. There was no sign of the Bolsheviks, but she guessed they must be hidden in the trees.

She knew that if the fighting came down the hill toward them they would be caught in the crossfire. They would have to make a run for it. "Azaylee," she whispered, "we are going to play a game."

Azaylee looked back at her confidently and her heart sank. The soldiers would shoot anything that moved. What if Azaylee was to fall?

She glanced back up the hill. The Tartar soldier in command of the machine gun had spotted them and was motioning her angrily to stay where she was. She sank behind the headstone again, sandwiching Azaylee between her body and the cool pink marble, whispering to Viktor to be still.

"Is this the new game, Missie?" Azaylee asked as the machine gun rat-tatted again from the trees, echoing around the hills and across the silken blue bay. Missie peered from the headstone, watching as the Tartar made his move. Now he had located exactly where the Bolshevik gunfire was coming from. He aimed his machine gun unhurriedly in that direction, feeding the ribbons of cartridges through with precise speed as he began to fire.

Missie clutched Azaylee's face against her breast, but she couldn't turn her own eyes away. She saw the Bolsheviks run from the trees, their hands held high in surrender. The Tartars showed no mercy. Their bullets sent the fleeing men spinning and twisting down the hillside, ripping them to bloody ribbons.

After sending one of his men to reconnoiter the woods to make sure all the enemy had been routed, the Tartar officer made his way toward her. He was tall and arrogant, and as well as a rifle he carried a huge old sword in an elaborate leather scabbard.

Missie flinched as his angry blue eyes inspected first her and then the child, wondering if this was the end. Then to her surprise Viktor stopped growling. Wagging his tail, he flopped at her feet and put his nose peacefully on his paws.

"Don't you know it is dangerous to walk in the hills these days?" he shouted in heavily accented Russian. "You might have been killed!"

"So might you," she retorted bitterly.

He grinned, showing a perfect set of dazzling white teeth. "That's my job. And I don't need any foreigners getting in the way." Putting his head on one side, he stared at Azaylee. "Xenia?" he said, surprised.

She stared back at him doubtfully. "Remember me?" he asked. "I used to make you and your brother laugh when I did this." Crouching beside her, he wiggled his mustache and pulled a funny face.

"Tariq!" She laughed delightedly as she flung her arms around his neck. "It's Tariq!"

He glanced at Missie and said, grinning. "My name is Tariq Kazahn. My father was head gardener at the Ivanoff villa. Misha and I used to play together as children whenever the family was down here on holiday. Of course I have not seen him in a long time. The army posted me to the Baltic, and then, when the troubles came, back down here, to Sevastopol. And now we are reduced to skirmishing in the hills!" His vivid blue eyes looked tired as he flashed her that white grin. "But we are not beaten yet," he added confidently. "This sword has been in my family since the time of Genghis Khan. It has killed many men in the name of freedom. We Tartars will fight to the end—and we shall win!"

Missie heaved a sigh of relief. He was a friend after all; maybe he could help them. She told him quickly what had happened.

Tears rolled down the Tartar's strong face but he made no move to wipe them away. "The prince was my friend," he said quietly. "I would willingly have died in his place."

"Please help us," she begged, "We need to get to Constantinople but it is dangerous. We have no papers and Princess Sofia might be recognized. The banks were taken over by the revolutionaries before we could get any money out, and now we have nothing, we are living on the charity of two old servants." She fell silent, waiting for his answer.

His blue eyes met hers steadily. "Trust me," Tariq Kazahn said softly. "It will be done."

Tariq Kazahn was a true Tartar. His bloodline went back to the sixteenth century, before Ivan the Terrible reduced the race to homeless nomads, forever roaming the bleak Russian steppes. Some of his ancestors had returned to Turkey, but others had settled near the Black Sea, where domed Islamic Tartar temples dotted the southern hills alongside Russian Orthodox churches.

A network of Kazahn relatives had soon covered the region, many of them working as fruit farmers or as cattle herders or tending the terraced vineyards of Georgia, but though they were reduced to menial tasks they never forgot that they had once been a proud ruling race, famed for their horsemanship and their fierceness in battle. And when the Russian revolution began in 1917, they had decided they were not about to let any upstart peasant revolutionary soldiers push them around and tell them what to do. They were prepared to defend their principles and were giving the People's Revolutionary Army a great deal of trouble.

Tariq was thirty years old, a big man, tall, with powerful shoulders and strong hands. He had thick curling black hair, a bushy black mustache, high Tartar cheekbones, and flashing blue eyes. When he smiled he showed a set of teeth as big and white as those of the fierce young stallion he rode with such ease and grace. And he was hot-tempered, impetuous, and intelligent.

Tariq was already a soldier in the army of the tsar when he met and married a Chinese woman of the Manchu race, and they had three small children: a son, Michael, named for his childhood friend Prince Michael Ivanoff, and two girls.

He had heard the rumor that the Ivanoffs were second after the tsar on the Cheka's death list and knew that unless he acted quickly, they would surely be killed.

He had promised Missie he would save them; now he had to figure out how. As always, he went to his wife, Han-Su, for guidance. She was living in an old fisherman's cottage near Yalta's waterfront and managing somehow to feed her family on the small amounts he sent her from time to time and on the vegetables she grew herself in the patch of fertile soil at the back of the house. Han-Su was a tiny, birdlike, graceful woman with shining black hair that she always wore in a heavy knot at the nape of her neck; her sloping dark eyes held centuries of wisdom, and Tariq had learned to trust her judgment.

"What shall I do, Han-Su?" he asked. "I have promised the girl that I will guide the Ivanoffs to safety. I will do it . . . I must do it."

"You must send them here at once," she told him. "Not under cover of night, because that is what the Cheka expect runaways to do. Let the child come first. She must carry a posy of flowers as if she is visiting friends. No one will suspect her alone. Later the young woman will take the dog for a walk. She will stroll along the seafront, maybe stop and have a cool drink in a café. She will wander along the shore, casually, until she reaches here. The old lady must wear peasants' clothing, a black dress, a shawl, a *babushka*. She will carry the basket of vegetables I will give you, and she will make as if to call at a few houses, selling them, making her way through the streets to this house."

"And after that?" he asked eagerly.

"You must go see the thief, Vassily Murgenyev. He is making a fortune issuing false papers using the collection of official rubber stamps he stole from the municipal offices and the foreign embassies. Tell him you want papers that will get three people to Constantinople and then across Europe. He will ask too much money but you will bargain with him. Meanwhile they will stay here with me. I shall speak with the harbormaster at Alupka, just along the coast. He is half Chinese and comes from my province. He will help get them a boat to Constantinople."

"Han-Su, you are wonderful," Tariq cried, hugging her passionately, but she merely smiled.

"Misha Ivanoff was your friend," she said calmly. "It is our duty to help his family. There is just one problem, Tariq. It will cost a great deal of money."

His face fell as he remembered that Missie had told him they had none, then he drew himself up proudly. "Leave that to me, Han-Su," he told her. "I shall find the money."

The following day he went back to the churchyard where he had arranged to meet Missie and told her what to do. Everything went like clockwork, and by the next afternoon the three of them and the dog were installed in the fisherman's cottage by the sea. For a week Tariq patrolled Yalta's hills, collecting a few rubles from each of the poor but loyal soldiers and the White Russian officers, knocking on the doors of people he trusted, explaining that he was helping refugees to escape. It was a risk, but one he took happily for he had undertaken the responsibility of his dead friend, Misha, and if it cost him his life he would not shirk it.

The night they were to leave for Alupka and the small fishing boat waiting to take them to Constantinople, Tariq arrived at the cottage bearing a bottle of good vodka. "None of this peasant-made rubbish," he said with a laugh, filling their glasses, "because tonight we drink a toast to the Ivanoffs. Long may they live."

After the toast Princess Sofia handed him a narrow suede box and said "Whatever happens will happen, Tariq. You have done your best and the rest is in God's hands. I am giving you and Han-Su this, with my gratitude and my son's. You are a brave and loyal man, Tariq Kazahn, and my son loved you as a true friend."

Tariq stared at the glittering diamond necklace lying on its bed of black velvet, stunned into silence.

"Your Highness is very generous to my husband," Han-Su said

quickly, "but of course we cannot accept such a payment. We are happy to help. You owe us nothing."

The petite Chinese woman and the tall Russian aristocrat eyed each other respectfully as Tariq snapped the box shut and held it out to Sofia.

"It is not a payment, Han-Su, and it will make an old woman happy if you will accept my gift," Sofia said firmly.

Han-Su bowed low. "I am honored, Your Highness," she replied.

Sofia and Missie rode the twenty hilly kilometers to Alupka on small, sure-footed donkeys, while Tariq carried the child. He also carried an automatic rifle slung over his shoulder and his old Tartar sword in its leather scabbard at his hip. It was dark and moonless but Tariq was used to it and easily spotted the waiting fishing boat. The vessel was as black as the night with all lights doused. As it slid quietly from the shore across the inky sea to Turkey, Tariq and his family prayed for Sofia and her granddaughter, though they knew they would never see them again.

=== 9 ===

One year after they had helped Missie and the Ivanoffs escape, the White Russian forces in the south were finally defeated and Tariq and Han-Su were also forced to flee with their children in a small, leaky open boat across the Black Sea. When they reached Constantinople it was Han-Su who, with a few quiet words, kept her hotheaded husband under control. Instead of selling Princess Sofia's diamond necklace on the back streets of the city, where she was afraid it might be recognized and traced back to them, and where anyway it would only have brought in a pittance, she sent it secretly to relatives in Hong Kong, where it was broken down and sold for enough money to give them a new start in life.

It was Han-Su who decided that the money should be invested in a small freighter traveling to the Mediterranean ports with cargoes of spices, silken carpets, brass, and silver and returning with vital machinery or, sometimes, guns. Meanwhile, the family lived frugally in a small, tumbledown wooden house atop one of the old city's many hills, close to its hub, the Galata Bridge spanning the Bosphorus.

With Han-Su's sharpness with money and Tariq's flair for promoting new business, the Kazahn Freighter Line soon began to prosper. Another ship was bought, larger than the first and newer and able to travel longer distances. Turkish manufacturers learned they could rely on Kazahn's ships and foreigners importing goods filled them on their return journeys. Tariq bought more ships and got more business and Han-Su banked the money. Within five years they owned a small fleet and a thriving enterprise. The foundations of the great Tariq Kazahn shipping empire had been laid.

After ten years they owned one of the world's largest shipping lines and were one of the richest families in Turkey. They had moved into a beautiful *yali,* an old summer palace at Yenikoy on the European shore of the Bosphorus. Its gardens were fragrant with jasmine and lemon trees, fountains tinkled coolly, and birds filled the air with their music. Whenever one of Tariq's ships sailed up the Bosphorus on its way from Europe to Asia, it would fly all flags and blast its siren as it passed the Kazahn *yali.* Looking handsome in the crisp white naval uniform and gold-trimmed officer's cap he always wore now, with one hand firmly on the precious Tartar sword at his hip, Tariq would salute proudly from his balcony.

But Tariq Kazahn never let any member of his family forget that they owed everything to the noble Ivanoffs.

"Without them, the Kazahns might still be peasants," he would roar at his children and later his grandchildren. "Their diamond necklace founded our fortune. The Ivanoffs are gone, many dead, others who knows where? But never forget that our first duty—our loyalty, our *sacred obligation,* is to the Ivanoffs. When I die, I shall pass that obligation on to you, my children, and then on to your children. This is my legacy to you. A Kazahn must never fail that duty."

Tariq's only sadness was that at the age of eleven his son Michael contracted a crippling disease that left one leg withered and useless. As the boy recovered his health he encouraged him to exercise, employing physical-education experts to improve his physique. As if to compensate for his weakness and his shambling gait, by the time he was a young man Michael Kazahn had the torso of a bull. On his specially made saddle, he rode his horse like a member of one of the Tartar hordes of old. He became a crack shot and a great huntsman and was always the life and soul of the family gatherings, for by now his two sisters were married and his parents were grandparents.

The years since their flight from Russia had passed quickly, but Tariq never let his family forget their background and the legacy of loyalty to his beloved Ivanoffs.

Michael was twenty-two years old and had his father's strong, dark good looks and hot temperament. Han-Su decided he needed a wife to calm him down. She also decided which girl she wanted him to marry.

Refika was eighteen, the daughter of a wealthy Turkish banker and his French wife. She was pretty with dark brown eyes and her mother's blond hair, and she was well educated with strong ideas.

This pleased Han-Su because she knew that the Kazahn men needed strong women.

She planned their introduction cleverly, choosing a sultry summer night with just the tiniest breeze drifting across the Bosphorus. Refika, wearing a pale-green chiffon dress with a jeweled belt encircling her narrow waist, sat between her parents, her ankles demurely crossed. Tariq fixed her with his piercing blue eyes. She was aware that he was observing her every move as they waited for Michael to arrive. His sisters were fluttering about offering sweetmeats to the guests while their husbands made small talk with Refika's father, and though Han-Su smiled as she apologized for her son's lateness, inside she was seething. Michael resented her matchmaking: She knew he must still be with the woman he kept in an apartment in the old city and that he was deliberately late because he wanted Refika to see him walk into the room. He wanted her to see that he was a cripple.

Refika's eyes met Tariq's and she smiled at him disarmingly. After walking toward him, she sat at his feet on a low ottoman covered with a fine silk carpet.

"Kazahn Pasha," she said in her soft, musical voice, "I have heard that you are a man among men, that those who work for you admire your courage as well as your business head. I have heard that everyone who knows you adores you; even that you are known as 'Sultan' Kazahn. I can see that you are a handsome man, better-looking than any of the young men I know, but your eyes are fierce when they look at me. This worries me, Kazahn Pasha, because you do not yet know me."

Tariq's jaw dropped and he stared at her, taken aback. "Fierce?" he repeated. "No, never . . . I am only fierce against my enemies or those who would cheat me."

"Am I your enemy then?" she persisted softly.

"No . . . of course not." She had him bewildered by her frankness.

"Then do you feel that I am going to cheat you? Or maybe cheat your son?"

"Cheat . . . no, no I don't think that. . . ."

She smoothed her soft chiffon skirts around her pretty legs and said, "Good, Kazahn Pasha. Then we have no problems between us, no secrets left unspoken. I hope it will always be that way." Lifting her head proudly, she stared at Michael, limping across the room toward them, his slanting blue eyes as fierce as Tariq's. "Like father, like son," she said, smiling mischievously, and Tariq knew that he had met his match. Refika would be the perfect wife for his son.

Michael's withered leg had not mattered to Refika. All she saw was a tall, bearlike, handsome young man, glaring at her as suspiciously as his father. But she had no fears. She knew what she wanted and, with all the skills learned from her French mother, she knew how to charm a man. By the end of the evening Michael was loath to let her go. He was used to the overt sexual charms of the series of women who over the years had occupied his apartment in the old town or else to the demure, well-brought-up girls who were too shy even to speak more than two words to him. Refika was a mixture of both. She was demure yet not shy, bold but not brazen, teasing yet not "knowing." Suddenly he was a man in love, and after a whirlwind courtship they were married on a rare rainy day in September.

Their son, Ahmet, was born "nine months later to the day," as Tariq would always explain with a proud roar of laughter just in case any Turk doubted the masculinity of the Tartar Kazahns. And three little girls soon followed.

Ahmet was a small, quiet boy, completely unlike his bold, brash father and grandfather. He looked like Han-Su, with her smooth black hair and dark almond eyes, though he had his mother's fair skin. Recognizing his intelligence, Refika and Han-Su insisted that he have the best education in spite of Tariq's protests at what he thought was his grandson's lack of proper masculine occupations such as riding, shooting, drinking, and women. He asked himself many times how such a child could have been born of two such strong, passionate people. Yet he was the proudest grandfather of all at Ahmet's graduation from the Harvard class of '54.

After two years at business school, Ahmet returned to Istanbul and the family business. Tariq watched him like a hawk, firing questions at him when he suggested changes or "improvements." But despite his misgivings, Ahmet's cool, calm confidence impressed him. "That boy's balls are in his brains," he told Han-Su, half mocking, half proud, as he gave Ahmet permission to build his first big oil tanker.

Tariq was seventy-three years old when Han-Su died in 1960, so peacefully in her sleep that he wasn't aware at first that she had gone. "She had no illness, no pain," he cried, bewildered, as his children and many grandchildren gathered around him, and he was not ashamed of the tears in his eyes, for true love has no pride.

With Han-Su gone, Refika and Michael became the official heads of the family. Michael was running the freighter line as successfully as his father had done, with his own headstrong flair and his wife's common sense. Meanwhile, Tariq filled in his days with long hours at the office, his only companion Ahmet, who was devoted to his work. Together, the old man and the young one plotted the rise of the Kazahn Shipping Line into a new empire of supertankers, fighting the Greeks for the lucrative oil business. Tariq would chuckle with delight as his grandson outwitted their rivals time and time again, displaying a coolness and nerve that Tariq said proved him a true Tartar Kazahn.

Ahmet was thirty-two when he met and married a pretty Swedish blonde and took her back to live with him and his grandfather at the big *yali* on the Bosphorus. Their daughter Leyla was born in 1966. She was a beautiful child with almond-shaped eyes in the true blazing Kazahn blue and heavy, silken dark hair; and of all his grandchildren and great-grandchildren, Tariq loved her the best.

Despite his age he was as upright and alert as a man twenty years younger, and, after a lifetime devoted to sons, this new girl-child enchanted him. As soon as Leyla was old enough, he began to take her everywhere. He took her to his huge office overlooking the Sea of Marmara, where she could play with the models of his ships and scribble on his desk pad, and to the stables where he kept his string of racehorses, and on trips on his yacht to the sunny Mediterranean ports. On her second birthday he had asked her where she would like to go to celebrate.

"With you, Grandfather Pasha," she had said, fixing him with a gaze he recognized as his own. "I want to go where you go when you are not with me." So he took her to lunch at the Yacht Club, where she was treated with all the proper respect of a grown-up lady, and where she ordered her favorite lamb kebabs and ice cream. And Tariq knew he was prouder of his little great-grand-daughter than of all his business successes and his fortune.

When Leyla was four years old, Ahmet and his wife decided to take her with them on a trip to Paris. When he heard the news Tariq said sternly, "You cannot take my granddaughter away from me. If she goes, I go."

Ahmet had glanced at his wife, shrugging his shoulders, and she had sighed resignedly. She had learned long ago that no one ever said no to her grandfather-in-law.

He was sitting on a bench in the Luxembourg Gardens watching little Leyla chase a ball across the grass when a woman spoke to him.

"Tariq Kazahn?" she said wonderingly. "Can it really be you?"

He glanced up, frowning. It was a face he remembered from the past . . . but then it had been a younger face, and the violet eyes had been frightened, terrified of the shooting . . . she had been clutching a small child to her, and there was a great amber-colored dog. . . .

"Missie?" His voice trembled as he rose to his feet, "Missie? Is it really you?" And then his arms were around her and they were laughing and crying together.

"I've never forgotten you, never," she was saying. "How could I when you saved our lives, and at such risk to yourself?"

"The Princess Sofia?" he asked eagerly. "And Xenia?"

Missie shook her head, "The princess spoke of you often before she died," she told him gently. "She said you were one of the bravest and most loyal men she had ever met, and that you were her son's good friend." She hesitated. "Like all of us, Xenia has a new identity. I doubt she even thinks about the Ivanoffs anymore." He looked down in surprise as she drew forward the small girl standing beside her and said, "This is her daughter, Anna. She is ten years old."

Tariq's eyes filled with tears as he looked at the fair, slender child, the last of centuries of the great Ivanoff dynasty. After taking her small hand in his, he kissed it. "My humble greetings, Princess," he said as she stared back at him, puzzled.

Calling to Leyla, he introduced his granddaughter proudly. "And now go play together," he told them. "We grown-ups wish to talk."

They watched as the two little girls hurried eagerly across the grass, and then he turned to look at Missie. There was no sign of gray in her smooth, seal-brown hair. She wore it fashionably shorter now, curling softly into her neck, and apart from a few lines of laughter—or tension—around her eyes, her skin was smooth. She was almost as tall as he and slender as a reed in her chic, cream-colored suit, and he thought admiringly that her long legs looked as perfect as those of a woman thirty years younger.

"Tell me," he asked. "What happened?"

He listened in silence as she told him the story of a life that had left them struggling between poverty and success, and always, like a pall over everything, the fear.

"You need money?" he asked, concerned.

Missie shook her head, "It's Anna I'm worried about. Her mother"—she shrugged—"is just like Anouska."

Tariq nodded. He knew what she meant.

"Anna needs family," Missie said, "and that's something I can't give her. I'm no companion for a child. I brought her to Paris for a change, a little holiday, but I know she's lonely. Just look how happy she is playing with Leyla. But you, Tariq," she said, turning to him with a smile, "you are as handsome as ever."

"I am a successful man," he said proudly. "The Princess Sofia's diamond necklace was the foundation of my good fortune. Without her generosity, I would have been nothing. I have never let my family forget this, and now at last we are able to repay some of our debt. Anna Ivanoff has a family. The Kazahns will treat her as their own daughter. Send her to us, Missie, and she will be a princess again."

Missie laughed and said, "Her name is not Ivanoff, Tariq, and she would not know what you meant if you called her that. She is not a Russian princess, she is just another little American girl. But thank you for your kindness."

"My yacht is at Monte Carlo. At least come and spend some time with us there," he said impulsively. "Think how the children will enjoy it." He waited eagerly for Missie's response, loath to let go of her. She was his one contact after all these years with the family he had adored and respected. He saw the hesitation in her face and bellowed suddenly, "No one says no to Tariq Kazahn."

Missie laughed as people turned to stare. "Oh, very well then," she agreed. "It will be good for Anna."

For Tariq the two weeks with Prince Misha Ivanoff's granddaughter as a guest on his yacht was the highlight of his life. Nothing could ever match this, he told himself as he watched his own granddaughter play with young Anna, just the way he and Misha had played together as children. The only trouble was, he didn't want to let her go.

"You say her own mother doesn't have time for Anna. Then why not let her come and live with me?" he begged Missie each night when the children had gone to bed and they were sitting on deck under the balmy Mediterranean night sky. "She will be as my own grandchild, my own blood. Just look how she blossoms here with us, she sparkles, she laughs. She and Leyla are like sisters. What have you got to lose, Missie? And you too are welcome; my house is big enough for everyone. I am a rich man, Anna will want for nothing. When I die, she will share my fortune. Just say she can come live with us, where she will be happy." He looked at her and added craftily, "Just ask yourself what Misha would have thought best."

His strong dark profile was etched against the midnight blue of the sky and Missie thought that in the half-light, he looked like a young man. But Tariq was old. Who knew how much longer he had for this world? And after he was gone, would his son and grandson still want Anna, the way Tariq did? She imagined the family outcry when it was known that Tariq had left part of his fortune to Anna and knew it would not be fair to put such a burden on them. No, Anna was her responsibility and hers alone. She must provide for her as she had always done and she must watch out for her safety as she always had done. But what about after she was gone? She sighed. She could only hope that God would be good to her and allow her time until Anna was old enough to take care of herself.

Night after night Tariq talked about Anna, using everything he could think of to persuade her, and Missie listened and said nothing. But she was tempted. After all, she told herself, Anna's mother scarcely cared whether she saw the child or not. But it was all so much more complicated than that. Though Anna didn't know it, she was an Ivanoff, and if her identity was ever discovered, she would be in danger. . . . She knew it was impossible, yet she felt herself weakening.

"She will have a real family, a real home," Tariq said proudly. "As a Kazahn she will be treated with respect."

But it was seeing how happy Anna was with Leyla that almost made Missie change her mind. Although Anna was six years older, the two children had had an immediate understanding and liking for each other. After two weeks, they were inseparable.

"I will agree to this," she told Tariq the night before they were to leave for Paris and home. "Anna may come to you for the summer holidays, three months every year."

"A million blessings upon you," he cried, his hawklike features split with a grin so wide that his big white teeth gleamed in the moonlight, though by now they owed more to porcelain than to nature.

Leyla hugged Anna tearfully when they left the next morning.

"I'll see you in a few months," Anna promised as she waved from Tariq's big Lagonda motorcar that was to take them to the station. "Don't forget me, Leyla."

Every year after that a pair of first-class tickets were delivered to Missie in America to take them by train and boat to Monte Carlo, where Tariq and Leyla would meet them in the yacht and take them to Istanbul.

Tariq was right: The girls were like sisters, and there was no doubt he loved Anna as much as Leyla. The whole vast Kazahn family became her uncles, aunts, and cousins, and Missie knew that Anna was happier than she had ever been, because they had given her the stability and continuity of a family life she had never had.

Where Tariq had had one adored great-granddaughter, now he had two; where before he had taken Leyla everywhere with him, he now took Anna as well, and every morning when he said his prayers, he gave thanks for being able to repay his debt of gratitude, honor, and love to the Ivanoffs.

When Tariq was ninety years old, there was a grand birthday celebration. The luxurious *yali* on the Bosphorus was filled with flowers and long tables were spread with a lavish buffet. Musicians played on terraces strewn with scented rose petals amid trees strung with thousands of colored lights. The five hundred guests had been instructed to wear traditional Turkish dress, and Missie thought the *yali* must have looked the way it did when it was first built in the time of the Ottoman Empire, three hundred years before.

Tariq enjoyed his birthday party surrounded by his family and friends, remaining until the last guest left at four A.M. After a short rest he was up at six as usual to say his prayers and sip his first cup of the sweet, grainy coffee to which he was addicted. At six-thirty he dressed in his white naval officer's uniform and gold-trimmed peaked cap, buckled on his sword, and strode out onto the terrace. To his surprise, seventeen-year-old Anna was already out there, leaning on the marble balustrade, gazing dreamily across the Bosphorus, golden with new morning sunlight.

When she saw him she smiled and said, "Kazahn Pasha," which is what she always called him. "Why are you up so early? You should still be sleeping."

Tariq laughed, ruffling her fair hair affectionately. Anna was a lovely girl, not a great beauty like Leyla, but tall and slender, with the strong Ivanoff bone structure and wonderfully expressive blue eyes. Right now they were beaming with love for him, and he knew that Misha Ivanoff would have been pleased with the way he had found to repay him.

"Shouldn't I be saying that to you?" he asked, leaning on the rail next to her. "After all, I am the great-grandfather and you are the child."

She put her hand over his and said, "I couldn't sleep. The party was the most wonderful experience of my life, Tariq Pasha. It was like a scene from a storybook. I shall never forget it."

"Nor I, my little daughter," he said quietly. "Look, here comes my ship, the *Han-Su,* named for my esteemed wife. You see, Anna, the men on my ships still expect to see their captain when they travel along the Bosphorus, even if he has been up late celebrating his ninetieth birthday."

His jolly laugh bellowed across the water as, with her beside him, he saluted the long gray ship gliding majestically past, its sirens blasting and the flag of the mighty Kazahn Line fluttering proudly in the breeze. And then, without another word, he crumpled at her feet.

"Kazahn Pasha," Anna screamed, cradling his beloved head in her arms. But Tariq's blue eyes were fierce no longer and she knew he was dead.

The funeral so soon after the joyful birthday party was a somber but grand affair, just as Tariq had always planned it should be. His solid bronze coffin, emblazoned with Russian and Turkish emblems, was drawn through Istanbul's narrow streets by eight matched black horses wearing tall ebony plumes; the old city's tangled traffic ground to a halt as the long funeral procession trailed slowly through the streets, getting stuck at every corner, and the service was accompanied by much wailing and crying, for the fierce old man had been well loved.

Afterward the procession wound its way slowly to the Asiyan Cemetery atop a hill overlooking the Bosphorus, where many years before Tariq had erected a beautiful marble tomb for himself and Han-Su, and where he had often gone to sit with her and watch his ships far below.

As he had promised, Anna shared in his estate, and to Missie's surprise, the family offered no objection. "Our father told us he was repaying a great debt," Michael, now the true head of the family and inheritor of the famous sword as well as the business, told her, "and naturally we shall honor that obligation. Besides, we all love Anna. She is one of our family."

So, after sixty years, Tariq had repaid his debt to the Ivanoffs and seventeen-year-old Anna was one million dollars richer, though of course a great deal of that was in shares in the Kazahn Shipping Line.

But that was long ago, and now, sitting alone in her Paris apartment, Leyla Kazahn wished with all her heart that she had never agreed to help her "sister," much as she loved her.

$$=== 10 ===$$

Düsseldorf

The flight to Düsseldorf was half empty and Genie sank back into her first-class seat thankfully. It had been a long night; she had had no sleep and the airport had been impossibly crowded. At least now she could be alone with her thoughts, and she was thinking about Valentin Solovsky. Not the Russian diplomat with a weight on his mind, but Valentin *the man.*

They had talked until five in the morning, sitting by the flickering fire as the storm howled around them, and at the end of it all she still couldn't recall his revealing a single vital personal detail. Yet there had been that flare of attraction between them. It wasn't just that he was so handsome. She had known quite a few attractive men in her time and most of them fitted into the genuine egomaniac category, to whom a woman was merely a decorative accessory. No, Valentin was . . . different. And she had to admit, there was also an exciting flutter of danger. His eyes had admired her, he had paid her subtle compliments, but he certainly had not made a pass at her. And she had had the feeling that he had known what she was thinking before she even knew it herself.

Perhaps it was some new Russian technique to relax the enemy, she thought, closing her eyes and putting on her dark glasses as the plane took off at last. If so, it had certainly worked: With Cal's plan foremost in her mind, she had told him about her job as a reporter and asked if she could do a "profile" with him in a new series she was thinking of doing for the network.

"Maybe," he had said with a laugh, "though I hardly think I'm important enough to qualify."

"Are you kidding?" she'd retorted. "Why, American women would just eat you up."

"Is that so?" he'd asked with a lazy smile. His deep voice had sent curls of anticipation through her stomach. Quickly remembering her mission, she told him the story of how much she had hated being sent to Geneva. "I thought the sale was trivial and unworthy of my talents as a reporter," she said, "but now I see I was wrong. I know the truth is going to come out sooner or later, and I want to be the reporter who breaks it to the world. I am an ambitious woman and this scoop would make my career. And besides," she added, glancing at him under her lashes, "I already know part of that truth—something no one else knows yet."

She sipped her brandy, waiting apprehensively to see if he would take the bait.

"It is common knowledge that both Russia and America wanted the emerald," Solovsky said, fixing her with those dark gray eyes that looked as if they knew too many secrets. "But I confess that in this matter I need a little help."

"What about the KGB?" she asked innocently.

He smiled, "There are times the KGB is of no use, times where we need a more subtle approach. Of course," he added, clasping his hands together and frowning, "if the KGB was involved there would be rules that must be obeyed. But in this case"—he leaned forward, staring deep into her eyes—"*if* I were to ask someone to help me, she would be responsible only to me. I alone would know her identity. No other person would ever know of her existence as . . . a helper."

"You mean a *spy,*" she whispered, a thrill of fear making her voice tremble. It had felt so different when she had said those same words to Cal. He was a friend; now she was negotiating with "the enemy."

Valentin sat back with a shrug. After summoning the waiter to bring coffee and more brandy he said in a matter-of-fact tone, "I believe that would be a very melodramatic description."

Genie licked her lips. This was the power of the Soviet Union she was messing with, and she had heard enough stories of people who just "disappeared" to make her think twice. *But she had to find out. It meant everything, not only to Cal and her country but to her.*

"Well, if you really need someone," she said, running a nervous hand through her blond hair, "maybe I could find out what you want."

"And what exactly is it I want?" he asked, leaning back against the pink-striped sofa cushions and smiling. "Can you read my mind, Miss Reese?"

"You need to know who bought the emerald."

He waited until the waiter had served their coffee. "And don't you want to know *why* we want to find out?"

"I already do; you want to find the 'Lady' so Russia can get the money."

His gray eyes were suddenly remote as he said, "And if that was true, are you not worried about what will happen to her when we do?"

Genie knew it was the billion-dollar question, but sitting here alone by the fire with Valentin Solovsky, Russia suddenly seemed as far away as another planet. It was down to basics, a woman and a man, and somehow she knew she could trust him. "I know *you* would not let her come to any harm," she said softly.

Valentin nodded. "You are a good judge of character, Miss Reese." He smiled as he took her hand. "I take it we can shake hands on the deal?" She nodded and he said, "Then the first question I am going to ask you is, Are you working with Cal Warrender?"

She felt the telltale blush rising in her cheeks as she said, too quickly, "Cal? Of course not. We are old friends . . . the same Washington social circuit, you know."

He nodded. "And now will you tell me who bought the emerald?"

She glanced at him warily. "Have we not already agreed to trust each other?" he asked. "I am a man of my word, Genie. You will have the exclusive story."

He took her hand again, gripping it tightly, and she thought they were not the smooth, too-soft hands of a desk-bound man; they felt hard and slightly rough. After taking a deep breath, she said, "This is probably not exactly the answer you expected. The emerald was bought by a dealer in Düsseldorf. His name is Markheim."

"Markheim?" Solovsky frowned, puzzled, then his brow cleared suddenly. "Of course, *now* I understand." His smile was so dazzling that she smiled back. "You see, Genie, you have already been of help. And now I'll tell you how you can help me."

Lying back in her seat as the aircraft circled Düsseldorf's airport, Genie thought of what she was going to do. It all seemed easy enough. Of course Valentin hadn't mentioned the other "secret" everybody was after, the thing Russia really wanted, but she knew about the money. Then when Valentin had told her whom she was to contact, all of a sudden things made sense. She grinned as she thought of what Cal would say if he knew what she was up to, but she had skipped out at the crack of dawn, deliberately missing their nine o'clock rendezvous. The romantic storm-tossed night was gone and in the cold light of day she had realized that the story was turning out to be bigger than she had thought. She was going to play this game her own way, and if she was clever enough she would find out the truth. And then she would be *sure* to have the exclusive.

The lobby of the hotel was bustling with pinstriped businessmen waving platinum credit cards. Genie's heart sank as she realized there must be a trade fair, but she had chosen the hotel precisely because it was large and she could get lost in the crowd. She sighed frustratedly as she waited in line to register.

"Of course, Miss Reese," the desk clerk said smoothly. "There is a message waiting for you."

"Oh, but no one knew—" she exclaimed, surprised, taking the envelope from him. "Hi, Genie," she read. "Sorry I missed you this morning. I'm just down the hall in 516. Why don't you join me for tea? Cal."

"Dammit." She groaned. Was he clairvoyant, or what? How the hell had he known she would be here? It wasn't going to be as easy to lose him as she had thought. In her room, she tossed the note onto the table and placed a call to her office in Washington, asking them to trace a private number for her. Then she hung her clothes in the closet, took a shower, and felt about a 100 percent better. The call back from Washington came just as she was drying her hair, and she wrote the number down and dialed it immediately.

After her conversation, she fixed her face and walked down the hall to room 516. As she tapped on the door a waiter emerged from the elevator wheeling a cart set with silver teapots, two cups, saucers and plates, a platter of tiny crustless sandwiches, and a small mountain of traditional German cream cakes. She stared at him, astonished, as he stopped outside Cal's room and the door was flung open.

"Great timing, Genie." Cal beamed at her. "You must have learned it from doing so much television."

"I want to know where you keep your crystal ball," she retorted, stalking into the room. "How the hell did you know I was here? And how did you get here before me? And how the hell did you know *exactly* when to order tea?"

He shrugged. "I'm the seventh son of a seventh son," he intoned menacingly, "and you know they always have secret powers." He laughed as she glared at him. "Okay then, I'll come clean—if you'll pour the tea. I'm sure you need it after your hectic day."

"How do you know how hectic my day was?" she demanded, blushing.

"I know *how* hectic," he replied, munching on a smoked salmon sandwich, "but not *why*. When you didn't show up at nine, I called your room. They told me you had already checked out. Now that wasn't quite the way we left things last night. Remember? When I last saw you, you were about to join our friend Solovsky for a little chat. I was concerned; I felt it was my business to find out where you had gone." He shrugged and took another sandwich. "It wasn't difficult. The concierge had booked your flight and your hotel. If you want to be a spy, Genie, you're going to have to polish up your act."

"Oh, dammit, dammit!" she exclaimed, slamming down the teapot, exasperated.

"Tut, tut . . . such violent language," he mocked.

"That still doesn't explain how you got here first, or the tea," she said with a sigh.

He smiled winningly at her. "Did anyone ever tell you how beautiful you are when you are angry? Blue eyes flashing, cheeks pink and rosy . . . okay, okay . . ." he added hastily. "I flew here by air force jet. I asked the hall porter to tell me when you arrived, allowed an hour for you to shower and freshen up—*et voilà!*"

"You're in the wrong business," she said icily. "You must come from a long line of private detectives."

"Nothing so grand," he said, grinning. "But now, let's get down to business."

She glanced at him over the rim of her teacup. His eyes had lost their laughter and no longer reminded her of a beautiful red setter. They were implacable as he asked for an explanation.

"I don't have to tell you everything," she replied defensively.

"Everything connected with last night you do," he said with a steely edge to his voice. "Remember? We made a deal. I want to know what happened with Solovsky and why you ran off to Germany without telling me. Anything could have happened to you. Besides, I thought we were in this together!"

"We are." She avoided his eyes, pretending to eat an enormous cream cake.

"You shouldn't eat that," he said reprovingly. "Think of the cholesterol—and the calories."

"Oh, all *right!*" She flung it back on the plate. "Solovsky wanted me to help him."

"And?"

"I said I would, if he would help me."

Cal stared at her but she was avoiding his eyes. "This is serious, Genie," he said quietly. "I'm a friend, I'm on your side, but you can't go around making promises to guys like Solovsky and not keeping them."

She shrugged. "What's so serious? He's just a man, like you."

"Not quite. *First* Solovsky is Russian, *then* he's a man."

She glanced up defensively. "I'm only doing what you asked—for *our* country, remember? Besides, he only asked me to do what you did—and he told me even less. But he did tell me about the billions."

"Did he?" Cal looked thoughtful. "But you still decided to skip out of Geneva without telling me?"

"I was just impatient to get started, that's all. I had some personal things to consider . . . I had to rearrange my schedule. I meant to call you as soon as I arrived."

"So? What's your next move?"

"I . . . I haven't thought it out yet. I'll let you know."

He nodded and glanced at his watch. "Fine," he said. "Remember to do just that. I've got one or two things of my own to take care of. You must be tired; after all, you had no sleep last night. Why don't you give me a call in the morning and we can discuss how to proceed?"

Suddenly he was all business and she found herself on her feet and on her way out of the door. The meeting was over! "But—" she exclaimed.

"But what, Genie Reese?"

His reddish-brown eyes were gentle again as he looked at her and she sighed with relief. "I thought you were really mad at me. I'm doing my best. I'm just not used to accounting to other people, I'm used to working on my own."

"No problem," he said abruptly. "Just don't disappear again without telling me. You got me worried."

She walked slowly back to her room feeling the pull of fatigue in her spine, wishing he had asked her to have dinner with him again tonight. But she told herself that anyway she would never have made it, she was just too exhausted. Too much had happened in too short a space of time and her whole life had been turned upside down. All she wanted was sleep—and tomorrow, somehow, she would get to meet the man who had bought the Ivanoff emerald. Though she wasn't about to tell Cal Warrender that yet.

Maryland

Missie pinned the brooch with the five diamond plumes at the neck of her blue dress, holding up the mirror to admire it. She touched the golden wolf's head, remembering when Misha had given it to her and the awful time when she thought she had lost it forever. The brooch and his photograph were her most precious possessions, along with Azaylee's childhood photographs and those of her beloved Anna.

Of course she had had other jewels, but this one piece had signified both her love for Misha and the end of an era, because when they had left Russia she had been plunged into a world she had not known existed.

She glanced around at her calm, luxurious suite, with its pale peach walls and silk curtains, the soft cream carpets and her beautiful antique Turkish rugs. Her familiar paintings hung on the walls and a fire glowed comfortably in the elegant marble fireplace. And outside, beyond the swagged peach taffeta curtains drawn against the cold night, were green lawns and shade trees and the lake with the swans and the mallards. Fairlawns was light-years away from Constantinople at the end of 1917.

Constantinople

They had arrived with only the few rubles Tariq had given them. Those had soon disappeared in payment for their room and board at a small wooden house high in the hills overlooking the Golden Horn.

Sofia had unpicked the jewels from Missie's skirt and Azaylee's pinafore and taken them to a Chinese merchant, who, after inspecting them for a long time, had said that the beautiful settings were worthless to him and he would pay only for the gems themselves. For a bagful of jewels worth a fortune, he offered the equivalent of two hundred American dollars. They had no choice but to accept.

Sofia had said it would be unwise to linger in Constantinople; the city was full of Russian agents and they must move on. Missie had been sent to buy them new clothes, simple, cheap, and serviceable, and within days they were at Sirkeci Station boarding the Orient Express en route for Vienna.

They had held their breath as the inspector checked their tickets and travel documents endlessly. But then he had smiled, handed back their papers, and clipped their tickets. *"Bon voyage,"* he had said, patting Azaylee's head as they filed through the gate onto the platform.

Sofia held Azaylee's hand and Missie carried a small cardboard valise containing their new clothes and the Ivanoff tiara hidden beneath a pile of underwear. "If all else is lost," she had told herself, "we shall still have the tiara. It is our insurance policy for our new life."

They were elated as the train finally departed, settling into the uncomfortable second-class compartment and telling each other they were finally free. But their troubles were not yet over. The Russian secret police were patrolling the train and their papers were inspected at great length at Kapikule and again at Belgrade, where the stony-faced guards returned them reluctantly as if disappointed to find nothing wrong.

"It's no good," Sofia had said. "If they catch us, they will kill us. And you too, Missie, even though you have no real part in Russia's drama." She had thrust a wad of money into her hand. "Take it," she had whispered, "go home to England, *milochka,* while you can. You are only a young girl, all your life is before you. Forget what has happened, forget the Ivanoffs. Please, I beg of you, go home."

Missie had stared at the money and then at the rolling Serbian countryside flashing past the window, thinking longingly of Oxford's beautiful colleges and pretty cobbled streets, the familiar bookshops and the tearooms, and beyond, the green expanse of the Cotswolds. Then she had glanced at Azaylee playing happily with her new Turkish doll and asked herself how she could leave an old woman and a child to fend for themselves.

Sofia had shaken her head despairingly when she had refused. "God knows what will become of us all," she had whispered tiredly.

Their hazardous journey had continued through Hungary to Budapest and finally to Vienna, where they had taken cheap lodgings behind the Opera House and soon discovered that there was a large transient community of White Russian emigrés. Sofia was still afraid but Missie talked to them in the coffeehouses and learned from them where the best places were to sell valuables such as icons and jewelry, and that they could not expect fair prices because the dealers knew the market was flooded with Russian refugees in dire need of money and were exploiting the situation, just the way the Chinese had in Constantinople. They told her there was no work and that many noble-born people were living in poverty; the lucky ones had found jobs as doormen in nightclubs or as waiters. They said it was even worse in Paris, that the Cheka were everywhere, searching out noble refugees who had managed to slip their net. Every day, they said, you heard of someone else who had just "disappeared." Vienna was no longer safe for those with something to hide, nor was Paris.

Sofia removed all of the smaller diamonds from the sunburst tiara and sold them cheaply, and with money again in their pockets, they began their long slow trek through Austria to the Italian coast, where they booked the cheapest passage to New York.

The *Leonardo,* out of Genoa bound for New York, was on its final voyage. It was old, its engines were obsolete, its fittings worn, and its furnishings shabby, but for two short weeks it was their refuge. Five months had passed since they had fled from Varishnya, where, lying in the forest, Missie had thought she was going to die. "I am only eighteen," she had told herself then. "I'm too young to die." Now she knew she wanted to live and she would begin her life right there, in New York.

Her long brown hair escaped from its black ribbon, blowing in the stiff breeze, as she leaned on the rail of the lower deck while the *Leonardo* steamed up the Hudson River, watching Manhattan's skyline coming closer and closer, wondering what lay in store for them now.

Their papers were checked carefully at Immigration, but there were a lot of Americans returning from the troubles in Russia, and the inspector was sympathetic. He smiled at Azaylee and patted the dog, and Missie and Sofia stared as the stamp was finally placed on their documents. They were really Americans now, and their new identity was official.

New York was big, sprawling upward and outward, noisy, dirty, intimidating, and bitterly cold. They found a small rooming house nearby that looked cleaner than the rest and counted their dollars and cents carefully while they searched for an apartment, but they soon found that an apartment was beyond their pocket: a couple of rooms maybe, and in the very cheapest area, the Lower East Side, where they could live unnoticed and unremarked on, just three more immigrants among thousands of others.

In the end, the only choice was between a dark room with a single window looking into an airshaft and a lighter, more expensive one with a window onto the street. Despite their poverty Sofia insisted they take the one with the window overlooking Rivington Street. It had a sink with a cold-water faucet in one corner and a shared toilet down the hall, and the furniture consisted of an ancient brass double bed, a small fold-up iron cot, a scarred unpolished wooden table, and four mismatched wooden chairs.

Missie could tell from Sofia's face that she was thinking that this was the end of the line, they could sink no lower, and she was determinedly cheerful as she rushed them back down to Rivington Street, shopping among the pushcarts for the cheapest cotton sheets and blankets and the thinnest towels. She bought eggs and butter and bread for their supper and a few meat scraps mixed with rusk and a bone for the dog; she found a piece of flowered oilcloth to cover the stained wooden table and a bunch of shiny evergreen leaves to brighten up the place because it was March and there were no fresh flowers. And that night when they sat down to a simple feast of boiled eggs and crusty bread, with the dog gnawing contentedly on his bone beside them, they smiled at each other, thinking maybe their little room wasn't so bad. And after all the running and hiding and the fear, it seemed a haven of peace and security.

As she tucked Azaylee into the sagging brass bed later that night, Missie said confidently, "Don't worry, Sofia, tomorrow I shall get a job and we shall soon have a proper apartment of our own."

Maryland

Now, looking back on those years, Missie smiled as she thought of the optimism of youth, when a boiled egg and a slice of bread, a roof of sorts over one's head, and a bunch of green leaves decorating the table was just a beginning. And tomorrow would surely bring success.

She unpinned her brooch and put it away in its little Cartier box, and took out the old photograph album. As she looked through it, she thought what a beautiful child Azaylee had been; so sweet, so quiet, so gentle. A dream child that any mother would adore. Poor Azaylee, poor little girl, orphaned so tragically, and so young. Who could blame her for what happened later? Certainly not she.

   She shut the album with a sigh as Nurse Milgrim came in bearing a tray with her nighttime cup of tea and her sleeping pill.

   Maybe tonight, she thought, just for once, she would not have the dream. But she knew she would.

$$=== 11 ===$$

It was another breathless New York day. The sun beat down from a brassy yellow sky, filling the stifling little room with the stink of fish and rotting cabbage from the pushcarts below in Rivington Street. The constant noise—of iron-rimmed wheels on the cobblestones and harsh voices bargaining shrilly in Yiddish, Russian, and Polish, of children crying and drunks cursing as they staggered down the street on their way back from the saloon—the dirt and gray grinding poverty filled Missie with despair.

She wished she could close the window and shut it all out, but then they would surely suffocate as the temperature soared into the hundreds. The cramped tenement room that had seemed like a haven the night they found it seemed to have shrunk, trapping them in its four walls. Sofia lay in the sagging brass bed, looking pale and ill though she claimed she was only resting, and Azaylee was sitting on the rickety iron fire escape, her thin arms clasped round her knees, watching the endless activity in the street four storeys below. Viktor's tongue lolled in the heat and Missie could see his ribs sticking out under their thin covering of fur and flesh. She knew that if she looked in a mirror she would see her own ribs sticking out just like Viktor's, but it no longer upset her. The desperate hunger of youth clawed perpetually at her stomach; lying in bed at night with only a bowl of thin soup and a piece of stale black bread inside her, she thought she would go crazy with her dreams of food: eggs, chicken, good bread, and sweet fresh butter. But she knew it was only because of Sofia's resourcefulness that they managed to eat at all.

She asked herself time and time again how a woman like Sofia, who had never even thought about food except to instruct her chef what to serve for lunch or dinner, knew how to shop and bargain among Rivington Street's pushcarts. But Sofia always came home in the late afternoon with a bag of vegetables bought for a few cents because they were bruised and shriveled, and by tomorrow would have gone bad. She would have a newspaper parcel with a bone "for the dog" on which the sympathetic butcher had left enough meat to flavor their meager soup, and occasionally she would buy cheap offal, liver, kidneys, even brains, to add to their diet. She had told Missie that she had often seen the villagers at Varishnya cooking such things, and now she learned how to make tasty meals from them herself. So with Sofia's ingenuity they ate, and meanwhile Missie looked for a job.

She had set her sights high, confident that she could get a position as an assistant to a professor of archaeology at one of the colleges: after all, she had learned firsthand about antiquities and digs. But the problem was she had no proper clothes, only the one blue skirt and a couple of simple cotton blouses, and there was no money to buy new ones or even a pair of decent shoes. Wages were low and by the time she had paid her fare on the Second Avenue el and the rent, she calculated there wouldn't be enough left over to pay for food and new clothes. She had considered getting a job as a maid because she knew they were given their uniforms, but all the grand houses on Fifth Avenue expected their maids to live in, and anyway, the wages were barely enough to keep them alive. She had tried for a job as a salesgirl at the new department store, Macy's, but knew instantly from the way the personnel officer looked her up and down that she was just not smart enough. It wasn't only her clothes, she thought despairingly, catching a glimpse of herself in a mirror. She *looked* poor. And that was the catch—*she was too poor to get a job.*

The high-summer sun beat down as she walked slowly along Delancey Street the next day, reluctant to go home and face them with the news that she had failed yet again. She stopped suddenly outside O'Hara's Irish Alehouse. The simple words chalked on a blackboard dazzled her as if they had been inscribed in gold: "Help Wanted—Apply Within." She had never been in a saloon in her life before, but she swung through the doors without hesitation. The fumes of whiskey, beer, and stale cigarette smoke and the smell of cabbage cooking somewhere in the back almost choked her, but lifting her chin determinedly she strode toward the burly man standing behind the counter.

Shamus O'Hara was a big, handsome forty-year-old Irishman

who looked as if he had been bred from a race of giants. Everything about him was oversized, from his head with its shock of curly red hair to his hands the size of hams. He wore a collarless blue shirt straining at the buttons across his barrel chest, the rolled sleeves showing forearms braided with muscle. An old striped tie was knotted around his middle and a small cigar was clamped between his teeth. He was checking the beer pumps in between puffs on the cigar and singing snatches of "I'll Take You Home Again, Kathleen" in a pleasant baritone voice with a thick Irish accent.

He stared in surprise at the girl asking him for a job. She was too tall to be called a waif because waifs were always tiny, and yet she had the haunted look of the hungry, that telltale yellowish tinge to her skin and deep-gray shadows under her eyes. But by golly, they were beautiful violet eyes, and her brown hair shone in the sunlight streaming in through the open doors. She was neat and clean in her white blouse and blue skirt, and she had ankles pretty enough to turn any man's glance. O'Hara thought she was a lot different from the usual rawboned, black-haired tired Irish women he saw in the saloon or at St. Savior's on Sunday, hidden under their shawls with a brood of ten or fourteen children flocking at their heels. With a bit of feeding up, this colleen might be a beauty. But as for giving her a job, it was hard work and she just didn't look up to it. Besides, his customers were a rough lot and she was obviously a refined sort of girl.

"Well . . . I'm not sure we be needin' anyone," he said doubtfully. A look of despair crossed her face and he sighed and said, "The trut' is y'don't look strong enough t' lift a pint of ale."

"Oh, but I am, I am," she cried, grabbing his arm eagerly. "I'll clean, I'll wash dishes, I'll serve . . . anything. Just try me . . . please."

Pulling herself up to her tallest, Missie tried her best to look "strong" as O'Hara looked her up and down speculatively and then said with a sigh, "Out o' the goodness of me heart then, but just on trial, mind. The pay's a dollar a night. Y'start at six and finish when I say the word—and not before. Understood?"

Too close to tears to reply, Missie nodded and rushed out of the saloon back to Rivington Street to tell them the good news. O'Hara followed her to the doorway, watching until she turned the corner of Orchard, wondering what her story was. Because in this part of the world, everyone had a story.

For a month O'Hara kept her busy. She swept the previous night's filthy sawdust from the floors and scattered fresh; she washed hundreds of glasses until her hands became red, chapped lumps; she polished the counter and scrubbed vainly at the beery circles staining the tables. Trying her best to get used to the smell, she carried heavy trays laden with a dozen pints of beer without spilling them and served them, anxious and unsmiling, to the rough crowd of stevedores, bricklayers, laborers, and whores who made up O'Hara's clientele. And at the end of each evening, she pocketed her dollar triumphantly and dodging the drunks who tried to manhandle her, she fled back through the dark streets littered with stinking refuse from the pushcarts to the room she now called "home."

Sofia would be waiting up for her with a glass of hot milk flavored with cinnamon, and Missie would always protest she was too tired to eat the plate of food she had brought home. "It'll do for Azaylee's breakfast," she would say, slipping a scrap to Viktor, who wolfed it down as if it were a peanut. She sipped her fragrant milk gratefully before subsiding, exhausted, onto the little iron cot that served as her bed, knowing that Sofia would wait until she slept before she climbed into the sagging brass bed beside Azaylee. But she never told her that she was afraid to go to sleep, afraid of the dream that came every night when she saw Alexei's terrified face and heard his voice begging her to help him.

Azaylee was the only one who didn't seem to mind her new circumstances, playing happily out on the dirty streets with the neighborhood's teeming population of children. Missie and Sofia would lean from the window watching her as, with Viktor always at her heels, she darted among the pushcarts, blond braids flying as she chased a ball or skipped rope or drew chalk hopscotch circles.

"Just look at those children," Sofia would marvel, "a bunch of ragamuffins and my granddaughter one of the worst." She would laugh as she said it but Missie knew it hurt.

There was one thing Missie hadn't told Sofia about her job at O'Hara's. The customers were a rough and ready lot, big, brawny Irishmen like O'Hara himself, though occasionally a "foreign-speaking" immigrant wandered in by mistake. Mostly O'Hara kept them in line with a mixture of Irish blarney and the threat of his fists. They were all right when they were sober but with a few whiskeys inside them, they became different men: men with one thing on their mind.

The saloon had some female customers, a few poor women burdened with too many children whose husbands beat them and who had taken to drink to escape, and then there were the whores. Missie tried not to notice as transactions were made over the stained tables, the man handling the woman like a piece of meat before he made his purchase; and she tried not to count the brief minutes before the fellow swaggered back from the alley, often still buttoning his pants. But toward the end of the evening their drunken glances were often directed at her.

The first time it happened she just froze. She stared down at the huge hand gripping her small breast like a vise. Its black-rimmed nails cut into her flesh, but she was too shocked even to feel the pain. Then she screamed. O'Hara came running, his shillelagh swinging as he hurled curses at the drunken workman.

"You filthy bastard," he roared, with a quick crack to the side of the man's thick skull. "Get your wanderin' hands off her . . . she's a respectable girl—and young enough to be your own daughter. If that's what you want you'll be off and find it elsewhere." Purple with anger, he hauled the surprised man across the room, blood spattering from his cracked head. "Take that!" he bellowed, planting a kick that sent the man hurtling through the swing doors onto the sidewalk. "A boot in the arse is all you're good for. And as for you," he said, turning to Missie, "I'll not be turning this place into a church social. Business is business, and if you can't handle the men by yourself, you're out."

Missie didn't tell Sofia what had happened, but the old woman knew something was wrong. That night as she massaged Missie's swollen ankles tenderly and rubbed glycerine into her raw, red hands, she said, "I cannot allow this to go on. You must leave the saloon."

Missie threw her arms around her desperately. "*Please* let us sell the jewels," she begged, "like we did in Constantinople. Surely we are safe now?"

Sofia shrugged and replied, as she always did, "These are not just ordinary jewels, they are heirlooms. Such grandeur is identifiable. They are as good as worthless."

"Then what about the money in Switzerland? We could go to a lawyer, we could have him send a letter with proof of your identity. I can't bear it, Sofia; you should be living like the princess you are instead of worse than the poorest Russian peasant."

Sofia went to a drawer and took out a newspaper clipping dated two weeks previously. "I didn't show you this before," she said, "because I didn't want to worry you."

Missie read the brief report. It talked of the atrocities being perpetrated in Russia, of the murder of the tsar and his family and the arrests and incarceration in *gulags* of innocent people. It said that the secret police were still searching for the Ivanoffs; that to the revolutionary regime they epitomized all that was wrong and decadent about "old Russia," that the Cheka still believed the two grandchildren had escaped with the Dowager Princess Sofia. Reliable reports from inside Russia stated that the secret police had scoured Europe for them and that the search had now spread to America. It said that if they were found, the fate of these young children was certain to be like that of the imperial family: brutal murder.

Missie finished her milk in silence. What Sofia had said was true, and there was no escape. A future struggling for each desperately needed dollar loomed in front of her, and her heart sank even lower, because she knew that somehow it was up to her to provide for them all.

O'Hara watched her with grudging admiration. She had spirit and she had guts and he liked that. She was cleaning the saloon as he lighted his first cigar of the day, and he grinned at her. "You're the sort they needed on the covered wagons, me girl," he told her as he watched her scatter the fresh sawdust over the shining clean floor. "You're pioneer stock."

Leaning on her broom, Missie watched as he drew in the smoke luxuriously. "That cigar cost one quarter of my night's wages," she told him. "Don't you think it's about time I had a raise?"

She laughed as he choked on the cigar, his big-boned Irish face reddening as he thumped his chest with a fist the size of a football. "B'jaysus, girl, you almost sent me out o' here feet first, saying things like that," he cried indignantly.

"Two dollars," she said, folding her arms belligerently, "and you know I'm worth it."

They glared at each other across the mahogany counter like boxers sparring in the ring and his green eyes twinkled suddenly. Running his hands through his halo of curly red hair, he said, "You've beat me, girl. Two dollars a night it is—but only because you're worth it."

Missie stamped her foot angrily. "Then damn it, why didn't you offer me it instead of making me ask?"

He leaned on the counter grinning. "Maybe it's because I like to see you get angry. Maybe it's because I wanted to see what the *real* Missie O'Bryan was like, instead of the tired girl who does her job and says little and never smiles. You know that today is the first time I've ever heard you laugh?"

"That's because I don't have too much to laugh about," she replied shortly.

O'Hara drew on his cigar, watching as she picked up her broom and began to spread the sawdust evenly across the floor. "I've seen you on the street with the little girl," he said, glancing at her ringless left hand, "but there's no man around?"

"Her father is dead," she said, not looking at him.

He nodded. " 'Tis a sad thing for a child to be without a fayther, and even harder on a woman left to bring her up alone."

Missie's head flew up and she looked at him, startled. "Oh, but . . . but . . ." she said, and then stopped herself quickly. Of course, everyone on Rivington Street thought she was Azaylee's mother.

That night there was two dollars in her pocket instead of one, and O'Hara himself filled a plate with boiled beef, cabbage, and potatoes and made sure she sat down for fifteen minutes to eat it. Faced with the huge plate of food, Missie suddenly lost her hunger, and she felt O'Hara's sharp green eyes on her as she put it into a basin to take home for Sofia and Azaylee.

After that, work at the saloon seemed to get a little easier, and sometimes O'Hara asked her to help at lunchtimes as well. He looked out for her, made sure the men didn't bother her, and he made sure she ate. His broad, handsome face always broke into a smile when he saw her and he paid her promptly. There were even a few precious dollars saved now, alongside the worthless jewels in the cardboard valise under the brass bed.

A few weeks later as she was carrying a heavy tray filled with Irish whiskey to a table of brawny shirt-sleeved men, sweating like pigs from the heat and the drink, Azaylee suddenly hurtled through the swing doors with Viktor at her heels. "Missie, oh, Missie," she screamed as everyone's eyes focused on her. "Come quickly! Grandmother—"

After thrusting the tray at the nearest man, Missie grabbed her urgently by the shoulders. "What's wrong? What has happened to Sofia?"

The child's blue eyes swam with tears, "She was standing by the stove stirring the pot. Then she cried out. She fell down, Missie. I couldn't wake her."

The streets were crowded with people spilling from their tenements in an attempt to catch a breath of cooler evening air, but Missie pushed them ferociously out of her way, dragging the child by the hand as they ran back home, the dog at their heels.

She tore up the steep wooden stairs and hurled open the door. Sofia lay by the stove; her eyes were closed but Missie could see a pulse beating slowly at the base of her throat, and she thanked God that at least she was still alive.

After arranging the pillow carefully under Sofia's head, she fanned her desperately. "Sofia, Sofia," she called, "you are all right now, everything's all right." But she knew she was lying, because Sofia Ivanoff looked very ill.

"It was just the heat," Sofia said weakly when she recovered her senses a few minutes later. "It was nothing."

But two weeks later it happened again, and this time she complained of the pain in her head. It was a pain that refused to go away no matter how much of the patent medicine in the deep-blue bottle Missie bought from the pharmacy and poured anxiously down her throat. She refused to see a doctor, saying she didn't need it, but Missie knew it was because they couldn't afford it. Then one morning Sofia could not get out of bed. Her left side was paralyzed.

Missie ran to Orchard Street to fetch the doctor, vowing she would earn the money to pay him somehow.

He was an old Jewish man, gray-bearded and kind. "I'm afraid the lady has suffered a series of small strokes," he told Missie gravely, "and this has led to bleeding in the cranial cavity. It is the pressure that is causing the pain, and this can only be relieved by operating." He glanced hesitantly at the young girl and the child standing side by side, their anxious eyes fixed on him as the life-giver, the bringer of hope. As he always did in these circumstances, he wished he had a different job. "I must be frank with you," he said. "She is an old woman. The operation is as likely to kill her as the stroke. All I can do is give her something to relieve the pain."

Missie gulped back the panic-taste of bile in her throat. "You can't mean . . . not that she might . . ."

"We all must die sometime, my dear," he said gently. "Believe me, it is far worse when my patient is young." He opened his worn black Gladstone bag. "I'm giving her an injection of morphine to ease the pain. I'll call in to see her tomorrow morning. Meanwhile you must take care of yourself and your child."

Missie glanced down at Azaylee, so blond, so pretty, and so helpless. *Her* child, the doctor had said. If Sofia died, then what everyone believed would come true. *Azaylee would be her child.*

Each morning she waited anxiously for the doctor to come, searching for him among the pushcarts and the crowds out on the street.

"She is no better," she told him worriedly a few days later. "The pain is back again. She tries not to show it, but I see it in her eyes."

"I will give her more pain-killers," he said patiently. "They will allow her to rest peacefully." He glanced sharply at Missie: she looked pale and worn out from lack of sleep and worry. "You should get some rest yourself, young lady. And make sure you eat properly."

Missie did not laugh because it wasn't funny. She hadn't been to work for a week and they were down to their last few cents. O'Hara had been kind; he had sent a woman around with a bowl of food every lunchtime, but she could not accept his charity much longer. And she knew if she did not return to the saloon tonight he would have to find someone to replace her.

At five o'clock she fed Azaylee a plate of their usual meager stew and gave her a hunk of the day-old black Russian bread, bought at Gertel's bakeshop on Hester Street, whose heady aromas almost drove her wild with longing. A whole fresh sesame bread spread thickly with sweet French butter was the peak of her desires, but she was forced to content herself with a small slab cut from a day-old sour rye loaf.

She washed Sofia, patting her fine-boned face with a fresh linen towel laundered by her own hands and dried in the sun out on the fire escape along with everyone else's laundry. There were days when she couldn't see the tenement buildings for the washing, and there were no secrets as to the worn state of their neighbors' undergarments. She lifted Sofia's head, urging her to sip the warm broth, but the princess only managed a smile and a few whispered words of thanks before she slid back into unconsciousness.

Her hand still clutched Missie's with a grip of steel and she thought with a shiver it was as if Sofia were clinging to life, that if she let go she might slip away into darkness and never find her way back.

After splashing cold water over her flushed face, she tidied her hair in the mirror and put on a clean cotton blouse. She was so thin her skirt hung from her hips rather than from her waist. She hauled it up and secured it with a wide leather belt.

She gave Azaylee a small blackboard and a few colored chalks bought for a couple of cents from a pushcart and said, "Here's something to keep you amused, little one. Watch over your grandmother, and if she needs me, you know where to find me." She hugged her, hating the idea of leaving her alone. "I'll try not to be too late," she promised.

Still Missie hesitated, her hand on the doorknob. Azaylee was sitting on a chair by the bed with the blackboard clutched in her hand, staring at her with huge, frightened brown eyes, but Missie knew she had no choice. If she did not work, they did not eat.

She called Viktor to sit by the door. "Stay," she commanded. "On guard."

He sat obediently, and she thanked God they had him or she would have been afraid to leave them alone.

"Love you, *matiushka,* little mother," she heard Azaylee call as she lingered outside the door, still torn between two duties.

"I love you too, *dushka,* dear one," she called back, running quickly down the stairs before she could change her mind.

The saloon seemed busier than usual that night and she was run off her feet, delivering full glasses and rushing around collecting the empties. But even the rough men who had pestered her asked after her grandmother and she thought that maybe, before the drink hit them, they weren't so bad after all. O'Hara himself made her a sandwich of rare roast beef and stood over her while she ate it, and at the end of the long evening he slipped an extra five dollars into her hand.

"You're a good girl, Missie O'Bryan," he told her. "Even though with a name as Irish as the Blarney Stone you're about as Irish as Zev Abramski."

"Who is Zev Abramski?" she asked, pocketing the money gratefully.

"Don't tell me you haven't been to Abramski's yet?" O'Hara exclaimed, with his big belly laugh. "You must be the only woman on the Lower East Side who hasn't. Zev's the Jewish pawnbroker on the corner of Orchard and Rivington. He'll lend twenty cents on your husband's Sunday shirt to get you through till Friday. He keeps most of the population around here alive—until Friday afternoon, that is. Then it's pay-up time—or the old man has no shirt for the weekend. And now be off with you, and good luck, Missie."

She would need it, she thought, hurrying back through the dimly lighted streets. Viktor recognized her step on the stair and wagged his long plumed tail in greeting. Azaylee was curled up on the bed fast asleep next to her grandmother. Breathing a sigh of relief, Missie poured milk into a pan, dropped in the cinnamon stick, and placed it on the little burner, remembering wistfully when Sofia used to make her bedtime drink.

She tiptoed to the bed, smiling as she saw Azaylee's thin arm thrown lovingly across her grandmother. But the smile on her face froze as she looked at Sofia. The old lady's eyes were closed and her face peaceful, but her lips were blue and when Missie touched her, she felt cold.

"No," she whispered, horrified, "no, it can't be." But it was true. Princess Sofia Ivanoff, encircled by the loving arms of her little granddaughter, was dead.

12

Rosa Perelman from downstairs sent her eldest daughter, nine-year-old Sonia, to Hester Street to fetch the doctor. After telling her other two daughters to look after Azaylee, she stayed with Missie until he came. The news flashed around the neighborhood and soon the room was filled with women bearing little gifts of food and drink and offering to help. As they laid out Sofia and dressed her in clean white linen, Missie wondered what she would have done without them. She placed Sofia's carved ebony cross in her cold hands and suddenly realized how thin and frail she looked. Alive, Sofia had always seemed so strong, so *indomitable*.

The first time she had seen her, Sofia had been on her way to an official court reception; she was wearing a gown of gold lace with a long royal-blue train trimmed with ermine. Diamonds sparkled at her throat and ears, a coronet of diamonds and rubies crowned her rich black hair, and she had carried a beautiful ostrich-feather fan. Now this great princess was reduced to the simplicity of death where jewels played no part and clean white linen was all that was needed.

"We've done all we can, Missie," Rosa Perelman said. "Now you'll have to be sending for the mortician."

Missie looked at her blankly. "Mortician?"

"The funeral parlor," Rosa explained patiently, "to see about the coffin and the burial."

Missie hadn't thought as far as a coffin and a funeral. She had no idea how much such things cost, but whatever it was, she didn't have the money.

"If it's money," Rosa said, reading her thoughts, "then you'll just have to contact the city welfare. She won't be the first around here to go to her rest in a free pine coffin. It's nothing to be ashamed of."

Missie glanced despairingly at Father Feeny. Sofia had been

afraid to attend St. George's Orthodox Russian Church on East Seventh Street, and had taken to worshiping at St. Savior's instead, and he knew and respected her. "She is right, my dear," he said, placing a sympathetic hand on her shoulder. "But I give you my word the old lady will be buried with dignity. She will have her mass before they take her to Potter's Field."

"Potter's Field?" Missie repeated, puzzled.

The women standing around the bed glanced apprehensively at each other; obviously the girl knew nothing about life—or death.

"The common graveyard, my dear," Father Feeny explained. "But you must remember that in the eyes of God all men are equal. Sofia is in heaven, and it is only her mortal remains that will be taken to a pauper's grave."

Missie flung herself to her knees by the bed. *They were planning to bury the Dowager Princess Sofia Ivanoff in a pauper's grave!* "No," she screamed. "No, no! You don't understand. She must have a proper burial, *and* High Mass. *I'll find the money somewhere.*"

Shaking their heads and whispering to each other, the women filed from the room, leaving her alone with the priest.

"You must not let these things trouble you, my child," Father Feeny told her. "You are only a young girl, and you have a daughter to look after. Let the old lady go to her rest without any more worry. I myself will call the welfare for you, it will all be over quickly."

"Never." Missie sobbed. *"Never, never, never. . . ."*

Father Feeny sighed as he knelt beside her to pray. When he had finished, he rose to his feet and said, "I'll come tomorrow morning and see to everything. Meanwhile, the church is always here to comfort you, my child, and remember that we believe in life everlasting. Tonight I shall say a prayer for Sofia's immortal soul."

Missie remained on her knees for a long time. Rosa Perelman had volunteered to look after Azaylee, and she was alone with Sofia. Her bitter tears gradually changed to a frown of worry as she wondered where she would get the money to bury her. There was only one answer.

The saloon was brightly lighted and busy. A crowd of men leaned up against the long polished bar while the whores queened it at the tables, sipping whiskey and laughing raucously, and a few poor women with shawls thrown over their pinafores sipped port and lemon in an attempt to blur the hard edges of their existence. Someone was playing popular tunes on the piano and a pall of blue cigarette smoke swirled and eddied beneath the flickering globes of the gas lamps like the fog off Ireland's shores.

O'Hara was behind the bar, pouring whiskey and pulling pints as fast as he could while a harried-looking young woman collected empties and delivered the next rounds. Missie's heart sank even lower. O'Hara hadn't waited, he had already given her job to someone else.

Wrapping her shawl closer, she pushed her way through the crowd to the bar. "O'Hara," she whispered, catching his eye, "I must talk to you."

He nodded and after calling to the girl to take over behind the bar, he signaled Missie to go into the back room.

She paced the Turkey carpet in the narrow little parlor nervously. It was the first time she had been in his private rooms, and this was the world of a man she barely knew. The furniture was heavy and dark and had obviously been brought over from the old country. There were a few faded sepia photographs framed in gilt on the walls and two massive chairs, stuffed iron-hard with horsehair and decorated with lacy antimacassars on either side of the cast-iron firegate. The mantelpiece was covered in red velvet trimmed with a bobble fringe and a galvanized tin bucket of coal sat on the hearth, alongside a tall vase containing the wooden spills with which O'Hara lighted his cigars. Missie guessed that everything must look just the way it had in his dead mother's house in Ireland.

O'Hara thrust aside the heavy red velvet curtain dividing the parlor from the bar. After covering the tiny room in two huge strides, he took her hands in his massive paws. "Missie, I'm real sorry. What can I say to comfort you, me girl? Only that she was an old lady and she must have had a grand life. 'Tis you I'll be worrying about now, left all alone with the little girl." He hesitated, then coming to a decision, he took a deep breath and said, "I've been thinking, Missie. Why don't you let me look after you and Azaylee? Sure and I've got enough to keep you in comfort and give you a decent home. And besides, what with Prohibition threatening, I've already got a few other irons in the fire. There'll be a fortune to be made, Missie, and I intend some of it to be mine. What d'you say to that?"

He grinned at her as if his idea was the simplest thing in all the world, and she stared back at him, stunned.

"But I can't," she exclaimed, horrified, "I can't just live here with you. What would people think?"

"Think?" he repeated, puzzled. "Why, they'd think nothing except that you're me wife. I'm asking you to marry me, Missie."

"Marry?" she repeated disbelievingly.

O'Hara shifted uncomfortably from foot to foot, then he suddenly folded his giant's body and went down on one knee. His broad handsome face blushing as red as his hair, he said, "Missie, I swear I've niver told this to another woman except me mother, but I'm telling you I loves you. You're the loveliest girl I've ever seen and you've got the kind of spirit that I like. I'm asking you properly to be me wife."

Missie's head swam. It was all wrong, a nightmare: She barely knew O'Hara and he certainly didn't know her, he didn't know the educated English girl who was Professor Marcus Aurelius Byron's daughter; he didn't know the same girl who loved Misha Ivanoff so passionately she could never forget him. *O'Hara didn't know Verity Byron!* All he knew was the poor skivvy washing glasses behind his bar and eating his charity food, the "widowed" mother of a four-year-old girl, though she doubted he even believed she really was a widow. And all *she* knew was the charming, brawny Irishman who ran his alehouse with an iron hand. Still, Shamus O'Hara was a decent man and he had asked her honorably to marry him. Of course if she did, then her money problems would be solved: Azaylee would have a home and a father and she would have a man to look after her, someone to lean on. The idea was suddenly tempting. She closed her eyes and Misha's face came to mind, proud and strong, his intelligent gray eyes looking directly into hers, and she knew it was all wrong. Azaylee could never have another "father" and she would never love another man.

O'Hara rose from his knees. "I can see by your face I've troubled you," he said. "And at a time like this as well. I'll be leaving you to think it over, Missie. Maybe afterward, you'll feel more in the mood to heed what I've said. Meanwhile," he added briskly, "are you all right for money?"

She stared at him blankly. She couldn't ask him to lend her the money now because she would be under obligation to him. Instead she said quickly, "I just wanted to be sure you would save my job."

" 'Tis yours, Missie, whenever you're ready to come back," he said, pressing her hands between his big ones. He held back the velvet curtain and she slipped from the saloon and hurried along Delancey Street, her eyes on the dirty sidewalk and her mind on her problems.

There was a light in the shop window on the corner of Orchard and Rivington. She glanced inside at the shelves stocked with a hodgepodge of goods, each with a little pink ticket affixed to it, and at the shadowy figure of a man behind the brass grille. *Zev Abramski, the pawnbroker,* she remembered O'Hara telling her. *"He keeps the Lower East side going . . . he'll lend twenty cents till Friday for your husband's Sunday shirt."*

Missie peered in the window for a while, thinking, and then she turned and ran around the corner, back to the room where Sofia lay dead with a cardboard valise full of jewels under her bed.

Zev Abramski was not a solitary man by choice, but for many reasons. He was twenty-five years old, short with a slender build and a pale complexion. His thick black hair was combed straight back, he had sensitive brown eyes, a firm mouth, and the long-fingered hands of a musician. He was extremely fastidious: He went twice a week to the public baths and every day he wore a fresh white shirt laundered free by a Chinese woman on Mott Street, who secretly used his pawnshop to finance her gambling at mah-jongg. Even on the hottest days Zev wore a sober blue tie because in his mind it established a psychological barrier between him and the ragged, shirt-sleeved populace who came to him to borrow money on their pathetic possessions.

He lived alone in two dusty rooms behind his shop, amid bits and pieces of furniture left unclaimed by their previous owners. The only thing he had ever bought was a lovely old piano that filled one room, and even that wasn't new. It came from a secondhand shop on Grand Avenue and it had taken him four years of weekly installments to pay for it. He had taught himself to play and though he was no maestro, it pleased him. Music, and the books piled in every corner and on every chair and table, filled the emptiness of his life when at nine-thirty every night excepting the Sabbath he turned the sign from "Open" to "Closed" and locked his shop for the night.

Zev had lived on the corner of Orchard and Rivington for thirteen of his twenty-five years, yet though he was well known in the neighborhood, where almost everyone had been his customer, he could not call any one of them his friend. He told himself it was because of the nature of his business, but he knew that wasn't true. He was afraid of friendship.

Every night, except Friday when he went to temple, he would walk down Delancey to Ratner's restaurant, where he would eat a bowl of mushroom and barley soup and *kasha varnishkes,* his favorite dish of bulgur wheat and noodles. Then he would walk back again, closing the door that led to his shop and to reality, and run his fingers across the ivory keys and dream. The dreams always began with his family. On the good nights they turned into the fantasies of what his life might have been, but more often than not, they simply retraced the story of his life.

The music flowed softly from his fingers as he summoned up the dim memories of his early childhood in the small *shtetl* on Russia's northern coast. When he was a child, summers had been green and sunny and he had run free in the tall, sharp forest grass, and winters had been wild and snowy and his feet had slid from under him as he had walked with his father across the frozen river. But no matter how cold it was, he was always warm and cozy in his padded coat with the little fur *chapka* covering his ears and muffling the sounds of the horse-drawn sleighs. He remembered clutching his mother's hand, running to keep up with her long stride as she hurried through the small town, eager to deliver her orders and get back home out of the arctic wind.

He remembered being put to bed in a wooden box near the stove and the sound of his father sighing as his sewing machine whirred through the night and seeing the finished garments hanging over the back of the chair the next morning. He remembered the vile choking smell of the communal privy in the yard and the flat smell of chalk on the teacher's blackboard on his first day at school; he remembered the sour smell of young bodies crowded into the small schoolroom and the sweet smell of the brown braided hair of the little girl sitting in front of him. He remembered straying from the muddy *shtetl* into the little town and the sound of his boots ringing on the wooden sidewalks and his fear as he stared at the malicious faces of boys who he knew for some reason were his enemies; and their laughter as they snatched his *yarmulke,* tossing it around like a ball while he stood stony-faced and silent, not knowing what was wrong, only that he was different. He smelled the familiar scent of his mother's skin as she kissed him and the heavy odor of beeswax candles burning brightly in the special silver candlesticks that had belonged to her mother's mother, and the aroma of the Friday night food, chicken soup and gefilte fish. Zev's tiny room would fill with loud, passionate music as he recalled the sounds that had struck terror in his heart, though he had never understood why . . . the knocking on the door in the darkness of night, the urgent whispered conversations between his father and his uncles, the words he didn't understand but which frightened him: "the temple burned to the ground, persecution, police, pogroms . . . injustice, murder. Jew!"

He was seven years old. The journey through the night, Archangel's dark streets and his mother carrying the precious silver candlesticks wrapped in a blue cloth, the dark ship and the smell of its cargo of freshly cut wooden planks and the terrifying noise they made slipping and crashing as the fierce North Cape seas tossed the small boat around. He saw his mother's frightened face and listened again to his father's voice intoning a prayer . . .

Then a big city, a bearded uncle and a house on a cobbled street; he was not to go out in case . . . *"In case what?"* he had wondered with a shiver of fear as they cut off his long side curls "for safety." He remembered men in dark suits gathering to say the Sabbath prayers and the same Friday smells, the same food, the same frightened dark eyes and low urgent voices. . . .

The big ship towering three storeys high had seemed like a giant whale swallowing them into its stomach along with hundreds of other immigrants. He remembered not knowing what "immigrant" meant. They were not allowed on deck, and on the journey he never once saw the sea. There was no air; it was hot, stifling. The endless sound of babies screaming, children quarreling, complaining of hunger and thirst, falling sick . . . the stench, the grim acceptance of degradation. And all the while the storms hurling themselves at the ship, lifting it and shaking it like a mad dog with a rabbit. The dank, rancid hold with its human cargo swelled with the sound of people praying, cursing, screaming in fear, vomiting. The sounds and smells were etched indelibly into his psyche to be triggered at any time, always releasing the same panic signals of fear, the sweating, the trembling, the lurching heart. . . .

His father fell ill. He could see him now, lying on the faded blue cloth that had covered the candlesticks, his face grim with pain as he shook with a terrible fever— "dysentery," the word went round the dark hold like a flame, and soon there were more pale, agonized faces, more sickness. Soon no one cared anymore about the filth and the degradation. They just wanted to die.

His mother went first, lying quietly beside his father while he watched them anxiously. Gradually her face lost its frown of pain and she seemed peaceful. Zev held her hand, happy that she was feeling better, but the hand grew colder, and then it became stiff and he screamed out, *"My mother is dead."* No one took any notice.

There were plenty of other dead people, mothers, fathers, children, infants . . . they were too sick to care. His father died a few hours later and Zev covered them both with the blue cloth, talking to them, pretending at first they were still alive. Then he broke down, wailing and sobbing until he was sick and his eyes were red and swollen. The next day the trapdoors above the hold were flung open and the captain ordered them onto the deck. Zev was filled with fear. He was alone and he did not know what to do, but the captain left no option. After kissing his mother and father, he put the silver candlesticks in his pocket and climbed the ladder after the others.

He smelled the salty breeze and the fresh easterly wind and saw that they were sailing up a broad river lined with tall, dark buildings. He watched to see what the others would do next. Sailors were pushing them toward the gangplank, their hands rough, their voices filled with disgust. He saw stern, official-looking men in peaked caps waiting for them, just like the police at home in Russia, and his stomach sank and his knees trembled as he waited silently for them to take him away. He listened to the questions they were asking other people, knowing he had no answers. He had no parents, nobody who knew him, no money . . . nothing. They would send him back to the ship, to death.

The family in front of him was large, five, six, seven children, no one could count they were running around so much, the baby screaming, the infants plucking at the tired mother's dress. "If there are no relatives waiting you will remain on Ellis Island and await deportation," he heard the official say. Zev held his breath, waiting for their answer. There were relatives, the man said, showing some papers. The official was impatient, eager to get rid of them and their smell; he barely looked. It was easy for Zev to tag along behind them, just another child among many. . . .

The big hall was filled with hundreds of people, all wailing and crying and laughing at the same time, but there was no one to greet him, no one who knew him. No one even noticed the small seven-year-old boy running from the hall, terrified they would catch him and send him back. He stopped, still as a frightened hare, staring up at the tall, dirty brick buildings, hearing new sounds, smelling new smells. Then he stared down at his feet in the new leather shoes his uncle had given him. *He was standing on America.*

Always at this point Zev would slam down the piano lid and pace his tiny room, unwilling to remember that small boy alone in a new country whose language he did not even understand, and the events that had happened next. After grabbing a book from one of the many piles, he would hurl himself into the sagging armchair with the stuffing spilling from its threadbare upholstery and immerse himself in the story of someone else's life so he would not have to think about his own.

To his customers, Zev was a soft-spoken young Jew with a middle European accent and a reputation for honesty in his dealings. Sure, like any other pawnbroker he offered only a minimum price on their goods, but unlike the others, he charged a reasonable rate of interest —*and* he didn't hurry to snatch away their possessions when they begged for another few days that gradually grew into weeks, until they could find the money to repay him. Zev Abramski did not smile much, but he was fair and the entire neighborhood gave him their business.

From behind his brass cage, Zev watched the world go by his window. He knew everyone, from the pushcart vendors to the rent collectors, the housewives and the whores, Father Feeny and Rabbi Feinstein. He knew which boy out playing stickball on the street belonged to which family, which man had work and which didn't, and which woman was cheating on her husband. He had noticed the pretty young girl with the shiny brown hair hurrying along the street. Sometimes she would be holding a blond child by the hand and a big dog would run in front as if clearing a path. She had a special quality, a ladylike innocence that caught his attention, and his eyes would always follow her until she disappeared from view. He had noticed her again earlier that evening, when she had stopped for a long time outside his window. He wasn't surprised therefore when the doorbell announced a customer and he glanced up to see her standing on the other side of the brass grille.

He knew at once that something terrible had happened. Her eyes were tired pools of gray shadow in her colorless face and she just stood there as if she had suddenly found herself in the wrong place.

"Gut evening," he said politely. "How can I help?"

Her face blushed a fiery red. "I need money," she blurted, thrusting out her hand and showing him the diamond.

Zev drew an astonished breath. Even without his jeweler's glass he knew he was looking at a stone of fine quality and at least four carats. He glanced at her again quickly, but she had wrapped her shawl around her hair, half hiding her face.

"Where did you get such a stone?" he demanded suspiciously.

"I . . . it was my grandmother's," Missie mumbled, wishing she hadn't come, but she had to get the money, she just had to.

"This is a fine stone, worth a lot of money. Why are you not taking it to a smart jeweler's uptown? For sure they'd give you a good price."

"I . . . because I can't," she said, placing both hands on the counter for support. "Don't ask me why, I just can't."

"It's because you have stolen it, the diamond!" Zev shouted angrily. "You bring such goods to my shop to get rid, and then I'm in jail . . . that's it, isn't it?"

Missie's colorless face became transparent and her violet eyes grew dark with fear. "Stolen?" She gasped. "Oh, no! No, I swear to you it's not stolen!"

"Then how only would you get such a diamond?"

"I told you the truth," she said shakily. She knew she was going to cry and hid her face despairingly in her hands. "My grandmother is dead," she said, sobbing. "And I need money to bury her so she won't have to go to a pauper's grave. But even to do that, I wouldn't steal."

Zev stared at her uncertainly. If what she was saying was true, he was sorry for her, but he just couldn't run the risk of handling stolen property; he had to stay as far away as possible from the police because he had his own secret to hide. Still, her reason for wanting the money was so noble and she looked so sad and young and vulnerable he wanted to help her.

"If you wish the money," he said more gently, "you must tell me honest how the stone came by your grandmother." He stared at her bewilderedly as she buried her face in her hands again, sobbing noisily. "Please," he begged, "in the neighborhood I know everybody's business. I give you my word, with me your secret is safe."

Missie lifted her face from her hands and stared at him, wondering if she could trust him. "She brought it with her from Russia," she said at last.

"Russia!" Now he understood. Many people running to escape had put their savings into diamonds. They were small and easy to hide and could be sold again when they reached the new country. But that meant that she was Russian too!

"Tell me your name?" he asked excitedly in Yiddish, but she just shook her head in bewilderment.

"Your name," he repeated in half-forgotten Russian, "and where you come from?"

"We are from St. Petersburg," she said warily. "My name is Missie O'Bryan."

"O'Bryan? Then your husband is not Russian?"

"My father's name was O'Bryan. I have no husband." She gasped and clapped her hand over her mouth. She had forgotten all about her story and now he had caught her out in a lie.

Zev turned away, embarrassed. "Excuse me," he muttered, "such a personal question I should not ask."

He picked up the diamond, inspecting it once again. He could feel her violet eyes fixed on him hopefully but he said nothing.

Missie knew he was waiting for her to tell him more, and how could she blame him? Where else would a poor girl like her get a valuable diamond if she hadn't stolen it? "My grandmother's name is Sofia Danilova," she said quickly. "We escaped the revolution, along with many others."

He pushed the diamond silently through the grille and she knew it was no good, he was not going to lend her the money. Sofia had been right after all. The jewels were worthless.

"Thank you, Mr. Abramski," she said sadly, putting the diamond in her pocket. "I understand."

Zev stared after her as she walked to the door; her thin shoulders drooped as if she bore the burdens of the world on her shoulders. She looked so pathetically young and alone: She reminded him of himself years ago, a boy all alone on the streets of New York with nowhere to go, no one to turn to. . . .

"Wait!" he called, banging his clenched fist on the counter.

She swung around, her eyes filled with fear.

"I will lend you fifty dollars only," he said. "Naturally, the diamond is worth much more, but I do not mean to cheat you. I will hold it until you can repay me, even though it may be a long time."

Missie felt a quiver of relief in her stomach, but she knew she must tell him the truth. She said quickly, "I earn twelve dollars a week working in O'Hara's Saloon. Out of that I have to pay the rent and keep my family. And with the threat of Prohibition, who knows how much longer even that job will last? I must tell you honestly, Mr. Abramski, that I may never be able to repay your fifty dollars."

"Some day your fortunes will turn," he said, opening the old wooden till and counting out the money briskly. He pushed the crumpled notes into the groove under the brass grille. "Fifty dollars. Let us call it a loan of trust."

Missie stared at the small pile of money that meant so much to her.

"Go, bury your grandmother properly," Zev said gently, "and *shalom aleichem.*"

"*Shalom?*" she asked, puzzled.

"It means 'peace be with you.'"

Her tear-swollen violet eyes met his and Zev knew they were eyes for a man to drown in, a man in love. "*Shalom aleichem,*" she replied softly. Then, after hiding the money under her shawl, she turned away.

The bell tinkled noisily as she closed the door behind her and Zev stared at the glittering diamond lying on the scarred wooden counter. In all the years since he had watched his mother and father die, he had never allowed himself to feel emotion—no matter what he had gone through, no matter what terrible things he had seen, no matter how despairing the stories he had heard—but now tears stung in his eyes. His heart had finally been touched by an unknown girl.

Missie's heart was breaking as she thought of the grand funeral that should have been Sofia's by right: the bronze coffin with princes and noblemen to carry her to her final resting place alongside her husband and the Tsars of All the Russias in the great Cathedral of St. Peter and St. Paul. The air would have been heavy with the scent of incense and flowers and the deep, sonorous chanting of a male choir, and the Metropolitan of the Orthodox Church himself would have conducted her service. Her family and all her many friends would have gathered to pay tribute and to mourn her, and afterward a lavish but dignified reception would have been held in her honor at the beautiful palace on the Moika Canal. But instead, there was just Azaylee and herself and two indifferent men from the funeral parlor carrying Sofia's cheap pine coffin down the four flights of narrow, malodorous stairs, cursing as it stuck at every bend.

Azaylee clutched her hand tightly. She was wearing a pink cotton dress and her long blond curls were brushed back and tied neatly with a black ribbon. She was pale but tearless and Missie felt glad there was no money to buy proper mourning because she knew Sofia would have hated to see her little granddaughter dressed all in black. Azaylee was carrying a posy of fresh flowers chosen from the pushcart that morning, and she bowed her head gravely to the watching women, who covered their heads with their shawls as Sofia's coffin was loaded onto the shabby hearse.

Silence fell suddenly on Rivington Street; the pushcart peddlers stopped their shouting, the women their bargaining, and even the children stopped their play as the hearse set off with Missie and Azaylee walking behind. With a great howl, Viktor broke his leash and hurled himself down the fire escape to join them, his flaglike tail cutting an arc in the air as he led the hearse, just the way it had as he led the sled through the forest on that cold, dark, terrible night in Russia.

Missie clutched Azaylee's hand even tighter. She lifted her chin high and stared straight ahead, afraid to catch anyone's eye in case she broke down and cried. Without Sofia, she felt alone and helpless.

She heard footsteps and turned, surprised to see O'Hara walking behind her, looking hot and uncomfortable in a stiff collar with his old striped tie knotted around his neck instead of holding up his pants as it usually did. He wore his special St. Patrick's Day shamrock-green suspenders and a black broadcloth jacket straining at the seams. "I thought I'd best give you me support," he whispered, clutching his black derby respectfully to his chest.

There was a sudden murmur along the street as another man fell into step beside him. Zev Abramski had broken his Sabbath to attend Sofia Danilova's funeral. Missie was torn between hysterical laughter and bitter tears as she thought of their ridiculous little procession: an Irish saloonkeeper and a Jewish pawnbroker, an English girl, a small child, and a borzoi dog escorting one of Russia's greatest princesses to her grave.

St. Savior's was lighted by a hundred flickering candles as Father Feeny said the beautiful Catholic mass, and as they lowered Sofia's coffin into the ground she thought wistfully that before there had always been hope, the thought that maybe this was just a charade they had to play for a while the way they used to at Christmas parties and that soon everything would return to normal. But as they threw earth onto Sofia's coffin, she knew it was real and forever. Before she had been a child. Now she must become a woman.

Azaylee tugged at her hand. "I want to go home," she wailed in Russian, "to my real home. I want Papa and Princess Maman. I want Alexei." Missie hugged her tightly, and their tears mingled. "I'm tired of this game, Missie," she screamed hysterically. "I want to go home, I want it all to be the way it used to be. I want Var-ishnya. *I want my grandmother Sofia Ivanoff back.*"

Missie's eyes met Zev Abramski's and she knew he had under-stood what the child had said and that she had lied to him. He knew now that they had buried Sofia Ivanoff, not Sofia Danilova.

His face was expressionless as he bowed to her and said, "My condolences. May your grandmother be your messenger to God in heaven." Then he turned and walked quickly away.

O'Hara stared after him, mystified, then he checked the pocket watch strung on a gold chain across his front. "I'd best be getting back to the saloon," he said, thrusting some money hurriedly into her hand. "A funeral always makes a person hungry, and there's to be no proper wake the way there should be. Buy yourself and the little one a good dinner and you'll feel better." His red hair curled wildly in the heat and he tugged uncomfortably at his stiff collar, mopping the sweat from his forehead with a large red-spotted kerchief. "Remember what I said before, Missie. I'll not be rushing you now, I'm a patient man. I just want you to know I'm ready whenever you are." And settling the small black derby on his halo of red curls, he marched back down the street.

As the diggers began filling in the grave, Missie followed him from the cemetery. But she wasn't thinking of O'Hara and his offer of marriage, nor of Zev Abramski. Like Azaylee, all she wanted was the impossible. She did not want to face tonight's despairing dreams and tomorrow's reality. She just wanted to go home to her father.

13

Istanbul

No one could say that Michael Kazahn was an old man: His eighty years sat as lightly on him as they had his father, and even though his hair was white, it was as thick and luxuriant as when he was twenty. His olive complexion was unlined, his bushy eyebrows and mustache black, and he bristled with energy. Of course he still used his ebony walking cane, but mostly he just waved it around to emphasize his point. And the fiery temperament he had inherited from his father had not changed one jot.

Ahmet Kazahn watched calmly as his father limped around the enormous office with its tall windows overlooking the Sea of Marmara, waving his cane and raging about the foolishness of women—especially granddaughters—and the trouble they were bringing to the house of Kazahn.

"Why?" he demanded, his thick black brows beetling angrily. *"Why,* I ask you," he repeated, banging his ebony cane so violently on the beautiful parquet floor that it snapped. "Bah!" He tossed it from him disgustedly and limped to his desk with the odd swinging motion of his paralyzed right leg that enabled him to cover more ground faster than a normal man. "Asil," he yelled to his secretary on the intercom, "fetch me another cane!"

"Why did they do this?" he demanded again of Ahmet. "Why did Anna not come to us—to the family—if she needed money? And—in the name of heaven—*why did she need the money?* Did not Tariq Pasha leave her enough? Is one million dollars not sufficient to keep an Ivanoff in the style to which she was accustomed? And why did Leyla, *your daughter,* help her?"

Ahmet sighed. He was used to his father's outbursts, but this was a serious one. "I suggest, Father, that instead of encouraging your blood pressure to new heights asking rhetorical questions, you ask the girls themselves." He shrugged. "A simple question, a simple answer. Then we shall know how to proceed."

"*Proceed?* Take a look at this!" He flung a Turkish newspaper at Ahmet's feet. "And this, and this. . . ." *The Times,* the *International Herald Tribune,* the *Wall Street Journal, Le Monde, Figaro.* . . . "Japan, Germany, everybody is talking about the sale of the emerald." He snorted. "*And especially Russia and America.* So? How long do you think it will take the CIA or the KGB to find out that it was Anna who sold the jewel?"

"Surely not. The secrecy of the Swiss banking system is sacrosanct."

"Of course it is," Michael roared, stomping his new cane, "but even in Swiss banks there are human beings—and there will always be one who can be bought. No, I tell you, Ahmet, we are in trouble. And I for one want to know *why!*"

After flinging himself back across the room to his desk, he pressed the intercom again and told Asil to get him a Paris number. He thwacked his new cane angrily against the side of the desk, bellowing with impatience as the answering machine picked up the call and Leyla's voice asked sweetly if the caller would leave a message.

"Leyla," he roared, "this is Kazahn Pasha. Why are you not at home when I call? Perhaps you are avoiding your family now? Because of all the trouble you are bringing upon us? You—and your sister, Anna! Where are you? And where is Anna? I order you to be on the next flight to Istanbul . . . *both of you.* And you can tell Anna she has Kazahn Pasha to reckon with!"

Slamming down the phone triumphantly, he beamed across the room at Ahmet. "There," he said, satisfied with his performance, "that should put the fear of God into them both. And so it should, because, my dear son, I have a feeling they are both in terrible danger."

Ahmet knew his father was right. The matter had escalated to global proportions. Who knew what the real story was behind the desire of nations to obtain the jewel? For some reason or other, they still wanted to find the Ivanoffs, and he had a feeling it was for more than the billions lying unclaimed in the banks. One thing he knew: He had better find out, and fast.

Back in his office, he dialed Leyla's number, waiting patiently for the tone before leaving a message telling her to obey Kazahn Pasha's orders and return at once with Anna. "You are both in grave danger," he added. "Come home so we can help you. . . ."

His next call was to a certain man in a small office on the waterfront at Piraeus. The man was a member of a well-known but impoverished Greek shipping family with access to every level of society, both business and social. He had been in Ahmet's secret employ for more than thirty years, ever since the beginning of the Kazahn Freighter Line, spying on their Greek rivals so that Ahmet knew their business almost before they did. Ahmet had paid him well over the years, but just enough to keep him wanting more. The Greek was a born spy, clever, sharp, and without scruples. He was the kind of character who sought out others like himself: In any country at any time, this man could find a "mole." And now Ahmet had the biggest job of his life for him.

Leyla breathed a sigh of relief as the Air France 727 roared down the runway and soared into the air. For a few seconds she could see Paris sprawling below, then the clouds closed in, the seat belt sign clicked off, and an anonymous female voice informed them that those who wished might smoke. Above the layer of cloud the sun shone in a clear blue sky and just a few hours away lay Istanbul.

She glanced at the empty seat next to her. Anna's seat. She had paced the courtyard outside the Louvre this morning, the airline tickets in her purse, but Anna never arrived. After two hours she had hurried back to her apartment hoping she had left a message, but this time no red light was blinking on her answering machine. She had waited until the very last minute before taking a taxi to the airport, where she had called again for her messages, but still no word from Anna, and she was worried sick.

Why had they done it? she asked herself angrily. *Why* hadn't Anna just gone to Kazahn Pasha and asked for the money she needed? But she knew why. Michael would have wanted to know what she had done with her inheritance and Anna didn't want to tell him. It was Anna's fierce Russian pride that had led to all this. Not that she had ever talked much about her ancestors, but apart from Missie and the Kazahns the past was all she had really ever had.

Leyla remembered the summer in Istanbul when she was eight and Anna was fourteen. They had been sitting on the terrace watching the sun set over the Bosphorus like a great scarlet cut-out pasted onto a gauzy-gold sky. A full moon was rising behind the darkening hills and the faint scent of night-blooming flowers drifted on the air. There were just the four of them: Tariq and Missie, Anna and Leyla, watching silently, each lost in his or her own thoughts as the sun slid quickly behind the horizon, leaving them wrapped in the warm blue-black dusk, soft as velvet.

Leyla was sitting on a silk-covered ottoman at Tariq's feet, and Anna was leaning against the balustrade, gazing over the dark water. "Missie," she had said in a quiet voice, "tell me about Varishnya and my grandfather."

Leyla glanced up at Missie sitting beside Tariq and saw him take her hand in his comfortingly. "Some things are too painful to remember," he told Anna. "The past is the past, it should be forgotten."

Missie replied quietly, "But she is right, she should know about her family. She should know the truth, the way it was."

The silence had seemed endless as they waited for Missie to gather her thoughts and then she had begun.

"The first time I saw Misha Ivanoff," she said quietly, "I was just sixteen years old and still considered a child; my long hair was tied back in a large floppy bow and I wore a simple white dress with a low, wide sash, white stockings, and little brown button boots. I was all alone in Russia, in the world really, for my father had just died and I had no other living relatives. I had traveled from the Crimean coast to St. Petersburg in the Ivanoff private train that seemed to me like a palace on wheels; in fact, it ran so smoothly even the wheels seemed cushioned. But if I had thought the train luxurious, nothing prepared me for the splendor of the palace on the banks of the Moika Canal.

"A chauffeur in the deep-blue Ivanoff livery met me at the station and drove me to the house in a wonderful de Courmont motor car, and as it drew up in front of a flight of marble steps a huge doorman, looking big as a bear in his blue coat with a blue bandolier studded with gold medals, sprang to open the door for me. I was stunned by the grandeur inside. The hall towered three storeys high, its creamy marble columns were embellished with carvings, and its soaring windows were draped in stiff golden silk. The floor was a checkerboard of black and white marble with an immense sweep of magenta carpet running from the magnificent double doors to the top of the marble staircase. And at its summit stood a tall blond man with his hand resting on the collar of a great amber-colored dog."

"Viktor," Anna breathed, coming to sit at Missie's feet. "The dog my mother always talked about."

Missie nodded. "When she was a child, Viktor was your mother's best friend. Her only friend," she added sadly.

"What next?" Anna demanded.

"Even though he was wearing an old tweed jacket, I thought he looked commanding and very Russian," Missie said. "He was very tall, his shoulders were broad, and he moved like an athlete. His blond hair was thick and very straight, and he wore it longer than was usual in those days, brushed back from his forehead. His eyes were slate-gray set very deep, and he had high cheekbones that gave his face rugged planes and angles. He was the handsomest man I had ever seen." She paused for a minute and then she whispered, "And I have wondered ever since if time really did stand still as our eyes met."

Anna drew in her breath in a little gasp and Leyla peered anxiously at her. They all knew that Missie had been in love with Misha, but this was the first time she had ever put it into words. The darkness had fallen, and as the moon sailed higher in the sky she could just make out Anna's fair head resting against Missie's knee as she listened.

"Your grandfather was one of the richest men in Russia," she went on. "As well as the villa at Yalta and the St. Petersburg mansion, there was the summer house next to the tsar's at Tsarskoe Selo and the country estate at Varishnya, your grandfather's favorite. It was the exact opposite of the St. Petersburg house. It wasn't the least bit grand, and it was one of the oddest houses I have ever seen. It was built all higgledy-piggledy, as if it had started out quite small and extra bits were added over the years as the family needed more space. It was L-shaped with wings sticking out and extra storeys stuck here and there, and the style was what I suppose you might call Russian rococo with a squashed-looking green-gold dome over the great hall. Outside, each bit of the house was painted a different color like a gay patchwork quilt. Inside there were no corridors, just a series of long narrow rooms that led one into the other, and all the floors were made of wide wooden planks, cut from the elm trees on the estate and polished to a beautiful mellow golden-brown slipperiness—just right for little feet like your mother's and her brother Alexei's to slide on. In summer, the tall French windows would be thrown wide to catch the breeze and even on the hottest days it was always deliciously cool. And in winter when the arctic wind howled outside, the huge tiled stoves roared in every corner and Varishnya was the coziest house in the world.

"And it was always full of people. All the old Ivanoff relations lived there, and their friends who had come to visit and somehow never gone home again: the maiden aunts, the widows, and the cousins. You always knew where they were by the smell of moth-balls and peppermint and the click of their knitting needles and the whisper of gossip. It was strange how they always seemed to know the latest scandals, even though they had not been to town in years.

"And then there were the servants. It seemed to take dozens of them to run the big house—it must have had close to a hundred rooms though no one had ever really counted, and of course even among the servants there was a hierarchy. At the top was Vassily, the butler and major-domo who had been there since Misha's own grandfather's time. He was old and very doddery, but Misha refused to ask him to retire. He said Varishnya and the family were the old man's entire life and that without it, he knew he would soon die." Missie sighed, thinking for a while before picking up the story again. "Nyanya was the next in importance. She too was old, though not as old as Vassily. She considered the nursery her own domain where not even Princess Anouska could tell her what to do. As far as children were concerned, Nyanya knew best. She had iron-gray hair covered in a white *babushka.* The ordinary servants wore blue aprons, but Nyanya's was white. It was the badge of her standing within the household, so even visitors knew she was a person to be reckoned with. I remember some days her hands would be so swollen with arthritis she couldn't bathe the children and she was forced to stand by, grumbling, while one of the dozen nursery maids did the job. But it was always Nyanya's lap little Xenia and Alexei climbed onto at night, and Nyanya who told them bedtime stories. And it was Nyanya they loved best, after their father."

Leyla frowned, wondering why Missie had not said "after their father *and mother.*" Anna never spoke of *her* mother either; it was almost as if she didn't exist, yet she knew she did.

"Then came the German tutor, and Anouska's personal maid and Misha's valet. They were both French and considered themselves very superior and a cut above the Russian servants. They were always whispering behind their hands and sweeping around the house in haughty silence." Missie laughed. "The old aunts always said they acted as if they owned the place instead of the prince, but in the end they were the last to leave Varishnya. All the others had disappeared days before, like rats from a sinking ship.

"Anyway," she went quickly on, "there were half a dozen chefs and a huge kitchen staff and dozens of indoor servants. I remember one young girl who did nothing but light all the lamps at night and take them away to clean the wicks in the morning. And another who did nothing but tend the enormous stoves. And then of course there were the dozens of gardeners and the man whose job it was to make sure the grass tennis court was the smoothest in all Russia. And the stables where the grooms looked after Misha's beloved horses. There must have been twenty or thirty of them. And the kennels where they looked after the teams of sled dogs and the pack of borzois.

"Your grandmother, Princess Anouska, hated to be alone, and the house was always crammed with people and there were endless parties. Sometimes we had to wear fancy dress or old Russian costumes, but no matter what she wore, Anouska Ivanoff always looked beautiful. She was the most gorgeous woman I have ever seen; she looked like a polished bronze figurine with her corn-gold hair and eyes like pansies. Even her skin had a sort of golden glow. She was young, only twenty-six or seven, and very gay, and when she laughed it made you want to join in. Only sometimes it seemed she couldn't stop laughing, as if she were acting gay and carefree but you could sense that underneath she wasn't gay at all. You never quite knew where you were with Anouska: One minute she was the life and soul of the party and the next she had disappeared. She would lock herself in her room for days on end and not even Misha could get her to open the door. Only her maid was allowed in with the trays of food he sent her, but they were always returned untouched. I remember thinking it very strange at first, but everybody seemed to accept it as a matter of course. It was just the way Anouska was.

"Misha was a good man," she said, looking at Anna. "He considered his servants and the estate workers and their families at Varishnya his responsibility. He looked after them with proper Russian tenderness, and they called him *batiushka*—little father. Every month he held a meeting in the great hall, where they were served beer and food, and any man was free to voice his grievance and know he would be dealt fairly with, even though Anouska always complained that the smell of their crude sheepskin jackets made the house reek for a week afterward. Each family had its own little house and every man had work. Long before the official reforms, the Ivanoffs had given every family its own *usadba,* a plot of land where they grew their own vegetables and potatoes. It had been a long time since anyone on the Varishnya estates had known the pangs of hunger.

"Misha had built a schoolhouse and paid the *klassnaya dama,* and he helped the brightest children with scholarships to a school in Moscow; he built them a clinic and paid the doctor, and he fought for the peasants' rights in the *Duma,* the Parliament. He did his best to convince Tsar Nicholas to do something to help them; he told him that everything he and Tsar Nicholas did for the people on their own estates, the tsar must do for all of Russia."

Missie shrugged and added with a sigh, "But of course the tsar's mind was on many other things. His son was desperately ill, and the Tsarina Alexandra believed only the mad monk, Rasputin, could cure him. Would that he could, then the tsar might have been free to devote his time to his country, and the whole history of Russia might have been changed."

She paused for a minute, thinking about her story, and then went on. "Anouska and Misha adored their children, Alexei and Xenia. By the time he was six, Misha had taught young Alexei to ride and to swim and even how to handle a rifle properly, and Alexei was devoted to him. The children were allowed to come rushing into his study no matter who was there or how important the meeting. If he was too busy, their father would kiss them and give them a piece of candy from the special Fabergé silver dish with the trick lid; it was shaped like a small hill with a palm tree on top and a little monkey hidden in the grass. If they pressed a special button the monkey ran up the tree and when he reached the top the lid opened. I remember Misha loved to watch the amazement on their faces. They could never figure out how it worked and it would always make him laugh.

"Alexei looked like his father: the same eyes, the same dark-blond hair and strong features. And Xenia was a beauty like her mother. Her hair was lighter, flaxen rather than gold, and her eyes were the bright bronze of enamel: I always thought they looked like the color of tropical butterfly wings. She had Anouska's lovely golden skin with the faint bloom on it. And she had her mother's temperament.

"Anouska Ivanoff was never still for a minute. She dashed between Paris and St. Petersburg, Varishnya and Deauville, Monte

Carlo, London, and Yalta, as if she were afraid to rest. And whenever she got where she was going, after a few weeks, or even days, she would become bored and off she would go again. The children were used to her absences and she always made a fuss over them when she came back, and of course they loved it because then there were always parties and the house was full of people again.

"Anouska bought all her clothes from Paris couturiers, and in winter she wore sumptuous furs, sable and arctic fox, and her shoes were made specially for her in London and in Rome. In each of the houses she had an enormous safe lined with soft gray suede where she kept all her fabulous jewelry: whole sets of rubies, emeralds, and diamonds like an Aladdin's cave. She adored violets and the *parfumiers* at Grasse in southern France created a scent especially for her. Of course it was called 'Anouska,' and nobody else in the whole world ever used it. And she always wore a bunch of violets pinned to her dress or her furs, so she always seemed to smell of springtime."

She fell silent, remembering. "Please go on," Anna urged.

Missie smiled at her and picked up her story again. "Varishnya was especially beautiful in the snow. Guests came on the Ivanoff train to the special little station at Ivanovsk and were picked up by liveried coachmen and driven by dog sled to the house. We always knew they were arriving by the jingling of the sleighbells, and we would rush outside to greet them. And of course the greatest favorite of all with the children and adults alike was the Dowager Princess Sofia Ivanoff, your great-grandmother.

"It was Princess Sofia who told me the story of your grandfather and grandmother's marriage. When he met Anouska, Misha was known as 'the catch of the decade.' The year was 1908 and he was twenty-four years old with an honors degree in archaeology from Oxford and two years of riotous travel behind him. He was tall and handsome and for some reason that mystified him, the young ladies of Europe and America had told him he was a heartbreaker. He loved all sports and kept his six-foot-five-inch body in peak physical condition, but riding was his favorite and he loved to play polo at Deauville. Anouska Nicholaevna Orloff was just eighteen years old and a niece of the tsar. Her family was a noble one but they were poor, and young Anouska was already a renowned beauty *and* a notorious flirt. Every eligible young man in St. Petersburg was in love with her, and your grandfather was no different. As soon as he met her he fell under the spell of her beauty."

Missie paused for a moment and then added, "You have to understand that flawless beauty like Anouska's is compelling: You just couldn't take your eyes off her; she was like a living work of art. Sofia said it didn't matter that Anouska was not well educated; she had a quick mind that picked up on all the latest happenings, and she would talk about the theater and the latest plays and novels as easily as she would the latest dressmaker or fashionable jeweler. And she was a wonderful dancer and always the star of any party. It didn't matter that she was selfish and petulant, and that sometimes she behaved strangely, not showing up at dinner parties arranged especially in her honor or simply disappearing for days on end. The young men still showered her with bouquets of flowers and love poems, as well as jewelry, which her mother always scrupulously returned. She had her daughter's reputation to think of, and the stakes were higher than a mere diamond bracelet.

"Misha could think of nothing else and for weeks she kept him dangling, playing him like a fish on a line. Sometimes she would see him, sometimes she wouldn't, and he was crazy with jealousy thinking some rival was going to snatch her from him. He proposed and after a week's consideration, when she left him to cool his heels alone in St. Petersburg while she went to stay with friends in the country, she finally consented to be his wife.

"Sofia told me their wedding was the grandest seen in Russia for many years. Anouska wore a cloth-of-gold train over cream satin and the great Ivanoff tiara with the huge ninety-carat maharaja's emerald that had been reset specially for her by Cartier in Paris. The tsar and all his family came to the wedding, and the ceremony was held in St. Isaac's Cathedral with its golden domes and columns of malachite and lazurite, but huge as it was, it was too small to accommodate all their guests. Afterward a lavish reception was held for everyone at the mansion overlooking the river Neva.

"Misha took his bride to America for a three-month honeymoon, and Anouska insisted on lingering in Europe on their way back. She needed more new clothes, more jewels. Misha was young and in love; he indulged her. Anything Anouska wanted, she could have. When she finally grew bored with shopping, she summoned her friends to the Ivanoff yacht and they all cruised through the Mediterranean, up the Bosphorus to the Black Sea, and back home to Russia.

"Sofia said that even then Misha knew there were problems. There were days when Anouska would refuse to get out of bed; her face lost all its color and her eyes looked far away. Sometimes she would just cry, not hysterically, just endlessly. The tears would run down her white, pinched face and Misha didn't know how to stop them no matter how he tried to comfort her, to coax her, to bribe her with the promise of presents. She just could not stop crying. Back in St. Petersburg things got suddenly worse: Anouska locked her bedroom door and refused to let anyone in. Misha summoned Sofia and she called Anouska's mother.

"Ilona Orloff told them Anouska was highly strung; she always pushed herself to the limits of her strength with endless parties and entertaining, and then she would just crash into this great depression for a while. The best thing was simply to leave her alone and wait for her to come out of it. But Sofia was worried and summoned an eminent psychiatrist from Switzerland. He told them that Anouska was manic depressive; he also said she was young and that a course of treatments would help her. So the young couple spent three months at a sanatorium in the Swiss mountains while Anouska underwent her treatment. When they returned she seemed better, and she plunged back into her old way of life as hectically as before.

"Now, Misha was a quiet man who enjoyed country life. In winter he liked nothing more than to sit by the fire at Varishnya, reading books on history or pursuing country sports, hunting wolves with his borzois and shooting in the season. Anouska only liked Varishnya when she could throw extravagant parties and fill it with friends from the world of the theater and the international riff-raff she seemed to collect on her travels. She was the most popular hostess and still the most beautiful woman in St. Petersburg. Gradually their lives began to take separate courses, and gradually too Anouska became more and more unpredictable in her actions.

"Alexei was born three years after their marriage, and for a time she was transformed: She doted on her baby son and took him everywhere with her, showing him off at every opportunity. But after a few months she was back to her old ways. Xenia came along three years after that in a desperate attempt by Misha to get his young wife back into his life, but she grew more and more erratic, and soon her behavior was causing gossip. There were rumors that Anouska had grown reckless, that flirtations had grown into affairs. Names were mentioned and the gossip swelled. But Anouska was so beautiful nobody minded her wild behavior, they forgave her anything. They said that every man in St. Petersburg was in love with Anouska Ivanoff. Except her husband.

"But Misha still looked after her; he cared for her as if she were a fragile porcelain doll who might break any minute, because he understood that the way she was was not what she wanted to be. Poor Anouska had no control over her emotions and actions; she was like a straw, drifting with the wind whichever way it blew. But when the great depressions came over her, she always came home to Misha."

"Oh, Missie," Anna whispered, and in the moonlight Leyla could see she was crying. "Oh, Missie, *now I understand.*"

Missie reached out her hand and stroked Anna's soft, fair hair tenderly. "There's something else I should tell you, Anna, now that you are old enough." She hesitated as if thinking how to say it, and then said quickly, "Your grandfather and I were in love with each other."

Anna's blue eyes opened wider and Leyla sat up straight, listening eagerly: It all sounded like a story from the Arabian Nights, jewels and princes and intrigue . . . Was Misha going to strangle his wayward wife with a silken cord, the way they had in the harem at Topkapi Palace?

"Missie?" Tariq said warningly, but she smiled and shook her head.

"Anna must know everything now," she said. "It is her right." And Anna reached up and took her hand as she went on.

"Even though I was only sixteen when I first saw Misha, it was love at first sight. And even though he was so handsome and a prince, and I was young and impressionable, I knew it wasn't just infatuation. It was like . . . like coming home, finding the one person in the world who is exactly right for you. Of course, he said nothing: It would have been wrong. But I knew he felt it too. My father had just died and Misha went out of his way to be kind to me, to try not to let me dwell on things. Anouska was away a great deal, and he took me to the opera and the ballet, always in a group of course, and to dinner parties at his friends' houses. And of course he showed me his beloved Varishnya. We rode around the estate together, visiting the school and the clinic, and dropping in on the workers and their families to take a glass of tea and see a new baby or even a new calf. I could see they loved him by the way they looked at him and the respect they offered. It wasn't smarmy or obsequious because *batiushka* was condescending to visit. He talked to them as equals, human beings with as many rights as he had, and they trusted him to look after them. The village children would rush to meet him, the boys competing to lead his horse and the girls dancing around in their swirling embroidered skirts and little scarlet felt boots. They were so pretty, so sweet then. . . ."

Missie sighed and Anna gripped her hand tighter. "Misha and I were growing closer, but it was a meeting of the minds, you understand. We never spoke of 'love.' That is, until my seventeenth birthday when he gave me a present, a jeweled brooch in the shape of the Ivanoff crest, and then he kissed me and said he loved me. How can I tell you what it felt like, to be in his arms? I can only say that I knew it was where I was meant to be. He told me he had not meant to say it, that he was married and anyway I was too young, but that if I went away his life would be empty.

"The war with Germany was going badly. Misha was an officer in the Chevalier Guards and he was often away at the front, and Anouska was away staying with friends; she spent more time at other people's houses than at her own. I wrote every day to Misha and sometimes I would get a reply, short, quick notes telling me he was well and missed his children and Varishnya and me, and always signed just 'Love, Misha.'

"I was alone in St. Petersburg with just the children and the servants for company. Of course by now I knew a lot of young people, but without Misha around somehow I felt as if I didn't belong and, anyway, I was in no mood for parties when young men were being killed at the front. One day I took Alexei for a walk. St. Petersburg was like Venice, built on an estuary with lots of little bridges connecting the islands, and this day we went to *Novoya Derenya,* the gypsies' island: It was Alexei's favorite and mine too. All the famous gypsy families lived there, and many years before an ancestor of Princess Sofia's had married a gypsy girl from the Shishken Tabor family. They were tall, good-looking people, with flashing dark eyes. All the men had big mustaches and the girls had long curly dark hair covered with gaily colored kerchiefs, and they wore huge earrings like gold circles. The men would play their balalaikas and guitars and sing and the girls would dance those wild stamping dances; they looked wonderful in their swirling skirts with scarlet sashes at their tiny waists, and we would toss a coin into the tambourine brought round by a swarthy, bold-eyed young gypsy.

"Alexei was a beautiful child, so blond in contrast to their darkness, and of course they knew who he was and always made a great fuss of him, inviting him into their houses and offering him syrupy drinks and little sweet cakes and fresh bread and their delicious jam. But this day one of the older women from the Massalsky Tabors beckoned to me to leave Alexei with her daughter and to come into her house alone. I was a little mystified, but I followed her into a back room.

"It was dark, just the light of a small red-shaded lamp; there was a round table with a red cloth and two chairs, and she motioned me to sit down. After going to a shelf, she took down a crystal ball. I remember smiling, thinking she wanted to make an extra ruble or two by pretending to tell my fortune.

"The light from the lamp flickered over her face as she gripped the ball in both hands and stared into its depths. I watched her silently. Her face was very lined and I guessed she must be more than seventy, but there was no trace of gray in her black hair and her hands were very beautiful, with long slender fingers and polished oval nails. When she finally looked up at me her eyes were mesmerizing, like dark pools, and I felt myself drawn to her. I leaned closer as she spoke, unable to take my eyes away.

" 'There has been sorrow in your life,' she told me, 'and you are alone in the world, yet you are surrounded by love.' I was amazed that she was right. I knew that the Russian women, who were obsessed by mysticism, believed the gypsies' predictions, but I had always been skeptical. I thought it was just an amusing game, a way to make money.

" 'It is not a love that will bring you happiness,' she said, and then she stopped. Then she said quickly, 'You are too young, you should return to your homeland, *you must not remain here.*' She took her eyes away from mine and stared back into the crystal and I followed her gaze, wondering what she could see in there. 'There is love and despair in your life, and happiness will not lie in the direction you think. Love will always rule your life, and because of it you will undertake a great responsibility.' She looked at me strangely and then added, *'A responsibility that could change the world.'*

"Of course I was intrigued, I wanted to hear more, but she suddenly pushed the crystal away from her and walked to the door, holding back the curtain for me. I took some money from my purse and offered it to her, but she put her hands behind her back and shook her head. 'God protect you, *malenkaya,* little one' was all she said.

"It wasn't long before her prophecy began to come true. Things were going from bad to worse in Russia. The war was a shambles, partly because the tsar was insisting on conducting it himself, and there were strikes and riots in the cities. Events happened quickly and the Bolsheviks gradually began to gain control. Many people were leaving Russia while they could, but others, like Misha, wanted to stay and protect their interests.

"He trusted his people, and why shouldn't he? He had looked after them better than their own fathers. His trust was sadly misplaced; they had fallen for the Bolsheviks' promises of riches and land for every man, and now, when we rode through the village, the children were whisked indoors by their sullen-faced mothers and the men avoided our eyes.

"One by one the servants disappeared. There was danger in the air and Misha tried to persuade me to leave, but I could not. It was my eighteenth birthday; Anouska was depressed and spent the day in bed. Sofia and Misha and I were dining with the old aunts and cousins. They had just toasted me in champagne, when suddenly there was a great hammering on the door.

"It was a friend, a doctor from the neighboring town, thirty kilometers away; he had come to warn Misha that the mobs were growing, that they were violent and that we should flee while we could. The house was thrown into chaos as we prepared to leave. The old people refused to go and so did Misha. He promised to join us in the Crimea within a few days. As we were leaving he said, 'Take care of my children for me, Missie.' I looked into his eyes and saw what was written there. And then he said 'I love you,' and he kissed me."

There was a long silence and Leyla held her breath, waiting for what Missie wanted to say next.

"I never saw him again." Missie's voice shook as she added, "You know the rest. Anouska was killed in the forest as we fled, and Alexei too. With Tariq Kazahn's help, Sofia and I escaped to America with Xenia."

The moon was high now, flooding the terrace with a strange white light as Leyla stared at Missie and Anna. Anna pressed Missie's hand to her cheek and she could see she was crying.

"Misha and I were never lovers," Missie said quietly. "I was young and innocent, and Misha was a gentleman."

"Oh, Missie," Anna whispered, "I'm so sorry, I should not have asked you. But I'm glad I know. Now I understand so much better."

"I'm glad, *dushka*," Missie said, "But it's all a long time ago, and your great-grandmother and I made a decision then to put it all behind us and look only to the future. And now that's what you must do too."

"I promise," Anna said. But even then, Leyla had wondered how she could ever keep such a promise.

Yet it seemed that Anna had. For years she had barely mentioned it, and then all of a sudden she had come to Leyla and told her she needed money. Urgently.

"Ask Grandfather," Leyla had said promptly. "If it's that desperate, of course he will give you whatever you need."

But Anna had refused. She said Tariq Pasha had already repaid the Kazahn debt of honor and this was her responsibility. And then she had told Leyla about the jewels.

It had all seemed so easy, the way she explained it, and when the diamond had sold so easily, they had dared to go further. Leyla had quite fancied her role as courier, slinking around Bangkok in dark glasses and making deals with the shady Mr. Abyss. Now she knew that had been the easy part. The hard part was yet to come: She had to face Kazahn Pasha's wrath alone.

14

Düsseldorf

The Arnhaldt mansion dominated the forested landscape, towering over the trees from the crown of its hill like a great gray mausoleum. It had been built by Ferdie's great-great-grandfather as a tribute to himself and the success that, in 1825, had taken him from his mother's small-town drapery business to the pinnacle of fortune as one of Germany's elite new steel barons.

By the time he had made his fortune and gained his title, Ferdinand Arnhaldt had had enough of making do with cheap gimmickry. He had built his mansion to last. It was of solid gray stone, with turrets and battlements, arched gothic windows and columned porticos, surrounded by gardens in the French style but lacking their charm and by hundreds of acres of parkland and forest. Indoors, the walls were paneled in rich woods; there were marble floors and onyx fireplaces, a carved Jacobean oak staircase taken from an English manor, and tall stained-glass windows that let in little light, giving it a gloomy, churchlike atmosphere.

Ferdie Arnhaldt sat in the oak-paneled study that had been his great-grandfather's, his grandfather's, and his own father's, in the same big burgundy leather swivel chair they had sat in, at the same massive partners' desk they had once used. On a pad of dark velvet in front of him lay the emerald. There was no question in his mind that it was the Ivanoff jewel, and the fact that it had been cut and that he had paid a great deal of money for it did not give him any cause for concern. In fact he considered it a triumph: Hadn't he snatched it from beneath the very noses of the competition? And the competition was as tough as they came. What did worry him was that he was over nine million dollars poorer and the identity of the "Lady" was still a mystery. The auctioneers had said they didn't know and the Swiss bank refused to tell him.

The metal castors on the chair screeched as he pushed it back, and he made a mental note to inform the housekeeper of the fact. The Arnhaldt household had always been run like clockwork, and he was not about to let standards slip. He could still remember his great-grandmother firing the butler for not being quick enough at opening the door when her automobile drew up outside. The fact that the man had been with the family for twenty years and suffered from arthritis had concerned her not at all. "I will tolerate nothing but the best," she had snapped when his father had protested that he liked the butler and he was used to him. "If he is no longer the best then he goes." And he had, only to be replaced by a succession of new butlers, none of whom could live up to his great-grandmother's tyrannical demands, nor to the old butler's qualities.

Still, Ferdie had learned his lessons young, and even today, when good staff was harder to find, it was impossible for him to let such things as a table improperly set or a telltale layer of dust on the tops of the picture frames or squeaking castors go without comment. He knew he was not popular with his household staff, or with his workforce at the five huge Arnhaldt engineering factories and at the ironworks, the smelting plants, the foundries, and the offices. He knew what they whispered about him: "The steely image of his father," they said, "and the iron fist of his great-grandmother." It was true, he did look like his father: the same light-blue eyes and blond hair brushed neatly back from the broad brow, the strong nose and powerful jaw, and the same tall, carefully disciplined body.

Ferdie's wife had accused him of being inhuman. Arlette was French and when he first met her she was frivolous and pretty in a cute doll-like way. She had black boot-button eyes, a cloud of dark curling hair, large breasts, and a very tiny waist. Of course there had always been girls available to young men as rich as Ferdie Arnhaldt, and he had never lacked for a glamorous companion on his arm, but wily Arlette had wooed him with all her sensual Parisian charm and before he knew it they were married. He had realized too late that she had married him for his money, but by then she was pregnant and he would never divorce the mother of his child. The fact that the child was a girl had at first been a great disappointment, but he had soon grown to love her. His little daughter had a combination of her mother's looks and the Arnhaldts' powerful will. Her picture still dominated his desk though she had been dead ten years now, killed in a horseback riding accident when she was only fourteen. Time had healed the wounds but never the bitterness of her loss.

Afterward he had decided it was expedient not to divorce Arlette, because she served as a good excuse to keep other wily women away from his fortune. Of course, should the need or desire arise he would divorce her in a minute. Meanwhile, he kept her in luxury in an enormous apartment in Monaco.

Ferdie walked across to the painting on the wall beside the fireplace. For a house of such richness and grandeur, filled with objects of such solid value, the painting was a nonentity: a mediocre woodland scene signed by an unknown artist. His great-grandfather had hung it there a century ago to conceal the wall safe behind it, in the belief that if he put a valuable masterpiece there it might get stolen and lead the thieves to even greater treasures behind.

After pressing the concealed button, Ferdie waited until the painting slid slowly to one side, and then he dialed the combination and opened up the safe. There was nothing in there of any value to common thieves, only to his enemies. It was stacked with papers and documents. He pulled out a brown manila envelope and carried it back to the desk. He sat for a long time looking at the photographs it contained.

The first picture was of his grandfather on the occasion of his second marriage. He had been fifty-two years old and looked the way all the Arnhaldt men did: tall, hard, and upright in his gray morning suit, his silk top hat held firmly against his chest. His bride was young and very beautiful, soft-faced with love in yards of bridal satin and lace. The second photograph was of the same woman, this time seated on a chair. She was holding up a hand to touch the smiling little blond girl leaning against her shoulder. The third photograph was faded and worn from much handling. It was of Princess Anouska Ivanoff wearing the famous tiara with the emerald.

For the umpteenth time Ferdie compared Anouska's face with the blond child's, examining them minutely, feature for feature. The resemblance was undeniable.

After pushing the photographs to one side, he took some documents from the envelope. They were a series of expired leases from the Russian Soviet Socialist Republic dating from 1920, giving the Arnhaldt Company the rights to mine lands on Rajasthan, previously the property of the Ivanoff family. Those mines contained the valuable tungsten necessary for hardening steel, without which the Arnhaldt factories would have been worthless. For over seventy years the Arnhaldts had been shelling out a fortune to the Soviets, knowing that their claim to ownership was invalid. Now the mines were even more valuable to an armaments business moving into new systems of warfare, and Arnhaldt would be held to ransom no longer. Ferdie intended to make sure this time that the mines were legally his. Just as his grandfather had tried to do, all those years before. And this time, *nothing* would stop him.

He glanced impatiently at his watch. It was one minute to three. In one minute the man he was expecting to telephone would be late. After pushing back his chair, he stalked the somber room counting the seconds and then the minutes. At five past three the phone rang.

"You are late," he said with a snarl into the receiver. He paused and then said, "I beg your pardon, I was expecting someone else." He picked up a pen and doodled impatiently on his desk pad, sketching the Ivanoff tiara and the gem lying in front of him.

"American television? Now, why would American television want to interview me? General interest, you say? Mm . . . a series of profiles of great men in industry? And to whom am I talking?" He dropped the pen and a guarded tone crept into his voice. "Well, Miss Reese, I'm not sure I can spare the time. . . . I see, well, why don't you call me again tomorrow. Yes, at my office."

He replaced the receiver thoughtfully. Genie Reese was the young American who had covered the sale for that American television network in Geneva. Could it be mere coincidence that she was calling *him* now? Or had she found out he had bought the emerald? If so, how? Surely not through Markheim? He was still puzzling over Genie Reese when the phone shrilled again.

It was the call he was waiting for, from his mole within the Swiss banking system. "Yes?" he said crisply. He listened for a while then he said very quietly, "I see. You were late," he added sharply. "Do not let it happen again."

After putting down the phone, he sat in his big leather chair, thinking. He had the answer to the mystery the world was puzzling over, but somehow it wasn't the answer he had expected. His contact had just told him that the seller of the emerald was the Kazahn Freighter Line, registered in Istanbul.

All the way in the taxi Genie asked herself why she was doing this. Was it to help her country—and to further her own ambitions? Or was it also because of Valentin Solovsky's beautiful gray eyes? Either way she was committed: Ferdie Arnhaldt was expecting her, and she could already see the crenellated gray roofs of the Haus Arnhaldt over the tops of the trees.

The house came into view suddenly at the end of a long straight gravel drive, looming behind a series of *parterres,* the clipped box hedges enclosing more gravel in stiff geometric patterns. The only human factor in the whole design was the ornate marble fountain stuck dead center of the carriage circle. Water sprayed from a dozen fanciful dolphins with Neptune astride the largest fish, his trident aloft as if he were about to go spear-fishing. The wind was blowing coldly from the east, sending the fountain spray over her as the cab driver held open the door. He threw her an admiring glance as she told him to wait, and Genie felt glad because at least it meant she looked good. She needed all the confidence she could muster for this meeting.

Before she even had time to ring the bell, a butler in pinstripe trousers and white jacket flung open the door, showed her into a formal anteroom, and asked her to wait. The square room was almost as tall as it was wide, and the walls were covered with drawings and photographs of the Arnhaldt factories from their beginnings in a tiny smelting plant near Essen to the massive engineering plants of today. The thick carpet was a dark plum red and there were matching brocade curtains at the gothic windows. Genie perched on the edge of one of the heavy carved oak chairs ranged around the walls, thinking it was like the waiting room of a Park Avenue dentist with not even a mirror for visitors to check their hair before being summoned into "the presence." She felt glad she was wearing the conservative beige Armani suit. With her blond hair pulled back she looked professional enough to discuss big business and just the teeniest bit glamorous. She shrugged: Hadn't Cal said she should use all she had got to further her career? Still, she was quaking a bit inside when the butler returned after a long wait and said the baron was ready to see her now.

She followed him up a wide flight of ancient oak stairs past several huge portraits of dead Arnhaldts and along a dark corridor. Baron Ferdinand Arnhaldt's study was as gloomy as the rest of the house. He was sitting behind a large leather-topped desk writing busily. He glanced up, waved her to a seat, and continued writing.

Genie sighed as she sank into the seat he had indicated. So it was going to be like that, was it?

Ferdie continued his writing for another few minutes. He was used to assessing people and had taken her in in that one quick glance. She was young, extremely attractive, and nervous. And yet she was also determined, otherwise she would not be there.

"So, Miss Reese," he said at last, coming around the desk to shake hands with her. "I am glad to meet you, though I'm not sure *why* we are meeting."

Genie fished in her purse and handed him some papers. "My credentials," she said with a smile, "just so you know I am who I say I am. And there's a fax from my network giving me the go-ahead on this interview. Now all I need is you to agree, Baron Arnhaldt."

He perched on the corner of his desk, taking her in silently with pale Prussian-blue eyes, and Genie's smile widened. "Of course the program would not just be for America," she said quickly. "There's also a wide European audience for a human interest story like this. After all, Baron, they say you are one of the world's wealthiest men, *and* one of its most interesting. I thought we might begin at the beginning, maybe with a tour of this house while you tell me the family history. And then perhaps a brief glimpse of the steel plants and your offices. I should mention that the other names on our list for possible interviews include Agnelli, Getty, the Duke of Westminster: all men whose families founded dynasties and who have taken the family businesses to even greater power and wealth."

She glanced apprehensively at him from beneath her lashes as she handed him a list of names. Would he, or wouldn't he?

Suddenly Arnhaldt smiled. Folding his arms across his chest, he said, "I must admit I'm flattered to be included in such an elite roster of names and to be told that audiences might be interested in someone as mundane as myself."

Genie smiled back, relieved. "I'm afraid I can't accept that statement, sir. I've been looking into a few of the facts about your family and your business. I find both aspects fascinating, as I am sure my audience will. For instance, your great-great-grandfather, the founder of the business, must have been quite a dynamic character."

"The first Ferdinand Arnhaldt. I am his namesake," the baron said thoughtfully. "Yes, I suppose each of the Arnhaldt men has made his mark in his own way. But of course, in this age of liberation, we must not forget the Arnhaldt women. For instance, the old lady with the drapery store whose only son founded the business. She was uneducated, poor and a widow, and yet it was her strength and wisdom that guided her son all the way to success. She translated all the knowledge she had gained in her dealings in her small business into larger concepts and Ferdinand Arnhaldt carried them out. She even insisted on living near the plant. She said if she could see the flames belching from the smelting sheds she knew the Arnhaldt business was safe. It wasn't until she was very old and her son built this house that she agreed to move. The rest of the Arnhaldt men seemed to take their cue from her: They always married strong women. My own great-grandmother, who brought me up after my mother died when I was still a child, would interest your viewers."

He pointed to the full-length portrait hanging behind his desk. It was by Sargent and showed a tall woman in a pale satin ballgown with pink roses in her dark hair. Her features were symmetrical and the ambience romantic, but her pale eyes stared haughtily from the canvas as if she were already impatient with the sitting and the artist and had more important matters to attend to. "Bossy" was the word that came to Genie's mind.

"I think she was probably the strongest of the Arnhaldt women. She ordered everyone around: the servants, the workers, the factory managers, the directors. Even my father, until he died, and then she went into seclusion and devoted her entire life to me."

Genie stared at him, amazed. She hadn't expected such intimate revelations, especially not at this early stage.

"I learned everything I know from her," Arnhaldt said quietly. "She became my mother and father, my business adviser, and my judge."

"Judge?"

He shrugged dismissively and changed the subject. "Did you come to Europe specially to see me, Miss Reese? Or did you have other business to attend to?"

Genie blushed. He had cleverly caught her off guard. "I . . . yes, actually. I came over to cover a jewelry sale. The one in Geneva with all the silly rumors about the Russian family. The Ivanoffs."

He smiled deprecatingly. "Surely no one believes that old tale."

"As a matter of fact, they do. And speculation has it, Baron, that you yourself might have been the buyer of the emerald."

She held her breath as Arnhaldt stood up and walked back behind his desk. He sank into the worn leather chair and placed his hands on the desk in front of him. His pale-blue eyes had turned to chipped ice as he stared at her and said, "Is this the real reason for your coming here today? To ask ridiculous questions about matters that do not even interest me?"

Genie shook her head and said quickly, "But you see, that is exactly the puzzle, Baron. I mean, *why* should you buy the emerald? It just doesn't make any sense. Unless, of course, you are a collector of rare gems?"

"I have no interest in emeralds, Miss Reese," he said harshly, "nor in diamonds, or rubies. My business is steel."

He pressed a button to summon the butler, then walked to the door and held it open.

Genie bit her lip angrily. The interview was at an end; she had blown it. Yet it was odd that he was so angry. *Unless he really had bought the emerald and was angry at being found out.*

As she stood up, she glanced curiously at his desk. Baron Arnhaldt was a doodler and his telephone pad was covered with all kinds of little drawings. She could swear that he had sketched the Ivanoff emerald and the tiara. Dropping her purse deliberately on the floor, she then knelt to pick it up and snatch a closer look. It was the tiara, all right, if only she could get her hands on it. From the corner of her eye she caught Arnhaldt's impatient glance and knew there was no chance. After picking up her purse, she walked regretfully to the door. "I'm sorry if I upset you, Baron," she said quietly. "It was only a stupid rumor. It really had nothing to do with my project. It was just that you asked why I was in Europe."

He nodded abruptly, holding out his hand. It felt as cold as his eyes as he said, "Good-bye, Miss Reese."

She was halfway down the corridor when she heard him calling her name. She turned, surprised. "Miss Reese," he said, "I'll let you know about the interview. It might be interesting after all."

She thought about it on the twenty-mile drive back to Düsseldorf, wondering what he had meant. Did he really want to do the interview? And did the sketch mean he really had bought the emerald? But Arnhaldt was an enigma, and whatever he had done, he wasn't telling. He'd surely been angry when she had asked. But she knew anger was not good enough proof for Valentin Solovsky; she would have to go into phase two of their plan.

She rethought his instructions. She was to go to Markheim's office in Friedrichstrasse later in the day, after working hours. Solovsky had said that Markheim's clients were international and because he had to allow for various time differences, he always stayed late to make his telephone calls. She was to tell him she knew he had acted as the agent and, in her role as a U.S. television reporter, she was to offer him a bribe to tell her whom he had acted for in the purchase, promising him absolute secrecy.

Genie gulped as she thought of the amount of the bribe. *One million dollars.* Oh, well, she told herself philosophically, they say all TV reporters are failed actors. How hard can it be to play the Mata Hari role anyway? Still, she wished uneasily that Cal was in on this. Back at the hotel, she called his room but was told that he had checked out. He had left a message asking her to call him in Washington. She sighed worriedly. Cal in Washington was too far away to be of any help—she was on her own. She waited until six-thirty and then took a cab to Friedrichstrasse.

Markheim's office was on the tenth floor of a large modern block with entrances leading from two different streets into an enormous marble foyer. There were arcades of shops and four banks of elevators. Even though it was late there were still a lot of people coming and going as Genie pressed the up button. Two businessmen stepped out as she got in. She tugged at her jacket and ran a nervous hand over her hair as the elevator slid silently upward.

The tenth floor was a wide empty corridor with suites of offices on either side. Markheim's was at the very end. She pressed the bell, staring at the spyhole in the solid-looking mahogany door, half expecting to see Markheim's eye staring back at her, but no one answered. She pressed the bell again, hearing it ring inside, but there was still no answer.

"Damn," she said, turning away despondently, "the one night I come to see him, he's not here." It meant that instead of catching the 9 P.M. flight to Paris to meet Valentin, she would have to spend another night in Düsseldorf and try again tomorrow. She wondered if maybe Markheim was on the phone and just couldn't answer the door right now. . . .

After retracing her steps, she rang the bell again and, when she got no response, tried the handle. Surprisingly, it was unlocked. She stepped quickly inside, closing the door behind her.

"Mr. Markheim?" she called, glancing around curiously. The small outer office was furnished tastefully with some excellent antique pieces and fine paintings, but then of course it would be. After all, that was Markheim's business. The lamps were lighted and there were two full cups of coffee on a small table in front of the pale brocade sofa. Genie inspected them: They were still warm so obviously Markheim must still be there. Perhaps he had just popped down the hall for a minute.

The door to the inner office stood open a crack and she called his name again, pushing it open. The lights were all on and Markheim was sitting behind the desk, half swiveled away from her. She caught her breath guiltily, feeling like a trespasser caught in the act.

"Oh, excuse me," she said, blushing, "I didn't realize . . ." Markheim did not move and she peered nervously at him. "Mr. Markheim?" Her voice faltered as she edged around the desk and looked at him. Markheim's glazed stare met hers, only Markheim couldn't see because he had a small round hole in the middle of his forehead and he was very dead.

Waves of panic hit her. She was going to scream, she was going to faint, she was going to throw up, she was in a room with a dead body. A *murdered body.*

With a strangled scream, she spun around, afraid she would come face-to-face with the assassin, but the room was empty. She looked back at Markheim. There was no mess, and the trickle of blood at the corner of his mouth had already congealed. A second wave of panic sent her flying from the room, through the outer office and out the door. Breathing hard, she stared down the silent, empty corridor. It had lost its former innocence and suddenly looked as dangerous as a minefield. What if the murderer had seen her go in? What if he was waiting behind one of those silent doors? To grab her, *to murder her as he had Markheim.* Genie tried desperately to remember what she had learned at all those self-defense classes she had taken before panic propelled her down the corridor to the elevator. She slammed her fist on the button, dancing up and down with fear until at last it arrived.

The two women inside glanced at her curiously as she jumped in, holding her finger on the down button until the doors closed and they began to descend. As soon as the doors opened she fled across the marble foyer and out into the crowded street, gasping in the freezing night air, waiting for her knees to stop shaking. Then she walked two blocks, trying to get a grip on herself before hailing a passing taxi.

Back at the hotel, she threw her things into her suitcase, called for a porter, went back down to the lobby, and checked out. Within half an hour she was on her way to the airport, where she went straight to the bar and had a large brandy, watching the minutes tick by until she could board her flight at eight-thirty. But it wasn't until it took off that she felt safe again. She was on her way to Paris and to Valentin.

15

Paris

As usual, Geneva airport had been crowded with groups of young skiers and harried businessmen. Valentin was late. He checked in at the first-class desk for the British Airways London flight. Carrying only his briefcase, he strode quickly to the gate. From the corner of his eyes, he could see the two men following fifty yards behind. They wore black overcoats and carried briefcases, but to him they stood out from the crowd as if they wore red KGB badges on their fur caps.

He settled into the seat reserved for him and a steward offered to take his coat, but Valentin shook his head. He accepted a copy of the *International Herald Tribune,* glancing behind him as the curtain dividing the cabins was suddenly pulled back and the KGB agent in the fur hat quickly scanned the seats. His eyes were expressionless as they met Valentin's, then he retreated obediently into the economy section as a stewardess shook her head reprovingly at him.

Valentin watched carefully as the last of the passengers boarded. When he heard the captain's voice over the intercom saying "Doors to manual, please, cabin crew," he stood up, grabbed his bag, and walked to the front of the plane. "Excuse me," he said apologetically to the steward, "but I have decided not to take this flight. Urgent business. . . ."

Within seconds he was striding back down the tunnel from the BA London flight toward the Air France desk. The flight to Paris was just boarding. He glanced back at the gate; the crowd had gone and there was no sign of the two KGB men. Valentin grinned as he thought of their faces as they waited for him later at Heathrow.

The hotel in the St. Germain quarter of Paris was small with a kind of faded charm. The *toile de jouy* wallpaper had bleached over the years to a pink blur and the bed was the old-fashioned French double that Americans always found too small. But the linen was immaculate, there was a bunch of flowers on the dresser, and the window faced onto a charming inner courtyard.

Valentin emerged from the shower, toweling his hair dry. After picking up his watch, he checked the time. Eight P.M. There had been no message from Genie so she should be on the nine o'clock flight. Unless she had changed her mind, of course. He doubted it. Genie Reese knew what she wanted and she was determined to get it, even if it took a little extracurricular activity. And anyway he had the feeling she wanted to see him as much as he wanted to see her. He knew it was wrong, he knew it was crazy, but there it was— he couldn't wait to see her again.

He dressed quickly in jeans and a beige crew-neck cashmere sweater and lay on the bed with his hands clasped behind his head, thinking. Before he had left Moscow, he had done his research carefully, intent on knowing every detail of the Ivanoff story and the mines. When Genie had told him about Markheim and the Düsseldorf connection he had put a fast two and two together: The Arnhaldts had been leasing those mines from Russia for years. So now he knew there was a third player in the game. Ferdie Arnhaldt.

He told himself that Genie had been a willing victim in his scheme. She wanted her scoop and he wanted the information. It was fair trade. Of course she had asked why the Russians wanted to find the "Lady," and that's why he had told her about the money.

"You have to understand," he had said firmly, "that after the revolution, Russia confiscated all monies and property. There was no more individual wealth: Everything belonged to the people. We believe it is *Russian* money sitting in the banks, not Ivanoff money. Unfortunately the banks refuse to recognize our claim. They will release the money only with the notarized signature of the Ivanoff heir, if one still remains. Naturally we are eager to find the 'Lady,' and we hope to persuade her that it is her duty as a Russian to help her own people by releasing the money to the Soviet Union." He shrugged. "After all, it is exactly what her ancestor the prince did in his small way."

"And if she refuses?" Genie had asked.

"Then we shall pursue our claim in the international courts."

"You won't . . . I mean, the 'Lady' is not in any danger?"

He had laughed. "The revolution was a long time ago. We are not savages. We are civilized men and women, just like you. We do not even want the money from the sale of the jewels. All we want is for her to return to Russia what is rightfully theirs."

Genie had breathed a sigh of relief as he had gone on to tell her what he wanted her to do. Then she had sat back on the soft striped sofa in the Hotel Beau Rivage, thinking.

Valentin had watched her silently, taking in her smooth oval face, the broad brow, her troubled blue eyes, and the soft mouth whose sweetness belied the professional hardness she assumed, like a cloak, to disguise her vulnerability. She was wearing a simple black dress and her blond hair shone under the lamplight, and he thought she was the loveliest woman he had ever seen.

She had caught the message in his eyes and known what it meant. "Okay," she said softly. "I'll do it, Valentin." And then it was back to business again as they had made arrangements to meet in Paris tonight.

He switched back the curtains and stared into the courtyard, automatically checking the windows opposite. All the shades were closed and a thin layer of snow covered the small, leafless trees. He was pretty sure he had lost the KGB men, but they were smart and you never knew. He thought of his father in Moscow. A worried man.

He had gone over his father's story a thousand times in his mind, and of course there was no doubt it was true. But try as he might, he could not think of himself as Prince Misha Ivanoff's grandson. His grandfather was the peasant, Grigori Solovsky, a man who had loved him and whom he had loved as only true flesh and blood can. It seemed unfair that the past should return to haunt his father. After all, he was just a helpless little boy when it happened. His only crime was to be the son of a rich, aristocratic man.

"I cannot let my father suffer for this," Valentin told himself again. "I cannot let him be exposed. Not because of myself, but for Grigori's sake too. Our whole family would be discredited. Why doesn't Boris see that?" The trouble was, he didn't know Boris's true game. Did he really mean to go through with his scheme against his father? Or was he simply intent on covering himself in glory by recovering the Ivanoff treasure for Russia and ensuring his place in the Wall of Honor in Red Square? But he knew Boris was an unpredictable man and a cruel one, and his father had said he would stop at nothing.

"Nor," Valentin vowed grimly to himself, "will I."

It was eleven o'clock when his phone finally rang. Genie's voice sounded shaky. She was downstairs in the lobby, and he told her quickly to come up.

He knew at once something was wrong. Her face was drained of color; her pupils were dilated, making her eyes dark. He put his arms protectively around her.

"What is it, *malenkaya*?" he asked.

She was shaking so much at first she couldn't speak; then all the pent-up fear and emotion she had kept under control on the journey suddenly cracked and she began to cry.

Valentin took off her coat and sat her down on the bed. He pulled off her smart brown cowboy boots and rubbed her frozen feet briskly. Then he went to the minibar and poured her a shot of brandy, standing over her while she sipped it.

She looked up at him, her eyes still brimming with tears. "It's Markheim," she whispered, "he . . . he's dead. Shot . . . murdered. . . ."

He sat on the bed next to her. "Where? Where did you find him, Genie?"

"In his office. I went there—after Arnhaldt—I was going to offer him the bribe like you said. Only . . . only . . . Oh, Valentin"— she dissolved tearfully into his arms— "somebody killed him just before I got there. It can only have been minutes! There was coffee, still warm. . . ."

He said urgently, "Did anyone see you go into his office? Or leaving?"

"Two women in the elevator going down. I don't think they noticed anything. Just that I was in a hurry."

She buried her face in his chest, crying quietly, and Valentin sighed as he put his arms around her. He wondered who had gotten to Markheim. And why? Either Markheim had accepted a bribe, told who the buyer was, and then been eliminated so he could not tell anyone else, or else the buyer himself had seen Markheim as a weak link and killed him.

"Genie," he said calmly, "what about Ferdie Arnhaldt? Did he buy the emerald?"

She sat up, dabbing at her face with a tissue he gave her. "I'm not sure. He certainly knew something about it because he reacted so violently when I mentioned it. He practically threw me out. He said he wasn't interested in emeralds and rubies." She glanced up at Valentin. The brandy had warmed her. She felt calmer now that she was with him. "Arnhaldt had been doodling on his notepad. It was right there, next to the telephone. Valentin, *he had drawn the emerald and the Ivanoff tiara.*"

"You have done well," he said, sitting beside her again. "I'm sorry about Markheim. Believe me, Genie, when I say I would not have sent you had I known there would be violence."

She nodded. His deep, dark-gray eyes that seemed to know so many secrets were absorbing her. She could not look away. She leaned toward him, drawn by his glance.

"And would you believe me, Genie, if I said I missed you?" he asked, taking her hands in his.

She nodded again.

He held her closer and her mouth parted under his as he kissed her; his hands were in her hair, caressing the nape of her neck, and he was stroking her tense aching back soothingly. And soon Markheim and Arnhaldt, Russia and America, were forgotten as he made love to her.

Much later, she lay curled beside him while he slept, feeling his breath on her cheek and the security of his arms around her, thinking about what she had heard about love at first sight. People always said it could happen, and maybe now she believed it.

=== 16 ===

A car was waiting for Leyla at Ataturk Airport. "Welcome home, Miss Leyla." The chauffeur beamed. "Kazahn Pasha is expecting you. I am to drive straight to the Kazahn *yali.*"

Leyla smiled, thinking it was typical of Michael Kazahn to expect her to obey him to the letter and be on the next flight from Paris. And of course he had been right. But she was surprised they were going to the *yali:* These days it was used mainly as a summer house. Both Michael and Ahmet had built spacious modern houses atop a steep hill at Yenikoy, where the double-height windows gave a dramatic view of the Bosphorus far below. She guessed the meeting must be a very important one since Michael believed that all walls except the *yali*'s had ears.

The journey from the airport seemed endless, and her stomach churned nervously as the chauffeur threaded his way slowly through the usual traffic jam at Eminonu and across the Galata Bridge leading from the old city to the new, driving at the usual Turkish breakneck speed along the shores of the Bosphorus toward Yenikoy.

It was a bright, cold day but she stared without noticing at the sun sparkling on the water. They passed Bebek, where she had gone to school, and the ancient castle at Rumeli Hisari, then through Emirgan, where the cliff sloped steeply up to beautiful Emirgan Park.

The old ugly docks at Istinye had been cleared away, leaving the beautiful sweep of the bay uncluttered, and now only a tiny shipyard remained with a few ships drydocked undergoing repairs. A vast red-hulled tanker displaying the Russian hammer-and-sickle insignia on its funnel and looking as big as a hotel lay in the deepwater mooring. Leyla glanced at it speculatively as they passed. The enormous superstructure in its bows threatened to tilt the ship on its end, and she knew the tanker must have had a dead weight of at least half a million tons, more than any of her father's ships, because Ahmet was always wary of potential ecological mishaps and preferred to play it safe.

The car slid past the silent, gloomy tanker, around the bend toward Yenikoy where the ferryboats hooted and fussed on their way to Tarabya. Then it turned sharply right through the huge wooden gates into the courtyard of the Kazahn *yali.*

Everything looked as it always had, right from Tariq Kazahn's time. The simple pale-green wooden façade with its white gingerbread balconies and fretwork screens; the cobbled courtyard with its shade trees, its Victorian lanterns, and the remnants of thousand-year-old columns and statues excavated from Anatolia. And inside, the contrast of great luxury: antique Turkish carpets and low, silk-covered divans, the great hall with its marble floors and glorious blue Izmir tiles, and the long, flower-filled terrace by the Bosphorus where the family had always gathered on warm summer evenings in the past. The house was full of treasures: antique Turkish silver and brassware, rare wall hangings from Bursa, ancient examples of calligraphy from Persia. There were porphyry columns and inlaid wall panels and a painted canvas ceiling that resembled fabulous Ottoman brocade. Leyla never walked through those big wooden doors without thinking of her great-grandfather, because when Tariq and Han-Su had created their family home, they had also created a living museum and a lasting memory of themselves.

They were waiting for her in Tariq Pasha's old study. Her father, Ahmet, hurried to embrace her, looking anxiously behind her for Anna.

"Where is she?" thundered Michael, limping toward her, his leg swinging and his cane thumping angrily on the marble floor.

"Oh, Grandfather, I don't know," she cried, bursting into tears.

She sank into a seat in the great bay window overlooking the Bosphorus, sobbing bitterly into her hands, and Michael stared at her nonplussed. "Don't cry, Leyla," he said gruffly, coming to sit beside her. "It's only your old grandfather in one of his tempers. You know it doesn't mean anything, it's just my way." He patted her dark head awkwardly.

"I'm not crying for you, Grandfather," she said, sobbing, "I'm crying for Anna. She was supposed to meet me. I had her ticket in my bag, and she just never showed up. There was no message, nothing, and after what you said, I'm so afraid."

"I called her at home and at work," Ahmet said worriedly, "and she's not there either. No one seemed to know where she is."

"If she's got any sense, she's hiding out somewhere," Michael shouted, "and if she has the brains I always thought she had, she'll be on her way here as fast as she can."

Leyla lifted her head from her hands, pushing back strands of wet hair from her tearstained face. "No, she won't," she said. "She's afraid to come home."

Ahmet glared at his father and said exasperatedly, "What did I tell you? You always roar and shout instead of asking simple questions. . . ."

"Never mind that now," Michael roared again, "let's get to the bottom of this story! Leyla, the first thing I want to know is *why* Anna sold the emerald."

"She needed money to pay for Missie's rest home. The bills are enormous. I had no idea these places cost so much until she told me. But only the best was good enough for her beloved Missie."

Michael nodded approvingly. "She was right. But why did she need money? What about the million dollars from Tariq Pasha?"

"Remember, Anna was only seventeen when she inherited the money. She paid off a lot of debts and bought the house in Los Angeles," she said. "They had bad advice and the rest just disappeared in bad investments. There was just enough for Missie to live on until she went to the nursing home." Leyla gripped her grandfather's hands tightly and said, "Oh, Grandfather, don't you see? Anna was ashamed to come to you and ask for money. She said the Kazahns had repaid their debt of honor and now the responsibility was hers. But it was impossible for her to earn enough to keep herself *and* cover Missie's bills.

"Then she called me and said she had thought of a solution. She told me that Missie had kept a cardboard valise under her bed for years. She had always supposed it held her personal mementoes, old photos, diaries, that sort of thing. But when Missie went to Fairlawns, she showed Anna these fabulous jewels supposedly worth millions and gave her the valise to look after. Of course she told her the story, and reminded her of the old warnings about the Ivanoffs, but Anna didn't believe it. She said that it was many years since the revolution, that Russia was different now—you know, *glasnost, perestroika*—we thought it didn't matter anymore. But we decided anyway to be careful. We put the diamond up for auction last year and it sold without any fuss. The emerald was so big we knew it had to be cut. Anna found out the name of a gem cutter and I delivered the stone to Bangkok. To a Mr. Gerome Abyss."

Ahmet nodded and said, "I know the name. He was well respected in Paris for many years, did a lot of work for Cartier until he was discredited. You took a big risk, Leyla. He might have ruined the stone. How much did you pay him?"

"I promised him ten percent. We thought the stone would bring in maybe two million, no more than that. Anna sent Abyss twenty-five thousand to do the job. The rest was to be paid later, after the sale." She smiled grimly. "Now Mr. Abyss is going to find himself a much richer man than he thought."

"Didn't you realize," Ahmet said quietly, "that a flawless emerald of that size is extremely rare? That it would be bound to draw the attention of the world's experts? Cartier must still have the original sketches and plans for cutting the stone and for the design of the tiara. Its every facet would have been noted. They would recognize it immediately as the Ivanoff emerald."

"We just didn't think anyone cared anymore." Leyla sighed. "It didn't seem that important. And anyway, *why* should anyone care about the Ivanoff emerald?"

Michael paced the room again nervously. "It's not just the emerald," he said, "it's the billions of Ivanoff dollars in the banks."

"Billions?" Leyla looked at him, stunned. "You mean the story is true? There really are billions of dollars? *And they belong to Anna?*"

"Of course it's true," Michael roared. "Your great-grandfather knew it. And so did Missie." He groaned. "She never told Azaylee or Anna because she thought it was still dangerous. The KGB has a long memory, Leyla, they are like the elephant that never forgets."

"There's more to it than that," Ahmet said in his precise tones. "My spy has excellent contacts. Not only did he trace the buyer, but he also found the reason why he was willing to pay any sum to get the jewel. And what he and Russia and America want." They stared at him openmouthed as he told them the story of the mines.

Finally he said, "Russia holds ownership documents known to be false and there is nothing America can do about it, *unless* they find the missing Ivanoff. In other words, *Anna.* If the Soviets find her, she will be spirited back to Russia. They will get the legally signed papers they need to lay their hands on the billions, and they will finally have the true Ivanoff signature on their title deeds to the mines." He shrugged his shoulders grimly. "And of course she will never be heard of again."

"Granddaughter," Michael said, taking Leyla's hands in his compassionately, "now you know why Anna is in such danger. We must try to find her, get her back to Istanbul. She will be safe here with us."

"You and Anna made a grave mistake," Ahmet said quietly. "Obviously Anna wanted to remain anonymous so you decided to deposit the money in the Kazahn account in Switzerland."

"We were going to tell you afterward," Leyla said quickly. "Anna thought it would be safer. She said it was a numbered account and no one would be able to trace it."

"Anna used the number of the Kazahn account in which her money was originally deposited many years ago. But the numbered account was changed recently, and she simply paid the check into an open account in the name of the Kazahn Shipping Line." Ahmet shrugged. "It would be easy for the buyer or any interested party to trace such a check, *if he really wanted to.* All it takes these days is a computer raider. . . . And I have no doubt that by now, at least one person, *the buyer,* believes that the Kazahns sold the emerald." He shrugged. "We must wait and see what happens."

"Tell me," Michael said quickly, "has Anna ever mentioned the name Arnhaldt?"

"You mean the German steel tycoon?" She thought for a moment. "Yes, I believe she did once. She mentioned that when she was packing Missie's things, she had come across a picture of Baron Arnhaldt clipped from a magazine. I remember she said she thought it was odd, but she didn't ask Missie about him. She said if Missie hadn't mentioned anything then, it either wasn't important or she didn't want to tell her."

"We believe," Ahmet said quietly, "that Ferdie Arnhaldt bought the emerald. Arnhaldt is a megalomaniac, like his father and grandfather before him. He is the armaments king and he knows if he can get his hands on those mines, he will control both the world's defense systems and its armaments supplies. He can hold the world to ransom. He bought the emerald because he hoped it would lead him to the 'Lady.' To Anna."

"But we knew nothing about the billions and important mines," Leyla cried despairingly. "We never imagined Missie's old stories could really be true. We thought that the past was the past and it was all over and done with."

"And so it probably would have been if it were not for those mines," Michael said abruptly. "One more thing, Leyla. Does Anna know where the original ownership deeds to the mines are? Because they are the one thing in the world everyone wants to lay their hands on."

Her dazzling blue eyes widened in horror. "Oh, Grandfather Kazahn Pasha," she whispered, "now I remember. They were in the valise with the jewels. It was just an old document, brown with age and crumbling at the edges. We thought it worthless but Anna kept it because it had the prince's signature and the Ivanoff seal. She said she would carry it with her in case she ever had to prove her identity at the bank. But she didn't know about the mines and the billions. Oh, Kazahn Pasha." She wailed. *"That document is in Anna's handbag."*

═══ 17 ═══

Major-General Boris Solovsky stared at the copy of the decoded message lying on his desk. It was from Valentin addressed to Sergei, and the message was brief. Valentin had found no positive evidence yet as to who had bought the emerald, but it was definitely not the Americans. He was following up several other leads. Meanwhile would Boris please call off his heavies because as a senior diplomat he was not used to such harassment. And besides, they were so clumsy and obvious, they stuck out like a sore thumb. He would report back in a few days.

Boris banged his fist angrily on his desk. Valentin was just like his father: arrogant, clever, and too good-looking.

He sat back in his chair, his shaved head gleaming under the lamp and his fleshy, brooding face set in a venomous mask. His jaw was tense with anger, deepening the lines from nose to mouth, and his jutting forehead seemed to lower itself over his small, sharp eyes.

He had always hated his foster brother. Right from the beginning, he had known Sergei was different: He had looked different, he had acted different, he had talked different—when he spoke at all, that is. That bastard Sergei had even *smelled* different.

When his father had first brought the boy home, he had told them that he was an orphan of the revolution, that his name was Sergei, and that he would now be their son. He remembered how his mother's pale-blue eyes had widened in sympathy as she had stared at the dirty, exhausted little boy. She had flung her arms impetuously around him, hugging him to her ample bosom, murmuring soft words of comfort. The first spark of bitter jealousy had flared in Boris's heart that day, and in the following years it had grown into a bonfire of hate, stoked by his father's strange pride in Sergei's every winning action.

When Boris was eleven years old and Sergei only seven, the younger boy could beat him at almost anything, and there was no doubt that his father was well aware of it. Grigori made no secret of the fact that he was proud of Sergei's progress at school. He had already skipped a couple of grades and was only a year behind Boris. It wasn't that his father ignored Boris. He went out of his way to praise his industry and efforts, but Boris had to work three times as hard to achieve reasonable marks. Somehow Sergei had made everything he did, from riding a horse to book learning, seem easy.

But there had been things about his new brother that his father did not know. Secret things that Boris knew because he slept in the same room with him, and sometimes Sergei talked in his sleep. And the strangest thing of all was that Sergei talked in a foreign language. Boris had not understood what language it was because he had never heard anyone speak anything but his own Russian dialect. He also knew that in the old days, unlike the peasants and the working classes, all good Russian households spoke French or English as their first language, and he suspected that Sergei was not what he was pretending to be. He had been determined to find out what he was saying but had only been able to make out a few names: "Papa" and "Maman," "Missie" . . .

He had forced himself to stay awake at night, straining his ears into the silence, waiting for Sergei to speak, until his mother grew worried at his shadowed eyes and white face and dosed him with an evil-tasting tonic she brewed from the bitter leaves of plants, just the way her grandmother had done when she herself was small.

One day they had been out riding, Boris, his father, and Sergei. There was a certain high wooden fence over which he had been practicing jumps for weeks, screwing up his courage every time he set his horse at it. Finally he had mastered it. Aware of his father riding behind him, he had kicked his horse into a gallop, hurdling the fence clumsily, managing to stay in the saddle only by clinging to the horse's mane. Behind him he had heard the thunder of hooves and his father's admiring cry as Sergei took his horse over the same fence as gracefully as if it had wings.

There had been no doubt that his new brother had been devoted to his father. He followed him around whenever he was home until, laughing kindly, Grigori would tell him to be off about his own business. Nevertheless, Sergei's gray eyes would be fixed unwaveringly on him like an eager pup awaiting his master's signal of a walk.

Boris had decided there and then that one day he would find out Sergei's secret, and then he would expose him to his father as a fraud and a liar. He vowed he would find out, even if it killed him. *Or killed Sergei.*

His hands clenched into two tight fists as he remembered that vow. If he had been cleverer, he would have killed Sergei years ago and been done with it. Now he would have to deal with both him and his son. Grabbing the message, he stalked across the red carpet to the heavy double doors. The two armed soldiers outside snapped smartly to a salute and he raised his hand in a perfunctory response, marching through the lofty halls, down the marble stairs, across the courtyard to his brother's office.

Sergei saw him coming from the window; Boris was nothing if not predictable. He was wearing the uniform he had devised for himself and which, like that of the old German SS, was designed to intimidate—military jacket glittering with gold epaulettes and a chestful of ribbons, cavalry jodhpurs though he had never been near a military horse, and tall shiny boots with built-up heels to boost his dwarfish height. His peaked cap, glinting with gold and flashing with red insignia, sat squarely on his bald bullet head.

Sergei thought of Grigori, wondering how such a fine man could have fathered such a psychopath. He remembered when Grigori had first taken him home and introduced him proudly as his new son. He had been too shocked to notice much at first, but he had liked his new mother immediately: She was warm and bustling and sang snatches of happy little songs when she was working about the house. But he thought sadly that she wasn't in the least bit like his beautiful, elegant Princess Maman. He had still hoped that his real father was alive and that one day he would meet him again. Maybe tomorrow, he'd thought in the beginning, then maybe next week, maybe next month . . . but as the months slid into a year, that dream had faded.

His new brother, Boris, was short and stocky with the lank black hair and sharp dark eyes of his peasant forebears. Sergei knew that the other dead sons had all been blond like their mother, and he wondered if Grigori had saved him because he looked like them. But right from the beginning he had understood that Boris hated him. He would feel his hawkish dark eyes boring into him as he sat quietly at the scrubbed wooden table in the simple three-room cottage that was considered luxurious by local standards, but which to him seemed poor and spartan. Even in the darkness of the room they shared at night he could feel Boris's inimical stare. Sometimes he thought he must be dreaming, but then he would catch the glitter of Boris's eyes in a shaft of moonlight and know it wasn't a dream. Besides, the only dream he ever dreamed was the one about his mother.

It was always the same. She lay on the snow in front of her captors, her long pale hair tumbled about her. Her pleading golden-velvet eyes met his for a fleeting second—and then her face exploded into a bloody redness, so glaring it burned his eyes. Screaming, he would fall to his knees, covering her tenderly with her fine dark sables, and then he would lie down beside her and bury his face in the softness of the fur, breathing the scent of the violets she always wore pinned at her shoulder until he was drowning in their scent. He would jolt awake, gasping for breath, the powerful scent of the violets still in his nostrils so strongly that he believed he was home again and she had come to kiss him good night.

He had trained himself not to cry out in case he woke Boris. He would lie quietly, bathed in the sweat of remembered horror, until the shaking had stopped, and then he would slide his hand cautiously into the straw filling of his pallet. His fingers would close around the smooth cabochon stone and he would sigh with relief that it was still there. There had been so much dark-red blood spilled on the snow that no one had noticed the ruby ring lying beside Princess Anouska. Now it was all he had left of the past, and in his heart he knew he would never have more.

Natalya and Grigori knew nothing of these dreams and the ring. They were his secret, as were his memories. In his waking moments he never allowed himself to think of the past, yet even though he had seen the orange glow in the sky that meant Varishnya was burning, there was always a tiny hope left that Papa was safe.

Grigori was his hero. He had plucked him from the jaws of death and had avenged the murder of his mother. He owed him his life and he determined that from then on everything he did would be to please his new papa. He would no longer be Alexei Ivanoff, a prince of all the Russias, but Sergei Grigorevich Solovsky, and he would make his new father as proud of him as he was of his own son. He wanted with all his heart to become the man Grigori wanted him to be. Yet somehow, try as he might, he was never able to forget who he really was and truly become that other person.

A few weeks after the incident at the fence he was riding back from the grandfather's house where he had been sent to help with the cows. There was a path running alongside the stream that he liked to take at a gallop. Here and there the trees crowded closer together, stretching their low branches across the path, and it had become a game with him to gallop as quickly as he could, ducking instinctively to avoid the overhanging branches. He smiled as he set his horse on the track, spurring him on to greater speed, and the animal snorted with delight, enjoying the game. He was aware of sunlight reflecting off the fast-flowing stream far below and of the breeze stirring the silvery leaves of the birch trees.

He could never be sure whether he actually saw the thin cord stretched between the trees in front of him, or whether, with his new awareness, he just suddenly sensed danger. He heard the horse's terrified whinny as he pulled its head sharply to the side and then they plunged together down the rocky bank into the deep-flowing stream. The horse rolled frantically in the water, struggling to its feet and shaking itself. Gripping a slippery boulder with one hand, Sergei managed somehow to hang onto the reins. The water was turbulent and icy, and a few yards downstream he could hear the roar as it tumbled and gushed into a gorge a hundred feet below.

Shivering with fear and cold, he climbed back on the horse and guided it through the mossy rocks to the safety of the bank.

He lay for a while across the horse's neck, waiting for the fear to subside. Then he dismounted and walked back along the track to where he had seen the cord. It had disappeared. He examined the branches, noting the broken twigs; then he stared around him, his spine prickling, sensing that he was being watched. But there was no sound, only the noise of the water rushing over the gorge.

Sergei walked back thoughtfully to his horse. He had been brought up alongside the peasants at Varishnya; his father had treated them as family, he had looked after them well, and in return they had taken young Prince Alexei out hunting with them and let him help around the stables where they had taught him their peasant tricks. One was how to garrote a speeding horseman by the simple method of stretching a thin taut cord across his path, just at the height of his throat. It never failed, they had said, grinning at his awed young face.

He rode slowly back to the cottage. He knew there was only one person who might want to kill him.

Boris avoided his eyes at the supper table that night, but Sergei said nothing. The pattern of their relationship was set. Through the years, from school to university, his own rise through politics and Boris's through the army, the rivalry had deepened. And there had been nothing Grigori Solovsky could do about it. Sergei knew Boris had wanted to murder him all those years ago, and he was still trying now. Every way he could.

There was no preliminary knock on the door. The head of the KGB simply strode in.

"Well, Boris," Sergei said quietly, "our mother taught us better manners than that. I might have been in a meeting."

"You weren't," he said, flinging the paper with the message onto his desk. "I've come to ask you if you know what this means. Or are you as much in the dark as the rest of us about Valentin's actions?"

"You? In the dark?" Sergei laughed. "What an admission for the head of the KGB. I thought you were supposed to know everything."

After placing his hands flat on the desk, Boris leaned across it, thrusting his face close to Sergei's. "Don't get smart with me, comrade," he whispered. "I know everything about you and your son."

Sergei looked him coolly in the eye. "Perhaps you are forgetting that the Party is meant to be the arbiter of the *people's* aspirations? Is this business in the interests of our country, Boris, or is it a *personal* vendetta you are pursuing? I thought your job was to use your men to find the 'Lady.' And Valentin's was to use *his brains.*"

Boris snatched up the paper, crumpled it into a ball, and flung it at the wastebasket. It missed and his face purpled with rage.

Sergei said mildly, "You never were any good at ball games."

"Why did your son not secure the emerald?" Boris asked tightly. "Who the hell did he let beat him to it? And why?"

Sergei shrugged. "You know the game, and the players. Why not take a guess?"

"Valentin was not sent to *guess.* He was expected to carry out his task efficiently. Now we don't even know where he is."

Despite himself, Sergei laughed. "It's a good thing the CIA can't hear us now, Boris," he said. "You must have had a dozen KGB men in Geneva, and yet you say none of them knows where Valentin is. That's ridiculous."

Boris thumped on the table angrily with his fists. "Well then, where the hell is he? He must have contacted you."

Sergei shook his head slowly. "I have no idea where Valentin is. Had he telephoned me, you would have known about it." He looked coldly at Boris: They both knew he tapped Sergei's phones. "I think we must just trust that he is getting on with the job, just as he said in his message, brother."

Boris spun on his heel and stalked to the door. Sergei thought how ridiculous he looked in his tall leather boots and military uniform, like a squat little marionette with the devil pulling his strings. Russia would be better off without a man like Boris Solovsky, and he knew he wasn't the first to think so. The rumors about Boris's behavior in his personal life were getting wider and more persistent: worse even than Beria's, they said. Boris had better watch his little jackbooted step.

Still, as the door slammed, he wondered worriedly where Valentin was and what he was doing. And why he had failed to secure the emerald and with it the identity of the "Lady." Because the message had not included the code words "best wishes," which would have told him that Valentin had found her.

18

Paris

Genie slept the way she had when she was a child, warm, dreamless, secure. For a blissful few hours Markheim was erased from her memory and the beautiful hard warmth of Valentin's body next to hers comforted her. The room was still dark when she awoke, just a faint gray blur where the window was. She rolled over, smiling, expecting to see Valentin's sleepy head on the pillow next to her. He wasn't there. She put a tentative hand onto the sheet on his side of the bed. It was already cold. Had he deserted her because she had screwed everything up and Markheim had been murdered? Was he afraid he would be implicated? Her heart sank as she contemplated the fact that she might have been a one-night stand, the cute American TV reporter playing at spies and the Russian diplomat afraid of a scandal. Then it leapt with hope again at a tap on the door.

"Bonjour, Mademoiselle, le petit déjeuner."

She shrank beneath the covers as a plump maid bustled in, turned on the lamp, and placed a tray of coffee and brioches on the table. Genie stared at it. There was only one cup.

"Monsieur said to wake you up at nine," the woman told her, pulling back the curtains. She peered from the window, tut-tutting and sighing. "Another cold gray day." She turned back to Genie with a smile and took an envelope from her pocket. "Monsieur said you would need a good breakfast. He asked me to give you this."

Genie waited until the door had closed behind her before she opened it. The note was written on a sheet torn from a Filofax.

"Little one," it began, "I must leave early on urgent business. You were sleeping so soundly I thought it best not to wake you. I shall never forget last night. I will call you in Washington. Please, eat some breakfast."

It was unsigned.

Genie sank back against the pillows with a sigh. She supposed it could be worse. At least he hadn't deserted her totally. But she hoped with all her heart that he *would* call her in Washington. She stared at the cup of coffee on the table and suddenly she was back in Markheim's elegant office; her spine was crawling with the feeling of something wrong and fear swept over her again as she remembered his face with the bullet hole between his blank, dead eyes.

After flinging back the bedcovers, she ran into the bathroom and was violently sick. Then she crawled back to bed and lay in Valentin's place, clutching his pillow and crying.

Later as she stood under the shower, washing away the imprint of Valentin's body, she decided she would take the next flight to Washington. She had had enough of this crazy amateur spy business. She took out her Filofax, she found the number, dialed Air France, and booked a seat on Concorde to Washington. She would be home in a few hours. And no doubt she would be waiting for Valentin to call.

Düsseldorf

Düsseldorf was a bleak city despite its prosperity. The industry that had made it wealthy had also taken away its soul, and its hotels were not places where people went for pleasure but for business. Each was as internationally anonymous as the other, but Valentin deliberately avoided them and selected one in the drab downtown area, away from the bright lights and smart restaurants.

There were no public rooms, just a plate-glass door with two flights of fake-marble steps leading to a lobby, a small, grubby elevator scratched with initials and graffiti, and a narrow staircase leading to the upper floors.

He was wearing jeans, an anorak, and a flat cap, and he carried a small brown case. He paid cash in advance and the old man behind the desk barely looked at him as he handed him his key.

The room was small and sparse with exactly enough space for the single bed, a table, and a tiny shower. Valentin looked at his watch. It was noon. After placing his bag on the table, he drew the flimsy flowered curtain, took off his shoes, and lay down on the narrow sagging bed. He thought of the bed he had just left, and of Genie, sleeping like a baby. Her blond hair fell across her face and her eyelids were still swollen from crying. One long slender leg was flung across him as she snuggled into the crook of his arm. She was very beautiful, she had smelled of roses and lilies, and he had wanted to make love to her again, but there wasn't the time.

He had turned away from her, dressing quickly. Then he quietly packed his bag and sat down at the desk. He had thought for a long while before he wrote Genie the note, then he had picked up his bag, walked back to the bed, and stared at her. The ultimate dangerous attraction. Leaving Genie Reese could have been the hardest thing he had ever done in his life.

Now he lay on the bed in the squalid German hotel, waiting for the hours to pass until it was night, wondering what he should do about her. Of course he should never have made love to her. It was the stuff all diplomatic scandals were made of, and if Boris ever found out, it would be just the ammunition he needed to disgrace him. He doubted he would, though. The KGB had lost his trail. For the moment, he was anonymous, and that was exactly what he wanted.

The hours passed slowly but he did not leave his room, even for food. At ten o'clock he stripped, showered, and dressed quickly in black trousers, thin black polo-necked sweater, black rubber-soled shoes, and the anorak. He placed an assortment of small tools— wire, fine cord, and a tiny detonator—in the special inside pocket of the anorak, put on the flat cap, and slid a pair of black woolen gloves and a black balaclava into his pocket, along with a small, powerful flashlight. Then he locked the rest of his things in his bag and, after locking the door behind him, walked quickly down the stairs and through the lobby. The old clerk glanced up briefly and then went back to the boxing match on television.

The car he had rented at the airport was parked two blocks away, a small black Mercedes—fast, the way Germans liked them for their autobahns. There was no traffic and it took him exactly fifteen minutes to drive the twenty miles to Haus Arnhaldt. He parked at the end of the wide lane that led to the rear of the house, switched off the lights, and waited.

He had done his research well. Haus Arnhaldt was built like a fortress, but there were no guards outside, no dogs. Just an electronic scanning device and an old security system. The place had never been burgled in 150 years, and nobody expected it ever would be. With his *Spetsnaz* training, it presented no problem to Valentin.

At midnight he put on the balaclava and gloves and jogged silently along the bridle path that led through the woods to the stables at the back of the house. There were no horses in the stables and no grooms in the cottages. He knew there had not been any since Ferdie's daughter was killed in the riding accident ten years before. Valentin slid into one of the stalls, flicked on his flashlight, and studied the plan of the house carefully. It was a photostat taken from a book in the public library and gave him all the information he needed.

When the second Arnhaldt had modernized the house, he had also installed a generator in the building next to the stables. Valentin glanced up at the house. There were no lights at the windows, just small ones over the main doors.

The door to the generator house was unlocked. Valentin slid inside and flipped the switch, cutting off the power and plunging the place into total darkness.

He had already figured out where the security scanners were likely to be. Avoiding them, he made his way cautiously to the back of the house near the kitchen quarters. Even though it was dark he knew from the plan he'd memorized exactly where he was going. The crenellated battlements made slinging a rope child's play, and he was up in a flash. After searching the acres of roofs for his bearings, he walked lightly over to the west wing, secured his rope to the battlements, looped it around his waist again, and lowered himself until he was standing on a window ledge. He took a deep breath. This was the tricky bit. If he were wrong all hell would break loose.

Working quickly, he cut a pane of glass, removed it intact, and slid open the window catch. He listened for a moment but there was no sound, and he breathed again. He had been right. The security system worked from the electricity supplied by the generator, and there were no supplementary batteries. The Arnhaldts were notorious tightwads, and Ferdie must have other things on his mind than updating a system that had been there since the 1950s.

The rest was easy for a man of his training. The study looked sinister in the thin beam of his flashlight as it picked out the dark-paneled walls, the somber paintings and heavy furniture. On the desk was the pad with the drawing of the emerald, just as Genie had described it. He turned the flashlight back on the walls, staring speculatively at the paintings. He knew that, with German logic, would be the place the first Arnhaldt had put his safe. Not behind the Sargent portrait though, nor the violent Hieronymus Bosch, nor the gloomy Rembrandt over the fireplace. He smiled as the light picked out the small anonymous landscape.

Safe-breaking is a difficult job, but this safe was so old it didn't even need blowing. He just fiddled with it for a while, listening as the mechanism clunked into place like an old player piano. He grinned as he swung open the door. Ferdie must feel pretty secure to leave his home as vulnerable as this. There was nothing much inside, just a couple of manila envelopes. *And a square blue leather box, just the right size for the Ivanoff emerald.*

It gleamed under his flashlight like pure green icewater, and he touched it tentatively. It felt as cold as it looked and he shivered. No matter what his father said, he could not believe that this immense jewel had belonged to his own grandmother. Yet he had been to the libraries and studied the photographs of the Ivanoff family, and when he had looked at Misha, it was himself he was seeing. *He* was the one who looked like Prince Misha Ivanoff.

He shut the box with a sharp *click* and returned the emerald to the safe. He opened the envelopes, glancing through the contents rapidly: the leases for the mines in Rajasthan dating from 1920 and granted to Arnhaldt by the USSR; a photograph of Princess Anouska wearing the tiara and two other pictures, one of a wedding couple and the other of the bride with a young girl. Startled, he flicked the light between the two faces, Anouska's and the little girl's, then he glanced back again at the wedding picture of Eddie Arnhaldt and his bride.

Valentin heaved a sigh of surprise: He had found more than he bargained for. There was something else in the envelope, a small piece of paper with the number of a bank account and a name. The Kazahn Shipping Line. He stared at it, memorizing the information, and then he replaced everything in the safe and locked it.

He glanced around carefully. Everything was exactly the way it had been except for the missing pane in the window. He stepped onto the sill, tied the rope around his waist, closed the window, and shimmied back up to the roof. Keeping low, he ran lightly back to his starting point and within seconds was back on the ground. He walked to the generating plant, flicked on the switch, and saw the outside lights flash back on.

He was back at the car within minutes and on his way to Düsseldorf. The whole operation had taken him less than two hours.

He left the hotel at seven-thirty the next morning dressed in jeans, anorak, and cap and walked to a nearby workman's café for a breakfast of bratwurst, eggs, doughy poppyseed bread, and three steaming cups of coffee. It tasted like the food of the gods. He drove the Mercedes back to the rental lot and walked across to the airport. There he went into the barber's shop, had a shave, and changed his clothes. Once more the smart young Russian diplomat in a conservative London suit, he boarded the flight for Washington.

19

New York, 1919

O'Hara threw open the saloon doors, letting the cold morning air in and the fog of smoke and booze out. He stood for a few minutes, his hands behind his back, the first cigar of the day at the corner of his mouth, inspecting his domain. He had lived on Delancey Street for twenty years and was one of its oldest residents, and sometimes he felt like he owned it. He knew everybody, the men were his customers, in work or out, for he always allowed them to run a tab until work came along. He knew their wives and knew how some were struggling to help their men while others were resentful, feeling life had cheated them. He knew their kids and their grandparents and aunts and uncles and lovers and the ins and outs of their lives because everybody's problems were hashed out over his mahogany counter, helped down with a few beers. And there had been many a quiet handout of a few dollars to the desperate, no repayment asked or expected. He liked Delancey. It was good-humored, there was no violence—only the occasional man cuffing his wife around or noisy family fight. He would be sorry to leave it.

He walked back inside and began to clean his pumps, restocking his shelves with whiskey and gin, tobacco, cigarette papers, and cheap cigars. In a few weeks all this would be gone, banned by the Prohibition Act; he would be out of business and out of Delancey Street. But he had got it beat. He had made his plans a long time ago.

When he first came to America he had been a raw lad of eighteen, fresh from Ireland's shores, big, brawny, and ready for what a new world had to offer. His brief schooling had ended at ten, but he could read and write and do arithmetic, and he had worked as a laborer in the fields. He wanted no more of the old country; he wanted "Life with a Capital L," and he knew he wasn't going to find it in the poor shebeen his ailing father had run in the bleak, windswept countryside overlooking Liscannor Bay. His father, Mick O'Hara, had been a weasly little man with a cough that dragged itself up from his oversized boots. He was rarely to be seen without a thin, ragged hand-rolled cigarette between his lips; it was there when he drew ale from the keg, it stayed there when he talked and even when he coughed. The only time Shamus had ever seen it removed was when his father ate, but that was over in a matter of minutes and it was back to rolling the next one. And to the next tot of whiskey, "to keep out the cold."

Mary Kathleen O'Hara knew her husband was killing himself but there was nothing she could do about it. She had long ago accepted the fact that one day he would drop dead and she would be left to fend for herself, and she had made her plans accordingly. But time went on and the tough old weasel still defeated death, coughing his way through yet another night. Mary Kathleen was a big, strapping woman herself, with the red hair Shamus had inherited, a high color to her cheeks, and flashing green eyes. She had been considered a looker in her day and she was still a fine woman at forty, but her life had been a rough one. When she was a young girl, the potato famine had devastated Ireland and millions had starved to death, including most of her family. When she met Mick O'Hara he was twenty years older than she; he fancied her and she knew that no matter how poor, men would always find the few coppers for a drink at his shebeen. Although he was small and sour and argumentative, Mick O'Hara offered a roof over her head and food in her belly. It was security of a kind, and she settled for it and tried to be a good wife to him.

Their only child was Shamus and at the time she had thanked God because more would have only meant more mouths to feed, but when she had realized that she was likely to become a young widow, she had wished she'd had more sons to look after her when her husband was gone.

In his typical cussed fashion Mick O'Hara took his time about dying, and Shamus was already seventeen when he finally went. After the funeral Mary Kathleen had walked with her son to the top of the Liscannor cliffs and they had stood there arm in arm, letting the fierce Atlantic winds sweep over them. It had felt like a cleansing to her, blowing away the tedious years when she had been confined to the three dark, mean rooms behind the bar with the constant sound of coughing and the smell of ale and death.

"Son," she had said, gripping his arm tightly, "across that ocean is a new world, a place where a man can make a fortune. I'm selling up the alehouse and giving you the money. I want you to go to America and make a new life for us, and when you are ready you will send for me."

Shamus still remembered looking down at her face, so proud and serene and sure; she had trusted him to take all she had in the world and multiply it, certain he would take care of her. He had vowed not to let her down.

When he first came to America, he traveled the country from coast to coast; he was big and muscular, and it was easy for him to get a job as a laborer, carrying bricks in Chicago, hauling crates on the docks in San Francisco and stoking furnaces at the steel plants in Pittsburgh, but he knew it was not going to make him a fortune. A year passed and though he still had the money his mother had given him, he was no closer to bringing her over and looking after her than he was before. He thought of her back home, waiting uncomplainingly for him to do what was right, and he knew he would have to find something.

He drifted back to New York, wandering the streets aimlessly, staring at the mansions on Gramercy Park and Washington Square and Fifth Avenue, wondering bitterly how people had made enough money to build such places, and he told himself that one day he would own one just like that. Meanwhile, he took a room over a saloon on Delancey Street and worked by day as a bricklayer on a construction site. He liked the building trade and he would have liked to learn more about it, maybe make his way up to foreman or even a manager, but there was not time; he always carried the dread in back of his mind that his mother would die before he was successful and he would be too late to keep his promise.

He enjoyed living over the saloon. The smell of whiskey and beer and the nightly noise were familiar and reminded him of home, and he offered to give the proprietor a hand of an evening, pulling pints of ale and slinging mounds of corned beef hash. He was a sociable young man who liked the masculine camaraderie of the saloon, and after six months, when the proprietor told him he was thinking of selling up and going back to St. Paul, Minnesota, on an impulse Shamus offered to buy it. Within two weeks the transaction was completed and he wrote his mother, enclosing her fare and telling her to come as soon as possible. It was only afterward that he reflected on the irony of the fact that he was bringing her to the brave new world to live exactly the way she had before, in three rooms behind an alehouse.

Nevertheless, Mary Kathleen had considered it a great step up in the world; she arrived from Liscannor with all her bits and pieces of furniture, and soon the rooms on Delancey Street looked exactly like the ones back home in Ireland. Mary Kathleen cooked up great batches of proper Irish stew as well as hash and boiled beef and cabbage and potato bread, and she served heaping portions at cheap prices. It didn't take too long for the word to get around the neighborhood that O'Hara's had the best and cheapest food around, and the ale was good too. They were on their way.

Mary Kathleen enjoyed her new role. Before, her husband had been the boss; now she herself was there every lunchtime and every evening, chatting to the customers and graciously accepting their rough compliments as she pocketed their money. Within a year they had money in the bank and in a few years they were prosperous. She kept telling Shamus that it was time he looked for a nice Irish girl to marry; he should settle down and give her a few grandchildren to indulge in her old age. After all, she said, he could afford it now.

Shamus knew he could afford it, but a wife and children demanded a man's time, and who would run the saloon if he wasn't there every night? No, marriage would have to wait. Five years later there was a fair amount of money in the bank as well as one or two little property investments Shamus had made up in the hills of New Jersey. Then Kathleen Mary died suddenly of a heart attack, still without her grandchildren and still living in three rooms behind the saloon.

As he buried her Shamus wept tears of anger and shame that he had never bought her a little house of her own where she could have passed her final years peacefully, and he told himself that when he finally did marry, no wife of his would ever live in three rooms behind a bar.

He reminded himself of that now as Missie swung through the doors, flinging him a brief smile as she hung up her coat and began briskly to sweep the sawdust and litter from the floor.

O'Hara watched her longingly. It had been three months since he had asked her to marry him, and he still didn't have an answer. In fact she had never mentioned it since the funeral, and he had held back, waiting patiently for her to recover from the blow of Sofia's death. But time was moving on: He was a man with important matters on his mind, a man who wanted answers—now.

His heart melted as he looked at her, working busily as though if she did her work in half the time she could escape earlier . . . but she could not. He paid her by the day and she was his as long as he needed her. It was his way of guaranteeing she would always be there. Except now he knew he needed her for a lifetime.

She felt his eyes on her and glanced up. He smiled beguilingly and said, "Missie, it occurs to me that you and I have never been alone together. Now you know I'm a busy man. The saloon opens every day and every night and that niver leaves a man a minute to himself, let alone for a woman. But tomorrow I intend on closing it —on one condition."

She stared at him, surprised. "What condition?"

"I'll close, if you will do me the honor of taking lunch with me."

She stared at him again, hardly believing her ears, and then she laughed. He felt the color rising in his face as she said, "You want to take *me* out to lunch? But why, O'Hara? We see each other every day except Sunday! And we eat lunch together here at this very counter every day too. So, why?"

He took a cigar from the box on the mirrored shelves behind the bar, lighting it busily. "I meant it as a surprise," he said sadly. "Dammit, Missie, I thought it would please you."

He ran his hand through his mop of red curls, looking pleadingly at her as she walked to the counter. She leaned her elbows on it, staring at him doubtfully. "O'Hara," she said, "maybe this is a mistake. I'm not the girl you think I am. You don't even know the real me."

"That's exactly why I want to take you out, so we can get to know each other better," he said, his old jaunty grin returning. "Away from here we can both be ourselves. Besides," he said, placing his large hand over hers, "I've something to show you. Something special." He could see she was intrigued and he added, "And I've something important to tell you."

After sliding her hand from under his, she began to polish the counter. "In that case I'd better say yes," she said calmly, "but remember, I will have Azaylee with me."

"Of course," he said, beaming, "of course Azaylee will be with you." He didn't care if she brought a whole troop of kids. She had agreed to come.

20

Missie hurried back to Rivington Street with her morning's earnings, a single dollar, in her pocket. She stopped at Zabar's pushcart and bought a spray of fabric roses and a length of yellow ribbon for fifteen cents, and blushing at daring to spend so much money on herself, she hurried up the stairs to Rosa Perelman's apartment.

Rosa's place could be called an apartment because it had two rooms, and with three children she needed them. Her husband, Meyer Perelman, was twenty-five years older; he was from Poland and spoke only Polish and Yiddish. Rosa was only twenty-five herself, and had been born right here on the Lower East Side, of Estonian immigrant parents. She spoke English and Yiddish, as well as a smattering of Russian, but very little Polish, so communications between them were limited. For two dollars a week she had added Azaylee to her own brood, and she fed and looked after her as if she were her own while Missie was at work. And over the weeks since Sofia died, she had become her friend. She smiled as Missie tapped on the door and walked in.

"*Nu, shane,* there you are," Rosa said, pleased. "You're just in time, I was fixing a glass of tea. And a little treat I saved for us."

She handed Missie a tall steaming glass and a plate with a few small biscuits. "From Gertel's bakeshop on Hester," she said, "and just like my own mother used to make." Her face lighted up as she took a bite. "Better, even. Don't worry," she added, noticing Missie's restless glance, "the children are out in the street, under my eldest, Sonia's, eye. And she knows she'll catch it from me if she takes that eye off them for one minute. Anyway," she added with a giggle, "it gives you and me a bit of peace to catch up on ourselves, doesn't it?"

Missie laughed. She liked Rosa. She was small and round with beautiful black shiny hair, dark brown eyes, and soft features, and even though matters were difficult between her and her husband, she always managed a smile and a joke. Nothing would get Rosa down for long. It just wasn't in her nature to brood on her misfortunes, the worst of which, Missie thought, was having been "sold" to her husband by her unscrupulous father.

It had all been arranged through a marriage broker, Rosa had told her. The matchmaker had said this man was big news in business in Philadelphia. He had come to the house to meet her family, and she had been shocked when she had seen how old he was—almost as old as her father. She herself was just seventeen, younger even than Missie. Meyer had been polite, but he hadn't smiled and his hand had felt sweaty when he shook hers. All evening he had practically ignored her, sitting around the table telling her father what a big man he was in cloaks and suits in Philadelphia, and she could see her father twirling his beard and looking interested and her mother smiling and bringing out the best glasses and the Shabbas tablecloth, as if he were the rabbi himself come to visit.

She had hidden her hands behind her back when he came to leave, refusing to shake his, and her father had glared at her angrily, apologizing for her bad manners. And there had been an unholy row that night when she had demanded to know why, if Meyer Perelman was such a big man in cloaks and suits in Philadelphia, he didn't yet speak English.

"He's from Poland," her mother had explained.

"So? And why then did he not attend night school like everybody else and learn to speak?"

Her father had slapped her then and called her an ungrateful daughter. There he was paying good money to the matchmaker and all she did was shame him in front of a good, honest man, a man who would work his fingers to the bone for her, a man who would give her everything, a house, fine clothes, jewels even. . . .

"Hah, jewels!" Rosa had said, laughing, as she glanced around the cramped apartment. "And houses and cloaks and suits! The big shot turned out to be a machinist in a small factory owned by his brother-in-law. He thought he was marrying into money by getting me; the marriage broker had told him I was an heiress to my uncle, Samuel Glanz, the one with the department store on Grand Avenue."

"And are you?" Missie had asked hopefully.

Rosa had shrugged, "He has no children, but knowing him, he'll leave what he has to the temple and let the relatives fight over the will. But Meyer still lives in hope. He drags those children over there every Saturday, rain or shine, to remind Uncle Samuel what fine nieces he has." She had thrown back her head, laughing so heartily Missie could see her throat pulsating. "It was all a fairy story," she said at last, wiping away tears of laughter, "and now I'm stuck with Meyer's sweaty hands and my kids have a father who still doesn't speak English. The people where he works make a joke of him. Each morning they say, 'Nu, Meyer, then have you yet learned to speak?' After all these years in America, it's a shame on him."

"How can you bear it?" Missie had asked, wide-eyed with horror at the thought of spending a lifetime with a man you didn't love.

"I've got my kids," Rosa had said with a shrug, "and maybe some day, when they are older, I'll leave him. I'll just bide my time until then, day by day."

Missie had flinched, imagining life taken day by day with Meyer Perelman. At least she didn't have that to put up with, she was her own person.

"You are excited," Rosa said, taking another biscuit, "I see it in your eyes. Something's happened."

Missie quickly explained about O'Hara and that she was going out to lunch with him on Sunday. "Look," she said proudly, showing her the bunch of pink roses, "I bought these for my old felt hat. I thought it would smarten it up a little. And new ribbons for Azaylee's hair."

Rosa admired the flowers and said, "So? Azaylee goes too? Then this is no affair? No lovers' rendezvous?"

"Of course not, silly," Missie protested, blushing. "I mean, well, you remember O'Hara said he wanted to marry me, but that was only because he was sorry for me. He's a very kind man, Rosa."

"And you are a very beautiful girl," Rosa said shrewdly. "Don't forget that, Missie."

Missie thought of Rosa's words early Sunday morning as she tried on the old felt hat with the pretty pink roses pinned on one side, turning her head this way and that in front of the tiny square of mirror, wishing she had something smarter to wear.

"Oh, Missie," Azaylee breathed, watching her, "you look beautiful."

Missie smiled at her, but she knew the mirror spoke the truth: She was too pale and her cheeks looked sunken and her neck too thin. She had lost the bloom of youth, and she thought that the only thing beautiful about her was the roses in her hat.

Azaylee was sitting on the very edge of her chair so she wouldn't crease her blue dress, swinging her white-stockinged legs and admiring her new boots bought from Zabar's cart yesterday. Missie had braided her hair and tied it with the new yellow ribbons, but stray curls had already escaped, framing her small oval face. Her skin had that golden glow Anouska's had, and her pansy-brown eyes that same dreamy look. She was an angel, a dream child, Missie thought, rushing over and hugging her tightly, and she couldn't love her more if she were her own. She was only four years old and she never complained about anything, accepting their one room as her home and Rosa as her aunt and the street as her playground. It wasn't fair, Missie thought, as she kissed her again, *it just wasn't fair.*

A horn honked loudly in the street. Azaylee leapt from her chair and rushed to the window. It honked again and she called excitedly, "*Matiushka*, it's O'Hara in an automobile!"

Missie stuck her head out of the window, staring down in astonishment at O'Hara, smart in a new brown suit complete with collar and tie, sitting proudly behind the wheel of a rakish yellow Stutz. He honked the horn again, waving to the awed faces sticking out of every window along the street. Then he opened the door, stepped onto the running board, and, removing his hat, he bowed to Missie.

"Oh, Azaylee!" She gasped, pulling her head in, embarrassed. "Now everybody knows I'm going out with O'Hara."

She flung one last anxious glance in the mirror and, taking Azaylee's hand, she hurried down the stairs.

"It's a grand morning, Missie," O'Hara called. "I thought it would be nice to take a little drive."

All the heads at the windows swiveled from O'Hara to Missie as she walked quickly to the car. He lifted Azaylee into the little bucket seat at the back and held the door open for her courteously.

"Bye, Rosa," Azaylee cried, waving excitedly at the Perelmans hanging out their second-floor window, but Missie refused to look. She knew everybody on Rivington Street was watching interestedly as O'Hara put the car into gear and they chugged noisily down the street.

"I just bought her yesterday," O'Hara said proudly, "and you are the first to ride in her. Well? What do you think?"

"It's beautiful, O'Hara," Azaylee cried, bouncing excitedly in her seat and waving at the passersby.

"It's lovely," Missie said, hanging on to her hat as he took the car around another bend, "but I might have preferred to make a quieter exit from Rivington Street."

O'Hara roared with laughter. "I promised you a proper day out, didn't I?" he said, glancing at her out of the corner of his eye. "And I'm a man of me word, Missie O'Bryan."

As they turned the corner into Orchard Street she laughed; there was something appealing about O'Hara's simple pleasure in the car and the sunny day and his treat. He was a man out to please and she sank back into the leather seat, allowing herself to relax and enjoy the ride.

Caged in his brass eyrie, Zev watched the long yellow car drive past; O'Hara was honking the horn and looking at Missie like he owned her, and Missie was laughing, looking like springtime in a big violet hat trimmed with pink roses. Jealousy burned like a flame in his heart. *"Ganzer macher!"* he shouted bitterly as they disappeared. "Big shot!"

"Where are we going?" Missie asked as the car bounced over the bridge, heading toward New Jersey's hills on the opposite side of the Hudson River.

"Wait and see," he said mysteriously. But there was a grin on his big, handsome face that told her he knew she would like it.

They drove along the banks of the Hudson for several miles admiring the view until they came to a large brick building set back from the road behind some trees. The sign said "Giorgio's Italian Restaurant," and Missie's eyes widened as she noticed the white damask tablecloths and matching napkins, the gleaming silver and crystal and the flowers on every table.

"I'm not grand enough for this," she whispered, embarrassed by her old gray coat and shabby blouse and skirt.

"You're grand enough for anywhere," O'Hara replied loudly, "and a lot better than any of the other women here."

He removed his new hat as the headwaiter shook his hand, greeting him like an old friend and showing them to a table near the window. "Good morning, Mr. O'Hara," he said, "and how are you today, sir?"

"Good, good," O'Hara boomed, grinning as a second waiter arrived bearing a champagne bucket. He nodded approvingly as he showed him the bottle and Missie's eyes widened.

"Champagne?" she asked, amazed.

"What else?" he said, reaching across and taking her hand. "On such a great day."

She blushed as the waiters smiled knowingly. O'Hara was giving them the wrong impression. They probably thought they were lovers or something. . . .

She stared at the foaming glass, remembering the last time she had had champagne. It had been her eighteenth birthday and Misha had poured it for her, and they had gazed into each other's eyes, knowing it might be for the last time. . . .

"Penny for your thoughts?" O'Hara said, but she shook her head, picking up her glass and toasting him instead.

"To you, Shamus O'Hara," she said, managing a smile, "and thank you for a lovely day."

"It's not over yet," he promised, "not by a long chalk." He gazed admiringly at her as she studied the menu. "You surely look a picture in that hat, Missie," he said gently. "You are the most beautiful girl I've ever seen."

"Yes," Azaylee said importantly, "I told her so."

O'Hara grinned. "And you, young lady," he said, tugging her braid, "had better watch out, because when you are as old as Missie, you're gonna be a knockout."

"What's a knockout?" she asked.

"Wait and see," he replied, taking a small parcel from his pocket. "Here, I almost forgot."

"A present?" she asked hopefully.

He nodded, "A present just for you, beauty."

She stroked the pretty red tissue paper, awed. "It's lovely," she said, her high childish voice trembling with excitement.

O'Hara looked at Missie and then back at the child, "Presents have to be opened," he told her, "so you can see what's inside."

She pulled off the paper carefully, smoothing out the creases before opening the box, gasping when she saw what was inside. "Oh, oh, look, *matiushka.*" She gasped. "Just look."

It was a doll, petite and perfect in every detail, from its porcelain face to its soft blond hair, its sweet little lace-trimmed coat and bonnet and tiny kidskin boots.

"What shall you name her?" Missie asked, smiling as Azaylee stroked the doll's face lovingly.

"I'll call her Anouska," she whispered, picking her up and holding her to her chest. "Anouska."

Missie felt as if she had been struck by lightning; in all this time Azaylee had never once mentioned her mother. She had hoped she had forgotten.

"But this is an American doll," she protested quickly. "Don't you think she should have an American name?"

Azaylee's eyes had that familiar faraway look.

"How about Kathleen?" O'Hara suggested. "It's a good Irish name, and the name of my own mother."

"Yes, we should let O'Hara choose," Missie agreed quickly. "Why not call her Kathleen?"

Azaylee hugged the doll to her cheek, closing her eyes and smiling. "Kathleen Anouska," she said. "Kathleen Anouska O'Hara."

O'Hara grinned as he poured more champagne. "The little one's got the right idea," he said, glancing significantly at Missie.

She looked away as the waiter appeared with their soup. "It smells delicious," she said evasively.

O'Hara smiled. "It is," he promised. "This restaurant is one of the best in New Jersey. I've been coming here a few years now, ever since I started some business interests in the area."

Missie realized suddenly that she was enjoying herself. The good Italian home cooking was ambrosial after her meager meals, and the wine went to her head; she felt mellow and relaxed as she listened to O'Hara's story of his life in Ireland and his beginnings in America.

"And now there's another beginning," he said, lighting a grander cigar than usual, watching as she sipped her coffee.

Azaylee yawned as the kindly Italian waiters plied her with candies and tiny *amoretti* in flimsy pink and blue wrappers, snuggling down on her big chair and hugging her new doll.

O'Hara stroked her hair gently and said, "There's a side of me you haven't seen yet neither, Missie. I'm a serious man and also a man of ambition. And that's what I want to tell you about today. But first I have something to show you, so let's be on our way."

He paid the bill with a flourish. After picking up the sleeping child, he carried her in his big arms, just as she carried her own little doll, and they left the restaurant with smiles and thanks and please come back again soon. He laid Azaylee down on the backseat, covering her with a plaid rug, and said wistfully, "It'd be grand to have a little girl like that, just grand." Then he helped Missie politely into the car, climbed in himself, and turned the car in the direction of the hills.

"Where are we going?" she asked as he threaded his way through rough country lanes, heading even higher.

"Not far," he said, smiling. "Just you be patient now."

They drove for another ten minutes, winding up a hill until they came to a cedarwood boundary fence. O'Hara got out to open the gate, and Missie peered through the tall elms and bushy chestnut trees that were shedding the last of their leaves.

"Almost there," O'Hara said, grinning as he drove up a newly graveled lane and stopped in front of a square, red-roofed house with a wooden porch. "It's bigger than it looks," he said proudly. "Inside is three bedrooms and outside is three acres. Them numbers sounded good enough for me, so I bought it. And besides, I bought all the rest of the land around here. Fifty acres of Smallwood, New Jersey, now belongs to yours truly."

He turned to Missie, his eyes hot with desire. "And it belongs to my wife, if you'll only say yes, Missie. I want to share it all with you, this house, the land . . . everything."

Her eyes opened wide with alarm and he held up his hand. "Before you say anything, let me just show you." He walked up the steps to the wooden porch, turning so he could show her his new estate. "As far as you can see, Missie," he told her proudly, "and beyond. That's my land."

She stared at the smooth, grassy slopes dotted with clumps of trees and the herd of black and white cattle in the distance, looking like toy farm animals. She closed her eyes, breathing the fresh country air, listening to the birds calling, and feeling the late autumn sun still warm on her face. She might have been back home in Oxfordshire. "It's beautiful, O'Hara," she whispered, "just beautiful."

"Come inside," he urged. "Leave the child to sleep. Let me show you around."

The front door had a curved fanlight with a stained-glass panel and the spacious hall ran all the way through to another glass-paneled door at the back, with a view of the garden. There was a square sitting room with a big fireplace and a separate dining room; there were polished wooden floors and diamond-shaped window panes, and a proper kitchen with a proper sink with hot and cold water and a proper stove; there was even electric light. A nice wide flight of stairs led to an upper hallway with three bedrooms, as well as a real bathroom with what O'Hara told her was the latest cast-iron enameled tub *and* a toilet.

"But it's a *proper* house," Missie cried, rushing excitedly from room to room. "It's lovely, O'Hara, it's really lovely—only—" She stopped, looking at him, puzzled. "Only how are you going to run the saloon and live here? It's so far away."

"That's what I wanted to tell you," he said, taking her by the shoulders and gazing into her eyes. "Missie, I'm closing the ale-house in a couple of weeks. The Prohibition Act will soon kill the trade and I'm getting out before the rest of them realize it. I've laid my plans, Missie, and this house is part of them. And so are you. I can run my new business from here. It's close enough to the rail-road and the port at Newark."

Missie's heart sank. If O'Hara closed the saloon she was out of a job. She felt faint suddenly and leaned against the veranda rail, staring at the pretty, bucolic scene below. "What new business?" she asked dully.

O'Hara grinned. "Oh, property, building, a little 'distribution' shall we say. It's real private up here, no one would know my business." He winked at her and then frowned; all the light had gone from her face and she looked about to faint.

"Missie, are you all right?" he demanded, gripping her shoulders protectively. "What's up, me girl? Have I shocked you then, with all me talk of new businesses? It'll be nothing *really* illegal, Missie, just skirting round the edges of the law a bit, selling moonshine— we've been doing it in Ireland for centuries. Why, I promise you it's nothing. And then I plan to use the money to build houses. There'll be lots of young couples anxious to move out of the cities into a place of their own in the country. Pleasant, cheap housing, that's what I plan to give 'em. You'll see," he promised, "once I provide it, they'll come flocking. And don't worry about the other part, Missie, my partners are in charge of that."

"Your partners?"

"Giorgio and Enrico Oriconne, the guys who own the restaurant we were just at. You have to meet them, Missie, they're real sweet Italian family men, you saw the way the waiters were with Azaylee, they just love *bambini*. But they're busy men themselves and they needed someone like me to front this business for them. Of course I've got me own investment in it and I tell you, Missie, I intend to make meself a fortune. No more pulling pints of ale for me. I'm a businessman from now on."

He looked at her soberly. "I always promised meself that no wife of mine would live behind an alehouse, the way me mother had to. And now I can ask you properly, Missie. I've bought this house for you and for Azaylee, for us and our children. Missie, will you please be me wife?"

She shook her head bewilderedly; he was so kind, so gentle, under his rough-and-ready surface, and so naïve. She looked at O'Hara waiting anxiously for her reply, and she looked at the house, with its pretty rooms and its garden and the acres of hillside that could be hers, imagining herself living here, filling it with new furniture, with paintings on the walls and flowers in crystal vases, and herself sitting out here on a summer evening, maybe rocking a new baby in a cradle. But no matter how hard she tried, she just could not fit O'Hara into the picture. She thought of Rosa tied to Meyer Perelman for the rest of her life and she shook her head again; tears rolled down her cheeks, and he put up a gentle finger and brushed them away.

"I can tell you're saying no," he said with quiet dignity, "but I'll tell you something, Missie O'Bryan, I'll never share this house with another colleen. I'll be waiting on you to say yes one day. And when that day comes, I'll be the happiest man in New Jersey."

The journey back was silent. O'Hara had lost all his bounce and Missie thought tiredly that it was all her fault. She hadn't meant to hurt him, but she had never encouraged him to think she might marry him. As the skyline of Manhattan came into view she told herself there must be more to life than this, there just had to be. And then she remembered the reality, that in a few weeks the alehouse would be closed and she would be out of a job. And there would be no money coming in.

=== 21 ===

It was a bitter cold February Friday. Zev stared at the people hurrying past his window, necks wrapped in mufflers, hands thrust into their jacket pockets, shoulders hunched against the wind. It was almost four o'clock and his regular customers had already been in and temporarily reclaimed their weekend items of clothing until Monday. Sometimes he thought his shop was just a wardrobe for the Lower East Side, since their clothes spent more time with him than they did on their owners' backs.

He glanced at his watch yet again; Missie was late. She came every week, sometimes with one dollar, sometimes with two. He hated taking her money when he knew she needed it, but she was determined to pay him back. And if he asked himself the truth, sitting here staring out of the window hoping to see her tall, slender figure hurrying around the corner, he was glad of the excuse to see her. Not that he ever said much beyond "Good afternoon, Missie" and "How are matters by you today?" but at least it gave him a few moments in her company, moments he would treasure later when he was alone in his room remembering exactly how she looked, the way her brown hair shone with golden lights, the curve of her cheek, the softness of her mouth, and the deep, deep violet eyes that could lead a man into her soul.

He sighed, checking that his new tie was straight. He was all spruced up for the Sabbath, but he knew it was really for her.

The bell pinged and he stared sharply at Mrs. Lipkin from Canal Street, coming for her Shabbas tablecloth. "You're late today, Mrs. Lipkin," he said, handing her the cloth and taking her money quickly, praying she would leave before Missie came.

"You too, Mr. Abramski," she said wearily. "I had to wait until my son brought home the money before I could reclaim. Better hurry and close now, it's almost Shabbas."

"I know it, I know it," he answered irritably, and she glanced at him in surprise as she closed the door. Abramski was usually so polite.

The brass hands on the big wooden wall clock moved one minute nearer to four and he stared anxiously at the window. It was already dark and he must close . . . but a few more minutes, just in case she was late. . . .

At ten past four he locked the door, turned the sign to "Closed," and walked sadly through to the back room. She had never been late before, and he knew now she wasn't coming. Though she hadn't mentioned it, he knew O'Hara had closed the saloon last week, and he guessed she was out of a job and didn't have the money.

Wearing his black overcoat and hat, he walked through the icy streets to *shul,* but he did not linger afterward among the families greeting each other on the temple steps.

Back in his room he lighted the Sabbath candles in his mother's precious candlesticks and sat for a while alone, thinking of Missie. She had already paid him eighteen of the fifty dollars and he knew that when she had paid all of the fifty, he would never see her again.

On an impulse he stood up, put on his coat and hat, locked the door carefully behind him, and strode determinedly around the corner. Rivington Street was still littered with the day's refuse from the pushcarts and bits of torn newspapers fluttered skyward in the icy wind; cats and dogs scavenged and fought for the fishtails and scraps of offal, and he wrinkled his nose fastidiously against the smell.

He knew where she lived. He had walked past her building many times and he paused as he always did, staring up at the window he knew was hers. A lamp glowed behind the thin curtain. He hesitated, glancing down at the ground and then back up at the window. Usually he just waited a while, hoping she might appear, but now he hurried across the street and into the building.

The hallway was crowded with the unwanted junk of a dozen families, a broken chair, splintered apple crates, an iron-rimmed wheel from a pushcart, papers and bottles, and the pervading tenement smells of garbage and urine. From behind the closed doors along the narrow stairway came the sounds of a shrill argument and a woman crying. A baby screamed, somebody laughed, and music blared loudly from a phonograph.

Zev climbed the ill-lighted stairs, avoiding the grimy banister that had been greased by a thousand filthy hands. "How can she bear it?" he asked himself again. "Such a *baryshnya,* such a lady."

He rapped on the door, coughing nervously behind his hand as he waited.

Viktor barked loudly and Azaylee sat up, yawning and rubbing her eyes. *"Matiushka,"* she said, "there's someone at the door."

She turned from the sink, astonished. "But who could it be?"

Azaylee laughed. "I don't know," she said.

Missie thought for a minute. It couldn't be the rent because she had paid that this morning, though she had no idea where she would get the money to pay next week's. Smoothing her hair, she hurried to the door.

"Excuse me if I am disturbing you," Zev said, taking off his hat politely, "but you did not come today."

Missie's hand flew to her mouth guiltily. "Oh, I'm sorry, Mr. Abramski, but I couldn't. I just didn't have the money. I . . . I'm afraid I'm out of a job, you see. Please, will next week be all right? I'm sure to find something by then."

She looked shaken and he realized that she thought he had come to demand his money. "No, no, is all right of course, not to worry," he reassured her quickly. "It was . . . I just . . . the fact is, I wanted to see you."

His dark eyes looked at her pleadingly and Missie stepped back. Holding open the door, she said, "Please, Mr. Abramski, won't you come in?"

The dog growled at him standing nervously just inside the door and the little girl said, "Hello, I'm Azaylee. Who are you?"

He coughed nervously. "Abramski, Zev Abramski, from Orchard Street."

Azaylee nodded. "My friend Rachel Cohen lives there."

"Won't you sit down?" Missie asked.

He sat politely upright on the wooden chair she offered and glanced around the room. Her home. Everything was spotless, a clean white tablecloth, clean white cotton curtains, and her coat and the hat with the roses hanging from a nail on the wall. The bed was discreetly hidden behind a lopsided wooden screen, and the damp-stained walls were naked except for a small square of mirror over the sink. It was a poor, bare room but there was a bunch of flowers on the table and it smelled sweetly of soap, and somehow, in the glow of the lamp draped with a scrap of pink silk, it looked more homey than any room he had seen since he had left Russia.

Missie sat at the table opposite him. "Excuse me, Mr. Abramski," she said, "it's not much of a place to ask you into, but maybe you would like a glass of tea?"

He shook his head. "Thank you, no. I came to ask you . . . I wondered only if you might take supper with me one night." The brim of his hat crunched under his fingers as he clutched it anxiously tighter; her violet eyes were round with astonishment, and she was looking at him as if she were really seeing him for the first time. He put up his hand to straighten his tie and she smiled.

"Why, Mr. Abramski," she said quietly, "I should be delighted."

His face lighted up suddenly. "Sunday would be nice?" he said quickly before she could change her mind. "I will come by your apartment at six o'clock."

"Six," she agreed. "I'll be ready."

At five-thirty on Sunday Missie took Azaylee down to Rosa's, then she brushed her hair, twisting it into a knot on top of her head. She rubbed her cheeks to bring the color to them, put on her hat, and asked herself dismally for the tenth time why she had agreed to have supper with Zev Abramski. He was a man she barely knew, a man who had lent her money, a man she had an obligation to pay back. She wondered for the hundredth time what he was leading up to by asking her to supper.

His knock came promptly at six. She threw on her worn gray coat and hurried to the door, afraid to ask him in when she was alone, worried about what the neighbors might think.

He looked neat and very foreign in his black overcoat and hat as they walked down the dark street together. "I know a café on East Broadway," he said, hesitating at the corner. "I have no car, like O'Hara. It's all right by you to walk?"

"Of course, Mr. Abramski." Turning up her collar, she hurried by his side but he kept to the outer edge of the sidewalk, maintaining a distance between them as if afraid of a casual touch.

The silence between them deepened as they walked. "And how are you, Mr. Abramski?" she asked desperately after they had gone a block.

"I am well, thank you," he replied.

Silence fell again and he glanced nervously at her out of the corner of his eye. Here he was, his dream come true, Missie O'Bryan was by his side and he could not think of a word to say to her.

He turned thankfully into East Broadway. "It's a Ukrainian café," he said stiffly. "I thought it would please you."

The café was crowded and noisy, filled with Russian voices and the sound of balalaikas and guitars. In the back room somebody was singing a familiar gypsy song; a samovar bubbled on the counter and there was the heady smell of warm poppyseed bread, and piroshkis, coffee cakes, and sour pickles.

Missie's face lighted up as they squeezed into a tiny table by the window. "It's wonderful, Mr. Abramski," she said, delighted. "It reminds me of a gypsy café I used to go to in St. Petersburg." She laughed, singing a snatch of the song, and the proprietor, a burly Ukrainian, stopped and spoke to her in Russian, complimenting her on her voice.

Zev gazed at her, thrilled. He had only ever seen her as the subdued, hardworking young woman, worn down with worry; now suddenly he was seeing the young girl she really was. She ordered the borscht, closing her eyes in ecstasy as she tasted the first mouthful and exclaiming how good it was, but then her face fell. "I should not be here with you, Mr. Abramski," she said guiltily. "I owe you so much money, it's not right that you should spend more on buying me supper."

"Are you not enjoying it then?" he asked worriedly.

"Oh, of course I am. Why, I haven't enjoyed anything this much since . . . since I don't know when," she finished hastily.

Zev breathed a sigh of relief. Summoning the waiter, he ordered a bottle of red wine. He was happy just to sit and look at her, his dream come true. She sipped the wine slowly, listening to the music as silence fell between them again.

Missie avoided his eyes, wondering what to say. They couldn't just go on saying *nothing*. She took another sip of her wine and said desperately, "Tell me about yourself, Mr. Abramski."

"Myself?" he repeated, surprised. "Why, there's nothing to tell."

"Oh, yes, there is," she said, emboldened by the wine. "For instance, are you a happy man?"

Silence fell again and he stared down at his soup. "I am happy to be here with you," he said at last.

"Thank you," she said, "but I meant, are you happy with your life? You see, when I was a child I thought everyone was happy, but now I'm finding out that there are really not very many *truly* happy people in the world. They are all fighting against something: poverty, illness, oppression, despair. Sometimes when I think of how different Azaylee's childhood is from my own, I want to cry. And sometimes I do, at night when I am in bed."

His dark eyes were sympathetic. The Russian music and the roar of conversation grew louder, isolating them in their own little corner by the window.

Somehow, she felt secure with him. The wine loosened her tongue and she began to talk about her childhood in England, and how her father had died in Russia, leaving her alone. "And that's how I came to live in St. Petersburg," she said, bringing her story abruptly to a close.

The waiter bustled by to clear their plates, bringing them a mound of golden crisp potato piroshkis, spicy sliced sausages, and a mountain of *kasha* with hot mushroom sauce. He refilled their glasses and called for another basket of breads.

She leaned her elbow on the table, propping her chin on her hand, and said, "I know you heard what Azaylee said about . . . about Sofia. I don't know why, Zev Abramski, but I know I can trust you." The Russianness of the restaurant, the familiar language, and the music were too much for her to bear her loneliness any longer; she had told no one her story, not even Rosa, her friend, but suddenly it all spilled out in urgent, frightened whispers. The flight through the forest with the jewels sewn in their skirts, the terrible murders, their escape to Constantinople and Sofia selling the diamonds for next to nothing. There was only the tiara left, she told him, with all the diamonds gone except the four remaining large ones. And the enormous, useless emerald. The food grew cold in front of them as she told him their fear of the Cheka and how she knew it would never stop. And how she dreamed every night about Alexei. She told him everything—except that she had been in love with Misha. "So," she said, lifting her head and looking at him, "now you know who I am, Zev Abramski, and why I am in this position. And you are the only person in the world who does."

She sniffed back her tears and he took out a fresh white pocket handkerchief and gave it to her. "I am proud that you have given me your confidence," he said quietly. "I shall never repeat a word of what you said. No one shall hear of this from me, I promise on my life."

His eyes were very gentle. "Eat," he said gruffly, "let the good food bring some color to your pale cheeks. Enjoy."

After that the silence between them seemed more companionable;

Zev seemed content just to be in her company, and, even though he was a man of few words, she was surprisingly content in his.

He walked her home silently afterward, still keeping to the edge of the sidewalk, and when they reached her door he asked if she would meet him again the following Sunday.

Missie hesitated. She really didn't know whether she should, but he had been so kind to her, and in an odd sort of way she felt close to him now that he knew all about her. "Six o'clock then, next Sunday, Mr. Abramski," she agreed. She said good night quickly and hurried indoors, aware that he was still watching as the door closed behind her.

Monday morning Missie awoke with a headache and a feeling of quiet desperation. The old-world charm of the Ukrainian café had faded and the relief of unburdening herself to Abramski had turned to fear. After all, she told herself nervously, you barely know him and Sofia wanted you never to tell anyone. . . .

She waited until she heard the Perelmans' door slam as Meyer left for work, and then she hurried downstairs to Rosa. Azaylee had stayed with the Perelmans last night, and the dog too; Viktor had transferred his loyalty from Misha to his daughter and refused to leave her side. Where Azaylee went, he went. It would be a problem when she went to school, Missie thought, and that thought triggered another nagging problem—the one about school. Misha's daughter couldn't just go around the corner to the rough local school. Why, she already knew more than she could learn there: She knew how to read a little, and she knew her alphabet, and she spoke French and Russian as well as English, though now her English had a distinct Yiddish accent like that of the rest of the kids on Rivington Street.

Rosa looked at her face full of woes and grinned. "So? You've come to cheer up my Monday morning? I should need such cheer!" She laughed as she poured Missie a glass of tea. "Well?" she asked, sitting down and gazing expectantly at her. "So tell me? About the pawnbroker—the clockwork man—you can set your clock and the days of the week by him. But you are the first to find out what makes him tick."

"I didn't find out a thing," Missie confessed, "it was me who did all the talking. Oh, Rosa, I told him everything. Things I was never supposed to tell." She stared at her, her eyes wide with panic. "Things I've never even told you."

"Best friends you don't need to tell," Rosa said, patting her hand comfortingly. "Whatever you might have done is all right by me. I know it can't be bad."

"What would I do without you, Rosa?" Missie said suddenly. "I'm so stupid, I know nothing. I don't even know how to get a job."

Rosa smoothed her flowered apron thoughtfully. It was a last resort but she knew Missie was at her wit's end. "There's always the *Chazir-Mark,* the Pig Market on Hester Street, where the people wanting jobs in the clothing factories go every morning to see if there's any work." She hesitated. "It's not really a place for a girl so refined like you, Missie, but for a few weeks maybe, until something else comes along. At least it would put a little money in your pocket. If you are chosen, of course," she added with a sigh. "There's always more workers than jobs. And the foremen have their favorites, the ones they know they can get most work out of for least pay."

"But I don't even know how to work a sewing machine," Missie said doubtfully. "All I know are useless things, like the date of an Egyptian tomb or the history of the ancient Babylonians—I never learned anything really *useful.*"

"You know those things?" Rosa asked, astonished. "You should be a professor, not a machinist. But need drives us to strange places, Missie, and it's all I can think of for you, now O'Hara's gone." She glanced shrewdly at Missie. "And what news by O'Hara?"

Missie shook her head, blushing. "None, not since he left for New Jersey two weeks ago. But then, I didn't expect to hear from him, not after I turned down his proposal."

Rosa sighed. *"Meshuganah,"* she muttered. "A good, strong man who would have kept you in luxury. What more does a girl want?"

"Love?" Missie whispered. Their eyes met across the table and Rosa reached out and took her hand. "Ah, love, Missie," she said bitterly, "I have a feeling that love ends up as just like this: one man, two rooms, and three kids. Nothing ever changes."

Missie hurried down Hester Street at six o'clock the next morning. It was beginning to snow and she turned up her coat collar, wishing she had taken the roses from her hat because the damp would ruin them. She hovered at the back of the crowd, taking in the scene. There were more men than women, some quite smartly dressed in overcoats, gossiping and buying coffee and knishes from a stall across the street, others just standing, shoulders hunched, their jacket collars turned up and their frozen hands thrust into their pockets, stamping their feet to keep warm. The women had wrapped their heads in shawls and waited quietly to one side, some young, some older. She felt out of place in her coat and too-smart hat and wished she had thought to wear a shawl like the others.

At six-thirty the foremen arrived, standing on a makeshift platform of orange crates, scanning the crowds and pointing out those they wanted. The women jostled to the front, eager to be noticed, but Missie hung back, waiting. The foreman wearing the black homburg caught her eye; he stared at her for a second and then passed on. She looked down at her feet dejectedly as he shouted, "That's all for today," and the chosen ones hurried off, their work chits clutched in their hands. "Try again tomorrow, darlin'" a hefty Irishwoman advised her. "Maybe you'll be lucky then."

The snow was a foot deep the next morning as Missie waited with the others, a shawl thrown over her head and icy water seeping through the paper-thin soles of her boots. The same man was there, the one in the homburg hat, and again he glanced at her, pausing, considering for a second or two. Hope lighted her eyes but then he passed on, choosing the woman next to her. Missie moaned and the woman said sympathetically, "Push yourself to the front next time, girl, that way he'll be sure to see you. They always notice the pretty ones," she added grimly.

She awoke late the next morning, coughing and sneezing as she threw on her clothes and hurried to the door. Slipping and sliding on the ice, she ran the four blocks to Hester Street. The foremen were already there, choosing, and remembering the woman's advice, she elbowed her way determinedly to the front. She stood there panting, clutching her shawl at her throat, her eyes raised to the men like gods on Olympus on their orange crates.

The man in the homburg was thin and wiry with sharply chiseled features and sharp black eyes. His thin lips curved in a half smile as he saw her and this time he nodded. "You," he said, pointing.

She glanced from side to side; did he really mean her? "Me?" she mouthed, pointing to her chest.

He nodded. "Come here and get your chit," he said roughly. His hand brushed hers as she took the slip from him. "Zimmerman's, three days, on Canal Street," he said sharply. "Don't be late."

Her feet had wings as she ran back to tell Rosa. After wrapping a slice of bread and herring in newspaper for her lunch, she ran all the way back to Canal and was at Zimmerman's promptly at seven o'clock.

Zimmerman's factory was a big one, running almost half a block over three floors. Missie crowded through the doors with the others, showing her slip to the foreman the way they did, edging through the narrow spaces between the sewing machines. The big Irish-woman she had seen the first morning on Hester Street smiled at her as Missie stared around, lost. "So you got yourself a job did you? Come, take this machine, there's more light over here by the window."

Missie sat down in front of the treadle machine, staring at it in bewilderment. A young boy ran past and thrust a basket heaped with cut and basted fabric at her.

The Irishwoman watched her shrewdly. "Sleeves," she said. "You've done 'em before, haven't you?"

Missie shook her head, "I've never even seen a sewing machine before," she confessed, "but I needed the job. I've a little girl to keep, you see. I thought I could learn."

The woman sighed. "Course you can learn," she said, "we all had to learn once. But you'd best not start on sleeves. Here, I'll show you how to thread up your machine and what to do, and then I'll get Sammy to change your basket for straight seams. Them's the easiest."

She was kind and practical and Missie found the machine wasn't difficult to work after all; in fifteen minutes she was sewing a straight seam. They were on piecework and she said guiltily, "But I'm taking all your time. You must be losing money helping me."

"I'll make it up," the woman said, smiling. "I know who you are. You worked at O'Hara's alehouse, *and* you worked harder than anyone he's had before. I've seen your little girl, she's lovely. My name's Mrs. McCready—Georgie to me pals. Well, best get on with it then, before the foreman catches us yapping."

The noise of the treadle machines and the fierce hissing of the big pressing irons, the clouds of steam, the shouted orders, and the press of bodies in the ill-lighted loft seemed to crowd in on Missie, but she put her head down and went to work; by eight-thirty the pile in her basket was beginning to diminish and she felt pleased with herself. Until Sammy came rushing by and filled it up again. By ten o'clock the noise had given her a headache, and the close press of bodies and dust was nauseating. Still, she knew she was lucky to have a machine within sight of a window. Mostly they were given over to the cutters and their big tables and enormous shears. At ten o'clock there was a ten-minute break and she joined the other women hanging out of the windows, smoking illegal cigarettes —cigarettes had caused serious fires in some sweatshops and many people had been burned to death. Missie hung her head out too, grateful for the icy air after the stifling workroom. Too soon it was back to the machine and the endless basket of "pieces." By twelve her back ached as well as her head and she felt exhausted. Apart from the ten minutes, she hadn't stopped work in five hours—and even so, her basket had only been changed once, while everybody else's had been refilled several times.

"Don't worry," Georgie told her kindly as she ate her bread and herring, "you'll get quicker as you get used to it."

At six-thirty they filed silently from the room, most too weary now for chatter and smiles.

Missie felt as if she had been sewing seams in her sleep, but she was at Zimmerman's promptly again the next morning, and the next. When it was over she waited in line triumphantly for her three days' wages. It was piecework so she didn't know exactly how much she had earned. "Too slow," the foreman said curtly, handing over her money. "Don't come back next week."

Missie's mouth dropped open with shock. "Oh, but I'll get better," she promised, "I'm learning."

"There's no time here for learners," he said curtly. "Move on."

She stepped out of the way so the next girl could be paid, feeling like crying, but crying would not get her a job. Nothing would, it seemed.

"Try the market again Monday," Georgie whispered as she passed her. "There's always another sweatshop needing workers."

She opened her hand and stared down at her three days' wages. It was exactly five dollars.

Missie sat opposite Zev in the Ukrainian café after supper on Sunday night, feeling like a failure. "I really tried, Mr. Abramski," she said sadly, "but I wasn't quick enough."

He shrugged. "You should not be working in a sweatshop, a girl like you," he said with a spark of anger. "I cannot let you do this, Missie." He coughed apologetically. "Excuse me, I meant Mrs. O'Bryan."

"Oh, no, please, call me Missie, everybody does," she said quickly.

His dark eyes lighted up. He smiled and said, "It would be pleasing if you would call me Zev."

She looked at him, thinking how seldom he smiled and how sad his dark eyes were, and she suddenly realized how *young* he was. Somehow she had always thought of him as just Zev Abramski the pawnbroker and never as "a young man." She thought guiltily that she was so full of her own woes that she had never even asked him about himself, only if he was a happy man, when he so obviously was not. She wondered what had caused the sorrow that lay behind his dark eyes. Leaning forward, she said impulsively, "Tell me about yourself, Zev. I know you were born in Russia, but where?"

Zev took a deep breath. He felt as if he were trembling inside. In all these years he had never, *never* told his story to a living soul. He only communed with the dead, in his dreams.

He drank deeply from his wineglass, wondering how to begin. How did people express their deepest fears, tell of their degradation, expose their innermost feelings to another? He stared into Missie's lovely violet eyes, warm, gentle, encouraging, and suddenly she leaned forward and took his hand. It was as if that one warm human touch unleashed a quarter of a century of pent-up pain.

He told her everything, about his family in Russia and their escape from the pogroms and how, as a boy of seven, he had found himself alone in New York. And then he stopped. He just could not go on.

She squeezed his hand understandingly and he trembled. After calling the waiter, he ordered another bottle of the rough red wine. He poured some and tipped up his glass, drinking deeply as if it were water to give himself the courage to continue.

"How can I tell you what it felt like?" he asked hoarsely. "A child, all alone in a new country whose language I did not even speak? I was too afraid to ask for help. I waited until some more people emerged from the hall and followed them. I walked and walked but it seemed to me I was getting nowhere, that I would never arrive because there was nowhere to go.

"When night fell I found myself in a maze of streets. They all looked the same, tall, narrow brick buildings with stone stoops. I slept under a stoop that night. The next day I walked again. I did not cry anymore. There were no tears left, just a terrible gnawing hunger. At night I rooted among the garbage for potato peelings, rotting fruits, and bones like an animal. And by day I walked. One night it began to rain, a hard lashing curtain, and soon I was soaked to the skin. Only my feet in their new boots from my uncle were dry. I found a cardboard box under a bridge and climbed in. I felt secure surrounded by my four cardboard walls, I was asleep in an instant. I was awakened by someone hauling on my collar and screaming at me. I saw a face, red, distorted, fringed with a matted gray beard. It was *his* box, his *home* I was sleeping in, and I knew he meant to kill me for it, like a mad territorial beast. I jumped out and ran away, running and running into the night.

"It was suddenly colder the next day and the rain turned to snow. I turned up my collar and kept on walking because I knew if I stopped I might never get up again. I asked myself, 'And what is there to get up for?' I would be better off dead. Then I saw a group of men and boys carrying shovels; they were being sent to clear the snow. I ran over quickly and joined them. The pay was fifty cents a day for as long as the snow lasted. I worked alongside the men, saying nothing, just shifting the snow endlessly, and at the end of the day I collected my fifty cents and went across the street to a diner and bought myself two frankfurters with sauerkraut. My first American food. I stuffed myself full of bread and I must have drunk a quart of milk and then I went outside and threw up. I thought, 'Such a waste, my fifty cents all gone.' The snow stopped after a week, but by then I had food inside me, and I had found a warm grating to sleep over where the steam came up from the diner's kitchen."

He hesitated. There were things he could not tell her, things he would never tell anyone about the men who had dragged him screaming from his warm hideaway, molesting him, and how he had bit and scratched and punched and fought until he had escaped; how he had run through the night across a great bridge, pausing in the middle, praying for courage to jump into the deep, dark, silent water below. But he was a coward and so he lived.

"Eventually I came by the Lower East Side," he said. "I saw an old man, a peddler, trying to push his little cart, but he was white-bearded and feeble. I ran across to help him, pushing it all the way to Rivington Street. For that he gave me a smile and a dime and asked me whose boy I was, and where I lived. I told him no one's and nowhere. He stared at me for a long time and then he said, 'So, it's an orphan, and speaking Yiddish only. I am old, I need a helper. Stay by me and help with the cart and I'll pay you each day fifty cents and bread and pickle for your dinner.'

"That night he took me home with him. He himself lived in a basement room on Stanton Street, but there was a lean-to shed where he kept his pushcart and that is where I slept. I worked six days a week and earned three dollars, I had a roof over my head and food in my belly, and at night in my shed I was safe. I was one step away from an animal, but at least it was a step.

"Mr. Zametkin was seventy-five years old. He had left his wife and family behind in Poland thirty years before and come to America to seek his fortune. He never found it and therefore he never sent for them. He heard many years later that their village had been destroyed in the pogroms and they had all perished.

"For three years I lived in the wooden shed on Stanton Street, freezing in winter and boiling in summer. I was not happy, I was not unhappy; I was just a 'being' who existed. I cannot remember ever laughing," he added quietly, "but nor do I remember crying anymore. I never went to school but I learned bits and pieces of English on the streets.

"One morning as usual I got the pushcart ready, loaded with the eyeglasses and scissors and padlocks and keys and bits and pieces that old Zametkin sold, and I waited for him to come to the shed as he did every morning at six-thirty. But this morning he did not show. After a while I walked around to his room and knocked on the door. There was no reply. It was never locked and so I went in. He was lying on the floor with his head bleeding and his eyes staring wide. I had seen that same frozen look in my father's eyes and I knew he was dead. More—somebody had killed him, hit him over the head, murdering him for the few dollars he carried on his person. I heard noises at the door and looked up; there was a sea of faces, all staring at Zametkin and then back at me, and I knew what they were thinking. That it was me who had killed him."

His voice faltered and Missie stared at him, spellbound, squeezing his hand tightly.

"The police came and took me away. I went quietly. I did not know what to say to them, only that he was my friend, that he was kind, that I worked for him and I would not do such a thing to old Mr. Zametkin. They put me in a cell and left me there. There was no window, just four stone walls, oozing water and slime. They turned off the lights and left me alone in the dark for a long time; I did not know whether it was day or night nor how much time had passed. I could hear the rustle of cockroaches and the whimper of rats and feel them brushing past me as I cowered on the bench. I felt the whole place was alive, seething with vermin. Every now and then someone came and thrust a plate of food at me and a tin mug of water, but I could not eat. No one came to see me, there was no one who cared. I fell into a despair so deep that nothing could remedy it.

"Then suddenly they came and turned on the light. 'Out,' they said to me. 'You are free.'

"They had caught the real murderer. He had killed a second man and this time someone had seen him. I was back on the streets again, verminous, filthy, and alone.

"I went back to my shed but it was already occupied by someone else's pushcart and there was a padlock on the door. I slept that night on the street again, and the next day I went to the public baths and asked to be deloused. I came back to Rivington and asked among the vendors if anyone needed help. I worked a little here, a little there. And then someone told me that Mr. Mintz the pawnbroker was ill and needed somebody to watch over his business. I was twelve years old and not a big boy, but I did not have the look of the young. I was already an old person and Mintz knew this. He took me as his assistant and let me sleep in the shop. His wife had died the year before and his only daughter had left home as a young girl and never spoken to him again. He never knew where she went or what became of her. For three years I looked after the business, earning five dollars a week. No raise was offered and I was too afraid to ask for one in case he gave the job to another. And all the while Mr. Mintz drank himself to death in the back room. When he died I was the only one to follow his coffin, and then I went back to the shop and continued as I had always done. Mr. Mintz's money was in a bank and I never touched it; I just signed a new lease with the landlord, telling him I was twenty-one even though I was only fifteen, and I carried on the business just like before. Nobody knew any different because I had been there so long already.

"I began to do things differently now, to smarten up the business, to think more about myself. I went to night school and learned how to read and write in English and I discovered the joy to be found in books. I could not read enough! I bought a piano and taught myself to play. But I always kept alone. I was too afraid to be close with anyone, in case they knew that I was not a legal person, that I had no immigration papers for America. I had no identity in this country."

Missie stared at him as he said finally, "I am not a person in America and not a person in Russia. I am no one. Just a pawnbroker."

Her heart was bursting as she took his hand and laid it against her cheek, "Papers are not important," she whispered, "it's *what* you are, *who* you are. And you are a man of courage. I *know* you, Zev, just the way you know me and about me. We have shared our secrets. Now you *are* a person."

Their journey back home that night was as silent as ever but he walked closer to her—not enough so that their hands touched, but closer. And when she said good night, she leaned forward and kissed him impulsively on the cheek. He knew that night as he returned to his shop that he was the happiest man on the Lower East Side of New York.

Rosa knew when Missie came through the door that she had not found a job. Her face was drawn and her eyes weary; even the flowers on her hat drooped.

"So?" she asked, determinedly cheerful. "It's not the end of the world to be out of a job. It happens to everyone." She stroked back her curly dark hair, smoothing the escaping tendrils into the knot at the nape of her neck, and then she put her hands on her hips and stared at Missie. The look of utter despair in her eyes frightened

Rosa, and she hugged her like a mother hugging a child. "It'll be all right, Missie," she whispered, "I promise you. Meanwhile, I have five dollars hidden in my old samovar—safe from Meyer's prying hands or it would all be gone on whiskey down at the union meetings. Take it. It's better off with you."

Missie shook her head. "I can't take your money, Rosa," she said quietly. "I know how you did without to save it."

"For friends, it's the same," Rosa said quickly, taking the money from the samovar and pressing it into her reluctant hand. "Only worry about yourself, one more to feed here is no problem." They looked at Azaylee sitting at the table eating supper with Rosa's three little girls, one so blond, the others so dark, and Rosa laughed and said, "She looks like a changeling turned up on my doorstep, brought by the gypsies in the fairy tales."

Missie sat at the table and Rosa put a glass of tea and a thick slice of bread spread with chicken fat in front of her. "A gypsy once told me that I would have a great responsibility, one that would change the world," Missie said thoughtfully. "Do you think she meant looking after Azaylee? But if she did then how would Azaylee change the world?"

"Maybe she'll grow up to become President of America," Rosa said, sitting next to Missie and helping herself to more bread.

"When I grow up," Azaylee chimed in, "I'm going to be a dancer."

"*Nu?* A dancer is it?" Rosa laughed. "A ballerina, no less?"

"A ballerina," Azaylee said firmly.

"You can't be a ballerina," Hannah retorted, "you don't have a dress."

"I can, I can," Azaylee wailed. She threw her bread suddenly at Hannah, and they fell to the floor, wrestling.

Missie stared at her, shocked. "Azaylee!" she cried, hauling her off Hannah.

"It's good she shows some spirit," Rosa said calmly. "Hannah's too bossy."

"I will be a ballerina," Azaylee said, glaring at Hannah, "you'll see."

"You have to take lessons to learn," Sonia, the eldest, said practically, "and you can't afford the cost."

Azaylee wasn't sure she knew what "afford" meant, and she glanced at Missie plaintively. There was a scratch across her nose and Missie could see the line of dirt under her chin where she had finished washing before she sat down to her supper. It can't go on like this, she told herself, it's enough, enough . . . just look what's happening to Misha's daughter.

"You want to tell me what happened?" Rosa asked glancing at the clock. Mayer was expected at seven and it was already half-past six. There was time, but she knew Missie would not stay when he came home; she knew she couldn't stand Meyer Perelman.

Missie shrugged. "The foreman at the Pig Market," she said, "you know the one I told you about, he picked me the first time for Zimmerman's? He picked me again this morning and sent me to Galinski's."

Rosa nodded. She knew Galinski's. It was a small operation, hand to mouth each week, picking up cheap itinerant labor when it was needed.

"There were only two other people there," Missie said, "a cutter upstairs by the window and Mr. Galinski in his office. He showed me a machine and told me to begin. I worked steadily until noon, and then I took a break. 'No pay for time stopped,' Galinski said, and I told him all right, I knew. Then he put on his hat and coat and went out for lunch. I went back to my machine and the next thing I knew somebody was standing behind me. It was the foreman who had hired me.

" 'Everything all right?' he asked me, coming closer.

"I told him yes and went back to work. He came even closer." Missie blushed as her eyes met Rosa's understanding ones. "Too close. He put his hand on my shoulder and slid it. . . ." Lowering her eyes, she whispered, "He said there would be work for me every day, that he could make it easy for me, and I would earn good money—if I was nice to him."

Rosa stared at her and said breathlessly, "What did you do?"

"I jumped up and picked up a pair of cutter's shears and I said that if he came near me again I would stab him where it hurt and he would never be able to molest another girl again."

Rosa flung back her head and laughed. "Missie O'Bryan," she exclaimed, gasping, mopping up her tears, "six months ago you never would have thought of that! You have become a true Lower East Side girl."

Missie glanced at Azaylee. "We both have," she said bitterly.

"Anyway," she concluded, "he told me to get out, so I did. He shouted after me that there would be no pay and not to come back to the Pig Market again if I knew what was good for me. So"—she shrugged—"that's that."

"You should go uptown, Missie," Rosa urged. "You are too good for them here. There are smart shops on Fifth Avenue where they make beautiful clothes for rich women. They'll need seamstresses, handworkers—anything would be better than the sweatshops. Take the five dollars," she urged, pushing it into Missie's hand. "Go tomorrow." Their eyes met as she added understandingly, "Before it's too late."

That night when Azaylee was asleep, Missie took out the valise from under the bed and opened it and looked at the tiara with its golden sunburst, naked of diamonds except for the four largest, and the huge ice-green emerald. She wondered what would happen if she walked into Cartier and said simply, "I would like to sell the Ivanoff tiara." Would they call the police? Arrest her maybe? Send her to jail for stealing it? She had no proof that it was hers, or that Azaylee was an Ivanoff. The only papers she had were the yellowing legal documents about some mines in India, and they were brown with age and the red sealing wax was breaking away from the pink legal ribbons.

She picked up the photograph and looked at Misha's dear face again, as she often did when she was alone. Sometimes he felt so close to her, as if maybe somewhere he was thinking about her too. After picking up the brooch, she pinned it to her dress and went to look in the mirror. The diamonds sparkled under the light and the rubies glowed mysteriously with their own fire. It was all she had of him, he had chosen it for her, he had held it in his hands and looked into her eyes to see her pleasure when he gave it to her. No, she could never, *never* part with it. She would starve first.

And so you will, she thought, replacing the jewels guiltily in the valise, unless you get a job this week. She looked at her old gray coat hanging on the nail and her hat and the tired flowers drooping on top of it. To get a job uptown she would have to be smart. It would take an investment. She looked at Rosa's five dollars and told herself that tomorrow morning she would go to Glanz's store on Grand Avenue and buy herself a new coat. She would pay a deposit and when she got the job she would pay it off at so much a week, the way all the women did around here. It was a risk, she knew, because the odds were she would not get a job. But she squared her shoulders resolutely. This time she was going to start right at the top. On Park Avenue.

She was at Glanz's as soon as it opened the next morning, choosing a simple coat of navy wool in the new, slim line. She bought a pair of kid gloves. Deciding she could not afford a new hat, she went back to Zabar's pushcart and bought a single imitation white gardenia to replace the roses on her old one. She polished her black shoes and ran excitedly downstairs to show Rosa.

"Turn around," Rosa said, inspecting her minutely from head to toe. "Give a look only, such a lady," she marveled, "as smart as any rich Park Avenue person."

Missie laughed excitedly. "Is my hat all right?" she asked, patting the gardenia doubtfully.

"Perfect," Rosa declared. "You won't need a job, you will get married when the employer sees you."

Missie kissed her, laughing, and Rosa ran to the window, watching as she strode down the street. "Like a deer she walks," she breathed admiringly. She leaned farther from the window. "Good luck, Missie," she called, waving and wishing with all her heart that she would return a new person. A person with a job.

=== 23 ===

The door at the top of the immaculate white marble steps was enameled a shiny purple and in the center was a large brass plaque with the flamboyant signature "Elise." A doorman in a smart buff uniform gleaming with gold buttons moved his bulk in front of it, folding his arms belligerently and glaring down at Missie, who stood hesitantly at the foot of the steps.

"What d'ya want?" he yelled.

Missie flinched and said hurriedly, "I . . . I've come about a job."

"What are ya? An idiot? Jobs go around the back, not in the front door! Get a move on, will ya. I don't want ya hanging around here. Hurry, hurry!" After shooing her away, he ran down the steps to open the door of a long royal-purple saloon car, smiling unctuously as he helped the elegant red-haired woman alight. Missie turned to stare. The woman was older, tall and wafer-thin and dressed with an understated flamboyance that drew your eyes to her. She turned her head and her eyes met Missie's, assessing her thoughtfully for a moment. She said something to the doorman and turned to look at her again; then she swept up the marble steps and disappeared behind the beautiful purple door.

"Hey, you!" The doorman waved his arm at her and Missie stepped closer reluctantly. "You got lucky with your cheek," he said. "That was Madame Elise herself. She asked what ya wanted so I told her a job, and she said to go round to Mrs. Masters and tell her that Madame sent you. She's the manageress of the workroom. Maybe she'll need an extra hand." He grinned suddenly, "Sorry I shouted, kid," he said, "but I was expecting Madame and she hates anyone cluttering up her steps when she's making her grand entrance. Tell Fred on the door I sent ya, and while you're at it, ask him to put me a dollar to win on Mawchop in the two-thirty."

"A dollar to win on Mawchop," she repeated, and then she turned and ran around the corner before Madame could change her mind.

Mrs. Masters was a dragon. She kept Missie waiting half an hour, and when she finally flounced into the room in a rustle of stiff lilac silk, she peered at her sitting on the chair by the door as if she were an intruder.

"Who are you?" she demanded. "Who let you in here?"

"Why, Joe showed me in. He told me to wait," she replied, standing up. "Madame Elise said there might be a job."

"A job?" Mrs. Masters's sharp eyes raked her from head to foot, and Missie knew she had priced her new coat and her tired hat and cracked leather shoes, and understood exactly where she was on the human monetary scale. Mrs. Masters looked like the kind of woman who prided herself on never letting anyone put anything over on her, and her eyes were permanently suspicious.

"And what can you do?" she asked haughtily.

Missie quickly abandoned the idea of telling her about the sweatshops and said instead, "I don't have much experience, ma'am, but I learned to sew from the nuns at school." She crossed her fingers behind her back, hoping the nuns would forgive her the lie.

"Nuns, eh?" Mrs. Masters was suddenly interested, "Of course they're still the best teachers. A lot of our girls are convent trained. Show me," she commanded, holding out her hands, and Missie peeled off her gloves, wishing her hands didn't look so red and chapped from all the washing and cleaning.

Mrs. Masters felt them and her nose wrinkled with disgust. "Too rough! We use only the finest, most expensive fabrics here: fragile silks and chiffons, laces, silver and bead embroidery. Why, these hands would wreck anything they came in touch with. No, I'm sorry, it's just not good enough. Good-bye, Miss . . ."

"O'Bryan," Missie finished forlornly. She waited for a moment, hoping for a reprieve, but Mrs. Masters had already turned her back and was examining fabric samples under the light from the window.

Joe, the old man guarding the back door, looked up from his *Racing Form.* "No luck?" he asked sympathetically. "Well, maybe next time. Hey, when you go by, tell Bill on the front door there's no runner called Mawchop in the two-thirty at Palisades."

Missie nodded. It was beginning to rain and she turned up her coat collar dispiritedly, wondering where she could try next. She turned the corner and walked to the front steps, remembering her message for the doorman.

"Hey, hey, you!" He came flying down the steps again. "You, drooping like a wishbone, come here!"

"I must have got your message wrong," she said, lifting her head to look at him. "Joe says there is no Mawchop running in the two-thirty at Palisades."

"Not Palisades, Saratoga, the idiot! But it's not Joe I'm wantin', it's you. Madame sent me after ya. Seems like she asked Masters where ya were and said she wanted to see ya herself. Right away."

Missie stared at him hopefully. "But why?"

He winked. "Who knows? Maybe she thinks you're a lady in disguise and will buy her entire spring collection. Anyways, it's up the front steps this time and into the salon. Hurry up now, ya don't want to keep Madame Elise waiting if ya know what's good for ya."

Bill hurried her through the marble hall up a flight of purple-carpeted steps into the salon and Missie stared around her, awed. It was an enormous room with graceful arched windows draped in stiff lilac taffeta, walls paneled in mauve silk and silver sconces with the palest pink shades. There were soft gray carpets and groups of pretty gilt sofas and chairs upholstered in moiré silk in every shade from purple to lilac, and cascades of specially dyed matching flowers were displayed on carved giltwood console tables along the walls. Three crystal chandeliers were reflected in the banks of mirrors, and two small lilac-gray poodles were sleeping on a purple velvet cushion at Madame Elise's side.

Madame Elise, wearing a cloud of violet chiffon, sat on a throne-like gold sofa at the far end of the room. "*Viens,* come here," she called. "Quickly, child, I don't have all day." Her shrewd gray eyes narrowed as she watched Missie hurry toward her, stumbling nervously.

"*Mon Dieu, les chausseurs*—the shoes." She groaned. "Take them off *immédiatement.* You will ruin my beautiful gray carpet!"

Missie slipped off her shoes and stood clutching them uncertainly in her hand.

"Off with the coat," Madame said. "Quick, quick!"

She shrugged off her coat and threw it over her arm.

"Melodie?" Madame called, and a young maidservant, pretty in purple with a frilly white organdie apron, hurried forward. "Quick, take away her coat and her shoes."

"Turn around," Madame said, waving her arm to indicate just

how she should spin. "Yes, yes, the posture is good, and the height
. . . too thin, of course, but that's good . . . and the long neck is
quite beautiful. Show me your legs," she commanded suddenly.

Missie stared at her, suddenly angry; she was being ordered
around and asked to show her legs, and she didn't even know what
the job was. Putting her hands on her hips the way she had seen
Rosa do, she stared at Madame Elise belligerently. "Why?" she
demanded.

"Why? How else would I see what your legs look like? And never
put your hands on your hips like that, you look like a fishwife, not a
mannequin."

"A mannequin?" Missie's eyes almost popped out of her head.

Madame Elise's foot tapped impatiently on the soft gray carpet.
"Why else am I interviewing you?" she demanded. "I have girls
standing in line to become an Elise mannequin and all you do is ask
questions. Now, let me see your face. Kneel here in front of me."

Missie knelt and Madame took her chin, tilting her face this way
and that. "Ah," she said, softening, "the eyes are a true violet, my
favorite color."

She smiled suddenly, "You are . . . unexpected," she told
Missie. "I did not expect you to turn up on my doorstep. You are
unexpectedly beautiful, and unexpectedly, you will become my new
mannequin. My favorite girl, Barbara, eloped suddenly with a millionaire from Texas." She sighed dramatically. *"All* my girls marry
millionaires—everyone knows that to be an Elise mannequin is a
stepping-stone into society. But my spring collection is to be shown
next week and I designed all the star evening dresses around Barbara. Only she had that quality necessary to bring out the sensuous-
ness of the fabrics. Now, you have the height, the build, the bone
structure, beautiful hair and eyes—and I can teach you the rest. We
will adapt Barbara's dresses to fit you and you will show them here
next week to the very cream of New York society."

She sat back, smiling triumphantly at Missie. "Oh, but I
can't . . ." Missie began, "I mean, I've never . . ."

"Of course you can," Madame Elise said calmly. "You will begin
today. But first some tea." Melodie appeared like magic with a tray
and Madame motioned Missie to sit beside her. "Beware *les émi-
nences grises.*" She laughed, indicating the two poodles. "They bite
when they are disturbed, especially men. Ah, they hate men. . . ."

Missie sat down gingerly at the edge of the sofa, accepting the
tea.

"*Eh bien,*" Madame said. "Now, what is your name?"

"Missie, Missie O'Bryan." She flinched as Madame tut-tutted, waving her hand in the air in distress.

"Oh, no, no, no, no . . . nevaire . . . I refuse to have a mannequin called Missie—like a maidservant."

"Well, *your* maidservant is called Melodie," she retorted.

Madame Elise laughed, running a hand through her luxuriant red hair. "Nonsense, her real name is Freda. *Mon Dieu,* I ask you?" She laughed again, waking the poodles, who began to yap shrilly, sending the lusters on the chandeliers tinkling.

"Actually, Madame," Missie said, "my real name is Verity." It had been so long since she had used it she had almost forgotten.

"Verity?" Madame cocked her head first this way and then that, studying her again. "*La vérité,* 'the truth.' Ah, but I like that, it is cool, calm, elegant. Virginal, almost. Yes, yes, it suits you. Verity you shall be. Now, off you go to the fitting rooms. We must try on those dresses."

Missie thought about her patched cotton underwear and stared at her, horrified. "Oh, but I can't . . . I mean. . . ." She was so humiliated she just wanted to die, and blushing, she said quickly, "You see, Madame, I'm a poor girl. I have no pretty things, my undergarments . . ."

"Ah! I understand." Madame Elise's face softened, and she leaned forward and patted her gently on the knee. "It is no disgrace, child," she said quietly. "We will start 'at the bottom' as they say. Melodie?" The maid came running and she said loudly, "Take Verity through to the lingerie department and tell them to equip her with whatever she needs. And only the best."

Turning to Missie, she winked. "There's nothing like the kiss of *crêpe-de-Chine* on the skin," she whispered, laughing naughtily.

It was six o'clock before Missie left Madame Elise's, and she ran all the way back to the Second Avenue el, clutching her hat with one hand and holding a smart lilac package printed with Elise's name in the other.

The journey seemed to take ages. When she finally reached the Lower East Side she ran all the way back to Rivington Street and up the stairs, tapping urgently on Rosa's door, bursting with her story.

Rosa stared at her, astonished, and then her face broke into a smile. "Is good news," she said. "No need to say it, I can see."

"Good news? Oh, *Rosa!*" Missie flung her arms around her,

twirling her around excitedly. "This isn't merely *good* news, it's monumental, it's startling, it's astounding, amazing, phenomenal. It's wonderful, fabulous, *exciting.* . . ." The four little girls sitting at the table eating supper stared at her, their spoons halfway to their mouths.

"So it's astounding," Rosa said practically. "So tell me how much you get paid."

Missie's face fell and she stopped dancing around and stared at her. "Oh, Rosa," she said, "I forgot to ask!" And then she burst out laughing. "What difference does it make?" she said airily. "I'm going to marry a millionaire anyway, all Madame Elise's girls do. She told me herself."

"You are going to work for Madame Elise?" Rosa said, awed. Then she added, "And since when did the seamstresses marry the millionaires, even at smart Paris shops?"

"But, Rosa, I'm not a seamstress, I'm a fashion mannequin." Missie whooped with excitement and threw her hat in the air. "I, my dear," she said in an exaggerated drawl, slinking across the room one arm outstretched and her head twisted over one shoulder in a vamp pose, "*I* am Madame Elise's new star mannequin." She laughed, turning back to Rosa, adding, "And it's all thanks to you. It's your advice that got me there and your five dollars that bought my new coat so I didn't look like the ghost of poverty in my old gray shroud! You, Rosa Perelman," she said, kissing her, "are my savior. And my very dearest friend."

Rosa grinned and ladled out a bowl of soup. "Sit, eat," she commanded, "and tell me all about it."

"First, I've got something to show you." Missie untied the violet ribbon from the pretty parcel. "There!" she said triumphantly, holding up a delicate camisole in the palest oyster-pink *crèpe-de-Chine.* Rosa sucked in her breath. After wiping her hands on her apron, she touched it gently with an outstretched finger. "Well?" Missie demanded.

"I've never seen anything like it," Rosa whispered, "so beautiful, so delicate. . . . Who wears such garments, Missie? It's sinful."

"Of course it's not sinful, it's *heaven,* Rosa. I'm wearing one now, and knickers with so much lace you could make five collars! *And* silk stockings and a corset so light it's like wearing gossamer. There's nothing sinful about it."

"It's sinful only when you wear it for a man," Rosa said quietly.

Missie stared at her, astonished, and said, "I never thought of that."

"No reason you should." Rosa turned to the children crowding around, exclaiming over the beautiful chemise. "Look but don't touch," she warned, sitting back at the table.

"Eat your soup, and then tell me all," she said, briskly cutting a loaf of rye bread and keeping an eye on the children's table manners while she listened to Missie's excited description of Madame Elise, her encounter with Mrs. Masters, the lilac salon, and the lilac poodles. Missie said that Madame Elise had been apprenticed to Poiret and Worth and now she was the most famous of them all; she had houses in Paris and London as well as New York and she traveled constantly between them.

"She has given me all these beautiful things," Missie said, awed, "so I won't disgrace myself with my patched cotton underwear anymore. Only it's called 'lingerie,' and oh, Rosa, I can't tell you how different I felt when the fitter slipped this wonderful chiffon dress over my head and I saw myself in the mirror. Madame took down my hair and smiled when she saw how long it was—it comes down to my waist. 'You must never cut it,' she said. And then they put powder on and rouge and stuff on my lashes, and a lipstick Madame calls 'Violette Elise,' her special color. It felt sticky and very scented, but I guess I'll get used to it. And the shoes, Rosa, little silver kidskin slippers with high heels and straps with diamanté buckles, and yards and yards of enormous pearls. . . ."

She sighed, staring dreamily into her soup. "I just couldn't believe it when I saw myself. I looked like another person." Her face grew thoughtful. "A new person," she added. "Verity Byron."

"Is that your mannequin name, then?" Rosa asked, propping her chin on her hand and looking admiringly at Missie.

She nodded. "Only for work though. Here I'm still just Missie."

Viktor cocked his head as the hall door slammed and footsteps sounded on the stairs. Rosa glanced at the old bracket clock and sighed. "I expect that's Meyer," she said, hurrying to the stove and stirring the stew, picking out the lumps of meat and filling his plate. "He likes his meal ready on the table as soon as he walks in."

"We'll be off, then," Missie said, gathering her things together hastily and grabbing Azaylee's hand. She hesitated. "Rosa, would you still be able to look after Azaylee for me? I don't know what the hours are yet, but Madame said they would be 'unorthodox,' whatever that means."

"It means 'long,' " Rosa said with a laugh. "Naturally I'll take her, don't worry. And, Missie"—she kissed her warmly on the cheek—"I'm pleased for you. It sounds real wonderful, like a dream come true."

Missie drew in a deep, satisfied breath. "Not quite," she said, "but it's a beginning."

She couldn't wait to get to Elise's each morning for the fitters to begin reshaping the glamorous dresses, but she was very aware of the jealous glances of the other models. There were three of them. Miranda, a blonde, Minette, a redhead, and Minerve, a raven-haired beauty, and Missie thought they were all far more glamorous than she and very confident. But Elise kept them away from her, guarding her as if she were a secret weapon.

She made her walk endlessly up and down the lilac salon, wearing a silk wrapper and high-heeled shoes, draped with pearls and soft fur boas, practicing her walk and poses, sighing when Missie did not get it right.

And on Saturday Elise herself pressed a little lilac envelope into her hand. "Your first week's wages, Verity," she said, patting her on the shoulder. "You are not as good as Barbara yet but you learn quickly and you are more beautiful than her."

Missie glanced at her reflection in the banks of mirrors along the wall, wondering if she really looked beautiful, barely recognizing herself. Surely this tall, languorous young woman with her rouged cheeks, her enormous shadowed eyes and pouting red mouth must be someone else? The long dark-green silk-velvet coat clung to her narrow hips and the amber-colored fox collar framed her face becomingly. "I look like a debutante," she told herself, surprised. And then she added slowly, "I look just the way Anouska used to look."

When she opened the lilac envelope later that night, she found four crisp ten-dollar bills. She knew Elise's dresses cost hundreds, sometimes thousands, but forty dollars for only four days' work! She could pay Rosa back her five dollars, pay her rent, pay off her new coat, buy Azaylee the new boots she needed, and there would still be enough left over for food. She could even pay Zev Abramski back ten dollars. Missie laughed; she just couldn't wait to see his face when she gave him the money and told him her story tomorrow at the Ukrainian café. Why, she could even take *him* to supper this time.

=== 24 ===

Zev stared at the ten-dollar bill lying on the table between them and then at Missie. She looked different: stronger, bursting with energy as if life's spark had somehow been rekindled.

"So," he said quietly, "you found luck with the job?"

"Oh, Zev, *what* luck. And *what* a job!" She laughed gaily and people turned to stare curiously at them as she began to tell him all about it. "Of course," she ended, "I haven't actually done a real fashion parade yet, and to tell you the truth I'm scared. I mean, it's one thing doing it for Madame Elise, but quite another with all those smart women watching. Besides, the other mannequins are jealous. I can see it in their eyes. It's because Madame Elise is paying so much attention to me and because a newcomer is replacing Barbara instead of one of them." She sighed. "Still, there's nothing I can do about that." He nodded silently and she eagerly. "Now I can give you ten dollars each week until my debt is paid in full, with the proper interest of course." She sighed happily, "Oh, Zev, you can't imagine what it will mean to me, not being in debt. Soon I can begin to look for a new apartment, maybe move farther uptown, put Azaylee in a good school!"

He stared at the ten dollars on the table. In three more weeks she would have repaid her debt and a few weeks after that she would be gone, back to the world from which she came. He felt a tugging at his heart as if a great weight were dragging him down. Missie was going to leave him. She was going to a carefree world full of light and laughter, a world he didn't understand but where he knew she belonged.

"Zev?" Her eyes held a question and he stared back down at the ten dollars, the symbol of her freedom.

"You are not happy for me?" she asked, puzzled.

"I am happy for you," he admitted, "but it means you will go away from here and I will never see you again."

"But of course you will." She took his hand across the table, gazing at him earnestly. "I looked forward all week to seeing you tonight, Zev. I wanted to share my good news with you. You and Rosa are my dearest friends." She smiled tenderly. "I'll never forget you, Zev Abramski, and 'uptown' is not a million miles away. We shall still keep our Sunday night dates here at the café. Why, they even save our table for us now, and they play my favorite songs."

He knew she meant it, but he knew it was not the answer to his problem. The gap between Missie O'Bryan's life and his own was immense. She was poor by circumstance, he was poor because he was born to it. She was educated, he was ignorant; she was tall, beautiful, any man would adore her; he had never been loved by anyone. And what was there to love in a young unattractive immigrant pawnbroker from Orchard Street?

Zev stared silently down at the sidewalk, seeming lost in his own thoughts as they walked back to Rivington Street. "Don't worry so," she whispered, touching his cheek tenderly as they said good night. "After all, I'm still here, aren't I?" She kissed him lightly and ran into the apartment house. "See you next Sunday," she called as she closed the door.

Zev waited until he saw the lamp go on in her room and then he walked slowly around the corner to Orchard Street. The shop door tinkled with the same sound he had been hearing for the last thirteen years, and for the first time the bell didn't sound like the ring of security. Instead it sounded like the knell of bondage.

He walked through to the small, dark, silent rooms he called home, turning up the gas lamps and noticing how worn and dreary everything was. There was no expression of a person in here, he thought, no one could tell it was Zev Abramski's home. He was just an ignorant immigrant Jew plying a mean trade, and all his dreams of sharing his solitude, his reading, his music, were gone; they lived only in his head. It was all meaningless. Missie was a lady, and once she had repaid her debt he would have no place in her life.

After taking off his coat, he sat at the piano and ran his fingers tentatively across the keys, playing a Chopin étude. He had always thought of this piece as Missie's music—soft, silken, gentle—but tonight he had seen another side of her. Suddenly he began to play a mazurka, a gay, dancing snatch of music that made him smile as he remembered her lovely face, so vivid with excitement. He might not be an artist, but he could paint his love in music.

Monday could not come soon enough for Missie. She was up at six, heating the kettles of water for the zinc hip bath and being as quiet as she could so as not to wake Azaylee, still sleeping the all-out slumber of the very young.

She paused by the sagging brass bed to look at her, promising silently that soon everything would change. They would have a proper apartment, she would go to a good school, there would be good food again, good clothes. Madame Elise would be their savior and she would do her very best to be a good mannequin.

"I don't want a *good* mannequin," Madame Elise told her angrily later that morning. "What I need for my clothes is a *great* mannequin, a wonder-girl, so *ravissante,* so alluring, and yet so ladylike that all those rich women will think they can be like that too if they buy Elise's dresses. Hold yourself taller, no, taller even than that . . . stretch your neck from your shoulders, stretch your spine from your waist, there, that's better. You walk so beautifully, Verity. Just relax, let your pretty head droop forward a little on that so, *soooo* fragile neck, remember you are clothed in gossamer, you cannot possibly look earthly. *Please,* Verity!"

She sighed loudly. Missie heard smothered laughter in the background and knew the other girls were enjoying her humiliation as Madame put her through her paces for the hundredth time that morning.

"Try again," Madame said loudly. "No, wait. Miranda, come here and show Verity what I mean."

Beautiful blond Miranda loped elegantly across the salon, one hand on her hip, the other arm swinging, her hand outstretched. She stopped in front of Madame and Verity, one foot prettily in front of the other, the fingers of her beringed hand spread at her throat, eyes disdainfully half closed as if she scorned to look at them.

"You see," Madame exclaimed triumphantly, "*that* is what I want. Exaggerate! *Viens,* Verity, try again."

It was a relief when Madame left for a consultation with one of her out-of-town clients at the Waldorf Astoria Hotel. The fitter told Missie she charged them a thousand dollars just to advise them on what colors to wear and what fabrics and styles would suit them best. "And then they come here and buy everything she has suggested," she told Missie with a laugh. "But you've got to hand it to Madame, those women leave the salon looking better than they've ever looked in their lives. Madame always says that's one of her secrets. The husbands are so pleased they don't mind paying up."

Missie touched the soft folds of her violet chiffon dress encrusted with tiny silver beads; it was beautiful and felt light as a breeze against her leaden limbs. She stared despairingly in the mirror, drooping with tiredness. The dress was sleeveless, cut in a deep V front and back, sashed around its low waist with a tasseled silver rope. The skirt was daringly short, cut to midcalf and draped over the hips with a floating panel at one side. She knew she should look like Ariel in it, but right now all she felt like was Puck.

"Can't turn an ugly duckling into a swan, can you?" Minerve's voice said mockingly behind her.

"And you can't make a silk purse from a sow's ear," Minette said with a giggle.

Tall, raven-haired Minerve strode toward her menacingly. "That's my job you've taken," she whispered threateningly, "but don't think I'm going to let you get away with it. I'll have you out of here before you know it."

Then she said loudly, "I'm having lunch with Alphonse today. That's the Duke di Monteciccio to you," she added for Missie's benefit, sweeping through the door.

The fitter sighed. "And she thinks she's already the duchess," she muttered. "It would be good riddance if she did get married and leave, she's a real trouble causer. Better watch out for her, darlin', or she'll steal your silk stockings, your job—and your boyfriend."

Missie decided Minerve was the least of her problems; the first was to learn how to stand like an Elise mannequin instead of the way that came naturally.

She practiced all afternoon at the mirror, stretching taller the way Madame had told her and drooping her neck forward until it threatened to break. She placed one foot in front of the other, copying Miranda, jutting her hip and clutching her throat, but all she looked like was a terrified silent movie heroine. And she sashayed up and down the salon bestowing haughty glares on an invisible audience of snobbish society women until her feet and her head ached.

"It's no good," she told Rosa despairingly later that night, "I just can't seem to do it right and I feel such a fool, mincing along the way Miranda does. Nobody walks like that, Rosa, so why should a mannequin, just because she's showing off the clothes?"

"Then why not do it your own way, instead of copying them?" Rosa suggested. "Do whatever feels natural to you, Missie. I'm sure it will work."

"I don't know." Missie sighed doubtfully. "Madame told me this is the way they do it in Paris, and I suppose she knows best. Anyway it's too late now, tomorrow is the big preview fashion parade. Oh, Rosa, I'm so scared. What if I make a mess of it? What if she fires me?"

Her face had lost all its happy glow. It looked white and pinched again, and Rosa couldn't bear it. "Of course it'll be all right," she reassured her. "You will look just beautiful and Madame Elise will sell all her dresses and you will marry a millionaire. After all"—she laughed—"that's the way you told me it would happen, didn't you?"

Missie laughed too, only she wondered why it suddenly sounded so hollow, as if she didn't really believe it anymore.

At the dress rehearsal the next morning, a small orchestra ran through tunes from the latest Broadway shows while workmen hammered the final nails into a wooden platform that had sprung up overnight down the center of the room. Hundreds of little spindly gold chairs were being carried up the stairs and cleaners were polishing chandeliers and windows. Soon a purple velvet carpet covered the platform and lilac chiffon drapes surmounted by Madame Elise's signature coronet disguised the entrance to the dressing room from which the girls would emerge.

Inside the dressing room was pandemonium, with fitters making last-minute adjustments while the girls complained their feet ached, sitting impatiently in front of the mirror while the hairdresser tried to make up his mind what to do with them.

When it came to Verity's turn, Madame warned him not to cut her hair. "But just here at the front," he protested, "a slight wave over the forehead, a few tendrils at the sides. . . ."

"*Eh bien,* a few tendrils is enough," she agreed. "I want it as glossy as a horse chestnut, long, straight and silky. We can put it in a chignon when necessary."

Dresses, shoes, hats, and complete ensembles were lined up with the proper accessories ready on shelves: gloves, furs, shoes, matching silk stockings, and the yards of the enormous *faux* pearls Madame had decreed should be worn by everybody this season, even those who could afford the real thing.

At three o'clock the great double doors to the salon were thrown open and Elise hurried to greet her guests. Verity stole a look at the audience rapidly filling the rows of little gilt chairs. The guest list read like a list of New York's elite four hundred, and to her surprise there were men as well as women, standing in the back, talking together and every now and then casting a discreet glance at the women. They were all dressed so smartly anyway she wondered why they needed anything new. But that was the lure of Madame Elise. None of them could afford to be seen in last year's fashion—only the latest would do.

She turned back to the dressing room, glancing at the clock. Ten minutes to go. Her stomach churned and she bit her lip nervously as she sat in front of the mirror while the stylist powdered her face and dusted her cheekbones with rouge, pursing her lips while she applied the Violette Elise lip rouge. "I feel like an actress," she murmured.

"And that's just what you are," the stylist replied. She looked at her in the mirror and smiled. "My, you look beautiful," she said.

Missie crossed her fingers, hoping she was right. One thing she knew, she didn't look a bit like Missie O'Bryan from Rivington Street.

Madame's little silver bell tinkled for silence and her voice came from beyond the curtain, telling her guests how privileged they were to be seeing a preview of her latest spring collection displayed by her sensational mannequins—and that afterward they could view any of the new styles privately in their own homes if they so wished. *"Eh bien,"* she announced, "now we begin."

The orchestra swung into a Gershwin tune from Ziegfeld's latest show. Minerve was ready in an ice-blue afternoon dress with matching shoes and stockings, a floral chiffon scarf trailing from her neck to the ground. With a toss of her head she slunk out onto the catwalk, and Missie heard a spatter of applause and murmurs of appreciation from the salon. Miranda followed in a pale lilac, and then Minette in sugar pink, an outrageous combination with her red hair that drew gasps of admiration.

It was Missie's turn next. She was wearing a travel suit in a creamy tweed with the new slouch hat pulled down over one eye, high-heeled cream buckled shoes, and half a dozen long ropes of fat, creamy pearls. As the curtains closed softly behind her she froze, staring at the sea of expectant faces turned her way. It's no good, she thought, panicked, I can't do it, I just can't. Her knees shook. She had forgotten everything Madame had taught her, she just wanted to run back inside. Minerve strode past on her way back down the catwalk, throwing her a contemptuous smile as she shrugged back through the curtains, but Missie just stood there, staring at the curious women staring back at her. She thought of Anouska: Hadn't she been just like these women? She realized suddenly that of course they were not interested in *her*. All they wanted to see were the clothes.

The thought gave her courage. Taking a deep breath, she strode down the purple platform in her usual long-legged loping walk, pausing here and there to smile at the ladies, extending her arm so they could see the cut of the sleeve, patting the new-style hat and turning her face sideways so they could see how it looked in profile. She stood for a few moments at the end of the platform, then spun around and, with a quick glance over her shoulder, loped back toward the curtains.

Safe in the dressing room listening to the polite spatter of applause, she wondered what Madame would think of her now. But she just could not walk the way the other girls did; she guessed she was just not cut out to be a mannequin after all.

She glanced up as Minerve sauntered past in a gold lace dress embroidered with sparkling copper beads. "Told you, didn't I?" she said with a snigger. "You can't make a swan from an ugly duckling."

The applause was very loud for Minerve, and Missie stepped despondently into the violet chiffon dress, searching the shelf for her silver kidskin slippers. They were not there and she glanced around, puzzled, spotting them at last on the floor under the dressing table. She picked them up, staring at them in horror; the narrow straps that kept them on were broken. Not broken—cut! She remembered Minerve's jealous smile. Would she stoop to such a thing? She glanced around in panic: The dresser had disappeared and all the maids were out in the salon, busy serving China tea and little cakes. Miranda and Minette were standing by the curtain waiting their turn, but anyway she knew they would not help.

She threw down the shoes in despair: It was the last straw; she knew now she was doomed to failure. She stared at her reflection in the big mirror and knew she looked beautiful. She remembered her confident promise to Azaylee that morning and was suddenly filled with a ruthless kind of courage, a do-or-die feeling. "Oh, what the hell," she decided. "Father always said when all else fails, improvise." After ripping the violet satin ribbons from Madame Elise's packages on the dresser, she slipped on the shoes and bound the ribbon under the instep, crisscrossing it and tying it in neat bows at her ankles. Then she took the pins from her hair, shook it free, and placed the jeweled aigrette low over her forehead.

"Hurry, hurry," the dresser called, taking her arm and giving her a push that sent her out through the curtains. Missie hesitated again, glancing around at the ladies. Then, tossing her head high and walking as tall as Madame could ever have wished, she swung slowly down the purple platform.

Madame Elise gasped, shocked by her appearance. What had come over the girl? And whatever had she got on her feet? She glanced around hurriedly at her ladies, surprised to see them leaning forward attentively watching Verity's every smooth, slinky move in complete silence. Even the men had stopped talking and were staring at her new mannequin. She turned to look at Verity again, standing at the end of the platform, the fluid folds of the violet chiffon clinging to her lovely limbs like a young Isadora Duncan, the sparkling silver beads catching the light as she moved. Her waist-length hair hung like a shining bronze curtain, the soft tendrils framing her face, and her huge wonderful eyes looked an even deeper violet than the dress.

Throwing back her head, Missie walked languidly back along the platform, stopping here and there, her hand resting on her tasseled beaded belt, the low neckline, the lovely skirt, but all eyes were riveted on her feet and the violet satin bows at her delicate ankles.

The curtain closed behind her and the orchestra changed rapidly to another show tune. The maids came to life again, hurrying around with more tea and cakes, and the gentlemen's heads lowered together as they discussed Elise's audacious new mannequin behind their hands. Madame closed her eyes. What had Verity done? Oh, what had she done? She had disobeyed her instructions, all her training, it was *une catastrophe!* She was aware of a murmur of conversation and then someone began to applaud, another took it up, and suddenly the applause became a roar; there were even a few bravos, though those were mainly from the men.

"Encore! Encore!" someone called, and Madame turned to look at the enthusiastic young society matron, a beauty in her own right and a true fashion innovator. She was one of her biggest customers.

She smiled graciously at her and quickly sent a maid to tell Verity to come out again please.

It couldn't be true, Verity thought, stepping out on the platform. Were they really applauding her? She loped along the platform once again, bestowing a smile here and there, pausing to let them admire her ribboned shoes, her egret feathers, her swirling folds of silk chiffon. She felt like laughing. Maybe being a mannequin was easy after all. "Do it the way that feels natural," Rosa had said, and maybe she had been right.

Minerve glared at her as she strode back into the dressing room to a thunder of applause but Missie merely smiled. "Another platitude to add to your collection, Minerve," she said sweetly. "Necessity is the mother of invention." As she walked to her dressing table she could feel Minerve's eyes on her shoes, and knew that it was she who had sabotaged her.

The rest of the fashion parade passed quickly, and to her surprise Missie enjoyed herself; it was fun being the center of attention, fun to feel young and beautiful. Afterward Madame Elise came to the dressing room to congratulate her.

"Everyone is talking about my new shoes." She laughed. "I don't know where you got the idea of the ribbons, Missie, but now everybody wants them. Mrs. Woolman Chase from *Vogue* said you personify the new feminine spirit, freed from the restrictions of war, able to be young again and soft and simple. 'La Vie Naturelle' is what I'm calling it, and believe me, Verity, it is a *succès énorme.*" She turned to the other girls suddenly. "And why can't you walk like Verity, eh? You, Minerve, looked like a marionette beside her. We have been invited to repeat our show at the Countess of Wensleyshire's on Sunday, and I want you all to walk exactly the way Verity does."

Minerve flung down her ropes of pearls and stood up angrily. "Never!" she shrieked. "I'll never take lessons from this little upstart."

"In that case," Madame Elise said icily, "you may find a job elsewhere. *Au revoir!*"

Minerve shrugged her shoulders. "The duke has asked me to marry him, anyway," she said haughtily. "I was only doing you a favor staying on for these shows."

"Congratulations," Madame said icily, but Missie stared after her anxiously as she flounced through the door.

"Don't worry," Madame Elise said, laughing. "There are a thousand Minerves, but there is only one Verity. Today you were *ravissante* for my ladies, Sunday you will be gorgeous and all New York will be at your feet—with their pretty little satin bows."

25

Azaylee sat on the edge of the bed watching Missie as she prepared to leave for the salon. Her blond hair was scraped back firmly into an uneven braid and her pansy eyes were sad. Viktor leapt onto the bed next to her and she curled her arms lovingly around his neck. The dog obviously adored her, and Missie hadn't the heart to protest anymore.

"What a picture," she said, laughing.

"We were going to take Viktor for a walk today," Azaylee reminded her aggrievedly, "but now you are going away again."

Missie bit her lip. It was true. She had been so busy the last few days there had scarcely been time for Azaylee, let alone poor old Viktor. "I'll make it up to you," she promised remorsefully. "I know it's Sunday, but this is special." She wished Madame Elise had chosen any other time for her show, but there it was, she had no choice. "Look," she said brightly, "how would you like it if we get a new apartment soon, maybe near the park so we can walk Viktor, with a lovely room just for you that you can fill with new toys? And how would you like to go to school with other little girls your age where they would wear a special kind of hat and coat called 'a uniform' so that it shows you belong. . . ."

"I already belong here," Azaylee retorted. "I don't want to leave Rosa and my friends."

Missie's heart sank as she sat beside her on the bed, "I don't want to leave Rosa either, *milochka,*" she said quietly, "but we would still see her. They could come and visit, maybe even stay over. Just think what fun that would be."

"It's fun here," Azaylee said stubbornly, clutching Viktor's neck even tighter and burying her face in his shaggy fur. "I don't want to change."

Missie stroked her hair silently. She could feel Azaylee's small body shaking with sobs and realized it was not just the idea of leaving she was crying about, but the insecurity of change. She was remembering leaving Varishnya and her father, her mother and brother; she was remembering leaving Russia and remembering leaving her beloved Sofia at the cemetery. Every time she had left a place, she had never seen the people she loved again.

When she dropped Azaylee at Rosa's later, Rosa said, "Good luck with the show. It's a fairy tale, Missie, a true real-life fairy tale. Maybe the millionaire will be there waiting for you today."

Missie doubted it and besides, she didn't care about millionaires; all she wanted was to earn enough to keep Azaylee and herself decently.

The week since the fashion parade had flown by. They had been kept busy visiting several of the grandest houses in New York so that the favored customers might choose privately. But it was Verity and *her* new style that was in demand, and even though Miranda and Minette had dropped their posed ways and were striving to become more natural, they didn't have the special look Missie had. Orders had flowed in for her violet dress, and variations of it were already being seen around New York, and *everyone* wanted the new shoes. She had spent most of the week being fitted for a series of new dresses Madame had hurriedly designed and the seamstresses had practically sewed them on her. And today they were to go out to the Countess of Wensleyshire's grand house as the high point of her annual spring weekend party.

There were six Delahaye limousines outside the Park Avenue salon waiting to transport them to Long Island. Madame rode in the first, alone with her chauffeur like a queen, and Missie had to ride with Miranda and Minette, neither of whom was speaking to her. It wasn't all a fairy story, she thought with a sigh, despite what Rosa said. But it *was* forty dollars a week and beautiful clothes to wear, because Madame wanted her mannequins to be her walking advertisements. "But I never go anywhere," Missie had protested.

"Nevaire? A young girl like you? *Tiens,*" Madame had exclaimed, "then it is high time you started."

The other four limousines carried the baskets of clothes, the dressers, and the hairstylist. The little procession wound its way through the sleepy Long Island Sunday countryside until they came to a pair of immense wrought-iron gates surmounted by huge carved griffons. A gatekeeper darted from the lodge to open them, and they drove on down a long gravel avenue and drew up in front of a huge white house. Beautifully dressed people were wandering across the lawns, where tables were set with silver and damask for tea and a group of young men in white flannels were playing tennis. A band played on the long terrace amid tubs of bright early-summer flowers, grown in the countess's famous conservatories specially for the occasion.

Missie was suddenly swept back in time to Anouska's wonderful parties—to a beautiful house just like this, young people scattered across the lawns laughing, playing games and always music in the air. . . .

"Come, Verity," Madame called, "the Countess is waiting."

Imogen, Countess of Wensleyshire was tall, thirtyish, beautiful, and spoiled to death by every man who had ever met her. The earl had been her third husband, an older man who doted on her, even dying conveniently when she grew bored with him three years ago. Now she maintained a stately home in Yorkshire, town houses in London and Paris, a penthouse in Manhattan, and an enormous sea-going yacht moored, now the war was over, at Monte Carlo. And she enjoyed doing what she did best, giving parties and looking for her next husband.

She stared curiously at Missie as she shook hands without smiling. "Ah, now I see what all the fuss was about," she said enigmatically. "Every man I know has been talking about Verity this week. I did not see Elise's fashion parade, but your reputation preceded you."

"I'm just the mannequin," Missie said quickly. "I'm sure it's the clothes they were talking about."

The countess's eyes narrowed into a smile; "The women, maybe, but the men . . ." She laughed, leaving the end of her statement hanging in the air.

"Elise, darling," she cried, turning to Madame, "come and have some tea and then I'll show you the ballroom where the parade will be held."

The ballroom was paneled in blue and cream like a Wedgwood vase with a little stage at one end. This time Madame herself organized her mannequins, parading them onto the stage and down the ramp to the lilting strains of a fifteen-piece orchestra.

As she strode onto the stage in Madame's latest extravaganza, a low-cut shimmering silver sheath overlaid with panels of dove-gray chiffon, Missie realized she was enjoying herself. It was as if she became someone else when she was wearing Elise's clothes. She felt she had power over these people, the power to make them look at her. She glanced around her audience, commanding them with her eyes, and then with an arrogant toss of her head she swung down the ramp, drifting languidly among them, pausing here and there to bestow a smile or extend a graceful arm so that the chiffon panels floated like gossamer wings. And of course she made sure that everyone noticed the silver shoes with the gray satin ribbons tied in pretty bows at her ankles. For the first time she was aware of the men watching her with as much interest as the women, and somehow their stares made her feel uncomfortable.

The applause afterward was tremendous. Everyone wanted to meet the famous Elise and her beautiful mannequins, and Verity found herself the center of an admiring crowd of young men. The afternoon had turned into a party; corks popped amid shouts of delight and glasses were laughingly filled with illegal champagne. A jazz band in striped blazers replaced the orchestra, swinging into a ragtime beat that sent dancers scattering eagerly onto the floor. Suddenly she felt let down, as if she had descended from some lofty, unreal pinnacle back to reality. She remembered she was really Missie O'Bryan from Rivington Street with all her problems. She did not belong here with all these smart rich people. After slipping away from the crowd, she stepped onto the terrace, breathing the early-spring scents of lily of the valley and winter jasmine, and she wandered through the lovely gardens, glad to be alone with her memories of Varishnya.

She sat on a stone bench overlooking the gray Long Island Sound, dreaming of how wonderful it would be to be able to afford a house like this for Azaylee, to give her everything she could ever want, the way her own father and mother would have.

"Good evening." A tall, well-dressed, middle-aged man was smiling genially at her. "Enjoying the fresh air? Or just dreaming?"

"Both." Missie smiled back at him. He had shrewd eyes and aristocratic features, and he was fanning himself with his hat.

He took off his jacket, mopping his face with a pale-blue handkerchief, and said, "Don't mind, do you? I can't stand hot weather. Bad for business."

He sat on the bench beside her and closed his eyes, listening to the fountain. "You're a mighty pretty girl, Miss . . . ?"

Missie blushed. Surely he wasn't going to make a pass at her? She glanced around anxiously, looking for an escape route.

agreed to become a Ziegfeld girl, or had he just assumed she had? She closed her eyes, trying to imagine herself on an enormous stage, dressed in gossamer and diamonds and dating stage-door romeos, and she wondered how she could even think of it. And then she thought of the hundred and fifty dollars "every Saturday, regular as clockwork" and she knew she would.

She shivered again. It was dark now. The false warmth of a too-early spring day had disappeared and the wind had a March edge to it. But she had lost all her mannequin's aloof poise. She was just Missie again and she didn't want to go back inside and face the party.

Tires crunched on the gravel and a long yellow car drew up in front of the house. She turned away as a man got out and ran past her up the steps. His footsteps stopped suddenly and then she heard them returning. As he drew level with her she could smell the smoke from his cigar.

"B'jaysus, Missie?" O'Hara's astonished voice said. "Can that really be you?"

She swung around, staring at him in amazement. It was O'Hara, all right, but O'Hara with a difference. His bright red curls were pomaded flat, he was wearing a sharp gray suit, patent leather shoes, and a gray silk ascot with a large pearl stickpin, and he was smoking a very large cigar.

He grabbed her hands eagerly, crushing them in his. "I turn out of a Sunday evenin' to make a delivery, and what's me reward? Why, Missie O'Bryan, the girl of me dreams!" He laughed uproariously. "That's what you get for being a man of your word. Delivery any time, day or night, that's O'Hara's motto, and I'm proud to tell you it's a successful one. I was waiting until I could prove it to you, but now you see for yourself—O'Hara delivering liquor to the nobs at prices they've never heard of in Delancey Street."

He stopped his monologue and stared at her again. "But just look at yourself now! You're a treat to behold, Missie O'Bryan, dressed in such finery!" He stiffened and said suspiciously, "Though I don't know where a girl like yourself would find the money for it. Nor what you're doing at the countess's party."

"I've got a job," she said eagerly, telling him her story about Madame Elise. She stopped, puzzled. O'Hara was staring down at his shiny black patent shoes, a troubled look on his face, and she asked him what was the matter.

"It's all wrong for you, Missie." He groaned. "You don't know what these people are like. I could tell you some stories about what I've seen at houses even grander than this one, stories that would make your hair turn white! They take up with a person one week and drop her the next. And when I think of you, my ideal, my colleen, flaunting yourself for them to see . . ."

"Flaunting myself?" she retorted angrily. "Just what do you mean by that, O'Hara? I show off perfectly respectable clothes so that perfectly respectable ladies will buy them." Pushing aside the memory of the men's speculative eyes, she added hurriedly, "And anyway, who are you to talk? Selling illegal liquor to people? At least my job is honest!"

O'Hara's face grew red with anger and he bit so hard on the end of his cigar he broke it in two. He stamped it viciously into the ground and then suddenly he began to laugh. "B'jaysus and if you're not right. Except in Ireland we don't consider selling moonshine illegal. And all I'm doing is giving people a little pleasure by giving them what they want."

"And so am I!" she retorted, stamping her foot.

"Is it a temper then you've been acquiring, along with your new job?" he asked innocently, laughing as she lunged at him, catching her hands in his. "I'm sorry, Missie, honest I am. I never meant to imply you were not a respectable girl. Of course I knows in me heart you are, but I guess it's just that I'd like you home safe with me, in New Jersey instead of showing clothes for a living."

She gripped his hands tightly. Despite her anger she was surprised how pleased she was to see his familiar handsome face, like a beacon of security among all the shiny New York society people. "I'm really glad to see you, O'Hara," she whispered.

He beamed happily. "Then grab your hat, Missie O'Bryan. I'm taking you out to supper to the best restaurant on Long Island."

Thrilled, she ran to find Madame Elise and tell her she was having supper with an old friend.

"An old friend?" Madame repeated with a skeptical smile. "Or perhaps a new conquest? Very well then, you may go. And tomorrow we will discuss the new 'arrangement' with Ziegfeld."

Missie had forgotten all about Ziegfeld, but as she ran to join O'Hara, she decided against telling him the rest of her story. Somehow, she just knew he would not understand. At least, not yet.

The restaurant was set back from the road behind some trees, like the one O'Hara had taken her to before. There were dozens of automobiles in the parking lot, but no lights shone from the windows and only a swinging carriage lamp lighted the sign "Oriconne's" over the front door.

"Are you sure it's open?" she asked nervously as O'Hara lifted a little brass lid and pressed the buzzer.

"Sure I'm sure, it's just private. You have to be a member, and they won't let you in if they don't know your face."

"But whyever not?" she demanded, astonished.

"It's a speakeasy. That means they are selling booze—O'Hara's booze," he added proudly. "They keep the window curtains closed and lock all the doors so they can get it out of the way, chance the police should arrive. Not that they will, with the payola the Oriconne brothers give them."

A tiny window opened suddenly and a face peered at them through the grille. There was the sound of the heavy bolts being drawn back and they stepped inside, then through another heavily padded leather door. Missie gasped as a wall of sound hit them. The long row room was crowded with people all talking at the tops of their voices over the noise of a jazz band. On a circular illuminated glass floor at the far end, couples were dancing, calling out to each other, and laughing wildly.

"See what fun they're all havin'," O'Hara said loudly, "and all courtesy of yours truly."

"But there are no drinks on the table," she said, surprised, "only cups of tea."

O'Hara winked broadly. "Sure and it's O'Hara's special tea they're drinkin'," he said in a loud voice as the headwaiter whisked them to a corner table.

"Can I get you something, sir?" he asked with a smile.

O'Hara looked at Missie and said, "We had champagne the last time we met, so why don't we make it a habit?"

"Why not?" she replied recklessly. Life felt good today, and anyway it was time for a celebration. She was going to be a Ziegfeld girl and make a hundred and fifty dollars a week. She told herself she would be doing it for Azaylee, but a secret part of her was enjoying the idea of being Ziegfeld's new star. And she wouldn't be in the least bit sorry to see the back of Rivington Street's grinding poverty, except for Rosa, of course, and Zev . . . Zev! Her hand flew to her mouth. "Oh." She gasped. "I completely forgot. I was to meet Zev Abramski at eight o'clock."

"Zev Abramski?" O'Hara repeated, puzzled. He frowned as she explained that she saw him Sunday nights at the Ukrainian café.

"We just have supper together, it's very simple," she explained quickly. "I mean, it's nothing like this, like you and me having supper here tonight. He's just . . . just Zev Abramski," she finished lamely.

"And what might you and he have in common, then?" he asked jealously. "Maybe you owe him money and he takes you out as a form of repayment?"

Missie's eyes flashed as she leaned across the table toward him. "How dare you, Shamus O'Hara," she whispered angrily. "Zev Abramski is a fine man and an honest one, and besides, we have a lot more in common than you think."

She sat back, thinking sadly of Zev, waiting for her at their table at the café, and hating herself for forgetting. I'll explain it all to him tomorrow, she promised herself, and I'll make it up to him next week; I won't forget again. She looked at O'Hara smoldering on the other side of the table and laughed.

"Whenever we meet, we fight," she said. "It must be your Irish temper."

"Sure and it's not me Irish temper," he boomed, banging his fist on the table so that the cups jumped. "It's your pig-headedness in not marrying me."

"I'll bet if I did marry you," she teased, "we would fight every night. You would still see things your way and I would see them mine. You would probably keep me locked up in your fancy house and expect me to cook and clean and bear your babies, just the way they did in the old country."

She laughed at his shocked face as he said anxiously, "Missie, I would niver do that! I'm a man of principles, and even though they don't extend to the selling of hooch, I'd niver treat me wife like that."

She sighed exaggeratedly. "What a pity you're not going to get a chance to try."

O'Hara groaned and poured more champagne. "Give a man a break, Missie, will you? I leave you struggling in Rivington Street and a couple of months later, you're a different girl."

"I am?" she asked, astonished.

"That you are, Missie," he replied solemnly, "but I still want you for me wife."

"Ask me again in a year's time," she said suddenly, "and I'll give you an answer."

He took her hand and held it tightly. "One year?"

"One year," she promised.

He smiled and said happily, "It'll be the longest of me life."

"Oh, no," she replied, sighing happily. "This time, it won't be."

Because for her, this time the year promised to fly by.

26

At twelve o'clock the next morning Madame Elise accompanied Missie to the New Amsterdam Theater. The auditorium with its gleaming gilt boxes was dark and mysterious; the safety curtain was covered with dozens of colorful advertisements for pomades and potions, sheet music, stores, and phonograph records; cleaning women were busy sweeping up the litter from the previous night's show, polishing the brass ashtrays and brushing the red plush seats. It brought back memories of childhood visits to the pantomime in Oxford and trips to the ballet in London, and Missie sighed, wondering what Professor Marcus Octavius Byron would think of his daughter now, about to set foot on the stage as a Ziegfeld showgirl. But she was desperate and one hundred fifty dollars a week had overcome any scruples she might have had. And anyway, wasn't it exactly like being a fashion mannequin, only better paid? Besides, she knew it would be fun. Fun? she thought, trying to remember the last time she had fun. Maybe fun meant a life without financial worries?

"*Vite,* quickly," Madame urged as Mr. Ziegfeld's secretary held open the door, staring curiously at her.

"Miss Verity." Ziegfeld hurried across the room, smiling genially. "Am I pleased to see you! See what it says here in the *Times*?" He thrust a copy of the newspaper at her, pointing out a quarter-page article devoted to Elise's spring fashion parade, and there was her own name in print.

"Elise's new mannequin Verity created a sensation when she appeared, clad in filmy violet chiffon embellished with silver beads and the most audacious little silver shoes strapped with violet satin bows at her deliciously delicate ankles. Verity epitomizes the new *Vie Naturelle,* Elise has said, and before too long you will see every woman in New York copying the way she wears her flowing nut-brown hair and her easy natural walk, though many will find it difficult to emulate Verity's long, long legs, her grace, her beauty, and her startling violet eyes. The word is out that Flo Ziegfeld already has his eyes on her and maybe soon we can expect a new Ziegfeld star."

"*Et voilà,* Ziegfeld!" Madame Elise said triumphantly. "I have created another star for you. First there was my little blond Maude who went on to marry the railroad millionaire, then racy, red-headed Jaquetta who you lost to the Hollywood movies, and now—Verity."

"The most beautiful of them all," he said, smiling.

"But I'm not beautiful, Mr. Ziegfeld," Verity said honestly. "I think I look like most any other girl."

"*Ahhh.*" Madame sighed, rolling her eyes. "How can this child be such a fool?" she muttered. "She is here to claim a place in theater history as a Ziegfeld girl and now she says she's just an ordinary girl on the street!"

"Take it from me, and I am an expert," Ziegfeld said briskly, "you have a different kind of beauty, Verity. Not flamboyant, I admit, but I've got enough flamboyants. What you have is beauty with class, and in my book that spells money."

"Florenz and I have already come to an agreement," Madame interjected quickly. "I will release you from your obligation to me and in return I am to design all your clothes, both for the shows and for your street wear."

"Hey now, just a minute," Ziegfeld protested, surprised.

"What? Is your new star supposed to walk down Fifth Avenue in a five-dollar coat? Is she supposed to dine at Rector's in a depart-ment-store frock? Wearing dimestore jewels? Come now, Florenz, where are your brains? No, I insist she is dressed by Elise, and no one else. It goes in the contract. And naturally, I will send the bills to you."

"Naturally." Ziegfeld sighed.

"And she is to be paid two hundred dollars a week, with a raise in three months' time, working or not."

Ziegfeld groaned. "You've got yourself a tough negotiator here," he told Missie with a wry grin. "Okay, okay, if you say so, Elise. And now, before you break the bank, I'd like to take you two ladies out to celebrate at Rector's."

Rector's was the New York showbiz world's swankiest rendez-vous and Flo Ziegfeld Broadway's ritziest producer, and the two were made for each other. The plush dining room was his home away from home and the maître d' greeted him like a treasured old friend, bowing deeply over Madame Elise's hand and even deeper over Verity's when Ziegfeld introduced her as his future new star.

"But of course." He smiled. "I have already read about Miss Verity in the newspapers."

"So has everyone else," whispered Ziegfeld, noting the excited buzz of conversation as every head turned to watch their progress to their table.

"Caviar!" he called loudly. "We're celebrating here."

"Excuse me, Mr. Ziegfeld, sir." An eager young man appeared at his side, notepad in hand. "I'm Dan James from the *Daily Star*. I couldn't help noticing you and Madame Elise, and I assume this lovely young lady is Miss Verity? Her new mannequin?"

"*Her* ex-mannequin, *my* new star," Ziegfeld said, beaming, "Tell your readers that, Mr. James, and tell them to come to see her. She's sensational."

"I sure will, Mr. Ziegfeld, sir, thank you." He bowed to Verity and shook her hand. "Nice to meet you, lovely lady."

"Y'see," Ziegfeld said, waving his arm expansively around the room, "all these guys have noticed you already. That's Tim Wells from *Variety* in the booth by the window, and I'll bet you ten bucks he'll be here next, even though he is lunching with Sally Vine— she's a Shubert showgirl. Not in the same league as you," he added disparagingly. "You will be a star before you even leave this room, Verity. Your name will be in all the papers tomorrow."

She sat quietly, taking in the scene, wondering if it was Madame Elise's fabulous cream suit that had suddenly endowed her with this magical beauty they were all talking about: There was no doubt she felt *lovely* wearing it. Whatever it was, she could feel curious eyes on her as she sipped a glass of orange juice. This was what it would be like onstage, she thought, blushing modestly, only worse. Except maybe it didn't feel so personal when you couldn't see the people looking at you out there in the darkened auditorium.

She sighed with pleasure as the waiter served the chicken in a creamy asparagus sauce. Ziegfeld had ordered it for her; and it looked delicious.

"Take it away, away . . . at once," Madame Elise commanded, waving her arms about agitatedly. "The girl has to think of her figure," she snapped at Ziegfeld. Turning to the waiter, she ordered him to bring a fresh green salad and a single noisette of veal, no sauce.

"Oh, but . . ." Verity protested, disappointed, as the chicken disappeared. Surely after starving because she was poor, they didn't expect her to starve now she was rich! "Can't I at least save it for Azaylee?" she asked, blushing again. Now she had done it, now she would have to tell them who Azaylee was.

"Azaylee?" Ziegfeld looked interested. "That your roommate? If she's as beautiful as you, send her around, we might find a job for her too."

"Azaylee is my . . . my little sister," she said quickly. "I've looked after her since our parents died. And she is beautiful—but she's only five years old."

They laughed and she laughed too, relieved. Azaylee had skipped from being her daughter to her sister in a single breath and suddenly all her problems were resolved. She was no longer the suspect "young widow" but a responsible elder sister. The relief at no longer having to play the young widow role was immense, and she ate her salad cheerfully, careful not to order dessert under Elise's watchful eye. But as they left, a discreet parcel was handed to her by the waiter. Ziegfeld said gruffly, "Tell Azaylee 'enjoy.' "

"In gossamer," Elise lectured her afterward, "there can be no extra pounds, not even ounces. I know some of those showgirls are famous for their curves, but they *wobble,* my dear, and the new *Vie Naturelle* will not permit wobbles.

"Tomorrow we will begin to design your new wardrobe." She waved her arms in her usual flamboyant gesture as the purple limousine took them back to Park Avenue. "We shall equip you from head to toe. Now we must discuss where you shall live, because of course you will need a new apartment, and I think I know exactly the place."

"But, Madame," she protested, "I can't move into a new apartment, I have no money. I mean, I have only what I earn with you."

"You forget," Elise said, "I no longer pay you. Ziegfeld does—two hundred dollars. And I know of a nice little apartment on Forty-third Street, close enough to the theater to be convenient and far enough away for discretion." She smiled, patting Verity's hand. "You didn't tell me about your little sister," she said reprovingly. "I thought you lived all alone in one room on the Lower East Side. But now you are going to be a star, you must move uptown. I will speak to Ziegfeld and he will advance you the money. *Mais non,* I insist, we will go right now and *regard* this apartment."

It was on the fourth floor, the same as Missie's room on Rivington Street, but that was where the resemblance ended. She flew around the big, gracious apartment, gasping with delight. "Just look at this sitting room," she exclaimed. "It's so full of light, and such beautiful furniture, big sofas, glass tables, soft carpets, even oil paintings on the walls! And the dining room has a *marble* floor . . . and two bedrooms, built-in closets, a *real* bathroom . . . and oh, a proper kitchen. . . ."

"Not too much cooking," Madame warned, smiling. The poor child had obviously been deprived; even a modest apartment like this was probably the finest she had ever seen.

Missie clasped her hands to her chest excitedly. "I must have it," she exclaimed, "I *must.* It's just *perfect.*" She paused, remembering she must also be practical, and asked anxiously, "But what does it cost?"

"Eighty-five dollars a week," Madame said, and Missie's face fell. "But perhaps, for you, we can get a reduction, maybe to seventy-five."

"Seventy-five?" It was still a great deal of money and she stared around again doubtfully. Poverty had become a habit. Only a few weeks ago she had been penniless; now she was discussing apartments that cost seventy-five dollars a week! But it *was* lovely and it *would* make all the difference to their lives, she just knew it would. There was sure to be a good school right around here for Azaylee, and she could get a maid who would look after her nights when she was at the theater. Taking a deep breath, she looked at Madame Elise, who was waiting for her answer, and said firmly, "I'll take it."

Madame nodded briskly. "You have made a courageous decision," she said, "and at last you have affirmed your belief in yourself. If Florenz Ziegfeld says you will be a star, you will be a star. *Eh bien,* I will have my lawyers take care of this, and now, back to the salon."

Later that afternoon a large wicker hamper was delivered, addressed to Verity. Inside were mounds of perfect fruits, each resting in its own bed of tissue: pears, apples, oranges, out-of-season figs and strawberries—and there was a roast turkey, lobster, fresh asparagus, and an enormous box of chocolates. Astonished, she tore open the envelope and read the note that came with it. "For Azaylee," it said, "so she should enjoy. Love, Uncle Flo." And wrapped carefully in tissue paper was a bottle of champagne. This time the note said, "Verity, for you—from my own private cellar, for your private celebration. Florenz Ziegfeld."

It was too much, Missie thought, bursting into tears, staring down at the note. Suddenly the world seemed filled with good people: people who took you to their hearts and showered you with kindness and thoughtful gifts. The terrible memories of Russia were pushed further into the background and the constant fear faded just a little as she read his note again. She no longer felt alone. If this was the world of show business, then she already knew she adored it.

Feeling like Cinderella, she changed from her smart cream suit into her old skirt and blouse and then Madame's chauffeur drove her and the hamper back to Rivington Street. She was too ashamed to allow him to carry it up the malodorous stairs, and, instead, she called to Rosa to come to help her.

"There is to be a party tonight," she told Rosa and the children as they peered excitedly at the closed hamper, dying for a look at its contents, "and you all are invited. And Meyer too," she added, glancing at Rosa, "if he wants."

"Meyer's at the union tonight." She shrugged. "It's better."

Missie beamed and said, "Be here at seven, Rosa, and bring plates and glasses. This is a celebration!"

Grabbing Azaylee's hand, she said, "Come on, baby, let's go invite Zev to our party."

They ran hand in hand through the streets as if they were both children, tumbling, laughing through the pawnshop's shabby door.

Zev glanced up from his accounts in surprise.

"Hello, Mr. Abramski," Azaylee said, still giggling, "We've come to invite you to our party."

He glanced quickly at Missie and she nodded, beaming.

"It's a celebration," she said. "Seven o'clock at my apartment."

"What are we celebrating, *matiushka*?" Azaylee demanded, tugging at her skirt.

"I'll tell you later," she promised. She remembered suddenly that she had not seen Zev to apologize and she said contritely, "I'm sorry, Zev, about Sunday. I just hated to miss our date but I was kept late at the fashion parade out on Long Island and I couldn't get back in time. I meant to come around tonight to apologize. But now it's a celebration instead."

She beamed at him and he stared back at her with black inscrutable eyes. He said stiffly, "You are under no obligation to see me. I understand if you are too busy."

"Oh, *Zev!*" She slid her hand into the little groove under the brass cage where the money was passed back and forth, touching his. "You *know* how much I was looking forward to seeing you. Please? Say you forgive me? And *please,* will you come to my celebration party?"

She cocked her head to one side, gazing at him beseechingly, and he felt himself weakening. He had sat at their special table as first the minutes passed and then the hours, aware of the waiter's sympathetic glances, and when by eleven o'clock she still hadn't come he had thought it was all over, that the romance that never was had disappeared forever. And now there she was again, charming him with her smile, softening him with her eyes, and he was happy again.

"I accept," he said, nodding.

Missie breathed a sigh of relief. "Then it's all set," she cried, grabbing Azaylee and whizzing to the door as Viktor barked excitedly. "See you at seven," she called, slamming the door behind her.

Zev closed early that night. He dressed meticulously in a clean white shirt and his best black jacket, smoothing his thick dark hair and fixing his blue tie just so. At five minutes to seven he locked his door and set off for Rivington Street. He had never been to a party in his life before, or to a "celebration."

Rosa Perelman opened the door, inspecting him up and down and shaking his hand pleasantly. "Come in, Mr. Abramski, we are all here," she said, smiling, "though Missie has enough food for fifty."

He stared in amazement at the table laden with good things, the colorful sweet-smelling fruits, the enormous pink-and-white lobsters, the turkey, the chocolates, and the bottle of champagne, and then he looked at Missie, puzzled.

"Quickly, Zev," she called, "open the champagne, we must drink a toast."

"I want some turkey," Azaylee demanded imperiously.

"I want never gets," Rosa said automatically. "I *would like* some turkey."

"So would I," Azaylee said, puzzled.

Missie sighed. "This child used to have good manners," she said, "and maybe she will again soon."

Zev pulled the cork clumsily and the children shrieked with delight as the wine fizzed onto the floor.

"Quick," Rosa cried, "the glasses."

They filled the tea glasses, allowing each child a little, then they held them solemnly in the air, looking expectantly at Missie.

She glanced around her audience, enjoying the moment. "All right," she said, "prepare yourselves for a big surprise. Two big surprises . . . no, *three.* Our first toast is to Mr. Florenz Ziegfeld, who so kindly provided this delicious hamper and this wonderful champagne."

"Ziegfeld!" Rosa exclaimed. *"The* Ziegfeld? *He* sent you this?"

"He sent Azaylee this," she corrected. "Here is his note, see for yourself."

They crowded around to look and Rosa said reverently to Azaylee, "You must keep this note for always because it's from a very famous man and it's written to you, 'to Azaylee.' "

"But what does he say?" she demanded, peering at it.

Missie laughed. "It says 'Enjoy,' and that's what we are going to do. Later I shall tell you the story."

She sat contentedly at the table, her hands in her lap, unable to eat she was so happy.

"Just look at those children," Rosa marveled, "eating lobster as if they were born to it, and enough meat to make up for all these years of doing without." She tasted the champagne and said wistfully, "I had champagne once before, when my uncle came over from Latvia. He brought it with him to celebrate his new life." She sighed and added, "He was knocked down by a brewer's cart a week later, and he never did get to enjoy his new life."

"The turkey is delicious," Zev said politely, refusing the lobster Missie offered him.

"Lobster is *traife*—not kosher," Rosa explained, "except for me, it doesn't matter. I have a more reformed outlook."

"Then more asparagus," Missie cried, "more champagne!"

"Only don't keep us in suspense," Zev said boldly. "We are longing to hear your surprise."

"Yes, yes, what's the surprise?" the children chimed in.

Missie held her glass aloft and said, "I want you to drink to Mr. Florenz Ziegfeld's new showgirl, Verity Byron." They looked at her, puzzled. "That's me," she added.

Their faces were so astonished that she burst out laughing. "Can you *believe* it? I am to be Ziegfeld's new star. *And* I am to earn two hundred dollars a week, 'regular as clockwork'—that's what he said; and 'working or not'—that's what Madame Elise said. She is to design my wardrobe—both on stage and off, though I expect to be so busy there won't be much free time."

They stared at her, shocked into silence. "Well?" she demanded. "Are you not pleased?"

"It's wonderful," Rosa exclaimed, "only tell me I am dreaming and tomorrow I will wake up and find a pumpkin in this room and a glass slipper on the stair!"

"You know what? I really think it was my little ribboned slippers that brought me luck." Missie turned to Zev and took his hand eagerly. "What do you think, Zev? Are you going to congratulate me?"

"Of course," he said quietly, "I can see it is a very good job, and the money is ten times a man's wage here on the Lower East Side. *Mazeltov,* Missie. I wish you well."

He downed his champagne quietly while she told them about the new apartment, and for him each delighted cry was like a knife wound. Azaylee had climbed sleepily on to Missie's lap and she was holding her close, stroking back her blond hair, telling her about her new room just as she had promised.

"*Matiushka,* what's the other surprise?" she asked sleepily.

"Why, the other surprise is that you will go to school."

"School?" Azaylee shot upright. "I want to go to school with Sonia and Rachel!"

Rosa sighed. "Why don't we talk about it later?" she suggested soothingly. "Meanwhile I have to get my children to bed."

Her little girls clung to her, sleepy with good food and chocolates and excitement. "I'll confess, I'll be sorry to see you go, even though my heart is bursting with gladness for you," Rosa said sadly. "But you have been through hard times, Missie, and you deserve such a reward."

Zev waited until they had gone and Azaylee had curled up on the bed with the dog at her feet, and then he drained his glass of champagne in a single gulp and said, "Missie, I'm not asking you to consider such a thing now, but one day maybe, if I was no longer what I am, would you . . . could you. . . ." It was no good, he just could not ask her to marry him. He said instead, "Would you consent to . . . to see me, still? I mean, when you are a star?"

She looked into his eyes sympathetically. There was something about Zev that touched her deeply: his sorrow, his loneliness, the polite, unemotional crust that she knew only too well covered wounds even deeper than her own. Stepping closer to him, she whispered, "Yes, Zev, I promise."

His arms went around her, and at last he was holding her close, close like lovers; he felt heady with love for her, he knew he wanted her. After letting her go he said roughly, "I must leave. Thank you for inviting me to your celebration, Missie. I wish you well in your new life."

His glance lingered on her as he stood by the door, and impulsively she ran to him and kissed him.

He put his hand to his lips, then he smiled and said good-bye, closing the door quietly behind him.

She listened to his footsteps on the stairs and the sound of the hall door closing, and then she ran to the window, watching as he disappeared down the street.

Zev paced his room all that night, occasionally picking up a newspaper, to read and reread the advertisement. It promised that a man could make a fortune overnight in the flourishing new movie industry in Hollywood. It said that people were flocking from back east to live the life of Riley in the land of perpetual sunshine and oranges; it said that everybody had a turquoise-blue swimming pool of his own and all the girls were beautiful. And that a man of integrity with a small sum to invest could become part of that scene simply by calling this number.

He stared down at the words that promised him everything. He knew that if he were ever to win Missie O'Bryan, he would have to become a different man, a man of substance, a man in charge of his own destiny. And this was surely the way to do it.

The next morning, instead of opening his shop as usual he turned the sign to "Closed" and went around to the offices of the *Ghetto News,* where he placed an ad of his own. "Business for sale," it said. "For details apply to Mr. Abramski, Orchard Street."

27

Missie lingered on the sidewalk in front of the theater, staring at the glittering marquee with its red, white, and blue lights spelling out "The New International Ziegfeld Follies. Starring from America, Fanny Brice. From Paris, Gaby Delys, from England, the Arcos Brothers" and in smaller letters, "Featuring the gorgeous Ziegfeld girls with the beautiful Verity Byron."

She wasn't a star yet, but her name was sparkling in lights on Broadway, people were gazing at her photograph displayed out front, and in a few short hours she would be on stage. Her stomach sank at the thought. It had all seemed so easy until now.

Then she thought of the money and cheered up. For two hundred a week she would smile the brightest of any girl, she would pose in her filmy chiffon robes and not mind that the men were staring at her legs and her bosom, artfully half revealed in Elise's draperies.

And anyway, the past two months had been the most carefree she had known since they had fled from Russia almost three years before. Everyone treated her like a precious object, and for publicity purposes she was also expected to be seen in smart restaurants with Mr. Ziegfeld and his friends; she had already had one proposal of marriage from a middle-aged titled Englishman fascinated by her newly created other-worldly good looks.

"You are a creature from a Scheherazade tale," he had whispered to her when she permitted him to escort her home after supper at Imogen Wensleyshire's Manhattan penthouse, but she had laughed and told him that her father was a professor and Oxford was a long way from Arabia, and that had soon dampened his ardor.

The move into the new apartment had been easy; there was nothing much to move, just herself and Azaylee, the dog and the two old suitcases, one with their few possessions and the other with the jewels. Azaylee's tears had turned to cries of delight when she had seen her new room with the big bed under its pretty pink-and-white quilt and her closet full of the pretty new clothes Missie had bought for her, and the parcels of new toys she had ransacked the stores for, squandering money lavishly and feeling like a princess herself as she told them happily, "Deliver them all, please."

Even Viktor had a new collar with a silver bell and a proper red leather leash as well as a silver bowl with his name inscribed on it, and she had filled it with prime steak and tasty dog biscuits that he had devoured in two gulps.

She had felt very proud that first night when she had walked around her new home; she had peered into her larder stocked with good things and laughed out loud to think she would never have to worry about going hungry again; she had looked at Azaylee, sleeping contentedly, and thanked God she had finally given her a proper home; and she had taken a long, luxurious bath in the beautiful white porcelain tub. Then she had put on a silk nightdress, courtesy of Madame and paid for under Ziegfeld's contract, and inspected her new clothes. Dresses, coats, suits, hats: everything suitable for a lady to wear on any occasion. And she had fallen asleep that night with a smile on her face instead of the usual worried frown. She felt like a carefree young girl again, freed from her burdens, and this time she meant to enjoy herself as she never had in her life before.

The next morning, Beulah Bradford had arrived and taken charge of them all. Beulah was a blessing in the guise of a middle-aged widowed lady who had already brought up six children of her own and had ten grandchildren living in Georgia. She wore a clean starched white overall and enormous white lace-up shoes and she moved about the small apartment like a battleship at full speed.

"Ah'm used to doin' for my own children," she told Missie. "Ah've been working for show-business ladies for more'n twenty years now. Ah knows all their ways, and the funny hours they keep, and no stories never get into the papers from mah mouth. Ah'm the soul of discretion, Miss Verity, and ah'm real thrilled to be lookin' after little Azaylee here. Takes me back to when my own were that age," she had added with a reminiscent sigh, "before they grew big and obstreperous."

Within a week Beulah was part of the family and had taken Rosa's place as "aunt in residence." She cooked Azaylee's meals and made sure she ate them, she bathed her, she washed and ironed her little dresses; she braided her hair and took her and Viktor for long walks in the park every afternoon where they met other children. Azaylee loved her and had a great time.

There were just two problems in Missie's life right now. One was that there simply had not been a free few hours to see Rosa, and the other was that money seemed to slip through her fingers like water.

Ziegfeld had given her a month's salary in advance so she could pay the deposit and the rent on her new apartment; she had paid back Zev and paid Glanz's for her coat; she had given Rosa back her five dollars and tucked another twenty into her pocket when she wasn't looking. And remembering working for poverty wages herself, she had insisted on paying Beulah a hundred dollars a month plus her uniforms and room and board, and even at that price she considered her a bargain. "When my salary goes up, so does yours, Beulah," she had told her frankly, "and that's a promise."

Of course there was enough money to live on, but it puzzled her that somehow the two hundred dollars didn't look like the fortune it had a few weeks ago. Especially when she had found out the fees demanded by New York's smart schools, not that they were exactly keen on having her custom. The genteelly snobbish spinster ladies who ran them had dropped Astors and Vanderbilts, Biddles and Bradleys, into the conversation like social confetti, looking askance at her when she explained that she was appearing in Ziegfeld's new Follies and looking skeptical when she introduced Azaylee as her little sister. If only you knew who this child really is, she had thought furiously, you would be swooning to have her!

Only one school, Beadles, had agreed to accept her, and Missie knew it was the best of all. The two Miss Beadles who ran it were down-to-earth smiling women from Boston, and their own background was socially impeccable enough not to have to boast of their pupils. On the contrary, all their girls wore the same smart little gray coats and skirts with wide-brimmed felt hats in winter and straw hats in summer and everyone was treated equally. The only trouble was the exorbitant fees, five hundred a term, payable in advance. She just did not have the money. She could not ask Mr. Ziegfeld for another advance, and anyway the thought of getting into debt again terrified her. She had vowed never again in all her life to owe anyone money and she intended to keep that vow.

She had hurried home and pulled the old valise from under her bed, taking out the contents and looking at them one by one, remembering Sofia prising the diamonds from the tiara with a hatpin and then selling them on the streets of Constantinople. The three huge remaining diamonds glittered under the light and the fourth that Zev had given back to her when she had repaid her debt was still wrapped in a scrap of velvet. She knew he was right. No one would believe they were honestly hers if she tried to sell them.

She looked at Misha's dear face, remembering every line, every glance from his gray eyes, every light touch of his hand, wondering why, when she was awake, he seemed like a dream. Only in her dreams did he seem real. The five-plumed diamond brooch lay on the bottom of the valise. She traced it again with her finger, remembering the night he had given it to her. It was her most precious possession. She stared at it for a long time, thinking of what to do. In the end she knew she had no choice. The brooch was an insignificant piece of jewelry compared with the valuable diamonds; she could easily make up a story that it was a gift sent to her by an unknown admirer. It was common knowledge that showgirls were often given expensive jewelry, and she had seen them showing off their diamond trophies collected from admirers, known and unknown. And anyhow, so much time had passed since the revolution and the Ivanoff murders. Surely no one would be interested now?

She debated the risk all that night, recalling that Cartier was lending Ziegfeld the diamonds she was to wear on stage. Then early the next morning before she could change her mind, she dressed carefully in Elise's cream suit, making up her face and choosing a flamboyantly feathered hat that looked sufficiently "showgirl." And then she called a taxi and told the cab driver to take her to Fifth Avenue.

She browsed nonchalantly along the velvet-lined glass cases in Cartier's hallowed gray halls, stopping to admire a diamond bauble here, a rope of pearls there as if she had not a care in the world other than choosing something delicious with which to adorn herself.

"Madame?" A pin-striped tail-coated gentleman smiled at her inquiringly. "Can I be of help?"

She smiled at him disarmingly. "I am Verity Byron. Mr. Ziegfeld informed me that you would be sending over some diamonds for me to wear in his next show. I wondered if I might see them first." She added doubtfully, "Perhaps I should have brought Madame Elise along to help? But no, I think with your good taste they are probably perfect. I would just like to add my approval before the final decisions are taken."

"But of course, Miss Byron, and it's a great pleasure to meet you." She adjusted her hat lower over her eyes, bestowing yet another sparkling smile on him, and he gazed at her admiringly. "May I say that you are every bit as lovely as your photographs," he said reverently, "and that Cartier are honored to be of service."

She sat on a little Louis Quinze chair, nervously drumming her cream-gloved fingers on the glass counter as he retreated to the safe in the back, emerging a few minutes later bearing half a dozen suede boxes.

He lined them up on the counter in front of her, opening them with a flourish and showing her the diamond necklaces and bracelets and enormous drop earrings that she knew Anouska would have adored.

"Please try them on," he urged. "If the necklace does not sit properly, just above the collarbone, then we can adjust it. And Madame has such slender wrists, I think the bracelets too must be altered. And how does Madame like this new design? The very latest snake bracelets from our Paris workshops?"

"Magnificent," she said, admiring herself in the mirror. "It makes my own little commission seem . . . well, trifling."

"And what is that, Madame?" he asked, eager to please.

She hesitated a second and then said, "I have a little souvenir, a present from an unknown admirer. . . ." She shrugged. "You know the way things are in the theater. It's a little garish for my taste, and besides, it means nothing to me. I would prefer to dispose of it, and as I understand it was bought from Cartier, I have brought it back to you."

"I understand, Madame, of course. May I see?"

She slid the brooch, wrapped in a silk handkerchief, across the counter to him, and he drew in his breath as he looked at it. "I see, Madame," he murmured. "Yes, a very *unusual* piece. I could quite understand that you would not want to wear it."

She watched nervously as he examined it minutely under his jeweler's loupe for what seemed a long time. Then he said, "This pin dates from the turn of the century and was made in our Paris workshops for a famous family." His eyes assessed her for a moment and he said smoothly, "It's a pity you don't know the name of the gentleman who gave it to you. It is always better with jewels like this to know the provenance. It facilitates the resale, you see."

"I'm sorry." She shrugged. "I simply have no idea. It was not important to me."

"Of course not, Madame, of course not. Well, I am pleased to tell you that with the quality of the gemstones and the Cartier workmanship this is now a collector's piece. We can offer you one thousand dollars for it."

Missie closed her eyes. A thousand dollars. She had hoped at the most for five hundred, enough for one semester's school fees.

"I'll take it," she said, opening her eyes and smiling.

The transaction was completed in a few minutes. After tucking the ten hundred-dollar bills into her purse, she smiled gratefully at him and floated out of the shop as if she were walking on air.

He watched speculatively as the door closed behind her, then he took the Ivanoff brooch and looked at it again. After going into his office, he placed an overseas telephone call. When it finally came through later that day, his conversation was brief.

"You asked us to let you know immediately, sir, should any of the Ivanoff jewels be offered to us for sale," he said. "As a collector, I think you will be very excited with this piece. Yes, sir, it is quite rare. It's a brooch in the form of the Ivanoff family crest: diamonds, rubies, and sapphires, set in platinum with a gold wolf's head. You would like it? Very good, sir." He listened for a while and then replied, "Yes, I remember you wanted to know, sir. It was a young lady who brought it in. A showgirl in Ziegfeld's new Follies, by the name of Verity Byron." He smiled, listening, and then he said, "In that case, I will hold it here for you, sir, until you arrive. Thank you, Baron Arnhaldt."

It was opening night and she was wearing Cartier's diamond necklace and snake bracelets with a dress of filmy silver gauze, flesh-colored silk tights, and her signature silver shoes, only this time with impossibly high heels. She had rehearsed in them a hundred times and practiced by herself a thousand times, and they still made her ankles wobble and still made her nervous.

Ziegfeld had said, "With all this publicity they'll be flocking to see you out of sheer curiosity. Almost as much as for Fanny and Gaby, although to tell the truth, Gaby's not so popular as she was. Pity, she's a lovely girl. The trick is to make them wait for you. That way their curiosity will be even greater. So we've featured you in the opening scene of the second half and again in the finale. That's all. I'm going to ration your appearances until they demand more!"

Unlike Elise's mannequins, the showgirls were friendly as well as beautiful; they knew she was frightened and they crowded around her encouragingly as she sat, drooping nervously at her dressing table. "Just stand where you're supposed to, walk when you're supposed to, and smile whenever you feel like it," they advised her. "There's nothing to it. You've already done it a hundred times."

The big dressing room she shared was full of flowers. There were bouquets for every girl, and the most popular ones had so many they had overflowed into the corridors. And she had flowers too, a huge bouquet of Madonna lilies from Mr. Ziegfeld with a note wishing her success; a spray of lilac-tinted blossoms from Madame Elise, telling her to remember she was *ravissante* and to stand *tall;* a posy of pink roses wrapped in silver paper with love from Azaylee, and a big bunch of spring flowers from Beulah, with affectionate good wishes.

"What more could any girl ask for?" she wondered, smiling. But deep inside she was scared, and she wished she had told O'Hara so that he could be here to protect her, because it was really tougher doing this all alone than she had ever imagined. She had sent Rosa and Zev tickets, but she was worried they might not come after all. Then just before showtime another bouquet was delivered. Two dozen deep-red, long-stemmed roses, with a card that said, *"Mazeltov* and success, with love, Zev." She clutched the roses to her, smiling. He hadn't forgotten her after all.

Even though the wind was blowing the rain sideways and the sidewalks were a minefield of puddles deep enough to come over the top of her shoes, Forty-second Street and Broadway were jammed with limousines and crowds of people gawping at the celebrities arriving for Ziegfeld's opening night. Rosa jumped the puddles expertly, pushing back the wet strands of hair and hanging on to her hat as she elbowed her way through. The ticket touts were doing a roaring trade on the corner, with seats in the stalls changing hands at fifty dollars each. She watched for a while, noting carefully who was giving the best deals, and then she approached one and offered him her expensive ticket. She drove a hard bargain as she did every day at the butcher's or the fishmonger's. After triumphantly pocketing fifty dollars as well as a ticket for a seat in the cheapest, uppermost corner of the balcony, she headed into the theater.

Her seat was to one side of the steep balcony, but at least it was near the front and she smiled complacently, glancing at the people around her. They were like she was, wet and poorly dressed, staring down at the glamorous audience in the stalls and dress circle, eager to share the luxury and fantasy that only Ziegfeld's sumptuous extravaganzas could provide. But unlike her, they did not know the new star of this show. *She* was here to see Missie, and she was keeping her fingers crossed for her.

The lights dimmed and the orchestra finished the overture and began to play the opening notes of Jerome Kern's new song as the curtain rose slowly on a sumptuous Arabian Nights scene. The audience gasped. Everything glittered in bronze and copper and gold, the dancers wore gold-spangled harem trousers and gold-jeweled boleros, the caliph sat on a jeweled bronze throne in his stiff gold-embroidered caftan, and the slaves were like gilded statues, their heads topped with sprays of shimmering osprey feathers. Oriental silk carpets and layers of shaded draperies lent mystery to the scene, and across the footlights stole the scent of sandalwood and myrrh and exotic eastern spices.

Rosa caught her breath along with the rest; she had never seen anything like this, never imagined a place filled with such sumptuousness. She was entranced by a fantasy world created by Mr. Ziegfeld's genius, and for a few short hours she was Mr. Ziegfeld's devoted slave. He promised her escape from the drabness of reality and gave her the stuff of dreams to remember. Ziegfeld knew what people wanted and he gave it to them—only more so and better, *and* he made a fortune doing it.

Rosa laughed loudly at Fanny Brice and cheered the Arcos Dancers and in the interval she sat quietly in her chair, studying the program. Missie's name was featured in the next scene, only of course now it was "Verity." She bought a box of chocolates from a passing vendor, stowing them carefully in her coat pocket to give to the children later. Then, clutching her hands together anxiously, she waited for the curtain to rise, praying "Verity" would be all right. After all, she thought worriedly, she's little more than a child herself. She crossed her fingers again, hoping that Missie had done the right thing.

At last the lights dimmed and the orchestra began to play a soft undulating melody, rhythmic and slow yet compelling. The audience leaned forward expectantly as a second blue gauze curtain rose on an underwater scene. Dancers in chiffon tunics in shades of turquoise through deep blue performed an elaborate ballet around a huge silver scallop shell in the center of the stage, while showgirls wearing sequined mermaid tails and fantastic headdresses made from sparkling shells swung to and fro in boat-shaped swings suspended from the ceiling. As the music rose to a crescendo the silver shell slowly opened to reveal a huge creamy pearl. Another crescendo and the pearl split in two and there was Missie in wisps of silver gauze with legs that seemed to go on forever, her arms open wide, her head thrown back, her hair falling in a shining cascade to her waist.

"Oohs" and "aahs" of admiration swept through the theater. A silvery light beamed down on her from a diamond moon half hidden behind the layers of blue gauze overhead, and she tilted her lovely long throat and held up her arms to it in supplication. A bevy of young men in blue tights and silver jerkins crowded around her, holding out their hands, and she strode forward, floating gracefully across the stage to a huge silver ramp descending slowly from above. As she stepped onto it she turned again to face her audience, flinging her arms wide, her violet eyes sparkling as she smiled, and then she was wafted up the ramp with her escort of young men to the moon in heaven above. Ravel's "Bolero" crashed to a climax as the curtain came down amid thunderous applause.

Rosa wiped a tear from her eyes. It was ridiculous, it was silly, but she had loved it and so had everyone else. All around her people were saying it was one of Ziegfeld's most spectacular scenes yet and that Verity Byron was a beauty, tall as an evergreen tree and fragile as the moonbeam she had represented. She was ethereal, subtle, had fabulous eyes, incredible legs . . . Rosa could hardly keep herself from crying out "But I know her! She's my friend! That's Missie out there on stage!" She couldn't wait until it was over and she could go backstage and see her.

The finale had Verity walking elegantly across the stage in a puffed violet silk crinoline as Marie Antoinette, carrying a huge ostrich-feather fan with a tiny chihuahua dog tucked under her arm, and the applause that greeted her was tremendous. As the final curtain fell, Rosa ran all the way down from the balcony to the street without stopping once, darting breathlessly along the alley behind the theater to the stage door. She wasn't the first; a line of smart men in dinner clothes, white silk scarves, and silk hats were already waiting, and the doorman was being kept busy passing their little notes to the girls, as well as several of what looked to Rosa like jewelry boxes.

"Hey, Mr. Doorman," she called, edging her way to the front, "tell Miss Verity Byron that her friend Rosa is here."

He threw her an indifferent glance and went on collecting up the little notes, sorting them out carefully and pocketing the ten-dollar bills that somehow slid from the young men's hands into his.

"Hey," she called again angrily, "you with the deaf ears, I asked you to tell Verity that her friend is here. Rosa's the name, Rosa Perelman."

This time he didn't even glance her way. She stuck her hands belligerently on her hips ready to call him a few names, but the smart young men were staring curiously at her and she didn't want to cause a scene and embarrass Missie. She would just have to wait here until she came out. Unless? After waiting until the doorman was heavily involved in his next transaction, she slid silently behind him through the stage door, running along the drab corridor before he could stop her.

"Hey," she called to a passing dancer, "which way to Verity Byron?"

"Upstairs, third on your right," she replied, continuing on her way.

The door was covered in little silver stars and said "The Ziegfeld Girls," and when she opened it there they all were, all twelve of them, laughing and talking at once, and all of them dressed to the nines in silk gowns looking ready for a party. Missie was in the very center, being hugged and kissed as they congratulated her, exclaiming over the shower of notes on her dressing table and the bouquets of flowers that were constantly being carried in.

Rosa thought she had never seen her look so lovely. She was wearing a beautiful red taffeta dress with the diamond snake bracelets around her upper arms and her lovely hair was swept up at the sides with diamond clips. But it wasn't the dress and the diamonds, she thought, awed. Missie didn't need them tonight. The poor, pretty girl from Rivington Street had acquired the beauty and sparkle of "a star."

"Rosa!" The other girls turned to stare curiously as Missie flung herself at the bedraggled figure standing by the door. "Oh, Rosa, I'm so glad you came. I got you a good seat so that you wouldn't miss anything. Tell me, what did you think?"

Her eyes searched Rosa's anxiously for approval and Rosa grinned. "Mr. Ziegfeld kept his promise," she said. "He made Missie O'Bryan into Verity Byron, the star. You were wonderful, Missie, just beautiful."

Missie laughed, then her face fell suddenly, "The only thing is,

Rosa," she said uncomfortably, "I don't actually *do* anything—like dance or sing or make jokes. All I do is stand there to be looked at."

"For two hundred a week—is enough," Rosa said firmly. "If Ziegfeld wants you to dance and sing, he pays a thousand."

"I suppose you're right," Missie said, laughing.

"The ticket I changed for fifty dollars also," Rosa said. "I couldn't sit next to the swells in the stalls dressed like this, could I?"

"Ohhh." Missie hugged her contritely. "Of course, I should have thought of it."

"No reason you should," Rosa replied softly. "You should forget all about being poor as soon as possible. Poverty does not make good memories."

"But there's *you,* Rosa," Missie retorted, "I will never forget you. You are still my best friend. And Zev." She looked at her, puzzled. "But, where is Zev?"

"You don't know?" she asked, astonished. "By the butcher, by the baker, by the carts, everyone is talking about it. How Zev Abramski sold up his pawnbroker shop and left for Hollywood. To make his fortune in the movie business. That's what they said."

Missie glanced at the flowers on her dressing table, "You mean he has gone?" she asked, shocked. "Without saying anything? Without at least telling me?" She felt let down, sad . . . like O'Hara, Zev had always been there, he had become part of her life, her friend . . . and now this.

"Believe me," Rosa whispered, patting her arm reassuringly, "is for the best. A young man like Abramski is not for you. And he knew it too. He left no forwarding address. It's better what he's done. Forget him, Missie, and live your own life. Like Ziegfeld said, 'Enjoy.' "

"It's time to leave for the party," the girls called.

Missie looked sadly at Rosa and said, "I have to go. Ziegfeld is throwing an opening night party at Rector's. Will you come and see me soon, Rosa? Bring the children?"

She clutched her arm, looking suddenly pathetically young despite the new veneer of sophistication, and Rosa replied, "I'll come when you need me. Don't worry, Missie, I'm still your friend." And with a wave and a smile, she disappeared down the corridor, sniffing at the irate doorman as she scampered past.

=== 28 ===

Eddie Arnhaldt sat in the aisle seat in the fourth row of the stalls in the New Amsterdam Theater, feeling vaguely irritated by Fanny Brice's comedy routine and wishing that Gaby Delys had been on longer. But what he was really waiting for was Verity Byron. In the interval he took a stroll round the foyer, smoking a special hand-made Turkish cigarette and inspecting the ladies, though he thought they compared unfavorably with German women: too slight, too breastless, too brittle. Not one of them in this foyer could compare with his mother when she was a young woman and even now that she was older, she was still stately and handsome. *And strong.* Eddie knew what he liked in women. He was the same as all the Arnhaldts; he liked them tall, full-breasted, and strong enough sexually to satisfy his appetite. And in Europe he had gained quite a reputation as a ladies' man.

As the second act bell rang, he crushed out his cigarette and strolled back to his seat, waiting impatiently for Verity's entrance. When the silver seashell finally opened he took out his opera glasses, studying her intently. She bore no resemblance to the Ivanoffs and neither was she his ideal, but if he was forced to sacrifice himself on the family altar, he was prepared to do so. And somehow, he did not think the task of seducing the delicious Verity Byron was going to be unpleasant.

When the final curtain fell he strolled around the corner to the stage door, arrogantly surveying the crowd of young men already waiting for the girls. He knew that this was not for him. His would be a more subtle approach.

His Mercedes-Benz limousine was waiting at the curb to drive him down Broadway to a florist, where he placed his order and then he told the driver to take him back to his hotel. A word in the bellboy's ear and a hundred-dollar bill in his hand guaranteed him a top-class beauty in the style he liked, and room service guaranteed him a supper of caviar and roast beef cooked "blue," as the French called it. Eddie preferred his steak almost raw and his women wild, and tonight he would have both.

Missie had been promoted to a dressing room of her own. Every night it was filled with flowers and notes from young men she had never met begging her to have supper with them, to lunch with them, to go to a party with them. Often a gift was enclosed—a pretty diamond ring, a slender jeweled bracelet, a sapphire and diamond pin in the shape of a lucky horseshoe. She always kept the flowers and always sent back the gifts, and she never dined with any man she had not been introduced to.

She had made her rules firmly; she was a Ziegfeld showgirl to earn her living, not as a piece of property to be bought for a trifling diamond bauble. The other girls laughed at her and told her she was crazy, that it was all part of the game, but she still could not do it. Besides, she was afraid. And she was too busy. She was taking singing lessons now as well as dancing and voice projection. Ziegfeld planned to expand her role in the next Follies: She was to sing a little song specially written for her by Jerome Kern and do a little dance with the chorus boys to help her, and if she was good enough she could play a speaking role in a little skit.

She smiled happily, pushing aside the night's trophies as she creamed off her makeup. Everything was going so well. Azaylee was happy at school, though sometimes the teachers complained of inattentiveness.

"It's just that she's dreamy," Missie had explained quickly. "Sometimes she gets lost in herself and quite forgets where she is." But the one time Azaylee never dreamed was in the dance classes. "Mime and Movement," it was called at Beadles, and the children would flutter about barefoot in skimpy chiffon tunics, plump little legs and skinny ones thundering across the floor, pointing their toes and swirling as Miss Beadle herself thumped out a tune on the Bosendorfer upright. But it was Azaylee who amazed them all; when the music began she seemed to quiver with excitement until it was her turn to flit across the wooden floor, arms arched over her head and her thin legs extended in a graceful leap. Azaylee in motion was a poem of grace, and even Miss Beadle said she should take ballet lessons.

So now twice a week after school six-year-old Azaylee took classes from an out-of-work Broadway dancer in a cold rented studio on Forty-second Street. Dora Devine put her through her paces at the barre in her little pink ballet slippers for one hour, and in little silver tap shoes she counted and tapped her way through a second hour. Then she returned home, flushed with success, to practice on the marble dining-room floor, driving them crazy with her endless tapping.

Missie looked up as her dresser came in. "Another note, Miss Verity," she said. "And a flower. This guy must be poor all right. Just one flower ain't gonna get him nowhere."

Verity took it from her. A single perfect creamy rose and a card that said "The Baron Edmund Arnhaldt." Nothing else, just the card with his name and the rose. Smiling, she put the rose in the big crystal vase along with the dozens of others and thought nothing more about it.

The following night he sent his card again, and another rose—this time fashioned in silver. It was charming and unusual and for once she kept it, putting it into a slender silver bud vase on her dressing table. The next night there was a gold rose, obviously antique and valuable, and she gasped with amazement. And the next, there was a rose of pale pinkish diamonds that sparkled as brightly as her smiling eyes. And this time the card said "Would you please have supper with me tonight? I am your devoted slave."

Missie hesitated. For once she was tempted. Then she decided she couldn't possibly do it. It was against all her rules. Besides, she had no idea who he was, or even what he looked like. He might be ninety years old and speak only German for all she knew. She went next door and asked Genny, one of the showgirls.

"Arnhaldt!" Genny exclaimed. "*Eddie* Arnhaldt. My dear, you've hit the jackpot. Arnhaldt is rich, rich, rich . . . he could buy every theater on Broadway if he wanted and never miss the money, he could buy every diamond in Cartier and not even flinch. He has yachts and castles and he's very handsome. All the money comes from muck and grime—steel and iron works, it's *solid* money. Verity, you're *crazy* if you don't see him—at least once. Just to test the water. I mean, after all, you can feel the man's got style. Just look at his approach!"

Missie dithered. Eddie Arnhaldt was becoming more and more intriguing, "Well," she said, "maybe just this once."

"Bravo," Genny cried, laughing. As Missie closed the door behind her she called, "Oh, by the way, I forgot to tell you. He also has a terrible reputation with women."

Her laughter followed Missie all the way back to her dressing room, but it did not change her mind. She was too fascinated by the mysterious Eddie Arnhaldt.

The long black Mercedes-Benz limousine with the tinted windows was parked in front of the theater, a uniformed chauffeur standing to attention in front of it. "Miss Byron?" he asked, whipping off his cap and opening the door for her. "The baron is waiting for you at Rector's, ma'am. He said to apologize but he has injured his leg and it is painful for him to step in and out of the limousine. He hopes you will forgive him for not being here personally, ma'am."

The chauffeur sounded like a parrot repeating his lines, and she thought, annoyed, that it seemed she was going to be kept in suspense just a little bit longer about Baron Eddie Arnhaldt.

Rector's was located between Forty-third and Forty-fourth streets, and its plush green and gold lobby was jammed with people desperate for tables. The ground-floor dining room with its ceiling-high mirrors and glittering chandeliers was crowded and from his table in the corner, Ziegfeld watched as Verity followed the maître d' up the sweeping staircase to the second floor, where there was a second dining room and also several private rooms. He was surprised to see her there alone. After summoning a waiter, he asked him to find out whom Verity Byron was dining with. When he heard who it was he wrote a quick note, asking him to deliver it to her right away.

Eddie Arnhaldt was at the window, staring down at the busy scene on Forty-third Street. As the door opened, he turned to look at her. There were compensations after all: She was beautiful, not merely pretty, though too slender for his taste. But her violet eyes were like jewels and her hair like silk and she walked like a dream. "I must ask your forgiveness again for not coming to meet you," he said, limping toward her with the aid of an ebony stick. He held out his hand to her, drawing her into the room as the waiter closed the door discreetly.

Missie glanced at him from under her lashes. Eddie Arnhaldt was handsome in a tall, arrogant-looking way, with pale-blue eyes and blond hair brushed straight back from his broad brow.

She realized suddenly that they were in a private dining room and took a surprised step back toward the door.

"But I can't have supper here, alone with you," she exclaimed, shocked.

He shook his head, smiling. "Our table is ready in the dining room next door, Miss Byron. I just thought you might prefer our initial meeting to be in private, in case you wished to change your mind." He smiled. "And in case I don't match up to your expectations. After all, you have never seen me before."

She stared at him, relieved. He really was very handsome, thin-faced and firm-lipped, lean and fit, with that confident air of a man in control of his emotions. And his life. "Oh," she said, smiling consideringly, "I think I could bear to have supper with you."

He took her arm in a courtly fashion as they walked to the door, "In that case," he said, giving her that smile again, "shall we join the other diners?"

She watched anxiously as the waiters helped him into his chair, aware of the curious glances from the other tables. "It's nothing really." He dismissed his injury. "I pulled a ligament playing polo yesterday. The damned foolish pony wanted to go one way and I wanted him to go another." He grinned. "I won, of course, but at a cost."

She stared across the table at him, fascinated. Half a dozen waiters hovered around their table anxious to fulfill his smallest command. He said, "I have taken the liberty of ordering our meal. I like to know in advance what I am eating so that the wine can be decanted. I am by way of being a wine connoisseur, and my cellar at home, at Haus Arnhaldt, has more than twelve thousand bottles, each a superlative vintage. I hope you appreciate good wine, Miss Byron, because tonight we are having some of the best."

She shook her head and he went on. "Even with Prohibition, it seems everyone is continuing drinking as normal." He shrugged contemptuously. "A ridiculous idea, of course. If a man wants to drink himself to death then he should be allowed to do so. And if he wants to savor the nectar made by man from the humble grape, then he should be allowed that pleasure."

A waiter approached and, excusing himself, said, "A note for you, Miss Verity."

She opened it, read it quickly, then looked up at Arnhaldt, surprised.

"Everything all right?" he asked a touch impatiently.

"Oh, yes, yes . . . quite all right, thank you. Just that Mr. Ziegfeld saw me come in and he wanted to say hello." She blushed. Of course it wasn't true. What his note had said was "Verity, take care." She wondered what he meant.

The baron leaned across the table and said quietly, "I must tell you, Miss Byron, that I have not stopped thinking about you since I first saw you, four nights ago on the stage of the New Amsterdam Theater. It is unlike me; I am a busy man. I am here in New York on business but I have not been able to get you out of my head." His eyes burned into hers as he added, "I cannot pretend with you. I have known many women in my life, but there has not been one that I have felt about so immediately the way I did you. You were not merely a star to that diamond moon on stage that night, Miss Byron, you were far more beautiful than the real thing."

Missie bit her lip, blushing modestly. No one had ever said things like that to her before and she did not know how to respond, but deep inside she was thrilled. She wondered if all the stage-door romeos talked this way, or if he was sincere. "Thank you, Baron," she said, fixing her eyes demurely on the damask tablecloth. "It's very kind of you to say so."

He laughed as the waiters swarmed around them bearing silver platters and said, "Not 'kind,' Miss Byron, just truthful." The waiter poured a pale wine and he sipped it, nodding approvingly. "I want you to taste this," he told her as the waiter filled her glass, "and tell me if it's not nectar from the gods."

She took a sip and her eyes rounded with pleasure; it was delicious.

As they ate he told her about himself, about how his grandfather had started the business from humble beginnings, how his father had been lost when the *Titanic* went down, and how he had been married at the age of twenty-three, only to lose his wife in a sailing accident off the coast of Dalmatia three years later. "My family seemed to be dogged by bad luck," he said finally, "but at least I have my son, Augustus—Augie. He's fourteen now, away at boarding school, and a true Arnhaldt." His ice-blue glance took her in as she stared at him, fascinated. "But tell me about yourself," he suggested, "where you are from, your family background."

"It's nothing like yours," she said, telling him quickly about Oxford and her father. He was looking at her, puzzled, and she said, "You are probably wondering how I came to be here in New York and a Ziegfeld girl. I . . . we . . . we were on holiday when my father died suddenly. I had to find a job to support myself and my little sister."

"Your sister?"

"Azaylee. She's six now, and at school at Misses Beadles'."

He nodded, "And is she as beautiful as you?"

Missie laughed. "Everyone asks that question, and the reply is always the same. No, she is not. She's far, far more beautiful. She has spun-gold hair and eyes like pansies, and she's just . . . just a dream child."

His eyes considered her as he drank his wine. "You obviously love her very much."

"Azaylee is all the family I have," she replied quietly.

"I would like to meet her," he said. "My yacht, the *Ferdinand A,* is moored here on the Hudson. Would you and Azaylee do me the honor of spending the day with me on Sunday? We can sail up the coast, have lunch. . . ." He leaned forward, gazing into her eyes, "Please say yes," he whispered.

His eyes lured her, yet she was uncertain. Despite his charm, there was something about him that intimidated her. Maybe it was his air of contempt for those beneath him—she had noticed that he never even looked at the waiters, just expected them to jump whenever he snapped his fingers. But she was probably being too hard on him. He was a man born to great wealth and not used to dealing with ordinary people. Life on his level must be like it had been for Misha—though she had never seen Misha treat a servant with anything other than courtesy. And yet he was so attractive and his eyes were begging her, caressing her almost. "I accept," she agreed breathlessly, telling herself that, after all, Azaylee would love it. Ziegfeld's note fell to the floor unnoticed as she left the table, blushing and smiling, and every head turned to watch them go.

On the way home he kept carefully to his side of the limousine, watching her as she chatted about Azaylee and about her life as a showgirl. She was exhilarated, alive, filled with a new excitement.

When the car stopped at her apartment he leaned forward and took her hand. "Till Sunday then?" he said, brushing her fingers lightly with his lips.

"Till Sunday," she promised, shivering at his touch.

The next morning when she awoke the apartment was filled with long-stemmed cream roses, and their scent was giving Beulah hay fever.

"I ain't seen so much pollen since my childhood in Georgia," she said, rubbing her reddened eyes, "but whoever he is, Miss Verity, he's surely stuck on you."

On Sunday at ten the limousine appeared to drive them to the Hudson River docks and the *Ferdinand A,* a 175-foot seagoing steam yacht with a full set of sails, polished teak decks, and gleaming brass rails. The captain and a crew of twenty were lined up to greet them, and Eddie Arnhaldt was waiting in the saloon that was filled with cream-colored roses.

Missie burst out laughing, staring around her in amazement. "But where do you find them all?" she asked. "The florists in Manhattan must have run out by now."

"They have," he replied. "These are from Washington, brought in this morning by railroad." His eyes caught hers. "Specially for you," he added quietly.

"*Matiushka*, this is wonderful." Azaylee ran excitedly into the saloon, stopping short when she saw the baron.

"This is my *sister*, Azaylee," Missie said, flashing her a warning glance to mind her manners. "Say hello to Baron Arnhaldt, Azaylee."

"Hello," she said shyly. "Thank you for inviting me onto your boat. It's beautiful. Are we going to sail soon?"

He stared at her thoughtfully. "Whenever you like, little girl," he said. "Just tell the captain we are ready and we'll be on our way."

They hung over the rail, watching as the big yacht sailed down the Hudson and out into the ocean. The air was soft, just a light ocean breeze, and Missie lay back in a steamer chair with her eyes closed, feeling relaxed and happy. She wondered guiltily what O'Hara would think if he could see her now. But O'Hara was always busy these days, traveling around the country—"Expanding his business" he called it. Besides, he still thought she was working for Madame Elise. It was a good thing he never set foot on Broadway because then he would know how she had deceived him. She thought about Zev, wondering where he had gone. She missed their Sunday nights at the Ukrainian café. And oddly enough, she really missed him too. There was only Rosa left to keep her feet on the ground, and she couldn't wait to tell her about Eddie Arnhaldt because he really was the most handsome and most charming man she had ever met.

The lazy sunny day drifted past like a dream. The baron spent a lot of time with Azaylee, showing her how things worked, treating her like a grown-up at lunch. Afterward they lingered on deck, inspecting the little seaports through his high-powered telescope and admiring passing boats until finally, pleasantly tired, they sailed back down the coast. Missie leaned on the deck rail with Eddie beside her, watching the full moon emerging from the horizon, and he said quietly, "I shall never forget the first time I saw you, but now I'm getting to know you I see so many other facets. I have enjoyed today, Verity." She wished he would take her hand as they gazed at each other longingly, or even kiss her—but he did not. And as she drove away in his limousine she realized that he had said nothing about seeing her tomorrow.

Ziegfeld questioned her about Arnhaldt the next day, and she told him enthusiastically that everything was all right. Eddie was delightful company. Why, he had even invited her out with her sister. He nodded brusquely and said, "Well, remember I told you first—take care."

She didn't hear from Eddie on Monday, or Tuesday, and when he finally sent her a note on Wednesday asking her to have dinner with him, she was overwhelmed with relief and happiness. He would send the car for her, he said, and would be waiting at Rector's. She dressed with special care that night in her red taffeta dress with flesh-colored stockings and matching red beribboned high-heeled shoes. She swept up her hair at the sides and pinned it with Cartier's diamond stars, she painted her mouth with Violette Elise and sprayed herself with Elise's special perfume, distilled from a dozen types of lilies. And as she checked her appearance in the mirror, she knew that for the first time she was dressing to please a man.

She hurried through Rector's crowded foyer, following the waiter up the wide stairs without a glance right or left. And this time when he showed her into a private dining room she did not object.

Eddie watched her carefully as she came into the room. She looked lovely in that dress, a tempting little morsel, if not quite enough for a man with such a large appetite. He smiled at her, remembering his duty. And by now he knew it was justified.

"Verity, you are so beautiful tonight," he said reverently.

She smiled, glancing nervously at the table set for two.

"I hope you don't mind?" he said. "This time I need to be alone with you. Please, I beg of you, don't say no. I must speak with you." His eyes gathered her to him and instinctively she stepped a pace closer. "Alone," he added quietly.

He limped toward the waiting ice bucket and poured champagne. "A toast to your beautiful eyes," he said, clicking his heels together and bowing slightly. Then he took a small parcel from the table. "I can't wait for you to open it," he said, his eyes admiring her.

She glanced up at him, smiling in surprise. "Go on," he urged, "please—open it."

She pulled off the ribbons and paper, gasping when she saw the diamond and ruby necklace, the matching earrings, and two matching bracelets lying on the burgundy velvet.

"The parure is an Arnhaldt heirloom," he said quietly. "I wanted to give it to you, Verity, because I am asking you to be my wife."

She closed her eyes, stunned. "But we barely know each other," she said, amazed. "We've only met a couple of times—"

"Does that matter?" he asked softly. "Do we have to meet a thousand times to know what is in our hearts? I am thirty-eight years old, Verity, I have been in love a dozen times, and I have loved casually a hundred. Believe me, I know the difference. And when lightning strikes you—or in this case"—he smiled—"a moonbeam—then there is no time to be wasted."

"But I—" she began.

He held up his hand to stop her. "I'm not a man who takes no for an answer," he said roughly. "Come here, Verity, come closer to me."

Hypnotized, she took a step toward him.

"Closer, I said."

She was next to him and then his arms went around her and his mouth descended on hers, crushing her with passion. He held her strongly but she did not want to escape, she didn't want to cry out. All she wanted was for him to keep on kissing her.

"Now," he said, lifting his face from hers and gazing at her triumphantly, "now say you don't want me as much as I want you, Verity Byron. Say you will be my wife."

"I will," she promised, closing her eyes as his mouth claimed hers again. "Oh, I will."

29

Hollywood

Zev was sitting on the veranda of the Hollywood Hotel, fanning himself with a copy of the *San Francisco Examiner*. It was nine o'clock in the morning. The clear desert heat made the backdrop of mountains look like cardboard cut-outs pasted against a deep-blue sky and the dusty street beyond the wilting flower beds looked like Main Street, Smalltown, America. Occasionally a car puttered by and in the distance he could see the big orange grove at the corner of Hollywood and Vine. He had thought he was coming to the glamour capital of the world and he had ended up in a village.

He glanced at his watch. At ten o'clock he was to meet Mr. Mel Schroeder to discuss his investment in Schroeder's new motion picture company. Sipping orange juice, he opened the newspaper, glancing at the headlines and the pictures on the front page. He stopped at the sight of a familiar face.

"Verity Byron Weds Armaments King," the headline trumpeted over the top of the picture of Missie, looking ethereally beautiful on the arm of a tall, unsmiling Prussian-looking man.

"Showgirl and former Elise mannequin Verity Byron, who created a sensation in her first appearance onstage this season, was married yesterday to the Baron Edmund Arnhaldt, multimillionaire steel and armaments chief, in a small private ceremony at Burkeley Crest, the palatial Long Island home of Mr. and Mrs. Florenz Ziegfeld. Miss Byron looked radiant in a cream silk georgette ensemble designed by Elise, with a tulip skirt and a cross-over neckline, cream silk roses at the hip and her trademark floating sleeves. She carried a bouquet of her favorite cream roses, and her rings were a seven-carat teardrop diamond and a wedding band of square diamonds, both by Cartier. She was attended by her sister, Azaylee, aged six, in shell-pink taffeta with Valenciennes lace, who carried a posy of violets.

"The bride's trousseau is by her former employer, Elise, whose beribboned shoes with their perky satin bows she made famous. The groom's presents to the bride included an heirloom ruby and diamond parure consisting of necklace, two bracelets, chandelier earrings, and a fine ring. The bride bought her husband a gold Cartier cigarette case, specially sized for the long Turkish cigarettes he smokes, inscribed with his initials in diamonds.

"A small luncheon was given afterward by Mr. and Mrs. Ziegfeld (the famous actress Billy Burke) and the house was a bower of cream roses for which it is said the bridegroom ransacked every florist on the East Coast.

"The happy couple sailed yesterday on the RMS *Majestic* for a Paris honeymoon. The new baroness has forsaken the stage to make her home with her husband at the famous Haus Arnhaldt in Germany."

Zev lowered the newspaper with trembling hands. A great anger was welling in him, the anger of a man forever forgotten, forever trampled upon. He was too late. Missie had married her millionaire and he would never see her again. She was the one person he had cared about, the only one to whom he had bared his soul, the only one he had loved.

The heat of anger faded, leaving him icy cool. His mouth set in a firm line as he told himself he would dismiss her from his mind, from his life. Forever. From now on he would think only of himself. Ambition stirred in him. If he was not to have love, then he would be a success. He thought of his meeting with Schroeder—the man would look at him in his black pawnbroker's suit and think he had another sucker here. Well, he would think wrong. Zev Abramski was in charge of his own life now. He was master of his own fate, and no one was ever going to make a fool of him again.

New York

O'Hara strolled around the dimly lighted nightclub, sizing up the room. It was pretty good, he thought, small enough to be exclusive and big enough to make a profit. There was a stage for the band at one end and a circular dance floor that he planned to cover with glass and light from beneath. There were revolving mirrored globes on the ceiling, and the floor was stepped up from the dance area in three tiers, each crowded with small tables. Of course it needed jazzing up with a new color scheme, black and white maybe to set off the women's colorful dresses, black carpets and tablecloths, silver lamé curtains. Yes, a bit of glitter would be just grand.

He stood in the center of the dance floor, hands in his pockets, envisioning the room with its glossy new look filled with the sounds of jazz music and the popping of champagne corks—at twenty-five dollars a time—and the laughter of wild, pretty young women. This floor he was standing on would be crowded with dancers flinging themselves about in the latest dances, and the men would be paying through the nose for the privilege of membership in King O'Hara's.

He nodded, satisfied, and the real estate agent standing by the door breathed a sigh of relief. "I'll sign the lease," O'Hara told him, "but not at the crazy price you are demanding. It's too far uptown. Not even the biggest sucker on Broadway is gonna pay you that kind of money."

O'Hara had done his homework. He knew exactly what he was going to charge: twenty-five dollars a bottle of scotch and ten for rye. He would even charge two bucks for a pitcher of tap water. He would have cigarette girls selling trinkets and souvenirs, kewpie dolls and boutonnières, at five bucks a shot, and any guy who didn't buy one for his girl was a cheapskate.

"We're talking Harlem here," he told the nervous real estate man, "and I'm being reasonable when I say I'll pay twenty-five percent less than you want."

The man gulped and nodded. "Okay," he said with a growl, "it's a deal."

"And that's for ten years, not five." O'Hara added as they walked to the door.

The man winced. "Aw, come on now, Mr. O'Hara," he said.

O'Hara shrugged. "Take it or leave it."

"I'll take it," the man said, scowling and slamming his hat on his head. "I'll have the lease ready for you tomorrow."

"Sure and that'll be just fine." O'Hara grinned as he watched him walk away. He stepped back on the sidewalk and looked at the façade of his nightclub. He could just see the sign out front: "King O'Hara's" in shamrock-green, his favorite color. He strolled jauntily along the sidewalk, his hands in his pockets and a smile on his face. He was going to be his own boss at last. He'd had enough of ferrying hooch for the Oriconne brothers, stocking their clubs and restaurants, doing all the work and taking all the risks as the front

man while they made all the money. He had seen how they oper-
ated: He had all the contacts and he knew the business like the back
of his hand. And after all, it wasn't a million miles from running an
alehouse on Delancey—only this time he stood to make a fortune.

After hailing a cab, he asked to be taken to a deli on Sixth Avenue. He would get himself a bite of lunch and maybe pay a visit to
Missie. He hadn't seen her in a couple of months, been too busy
traveling to Chicago and back on Oriconne business, but he guessed
she had been busy too. She had said that Madame Elise worked her
girls real hard. He sure had missed her, but he was playing it her
way, waiting for a year like she'd asked, and at the end of it he just
knew it would pay off. By then he would be a rich man, famous too,
probably, as the owner of King O'Hara's, and she would become his
wife; queen to his king.

Sliding into a booth, he ordered pastrami on rye and a celery
tonic. He took out a notepad and wrote down some figures, smiling
as he added them up. He sipped his drink, waiting for his pastrami,
casually picking up the newspaper lying on the table. He wasn't
much of a readin' man, he was too busy for that, but he glanced
through it idly and almost choked on the celery tonic when he saw
the picture of Missie on the front page. He scanned the report
quickly, scarcely able to believe what he was reading.

"B'jaysus," he roared angrily, clearing the table with a single
blow of his arm. After throwing a couple of dollars onto the
counter, he strode from the deli and took a cab over to Missie's
apartment.

"She's gone, sir," the porter told him smugly, "she and the little
girl. The maid went too. All of them. To Germany. Married a millionaire," he added with a grin, "like all good showgirls."

His virtuous Missie a showgirl? And he must have been the only
man in New York who didn't know it! O'Hara strode down Broadway to the New Amsterdam Theater, burning with anger. Workmen
on ladders were taking down Verity's name from the marquee but
her picture was still out front along with the others.

O'Hara stared at it for a long time. Tears stung his eyes and he
doubled up in physical pain. Missie had promised to give him an
answer in a year's time. *She had promised.* And now look how she
had cheated him, working as a showgirl and running off with some
millionaire. His colleen, his love. If she was here now he would have
strangled her with his bare hands. He would have hanged for Missie
O'Bryan.

Eddie had reserved two suites on the *Majestic*, one for himself and Missie, and the other for Azaylee and her nurse, Beulah. He was pleased with his bride as they boarded the ship; she looked beautiful and she also looked like a lady in her elegant Elise violet coat with the sable collar. The steward showed them into their staterooms and she spun round laughing with delight.

"But it's wonderful, Eddie, just marvelous," she cried, racing from room to room, counting. "A sitting room, two bedrooms, two dressing rooms, two bathrooms." She was as excited as a child and his eyes were speculative as he studied her; perhaps tonight would be more interesting than he had thought after all. He glanced at his watch. They were to sail on the tide at six, and dinner the first night out would be early and informal. Suddenly he could not wait for it all to be over with, to have her in bed with him.

Azaylee rapped on the door, then rushed in with Beulah at her heels, as excited as Missie. "Did you know there's a promenade for walking dogs on the very top deck?" she demanded. "And a special lamppost for them, and kennels? Missie, we could have brought Viktor, after all."

"Darling, Viktor is too old to travel anymore," she replied soothingly. "He's much better off with Rosa. You know she will take care of him. Besides, we shall see him lots. Eddie says he has so much business here we shall be back and forth across the Atlantic like yo-yos."

"Truly?" Azaylee's face brightened, but she said sadly, "I shall miss him so much, though, *matiushka.*"

Missie shooed her out onto the deck. They watched for a long time as the tugs pulled the big ship from her berth and Manhattan's burgeoning skyline faded into the distance, feeling the deck rolling under their feet as the *Majestic* took to the open sea.

Missie could not help but remember that last time she had stood by the deck rail, four years before, waiting for her first sight of the great city and wondering what her new life held in store for her. Now she was leaving Sofia behind, buried in an alien land; and her friend Rosa who had become as dear to her as Azaylee, and the two men who had helped and encouraged her. But she was married to a man she was crazy about and at last Azaylee would lead the kind of life that was hers by birth. She hoped Misha would have been proud of her. Even though she was married to Eddie, she knew he would always be her first, true love.

They dined quietly, alone at a table in the corner in the huge dining room with its dramatic staircase where society and celebrities descended in style, pausing first at the top so that everyone might see them. Eddie poured wine with a liberal hand and afterward they took a stroll around the promenade deck, lurching and laughing as the sea roughened. He put his arm around her protectively, glancing at his watch. "It's getting late," he said, turning toward the staterooms. "Shall we?"

The stewardess had unpacked for her and Beulah had arranged all her things the way she knew she liked them; her face creams and powders in shiny crystal pots were laid out on the dressing table next to her silver hairbrushes and the tall spray flacon of Elise perfume. Her beautiful new dresses hung neatly in the closets, her hats in their lilac boxes stored on shelves above, and her lovely new shoes lined up in rows below. A wonderful mink coat, Elise's wedding present, was shrouded in its own special bag, and the case containing her jewels was locked in the safe in her dressing room. I am a rich woman, she thought, amazed. I can have whatever I like, do whatever I want. Just like Anouska. But the only thing she wanted was her new husband, waiting impatiently for her in their bedroom.

After casting off her clothes, she bathed and put on one of her trousseau nightdresses. Elise had really gone to town on this one, pure white finest silk *crêpe-de-Chine,* slit to the waist front and back and lavished with ecru lace. She brushed her hair until it shone, letting it fall forward over her half-naked breasts. Then, putting on the matching peignoir and the satin slippers, she sprayed herself with the lily perfume. Taking a deep breath, she walked slowly into the bedroom.

Eddie was sitting on the couch, wearing a navy silk robe and matching pajamas, reading a newspaper.

He glanced up as she came in, then his eyes narrowed and a faint flush stained his cheeks. "My dear Verity, you look . . . charming," he said quietly.

He turned off the lamps, leaving on just the one near the bed. "Come here, to me," he said, striding across the room and taking her in his arms.

His rough kisses took her breath away. They were different from before, urgent, demanding. "Please, please, Eddie," she murmured, gasping as he took his mouth from hers at last. "Let me breathe!"

Laughing, he took her to the bed, pulling off her peignoir and the lacy straps from her shoulders, burying his face in her breasts. She trembled in his arms, not knowing how to make love to him.

"Eddie, you'll have to show me, tell me what to do," she whispered, stroking his smooth blond hair.

"Take off the nightdress," he commanded, standing up and shedding his robe.

Blushing, she did as he asked, sitting on the edge of the bed, her hands modestly clasped in her lap.

"That's better," he said in a sort of groan, pushing her backward onto the bed. And then he was on top of her and his fingers were plunging cruelly into her and she moaned in pain.

"That's it," he cried excitedly, "I like to hear you moan." Suddenly he was thrusting himself into her, again and again, harder and harder, and she was screaming with the pain. She pleaded with him to stop, gazing at him beseechingly through her tears. But his eyes were closed, his head thrown way back, his face a grimace of pain and ecstasy as he reached his climax and toppled down onto her, breathing heavily.

After a few moments he got up. Without even looking at her, he walked to the bathroom and closed the door. She heard the sound of water as he turned on the shower and she closed her eyes again, stunned. She wondered if this was what making "love" was all about, and if so how anybody could ever call it love. And how could anybody enjoy it, the way all the showgirls had told her you were supposed to? There had been no tenderness, no loving caresses, just a brutal transaction between two bodies.

He returned from the bathroom wrapped in a robe, looking clean and refreshed and perfectly normal, as if nothing were wrong. "I suggest you take a bath," he said coldly. "You will feel better in the morning."

"Eddie?" she whispered, sitting up and clutching at his hand. "Is it always like this? The first time?"

He shrugged. "Some women like it more than others. It's up to you, Verity, whether it gets better—or worse." His pale eyes were cold and expressionless as he said, "I'm going to bed now. Please do not wake me in the morning. I asked the valet to bring me my breakfast at ten. You may do whatever you please." And without a second glance he strode into the other bedroom. She stared disbelievingly as the door closed and she heard the sound of the key in the lock, and then she turned her face into her pillow and wept because all her wonderful romantic dreams had come to nothing.

They met again at lunch the next day. He was urbane and charming in public and aloof and silent in private. Dinner that night was a grand affair, and Missie decked herself up in her most beautiful gown, a soft, rustling sea-green silk with a beaded shawl like a peacock's tail. She wore diamond stars in her hair and the diamond snake bracelets Cartier had given as a wedding present to the wife of their favored customer. Eddie looked handsome in his hard, military-looking style, and she thought wistfully that they made a beautiful couple as he escorted her down the wide staircase to the captain's table.

She was seated between the captain and a famous English cabinet minister, who had seen her onstage at the New Amsterdam Theater and told her he would forever be a devoted admirer. She did her best to sparkle and be amusing but most of the time she was watching Eddie covertly through her lashes, flirting and chatting intimately with the tall, blond German countess Gretel von Dussman, whom he obviously knew well.

Afterward she undressed and prepared for bed in another of Elise's alluring confections, wishing she had brought some of her old cotton nighties with her. She waited nervously for Eddie to arrive but though she heard him moving around in the next room, he did not appear. Later she heard his door slam and the sound of his footsteps disappearing along the corridor, and she climbed sadly into bed. He must be so disappointed in her that he had decided to try his luck at the casino instead.

The pattern of their days on board fell into a regular routine. She would rise early and have breakfast with Azaylee and then they would take a walk around the decks, maybe try their luck at a game of quoits or shuffleboard. At eleven they would sip a cup of hearty bouillon on deck, brought by an attentive steward, and at one they would join Eddie for lunch.

Though he did not seem to have much to say to her, Eddie certainly went out of his way to charm Azaylee. He bought her trinkets and little gifts from the shop and spoiled her with chocolates and cream cakes. Missie thought she bloomed in his presence, like a little girl who had finally found a father.

Missie always sat with Azaylee while she had her supper, and then she went back to her sumptuous stateroom and the nightly ritual of preparing for dinner. She wore a different Elise gown in a different color scheme each night, drawing admiring glances as she descended the stairs on the arm of her handsome millionaire husband. And each night she watched him flirting with Gretel von Dussman, and each night she waited in vain for him to come to her.

On the last night before the ship docked at Cherbourg, she dressed in the red taffeta she had worn when he asked her to marry him, and for the first time she wore the Arnhaldt heirloom rubies and diamonds. She lifted her head proudly as she strode down the steps, searching the sea of faces turned toward her until she found Gretel von Dussman's malicious smile. She smiled back sweetly as she took her seat at the table: She knew the big, overblown blonde could not hold a candle to her tonight. Elise had given her a good grounding in how to hold an audience, and Ziegfeld had taught her well. Even Eddie could not keep his eyes off her tonight. Every time she glanced up he was staring at her.

He walked quietly back with her to their suite, opening the door to let her pass, following her in, pulling off his tie and jacket and ripping off his shirt like a madman. Then naked, he came toward her. She stood silently, terrified of the brutal look on his face. After turning her around in his arms, he unbuttoned the taffeta dress, letting it slide to the ground with a silken rustle. Slowly he removed her chemise, running his hands across her breasts while she gazed at him with fear in her eyes. He removed the rest of her undergarments, leaving her naked and shy, except for her stockings and the brilliant fire of the rubies.

She kept her eyes on his face, afraid to look at what was happening to him, terrified of what he was going to do.

Cursing angrily in German, he suddenly pushed her from him, sending her reeling across the room. "You stupid little milk-fed child," he said with a snarl, his passion subsiding as he threw on his clothes. "Have you no idea at all what excites a man? Don't they teach you these things at the New Amsterdam Theater? Why, even the meanest girl on the streets understands a man's passions better than you."

He stood looking at her, fully dressed, smoothing back his blond hair. "Put your clothes on, for God's sake," he said contemptuously. "One day I'm going to show you how not to be a lady in bed. But tonight I've got better things to do." And with that, he turned on his heel and stalked from the room, slamming the door behind him.

Much later, she heard him return. She could hear the clinking of glasses and the sound of a woman's laughter and then later, their animal groans of passion, the cries and commands as the woman goaded him on. Missie buried her head in her pillow, shutting out what she knew only too well was happening next door. Gretel von Dussman was satisfying her husband in a way she never could.

She was up early, waiting on deck as the *Majestic* docked at Cherbourg, and she stared at Eddie as he sauntered toward her. He was immaculately dressed as always, and she wondered how it was that his saturnine, freshly shaved face showed no marks of the previous night's activities. Eddie, clothed and a gentleman, was a different man from Eddie, naked and brutal with passion.

He said abruptly, "I have decided that we shall not visit Paris after all. I have canceled our reservations at the Hotel Bristol and we shall go directly to Germany."

Azaylee's face fell and he put his arm around her shoulders. "Don't you want to see Haus Arnhaldt?" he asked, smiling. "Your new home?"

"Oh, yes, yes, of course," she replied excitedly.

He shrugged. "Then Paris will wait until you are a little older."

The journey by train and automobile was a long one, and Missie was exhausted when the car finally turned into a long road that wound its way between dense, gloomy woodlands, emerging at last at a series of formal landscapes of box hedge and gravel, with not a flower in sight. She stared in dismay at the forbidding gray house. As she watched the big doors were flung open and a butler appeared on the steps, marshalling a troop of household servants into line to receive their master and his new bride.

The butler hurried to open the door, clicking his heels and bowing, introducing himself as Manfred, and Missie walked down the line of servants, smiling and saying hello as each girl bobbed a curtsey and each man bowed.

The tall, regal-looking woman waiting in the shadows of the hall watched the little charade taking place outside. Her glance took in Missie and then dismissed her and moved on to the child. She caught her breath. Eddie had been right after all; the resemblance to Anouska Ivanoff was uncanny. She smiled. Her son had done well. In one move he had accomplished what they had been hoping for for years. She had no doubt that this was the Ivanoffs' missing daughter, left for dead by the Russians in the forest four years ago. But now she was also Eddie Arnhaldt's "daughter."

Their plan was long-term. After all, the child was only six. But it would be worth the wait. She would instruct her lawyers to prepare their case, and when the girl was eighteen, she would be revealed as the Ivanoff heiress and the legitimate owner of the Rajasthan mines.

The new bride, Verity, was important for the moment because she would be needed as a witness—and they would not hesitate to use force if necessary to get her to tell them the truth. Meanwhile, Eddie would be a dutiful and indulgent father and naturally, when she was of age, Azaylee would assign the mines to him. By then she would be as true an Arnhaldt as they were. She would be married to her beloved grandson and Augie would inherit everything.

She swept forward to greet her new daughter-in-law, smiling coldly and offering her cheek for a kiss. "I hope you will be very happy here," she said, her glance shifting quickly to Azaylee. "And you, child," she said, allowing a little warmth to creep into her voice, "you have come to brighten up our days with your youth. Haus Arnhaldt welcomes you. And I want you to remember that from now on, this is your home."

30

Düsseldorf

As each day dragged by Haus Arnhaldt felt more and more like a prison. Missie's rooms were on the second floor opposite Eddie's but he never came to see her. He was away most days at the Arnhaldt offices in Düsseldorf or at the plant at Essen and he was often away at weekends, hunting or attending parties without her. She suspected he was still seeing Gretel but she could not be sure, because she had not been out of Haus Arnhaldt and its grounds since they arrived two months ago. In fact, she had never seen him alone since that night on the *Majestic,* and she could not decide whether she was relieved or sad. After all, she was a bride. Even if things had started out badly because she was so ignorant, could they not at least make up and try again?

She decided to be as charming and sweet to Eddie as she could, dressing with great care every night for dinner in the vast, echoing gothic-paneled hall lighted by lugubrious antler's head sconces. But each night it was as if she were invisible. Manfred and a posse of servants served them silently, and Eddie and his mother, the Baroness Jutta, spoke only in German, of which she understood not a word. She might just as well have been a fly on the wall for all the notice either of them took of her. Aware of the curious glances of the servants, she ate her food quickly and excused herself as soon as possible.

She trailed up the wide oaken stairs and back down the gloomy corridors to her rooms in despair. If it was not that Azaylee was enjoying herself so much, she would simply have told Eddie she was leaving and that would be that.

And where would she go? she asked herself, staring out of the window and seeing only the dark woods in the distance. She was in Germany, she had no money of her own, Eddie never gave her any.

Things were simply "provided": Rich people had no need for money.

It was different for Azaylee. She had a light, sunny suite on the first floor, with a cozy bedroom specially decorated for her in fresh green-and-white cotton chintz, and an enormous playroom stacked with new toys and games. There was a schoolroom where a governess gave her German lessons daily and a bedroom and sitting room for Beulah where Missie joined them each day for five o'clock tea. It was the highlight of her dreary life and she looked forward to it. Between Azaylee's riding lessons on the new pony, the swimming lessons in the enormous indoor pool, the ballet lessons every day in Düsseldorf, and the endless German lessons, tea was almost the only time she saw her.

Beulah shook her head unhappily. "Ah don't like it, Miss Verity," she said in a loud stage whisper, "ah just don't like what they're doin' to that child. Fillin' her head with Arnhaldt talk, 'bout how rich they all are, and telling her she should only speak German now she has a German daddy and is a little German girl. What about you, Miss Verity? You're her sister, ain't yuh? So why ain't they giving you German lessons so you can talk to your German husband? No, there's sump'n funny goin' on here. Ah'm tellin' you, Miss Verity, they's takin' that child away from you and me bit by bit. Soon all we'll have left is a little German *fräulein.* Don't ax me why, but that's the way it's goin'."

Missie thought about her words, alone and sleepless in bed that night. It was true, they kept Azaylee deliberately busy, they did keep her away from her, and they were teaching her to speak only German, praising her fluency even when she made mistakes. But why? She considered the possibility that it was because they really loved her, but then she remembered Eddie's cold Prussian-blue eyes, so like his mother's, and knew that was not true. It was no good, she thought desperately, it was time matters were straightened out between them. And if it meant it was the end and she had to return to New York and face up to the shame of her broken marriage, then so be it.

The next day was a Saturday and for once, Eddie was home. Deciding there was no time like the present, she dressed in a pretty blue woolen dress, put her hair neatly into a chignon in the hope that it made her look older and more commanding, and hurried downstairs to his study.

She tapped on the door, calling his name, waiting nervously.

There was no reply and her heart sank as she realized he might have decided to go out. Now she had made up her mind she wanted action. Calling his name again, she opened the door and peered in. The study was empty but she could smell the pungent Turkish cigarettes he smoked and a book lay open on the desk. Thinking he had probably just gone out for a few minutes, she decided to wait. She had seen Eddie's study only once before when his mother had taken her on a tour of the house, and she wandered around staring curiously at the objects on his desk. The massive silver lamp, three telephones, an enormous ugly brass ashtray, and silver models of various Arnhaldt guns. She thought disconsolately that everything in Haus Arnhaldt was grand and oversize. Even the books on the shelves were all fat, worthy leather-bound tomes.

She inspected each of the paintings, stopping suddenly at a small landscape. But she was not looking at the painting, she was looking at the open safe that it was meant to conceal. And there staring back at her was a familiar object, an object she had thought she had lost forever: Misha's brooch, which she had last seen at Cartier in New York.

She clutched her throat as the horrific memories crowded back, hearing Sofia's warning voice telling her over and over again that it would never be safe to sell the jewels, that the Cheka never slept and never forgot, that sometime, somewhere in the world, someone would be waiting for the Ivanoff gems to surface. And then they would act.

But there was something else that looked vaguely familiar, a legal document with a red seal. She picked it up and read the heading: "Lease of the Ivanoff Rajput Mine to Arnhaldt by The Union of Soviet Socialist Republics," dated January 1, 1918, signed and sealed by Michael Peter Alexander Ivanoff on this date. She stared at it, puzzled. It could not be true; Misha was already dead when this document was signed.

Panicked, she remembered the Arnhaldts' wooing of Azaylee and realized they must know who she was. But what did they want from her? Were they in league with the Cheka? A million possibilities flooded through her head, each more terrible than the last, as she stared, frozen, at Misha's brooch. Instinctively she reached out, took it, and slipped it into her pocket. She spun around horror-struck as she heard Eddie's loud voice outside giving instructions to Manfred. She glanced around helplessly, but there was no escape.

She pushed the lease back into the safe, shutting the door with a clang she felt sure could be heard a mile away, and quickly thrust the painting back in place. Then, picking a book at random from the shelf, she ran back to the other side of the desk and sat in the big red-leather wing chair.

Her spine crawled as the door opened; she flicked through the pages, pretending not to have heard, and after a few seconds Eddie said, "Are you here for a reason? Or just curiosity?" He walked toward her and took the book from her hands. *"A Study of Ballistics* —in German? Really, Verity, if you are looking for an excuse to spy on me, you can do better than that."

"I did not come here to spy on you," she said indignantly, "I came—" She stopped, remembering that she could no longer say what she had intended to say. She could not tell him they were leaving because now she knew he would never let them go. "I came to ask you why you don't speak to me anymore," she said instead.

He shrugged. "I thought it was decided on the *Majestic* that we had nothing to say to each other. I made a terrible mistake, Verity. You are not the girl I thought you were. But I will not divorce you. You may stay here at Haus Arnhaldt and live like a lady. The young Baroness Arnhaldt." His thin lips twisted into a cruel smile as he added softly, "For the rest of your life."

She gasped, wondering, terrified, what he meant. Did he intend to kill her and take Azaylee? All she knew was they must leave here as soon as possible, and in secret.

She stood up and walked past him to the door. Flinging back her head, she met his eyes across the room. "I am still hoping that we can work things out between us, Eddie," she said quietly. "I will do my best to please you from now on."

It took all her self-possession to walk and not run back through the hall and up the stairs to her room. All day she worried about how to escape from Haus Arnhaldt. The place was a fortress and twenty kilometers from the nearest town; she couldn't just pack and ask the chauffeur to drive them to the station in Düsseldorf because he would never do anything without first asking Baroness Jutta. And even if they attempted to walk, she knew they would be missed and brought back. Besides, Beulah was too old for such an expedition and Azaylee too young. She groaned, holding her head in her hands despairingly. All she could do was watch and wait her opportunity, and meanwhile she would tell Beulah to prepare for their flight.

The old woman was thrilled when she told her they were leaving.

"It just cain't come soon enough for me, Miss Verity," she said, grinning. "Ah cain't wait to git the hell outa here."

The opportunity came sooner than she expected and in the most satisfactory way. The detested Baroness Jutta fell while walking in the park and broke her hip. A world-famous bone specialist was summoned from Paris and Eddie was told the fracture was a complicated one. The baroness would have to be taken by ambulance to the doctor's private Paris clinic, where he could treat her personally. If not, he feared she might never walk again.

Eddie was white-faced and tense as he made the arrangements, and Verity saw her chance. "Your poor mother," she said sympathetically. "She will be so lonely in Paris, away from her beloved Haus Arnhaldt. Why don't you let Azaylee go along too, to cheer her up? You know how she adores her."

His eyes were worried and she knew he had barely heard her. "She really does adore Azaylee. You know how she makes her laugh," she persisted.

"The baroness is right," the doctor agreed. "The psychological outlook of a patient, especially a patient of the baroness's age, is important. If she has family members around her, so much the better. It's an excellent idea."

"Then why don't we all go?" Verity cried, clapping her hands together delightedly. "After all, Eddie, you promised to show Azaylee Paris, didn't you?"

He glared at her, unable to say no in front of the doctor without looking foolish. "Oh, I suppose so," he agreed sullenly, as she fled from the room to tell Beulah the good news.

They packed quickly, just enough for a few weeks' stay in Paris. Eddie left, following his mother in the ambulance, but they were to travel by train and meet him later at the Hotel Bristol.

When the train drew into Paris, it was an easy matter to take a taxi to the Gare du Nord instead of the hotel. After leaving Azaylee and Beulah at the station, Missie went to the Rue St-Honoré. As she walked into the smartest jeweler's she could find, she tilted her nose arrogantly in the air, removed the enormous diamond from her finger, and told them she wanted to sell it.

Without batting an eyelid, the worldly-wise Frenchman agreed it was a fine stone and offered her three thousand dollars. She took it with a smile and went immediately across the street to Thomas Cook and bought second-class passages on the liner *America,* sailing for New York that evening. Then she dashed back across Paris to the station and they caught the first train to Cherbourg.

By seven o'clock that night they were on board and on their way to New York. And this time Missie did not even look back. She was afraid to, because she didn't know what Eddie Arnhaldt would do when he found they had gone.

31

Istanbul

Gerome Abyss rose early from his bed that morning for the first time in years. He threw off the stale sheet, walked barefoot across the dingy carpet to the bathroom, and inspected himself in the unframed rectangle of mirror. The bright morning light was not flattering. His face was puffy, folded, straining at the seams. His stomach churned and beads of sweat trickled down his back as last night's alcohol attacked his liver. Suddenly he doubled over with pain. After a few moments the pain lessened and he straightened up and stepped into the shower. Maybe now that he was rich he would go to one of those new clinics, try a cure. "Cure" they called it, as if it were a disease, when any man with any sense knew it was a pleasure: mostly the pleasure of oblivion, but still a pleasure.

As he soaped himself he stared at his body, larded with fat like a white whale's blubber. Maybe he would lose a few pounds too, now that he was rich, and get himself some smart suits. Like he used to have in the old days when he was Gerome Abyss, the best gem cutter in the world. When companies like Cartier begged for his talents and paid him a fortune. Not as much as he'd gotten for cutting the emerald, of course, but in those days it seemed to go much farther.

And maybe, now that he was rich, he would set himself up in business again. He might let it be known, discreetly of course, to his old contacts at the big jewelers that it was he who had cut the Ivanoff emerald. It didn't matter that he had given his word never to tell. After all the excitement the sale of the emerald had caused and the amount of money it had made, that beautiful girl with the long black hair and slanting blue eyes would not be selling anything else for a long time. Leyla Kazahn. He knew her name now, but he didn't know how she came to have the emerald, and what's more he didn't care. Last night a banker's draft for over $648,000 had been delivered to him at the Locanta Antalya, the local bar where he did his drinking. He was a rich man.

The open razor drew blood under his unsteady hand as he shaved the five days of gray stubble, and he flinched. He thought about the newspapers again. They paid a fortune these days for an exclusive. With a story like this he could have the whole world competing. He grinned, showing a broken line of dirty yellow teeth. Yes, he could become even richer. More than that—he would be famous.

He took a shirt from the closet, inspecting the grimy band around the collar; it would have to do. The old white sharkskin suit was yellowed with age, sweaty and creased, and it looked ridiculous on this cold spring day. But a white suit had always been his trademark, that and his panama, his lucky hat.

Setting the battered panama with the scarlet band at a jaunty angle, he walked across the room to the door. With his hand on the handle, he stared around. He wanted none of the few miserable possessions that were his. He would never come back here again. He patted the pocket with the bank draft, reassuring himself. He was a rich man now.

The counter clerk at the Banca Stamboul noted the size of the check and the appearance of the client and called the manager. Abyss was uncomfortably aware of his scrutiny as he took in the size of the draft drawn on a reputable Swiss bank, and then his appearance, checking it with the picture in the passport in the name of Mr. Georges Gerome.

"Of course, Mr. Gerome, we will be delighted to open an account for you," the manager said at last. "I myself will take care of it. Just tell me what sort of account you would prefer. May I suggest a short-term deposit at our highest interest rate while you make up your mind about investments? And a reasonable current account, for ready cash and so on?"

Abyss nodded. "Put a hundred thousand into a current account and the rest on deposit. And I'll take ten thousand cash now, in dollars."

He toyed nervously with the spoon in the Turkish coffee they had given him while he waited. They were taking their time and he sweated, wondering if something had gone wrong.

"Here you are then, Mr. Gerome." The manager returned, smiling. "We just need your signature here, sir, and here."

Abyss wished his hand wouldn't shake so. His scrawled signature looked like a forgery. He glanced up nervously but the manager's smile seemed glued on.

"And here is your ten thousand dollars, Mr. Gerome. May I welcome you to the Banca Stamboul. If you encounter any problems, or wish to discuss investments, anything at all, I should be pleased to advise you."

Abyss grinned as he walked through Taksim Square, unaware of the small man in the brown coat ten paces behind. The ten thousand dollars made a satisfying bulge in his jacket pocket and he grinned again. First he was going to check into a suite at the Hilton Hotel, then he was going shopping. Four dozen new shirts, custom-made of course, a dozen nice suits, underwear, socks, shoes . . . and a new lucky hat. He didn't need the old one anymore. Laughing, he tossed his old panama at the shoeshine man sitting on the corner of the square and the old boy grinned back, his toothless brown face creasing like a cracked walnut. Abyss decided that he liked Istanbul. A man was treated like a prince here—*and* he could live like a king.

The neon sign on the bar on the corner caught his eye and he hesitated. Just one drink wouldn't hurt and after all, there was no hurry, the Hilton would still be there in an hour. He laughed, telling himself it was the same with sex; he could heighten the pleasure by delaying the ultimate event. And that was another thing money could buy, something he hadn't had in a long time: sex.

He didn't notice the small shadowy man in the inconspicuous brown jacket slip into the bar after him and take a seat by the door.

Abyss surveyed the array of bottles behind the bar happily. He had never really thought the girl would pay up. He had thought twenty-five thousand was as much as he would get, and that had already slipped through his fingers like water. It had cost him ten thousand alone for the new passport, and then there had been boats, planes, trains, hotels . . . all the long-drawn-out palaver of hiding. But no more. Now he could have whatever he wanted.

He chose a double-malt scotch, savoring it on his tongue before tossing it back and ordering another. "And one for yourself," he said magnanimously to the barman. The man nodded, pocketing the money. He'd met a million like Abyss. They came and they went.

Abyss crouched low on the barstool as the pain hit him again. *Merde,* it was really getting bad now. Maybe he really would have to give up the scotch. Sweating profusely, he staggered from the bar.

The little man was beside him in a flash. "Are you all right?" he asked in French.

Abyss stared at him in surprise, then he groaned as the pain hit him again. "I need to get to a hospital." He gasped, clinging to the man's arm to stop himself from falling.

The taxi cruising slowly at the sidewalk pulled to a stop and the little man helped him into it, then he climbed in beside him and slammed the door. The taxi took off, its wheels screaming as it lurched around the corner and down Siraselvileh Caddesi, heading back toward the bridge and the old town.

The news merited only five lines in the morning's newspapers. The body of a man had been found floating in the harbor at Unkapani. He had not drowned, he had been stabbed to death, and the dagger was still embedded in his back. Robbery was not a motive, since the sum of ten thousand American dollars had been found in his pocket. He had been identified as Mr. Georges Gerome and police were investigating further.

=== 32 ===

Cal read the morning papers standing by his window overlooking the Potomac and Theodore Roosevelt Island, drinking his breakfast coffee. The hot news was Markheim's murder. His body had been found by a cleaner, and, because his connection with the sale of the emerald had come out, the papers were having a field day. He wondered if Markheim had told his assassin the identity of the buyer before he was killed, and who the killer was. Maybe Valentin Solovsky?

The cup rattled against the saucer as he put it down, remembering Genie and Solovsky. He had not seen or heard from her since Düsseldorf. She had gone off again without telling him and then he had been called back to Washington.

He remembered Genie's scared blue eyes and his own voice promising her there was no danger. "There's really nothing to be afraid of," he had told her blithely. "It's the Ivanoff woman they want, not you. Besides, you're no Mata Hari." But dammit, Genie had turned out to be just that, determined to do her best for her country, just the way she always did in her job as a reporter. Like a fool he had sent her into a world of danger he had not anticipated.

He glanced worriedly at his watch, reading the date and time as if it might tell him where she was.

After picking up the phone, he called her producer. "Oh, sure," he said, "we heard from her this morning. And about time too!"

Cal thanked him—and thanked God at the same time. Genie was okay. She was on her way home. And as soon as she got home he was going to see her and tell her to forget all about it. He wanted her to forget he ever asked her, to forget it ever happened. He just wanted her to be the tough, vulnerable girl reporter again, safe in her own world. He smiled ruefully as he dialed the florist and ordered two dozen cream roses to be sent to Ms. Genie Reese, with a card that said simply "I'm sorry. Love, Cal."

He hoped she would believe him.

His thoughts turned grimly to Markheim's murder. He switched on the television, wondering if there might be something more on the early news. Suddenly there was the Russian at Dulles Airport, battling his way through a crowd of reporters and cameramen.

Valentin stared, surprised, into the TV camera, then he turned and scanned the crowd blocking his way. Half a dozen men in dark glasses materialized from nowhere, pushing back the reporters and opening up a channel for him to pass through.

"You were at the sale in Geneva, Mr. Solovsky," a reporter called, thrusting a microphone at him. "Can you tell us why?"

Ignoring him, Valentin moved forward. "What about Markheim's murder, sir?" the reporter persisted, but Valentin simply thrust the microphone away and walked on. He glanced angrily at the security men and they closed ranks in front of him, shunting the reporters backward out onto the street. There was no embassy car waiting and Valentin stepped quickly into a cab. The cameras were still flashing as it drove away.

Cal whistled softly. He had thought he could handle the Ivanoff case diplomatically, but now things were getting out of hand. He needed help. He punched the phone buttons again, got Jim Cornish at CIA headquarters in Langley, Virginia, and asked him about Markheim.

"They got him, all right," Cornish told him. "And Abyss. The info came through this morning from Istanbul. It's all in the NID, waiting on your desk. Yes, Abyss is very dead—with the dagger still sticking out of his back and ten thousand dollars in his pocket. Pretty gruesome stuff, uh?"

"Well, I'll be damned," Cal said thoughtfully.

Cornish laughed, a hearty belly laugh, and Cal winced, holding the phone away from his ear. "That's a pretty mild statement, considering," Cornish said.

"You've heard cusswords before, no need to hear more from me this early in the morning." Cal bit into his whole-wheat toast thoughtfully and said, "So I was right about Istanbul, he was there all the time."

"Good a place as any for a man to hide out, I guess. And the ten thousand must have been his payoff."

"It's not enough. Abyss had to have been paid more than ten

grand. But the fact that he had it in his pocket must mean he had only just been paid. *So where is the rest of the money?*"

"A bank account?" Cornish guessed.

"Exactly—and a brand-new bank account, I'll bet." Cal's mind raced ahead. "Do me a favor, Cornish, will you? Check all the banks in Istanbul and see where Mr. Georges Gerome opened a new account. Or maybe the bank manager has already come forward and told the Turkish police?"

"Doubtful. The mention in the papers was a small one, anyone could have missed it. But okay, we'll follow that up."

"And when you find the account, ask how the money was paid. A check? A banker's draft? Find out if it was from a Swiss bank and if so, which one."

"Will do," Cornish said irritably; he didn't like to be told how to do his job.

Washington sparkled under a bright blue sky as Cal drove along Virginia Avenue. He cut across Eighteenth Street and made a right on Seventeenth, heading for his office in the West Executive Wing of the White House.

A bunch of reporters were hanging around the west gate, and as he nosed his car through the crowd he wondered who they were waiting for. Lights blazed as TV cameras focused on him, and he suddenly found himself staring into a microphone thrust through his open window.

"Mr. Warrender, can you tell us what you were doing in Geneva?" someone demanded.

Cal remembered Valentin had kept his mouth shut at the airport and simply shook his head.

"What's the story on Markheim's murder? And we've just heard about Abyss. Who do you think is knocking them off? And why?"

Cal shook his head again thankfully as Security let him through. As the gates clanged shut behind him he could see the cameramen outside still filming. He wondered if Genie Reese was home yet. He'd bet his bottom dollar hers would be the first call he would get this morning.

After asking his secretary to get him some coffee, he sank wearily into his chair. A copy of the NID Cornish had mentioned was waiting for him. The National Intelligence Daily contained a summary of the latest reports from American agents all over the world, using electronic eavesdropping equipment and satellite spy photography as well as news reports. Sometimes what it contained was useful, sometimes not. The NID with its red and black flag emblem was sent to the President and circulated to officials with top-secret clearance or higher at the Defense Department, the State Department, and the CIA. Today there was one page devoted to the latest on Markheim's murder: that all his business ledgers and diaries were missing and that intelligence suspected it was a "wet" affair—Russian slang for an assassination, "wet" meaning "blood." There was also the pick-up on the Georges Gerome/Abyss murder in Istanbul.

Cal knew that the "Early Bird"—the cut-and-paste distillation of the major news articles and hot information taken from the nine major newspapers as well as the wire services and the three TV networks and also circulated to the top brass—would not have picked up on it yet. But by tomorrow everyone on "the loop"—the important short list of people who received high-level information first—would know the details, and it would be hot Washington gossip. He had to make a move. He sat back in his chair, his eyes closed and his arms folded, thinking. Whoever the "Lady" was, she was in terrible danger. The Russians meant business. And he was sure now there was somebody else besides the two nations who wanted the mines.

He called the CIA again. "Cornish," he said, "do we know what the Russians have been doing with those Indian mines all these years? I mean, were they working them?"

"I guess so," Cornish replied, "but we were never given the go-ahead on the Ivanoff thing, so we've never really explored all the angles."

"Start exploring," Cal retorted as clues clicked into place in his mind. "We know the mines are valuable because of the tungsten, and that tungsten is vital to steel production. And who is the world's largest producer of steel and *armaments?*"

"Jesus, Cal, you don't think . . . ?"

"Arnhaldt is in Düsseldorf," Cal said, "and so is—*was*—Markheim."

"I'll get right onto it," Cornish said. "Be back to you later today."

Cal grinned as he put down the phone. He just might have cracked the mystery of the third player in the Ivanoff game. He'd bet his last dollar Arnhaldt had bought the emerald. What would Genie Reese think about that? He would give her a call later, maybe ask her to dinner. Sure, she had upset the hell out of him with her recklessness, but there was just something about her. Perhaps it was that her determination matched his own; she was a trier, he would certainly give her *E* for effort. He pictured her sitting opposite him on the banquette at the Hotel Beau Rivage, remembering the way her blue eyes had widened when he told her about the billions and the way she pushed her hand through her long blond hair when she was nervous, and he remembered the mouth that was too vulnerable for the role she was playing. Yes, he liked Genie Reese, he really liked her.

It was five-thirty in the afternoon when Cornish called him back. He said the facts about Arnhaldt operating the mines had been confirmed and he was following it up. Also intelligence from Düsseldorf said that Markheim had accepted a large bribe from someone, probably KGB agents, to divulge the name of his client, and there was no doubt that the Russians now knew about Arnhaldt. Cal nodded; it was as he expected. He told Cornish to let him know if they were able to come up with anything else, and then he glanced at his watch. Genie hadn't called him so he would call her.

"Hi," she said. "Thank you for the flowers. They're beautiful. They smell like a summer garden."

"You're welcome," he said, relieved to hear her voice. "Is my apology accepted?"

"Oh, sure. There's really nothing to apologize for."

"Yes there is, but nothing we can talk about over the phone." She didn't reply and he said quickly, "Are you all right?"

"Why shouldn't I be?" Her voice was cautious.

"Well, you skipped out on me again in Düsseldorf. I'm just glad to hear you're back safely, what with events there."

"Events? Oh, yes." She hesitated and then said quickly, "Cal, I'm really glad you called. Can you see me tonight?"

He smiled. "You beat me to it. I was going to ask you to have dinner."

"Dinner? Well, maybe. . . ."

He thought it wasn't the most enthusiastic acceptance he'd ever heard but he really wanted to see her. "Shall we say eight o'clock then? The bar at the Four Seasons? We'll take it from there."

"I'll be there. Cal? Watch the six o'clock news tonight, will you? I think maybe we will have something else to talk about."

He put down the phone with a frown, wondering what she had meant. He sure hoped she wasn't going to make another dumb move like she had with Solovsky. He hadn't expected her to go that far. But Genie was a high flyer, aiming for the top. And because of him she was playing a dangerous game to get there.

He glanced at his watch. It was a quarter to six. There wasn't time to get to the television station and find out exactly what she was up to before she went on the air. Goddamn, why did she always act without asking him first? Who knew what Solovsky had told her to do? He switched on the TV angrily, waiting for the news.

Genie didn't need her notes on the autocue. She knew exactly what she had to say. She stared at the studio clock as its hands ticked slowly toward the hour. Valentin had been home since this morning and he still had not called her. And maybe now he never would. Tears pricked her eyes and she bit her lip. She couldn't cry now, she would be on camera in a few minutes. Besides, she had cried enough in the last couple of days to last a lifetime. What had happened to the old Genie, the jaunty, fearless reporter? She's still here, she reassured herself. After all, look what's she's going to do now.

She gripped her notes tightly as a makeup girl fussed with powder and lip brush. She knew there was only one sure-fire way to bring all the players in this game into the open. And only one way to find the murderer. It was the biggest gamble of her life, but one she was prepared to take.

She had made the decision that morning and gone straight to the network director. He had listened carefully and asked several pertinent questions, and then he had agreed to let her do it. "But you'd better deliver," he'd warned. She had shivered. If she didn't deliver her career was through. And maybe her life.

At four minutes to six the phone rang and the voice on the other end melted her into sudden softness.

"Valentin," she whispered.

"Genie, I must see you," he said urgently.

"Yes, yes . . . of course. . . ."

"Your place," he said tersely. "Seven o'clock."

He rang off as the hands on the clock moved to three minutes before six.

"Okay, Genie," the director called, "let's have some action here."

She took her place behind the big curved desk, blinking in the battery of lights as the makeup girl powdered her brow yet again, staring numbly ahead as the music intro'ed and the credits unrolled on the monitor. She was quite calm now. She was ready.

Cal slumped in a chair in front of the TV set, his jacket off, his tie loosened, and a can of Miller's at his side. The credits had finished, the international headlines were read, and then the anchorman said, "First our reporter, Genie Reese, has some important revelations on the strange case of the Ivanoff emerald."

The picture changed to Genie, cool, unsmiling, and tailored in a blue silk shirt that matched her eyes. Her hair was drawn back into a velvet bow and there were pearls at her throat and ears. Cal thought that she looked like a girl who would smell deliciously of Chanel No. 5.

Genie faced the cameras seriously. "It seems the case of the Ivanoff emerald and the speculation as to the identity of its owner, the unknown 'Lady,' has reached new depths with the murder of the agent in the purchase, Paul Markheim, in Düsseldorf, and now also the murder in Istanbul of the man thought to have cut the stone, Gerome Abyss. People are asking if the old story is true after all, and if the KGB is still on the 'Lady's' trail. Or maybe it's the CIA? Or—and this is looking more and more likely—is there a third player in the drama?

"There is only one person who can answer those questions, only one person who can stop this trail of murder and mystery, and that is the 'Lady' herself. I have been making my own investigations into the Ivanoff affair and I now know *who* the 'Lady' is. In three days' time I shall present a taped interview with her, here on the six o'clock news on station WXTV. Be watching."

"Genie," her producer said through the ear mike, "you'd sure better have got it right, because all hell is about to break loose."

"That's exactly what I want," she replied simply.

"Okay," he said, "the limo is waiting to take you home. It'll be at your disposal for the next week, and a couple of heavies will be mounting guard on your house as soon as they can get over there. Okay?"

"Sure." She glanced at the clock as she gathered her things together. "I'll see you guys in a couple of days then."

The producer glanced after her worriedly as she walked from the studio. "I sure hope we did the right thing," he said.

For a few seconds Cal was frozen in his seat. Then he leapt to his feet, yelling at his secretary in the next office to get him the TV station on the phone. The girl had gone home. Groaning with frustration, he found the number and dialed it himself. It was busy, and he guessed that after Genie's sensational statement the switchboard was jammed.

Flinging on his jacket, he slammed from the office and took a cab over there.

"Sorry, Mr. Warrender," the man at reception told him, "but Miss Reese has already left."

"Where's she gone?" he demanded.

The man shrugged. "I can't say, sir."

"Goddamn," Cal said savagely. "Let me talk to the station director."

"He's gone too, sir," the man said, avoiding his eye.

He strode to the pay phone in the lobby and dialed her home number. He let it ring for a long time but there was no reply, not even her answering machine. He wondered where the hell she was, cursing himself again for involving her in what had turned out to be a dangerous game. There was no way to reach her. He would just have to wait until their date at eight o'clock, and then he was going to tell her she wasn't leaving his sight for a minute until this affair was over, even if he had to move in with her! Dammit, didn't she realize she had just told *the world* that *she* knew who the "Lady" was? Didn't she even consider what a dangerous position she had put herself in? Gloomily he took himself off to the Four Seasons to wait for her.

He sat in the pleasant flower-laden cocktail lounge, nursing a drink, listening to the piano music and watching the ebb and flow of Washington's bright young things, checking his watch worriedly every ten minutes. Eight o'clock came and went. At ten past his name was paged. There was a message from Genie saying she couldn't make it. He called her number again and got no reply. He called the operator, got the home number of the station director, and called him.

"There's no problem, Mr. Warrender," he said. "Obviously we thought about the risk. We put a limo at Genie's disposal and two bodyguards on her house. I shouldn't worry. She said she might be going away for a couple of days. She also said she knew she would be okay."

"Wanna bet?" Cal said with a snarl, slamming down the phone and heading for the parking lot.

He covered the distance from Foggy Bottom to N Street in five minutes flat and sat in the car, staring at Genie's house. It was dark. Fear gripped his throat as he walked up the steps and peered at the windows. All the curtains were drawn. He hesitated, his finger on the bell, then he tried the door handle instead. It opened under his touch and he stepped warily inside, calling her name. He heard a distant muffled bark and remembered Genie had a dog. He groped for the light switch, to the left of the door. The hall was tiny, a few feet of polished floor with a pretty rug and an antique console with his two dozen cream roses arranged in a tall crystal vase.

"Genie?" he called again, opening the door leading off to the left. He turned on the light and stared at the empty room. Oriental rugs, white sofas, flowers, soft lights—but no Genie. The door on the other side of the hall refused to budge and he put his shoulder to it savagely. It gave suddenly and a huge dog flew at him, lathering him with excited licks, barking with joy at being freed.

"Okay, okay, boy," Cal said soothingly, trying to push the door wider. "Where's Genie, eh? You tell me, boy." He slid through the gap into the kitchen, peering behind the door to see what was stopping it. Two men lay on the floor, their wrists and feet bound and their eyes and mouths taped. They were ominously still. He dropped to his knees, feeling for a pulse. It was slow but they were alive, and he guessed they had been drugged. He searched the rest of the house quickly but there was no sign of Genie.

There was a wall phone by the kitchen counter. He called an ambulance and the police and then the FBI, and told them Genie was missing. Then he called Cornish at home and told him to get his ass over to his office right away.

Even though they saw him every day, the White House Security detail at the west gate still checked his pass and the marine with the machine gun inspected his car before they let him through the gate. Cal thought furiously that it made no difference that he was in a tearing hurry, but he knew they were right. They could never afford to take chances.

Lights were still on in some of the offices and a presidential reception for some foreign dignitary was going on. The White House never slept. Cal checked his messages with the switchboard. There was just one and it wasn't from Genie. In fact, it wasn't from anyone he knew. He dialed the number and asked for Nurse Sara Milgrim.

She was calling from Fairlawns for one of the residents, Nurse Milgrim told him. It was difficult for the lady to call herself, you see, because she was ninety and a little bit deaf. She knew about him from the newspapers and had seen him on television, and was most insistent she had to see him personally. "She said to tell you she would only speak to you, sir. I don't know what she means but she said it had to do with," Nurse Milgrim lowered her voice. "It had to do with the Ivanoff emerald."

Cal sat up straight. Cornish would have to wait. "Who is she? What's her name?"

"Why, Missie O'Bryan, sir." Nurse Milgrim's voice faltered.

"O'Bryan, you say. Right, tell her I'll be there right away. And thank you, Nurse Milgrim, for taking the trouble to call me."

"I did it for her, not you," Nurse Milgrim said tartly. "And when you get here, remember she's an old lady. It's very late and I don't want you upsetting her."

"I promise," he agreed with a half smile.

Maryland

Missie glanced at herself in the hand mirror, patting her hair shakily, making sure that Milgrim had done a good job and she was looking her best for her visitor. A bit of the old vanity returning, she thought with a tired smile. It seemed everything from the past was returning to haunt her in her old age. Except Anna. Why hadn't she called? Or come to see her? Hadn't the murders of those two men convinced her what a dangerous game she was playing?

She shook her head and put away the mirror. She slept so little these days she was always glad when the early TV programs came on to keep her company. But she hadn't expected to see Misha's eyes looking at her from the screen this morning. Nor had she ever expected to hear the name Solovsky again. And now suddenly Anna was going to be exposed on television and she was afraid for her life.

She had wondered desperately what to do. She knew of no one who could help, except maybe the President. And that was when she had seen Cal Warrender on TV. They said he was the young man investigating the Ivanoff mystery and she remembered reading about him in the newspapers, "an up-and-coming young politician," they called him, and "a man to watch." They even said he had the President's ear and that his views were respected, and he was always pictured at those Washington parties. Suddenly he had seemed the answer to her prayers. Surely a man who had the President's ear and who was also involved in the Ivanoff affair would understand what she had to tell him. He would help Anna. No doubt Milgrim thought she had finally gone round the bend with all her talk of the Ivanoff emerald, but she had been forced to use the name in order to convince Mr. Warrender to see her.

Her hand trembled as she took out the beautiful jeweled frame with its photograph of Misha. She placed it on the table beside her, displaying it for the first time in more than half a century.

"Well, Misha," she said softly, "I'm going to have to break my promise after all. I'm going to have to tell them Azaylee's story. Because if I don't, my darling, then what you feared will come true and they will kill your granddaughter."

After folding her hands in her lap, she sat quietly, waiting for Cal Warrender to arrive.

Missie was not what Cal had expected from an old lady. She had the kind of regal beauty even age could not wither, with her up-swept silver hair and her magnificent violet eyes that were assessing him so anxiously.

Nor was Cal what Missie had expected. "You are younger than I imagined from television," she complained in a voice as silvery as her hair, "but then, everyone seems impossibly young to me these days. Even my doctors are young enough to be my grandchildren."

He smiled, "Do you have many grandchildren, then?"

She shook her head. "Only the one, by proxy as you might say. And thereby hangs the story. Please sit down, Mr. Warrender." She waved her hand to the chair pulled close beside her, as Nurse Milgrim hurried in with a tea tray. "This may be a long night."

"Not too late now," Sara Milgrim warned anxiously. "Remember we haven't taken our pills."

"I have no need of pills tonight," she replied, shaking her head impatiently. "There's work to be done." Her eyes were fixed on Cal's as she added, "And I am hoping that this young man can do it for me."

Milgrim handed him a cup. "It's Earl Grey," she said, glancing at him disapprovingly. "It's all she drinks."

"That will be all for the moment," Missie told her haughtily. "Mr. Warrender and I have a great deal to talk about. Please do not disturb us."

The nurse's worried eyes met Cal's and he said reassuringly, "I'll take care of her. If I see she's getting too tired, I'll send for you—and a fresh supply of Earl Grey."

As the door closed behind her Missie said agitatedly, "There's no time to be wasted, Mr. Warrender. Anna Ivanoff is in great danger." She nodded her head as he reacted to the name. "Yes, she is Misha

Ivanoff's granddaughter. You see, here is his photograph." She handed him the beautiful frame with its princely crest. "Anna is the daughter of Xenia Ivanoff, who escaped with me from Russia in 1917. It is a long story, most of which you have probably guessed by now, but I will fill in the details. And I will also tell you what happened to Misha's son, Alexei."

The old fear flooded through her again as she looked at Cal, wondering if she could really trust him, a stranger she only knew about from the press and her television set, but she had no choice. She was too old to be of any help now to Anna. Someone else must take over her role.

"It all began on the night of my eighteenth birthday," she said softly. "We were at Varishnya, and even as we drank the champagne, we knew it was unlikely we would ever see each other again. . . ."

The miniature tape recorder in Cal's pocket made a faint whirring sound as he switched it on, but she didn't hear it, and he listened, fascinated, as she unraveled a mystery for him that had captured the attention of nations for over half a century. He nodded when she finally told him about Eddie Arnhaldt; his suspicions had been correct—there *was* a third player in the game.

At last Missie leaned back in the chair, a flicker of exhaustion crossing her face, and he said worriedly, "This is very hard on you, ma'am, reliving so much fear and emotion. Maybe I should go now, and let you get some rest."

"No," she said, straightening her already ramrod back. "I've only told you the beginning. Now I must tell you the end. It's important you know everything for Anna's sake. But perhaps I'll take a small glass of brandy, if you wouldn't mind, Mr. Warrender."

"Look here, ma'am," he said, pouring the brandy and handing it to her, "you cannot go on calling a man to whom you are baring your soul 'Mr. Warrender.' Please, won't you call me Cal?"

She smiled. "Is it short for Calvin?"

He shook his head. "Callum, for my Irish ancestors."

Her eyes grew dreamy. "Ah, I knew an Irishman once," she said, forgetting she had already told him about O'Hara. "A strong, brawny, red-headed charmer of an Irishman. . . ." She sipped her brandy, thinking, and then she began.

"When we returned to New York from Germany, I left Azaylee and Beulah at a small, anonymous hotel on West Fifty-seventh

Street, the kind used by traveling salesmen and the like. And then I went immediately down to Rivington Street to find Rosa. . . ."

New York

The dark, sharp-faced young woman who answered Rosa's door looked her slowly up and down, obviously impressed by what she saw.

"*Nu*, so what does such a smart lady want with the Perelmans?" she asked, staring enviously at Missie's expensive blue coat.

Missie peered past her into the room she knew so well, only now it looked different, strangely quiet, neat and tidy with no children's clothes and toys scattered around. Yet there were the same old sticks of furniture and Rosa's bits and pieces of china and pots and her Shabbas candlesticks. It was all Rosa's and yet it didn't look like Rosa anymore. She hardly dared ask where Rosa was, she was so afraid something bad had happened to her.

The young woman shrugged. "Gone," she said, "and good riddance to her. What a man like Meyer Perelman was doing with such a lazy slut I'll never know. Every night he would come to the union meetings and tell me about how lazy she was, how she neglected his kids, squandered his money . . . so finally he kicked her out." Her hard dark eyes were defiant as they met Missie's. "Soon as he is divorced he will marry me. I will be the new Mrs. Perelman."

Missie gripped the doorpost, numb with shock. "Where did she go?"

The girl shrugged. "Meyer was too good to her. Even though I said he should not do so much, he gave her money to feed the kids. Next we hear she's taken off and gone to California. Hollywood, no less." She smirked disparagingly. "Maybe with her looks she thinks she's gonna be a movie star. She should be so lucky!"

"*Where* is she living?" Missie stamped her foot angrily.

The girl shrugged. "Meyer doesn't know, and what's more he doesn't care."

"But what about the children?"

The girl stared at her thoughtfully for a few moments, "You know, kids is kids," she said finally. "Meyer says he can have a dozen more kids if he wants." She shrugged again, aiming a lazy, malicious smile at Missie. "A young woman like me can give a man like Meyer Perelman everything he wants."

Missie thought of Rosa and her girls, kicked out of their pitiful home for the sake of this hard-faced bitch, and she wanted to kill her. She reached out suddenly and slapped her hard across her cheek. "Don't you *ever* call Rosa Perelman a slut again," she cried. "It's you who are the slut, living here openly with a married man. A father who cares nothing for his own children! You and Meyer Perelman deserve each other."

Fighting back her tears, she turned and ran down the stairs, nauseated by the scene and the familiar reek of rotting vegetables and fish. Outside, she stopped and looked around at Rivington Street: The vendors were still loudly hawking their wares and the women were still proudly striking their bargains; dogs and cats and small children still lurked underfoot among the pushcart wheels. Nothing was different—and yet everything was changed. Sofia was gone, and O'Hara; Zev, and now Rosa. She knew she no longer belonged there.

After stopping to buy an enormous bunch of flowers, she walked quickly to St. Savior's, where she went inside and lighted a candle for Sofia. Then she placed the flowers on her grave and sat for a long time, remembering. Finally she thought about her future. She could hardly go to O'Hara and ask him to help her, not after she had gone and married someone else. And now Zev had disappeared too. She must just go to Hollywood and find Rosa.

After hurrying from the cemetery, she took the el back up to Second Avenue and hailed a cab. On an impulse she asked the cabbie to drive past the New Amsterdam Theater, peering from the window at the marquee blazing with familiar names. Only now there was a new "featured" Ziegfeld girl. Verity Byron's brief spurt of fame was already forgotten and she was yesterday's news, the one who had married the millionaire and gone to live in Europe.

She had two thousand four hundred dollars in her purse, no small sum if used carefully, and she had certainly learned how to do that. She would have to find a new way to make her living, for now she had two enemies to hide from, because Eddie Arnhaldt was as ruthless a foe as the Cheka. But Hollywood was a place where everybody gave themselves a brand-new name and a new family history and became someone else for the benefit of the silver screen. It seemed to her to be as good a place as any to find anonymity.

$$=== 34 ===$$

Hollywood

Rosa's Hollywood living quarters were very little different from New York; a single room instead of two, a few sticks of furniture, an old bed where the four of them slept top and tail, a kitchen shared with the other boarders, and a bathroom down the hall. The only change was that this was on the ground floor of a weatherboarded house with a porch tacked onto the front, a square of rusty grass beyond, and a view over the Hollywood Cemetery. And it was on the wrong corner of a street called Gower, where Sunset met Santa Monica.

Its disadvantages were that it was dismal, cramped, and hot as hell in the long summer and dismal, cold, and damp when it rained in winter—which it did occasionally and more heavily than she had been led to expect. Its advantages were that the view of the flowery Hollywood Hills with their backdrop of purple-bronze mountains offered a daily changing feast for her eyes, sometimes tipped with the pale blush-gold of daybreak when the air sparkled like crystal, sometimes broiling to a brown noonday crisp, and sometimes glazed with a roseate varnish as the giant red sun shifted westward over Santa Monica like some epic D. W. Griffith movie set in the sky.

Rosa was in love with Hollywood, only she wasn't so sure Hollywood was in love with her. She loved the palm trees and the pepper trees, the yucca and oleander and hibiscus; their colors made her feel like a tropical flower herself, ripening and unfolding her yearning petals in the sun—though what she yearned for she did not know. She loved the make-believe she saw enacted daily on the streets where "thieves" fled with swag bags while black-eyed "damsels" in yellow makeup screamed in distress as the cameraman turned his reels frantically to keep pace with the action. She loved seeing faces familiar from magazines at the corner drugstore in Hollywood where she worked, laughing and drinking sodas just like regular people, or stepping into their luxury automobiles, swanky imported Rolls-Royces and Bugattis and de Courmonts. Once she had even served the personal maid of the Nation's Sweetheart herself, who had come by to pick up the special cream Miss Pickford used to keep her skin beautiful for the benefit of her fans. But most of all, she liked the way her three kids were able to play outdoors in the sunshine, away from the grime and filth and dangerous traffic of the Lower East Side. Poor they might still be but they were healthier and happier, not least because Meyer was finally out of their lives. Yes, there was no doubt about it, Rosa told herself, smiling as she sat on the porch in the cool of the evening, she felt like a woman again, a young girl even. Finally. After all these years and three kids.

And her kids were something else again. Sonia loved Hollywood High and was already determined to be a teacher, though where she would find the money for college she didn't know. Hannah and Rachel were as movie-crazy as their mother and wanted to be in pictures, and Rosa was as ambitious for them as any true stage mother. She would do the rounds of the casting offices at the nearby studios, a neatly brushed and furbished child on each hand, starting with National on the opposite corner from the house and progressing through Metro at Romaine and Wilcox, Famous Players-Lasky on Selma, Chaplin at La Brea, and Griffith on Sunset. They were all within easy walking distance—the rest were out because they would have meant trolley-car fares.

The girls were pretty like her, with merry dark eyes and tumbling dark curls, and their plump, smiling innocent faces had already gained them several small roles as "walk-ons"—just one step up from extras really, but at least it meant the casting directors knew them by name, and there was always the chance they would think of them when the perfect role came along. That's the only way it was in Hollywood, they had told her: One day you're nothing, the next a star! And Rosa believed it.

Meanwhile, she worked at the drugstore and earned her own money. Of course it wasn't enough, but under this wonderful California blue sky and warm sunshine, good fortune was always just around the next corner. Hollywood bred hope in a thousand hearts, and Rosa's was one of them.

She rocked slowly on the porch, enjoying the peace. Occasionally an automobile would stutter past but mostly there were only the bird songs and cicadas to disturb her. Sonia was studying and the other two were playing with the kids from next door, probably racing illicitly around the gravestones in Hollywood Cemetery's four acres. The sun dropped low in the sky, sending a dusty golden light through her closed lids as she drifted contentedly, feeling a million miles away from Meyer and the Lower East Side. And from Missie, whom she missed like crazy. But she was thousands of miles away now—as far away as the stars. Her own life might not be the fairy tale Missie's was, but she had found a sort of peace.

She barely heard the sound of footsteps approaching, and she thought she must be dreaming when Missie's voice said, "There you are, Rosa. At last!"

But it wasn't a dream and Missie wasn't as far away as the stars. She was right there, with her back to the sun so she couldn't see her face properly, but she knew she was smiling.

"Missie!" she cried, leaping up and holding out her arms. "Such a surprise! Oh, am I glad to see you!"

They hugged each other tightly, tears of joy mingling as they stumbled through their stories. . . .

"You first," Rosa said, laughing. "Tell me all about your wonderful new life. And what are you doing here?"

"But it's not wonderful," Missie exclaimed. "It was a nightmare! I've run away, and that's why I came to find you. The woman at Meyer's place told me you had come to Hollywood. I knew the children would be in school so I went to each one and asked if they had any Perelmans on their student roster." She grinned. "I'm getting quite good at detective work."

"Then you know what happened to me," Rosa said bitterly. "So? Tell me all."

Missie nodded. "But first, what news of Zev? Is he here in Hollywood?"

"No one seems to have heard of him." She shrugged. "No news is bad news, they say. Maybe he went back to New York and pawnbroking."

"I would have liked to have seen him," Missie said wistfully, surprised how disappointed she felt. Zev had been part of her life, like O'Hara, and now it seemed she had lost them both.

"Very well," she said, "now I'll tell you what happened. But this time I'll tell you everything from the beginning. No more secrets."

Rosa listened in silence and then she said practically, "Okay, so now what?"

Missie eyed her doubtfully. "I don't know. All I knew was I must find you. I have just over two thousand dollars left—I thought I could get a job."

"*Two thousand dollars!* Why, you could buy this house for a lot less than that!" A thoughtful expression crossed her face as she considered what she had just said. "Missie," she exclaimed excitedly, "I think I have just found us an answer."

The Rosemont Rooming House was on Fountain Avenue between La Brea and Seward. They had chosen it because there were a dozen movie studios nearby, and therefore it was handy for aspiring actors and actresses to do their daily rounds. The ramshackle weatherboarded house had been patched up and given a coat of paint with green trim at the windows and doors, and it now offered half a dozen freshly decorated double rooms and two singles, with board extra for those who wanted it.

Missie and Rosa had worked hard to make it the sort of clean, airy place they wished they could have found when they had needed a room, and the big central hall had been turned into a sitting room filled with comfortable secondhand chairs, a card table, a tea table, a piano, and a Victrola. The chairs spilled out onto the wooden porch overlooking the white and pink stucco houses opposite, and the tree-lined street was as peaceful as a country lane.

The bungalow in the back garden became their own living quarters, where the girls slept two to a room and Rosa and Missie each had their own small rooms. Beulah had refused Missie's offer to pay her fare back east plus three months' wages and had decided to stay. She had her own room behind the kitchen at Rosemont, where she was now officially housekeeper, though for the moment unpaid. And Viktor, the dog, was master of the choicest shady spot on the front porch.

The only trouble was, they didn't yet have any boarders and the money had almost run out.

"We must advertise," Missie said as they glanced worriedly at each other across the dinner table. "We shall get the girls to hand-letter some leaflets and distribute them to the studios."

They trudged around Hollywood dropping their leaflets in every waiting room at every casting office, and two days later they got their first boarder, a bright fair-haired young man with a pleasant round face and thick glasses. His name was Dick Nevern and he was an aspiring director. He took the smallest single room and paid one month's cash in advance, peeled, Rosa noted as he handed it to her, from a very small roll of bills.

Because he was their only boarder they decided he might as well eat with the family, and he kept them entertained with stories of his home out on the vast wheat plains of Oklahoma, where life drifted slowly and inevitably from the old red schoolhouse to teenage square dances, to work on the family farm and marriage to the girl next door, to a rocking chair on the porch and dungarees, a wide-brimmed hat, and a straw in the corner of your mouth as you dozed the time away and swatted flies.

"So what makes you think you can be a movie director?" Missie asked.

Dick took off his thick glasses and polished them, peering at her with myopic red-rimmed eyes. "Y'jest learn how to really see things out there on the plains. There's sumpin' about all that space, those broad horizons, that stretches the eye, puts everything into perspective, every tree and every object into its rightful place. I've rearranged that landscape so many times I reckon it'd be child's play to do what Mr. Griffith does. It's characters I'm not too sure about. I haven't had much truck with strangers. . . ."

"You'll do just fine," Missie reassured him. "You're having no trouble with us."

"And how long do you give yourself before you become this big director like Mr. Griffith?" Rosa asked, thinking worriedly about her rent.

"Ah've given myself exactly three months, that's 'bout as long as my money will last." He finished polishing his glasses, put them back on his blunt nose, and beamed at them. "That's time enough, don't y'think?"

Rosa sighed. She could just see the way it was going to be with a rooming house full of young hopefuls with no money. Maybe it hadn't been such a great idea after all.

Hollywood was swarming with eager young people, and within two weeks Rosemont was able to hang the "No Vacancies" sign on the gate. They had the twins, Lilian and Mary Grant, aged nineteen, blonde and beautiful with round blue eyes and long curling hair, accompanied by their mother, Mrs. Winona Grant, all the way from Stamford, Connecticut, who told them her daughters were "just brimming with talent. They've learned since the age of six at the local Barrymore School of Mime and Dance."

Then there was Millie Travers, aged twenty, from Des Moines, with a valise full of old copies of *Photoplay* and her pretty red head full of dreams; and feisty young Ben Solomon from Newark, New Jersey, who wanted to be a comedian like Harold Lloyd and who had worked his way across the country playing every small club that would have him. There was forty-year-old Marshall Makepiece, who had played Broadway and San Francisco and everywhere in between in his up-and-down acting career and who thought he recognized something familiar about Missie, but he just couldn't put his finger on it. . . . And there were Ruth D'Abo, Marie Mulvaine, and Louise Hansen, who were all fully employed as Mack Sennett Bathing Beauties and from whom at least Rosa knew she could be sure of the rent.

The old weatherboard house brimmed with life and youth. It took Missie's mind off her fears and Rosa's off Meyer, and it brought in enough to cover their needs so even if they were not making a fortune somehow it didn't seem to matter. And the children thought the boarders were just one big extended happy family.

Eight-year-old Azaylee still missed her pony and her beautiful room at Haus Arnhaldt and the servants and the fuss everyone made of her. And she missed the fact that she'd only had to mention something, a doll, a dress, a game, and it was hers. She had been waiting eagerly for her new stepbrother, Augie, to come home from school to be her companion, but now she couldn't wait to race home from school with Hannah and Rachel, her books clutched under her arm, flaxen braids swinging, eager to hear who had got work today and what the Bathing Beauties had been up to. But her real idols were the twins.

Lilian and Mary left for the studios each morning after a dawn breakfast, watched by their eagle-eyed mother, who knew only too well their craving for sugarcakes and honey and Beulah's apple turnovers. "Think of your figures," she would chide them as they eyed Beulah's hot biscuits longingly. "Take care of your complexions," she would say, pushing away the chocolate cake at supper. "Remember there's a lot more to being a movie star than just talent." So, fortified by orange juice, cereal, and fresh fruit, the twins made the rounds of the casting offices, smiling blandly at the women and a little more roguishly at the men, and they returned wearily each afternoon, still jobless, to take their "beauty sleep," as their mother called it. They were up again at four, for an hour's dance practice in the sitting room. Mrs. Grant played the piano and Azaylee watched, breathless with admiration, as they stretched and leapt and pitter-pattered around on their toes, until, overcome with excitement, she would dance along with them, copying their movements exactly, her long coltlike legs wobbling as she balanced on tiptoe, her thin body swaying in time to the music.

In no time at all she was accompanying them to their daily classes at the Berkley School of Dancing on Santa Monica Boulevard, and when she was there she just knew she was the happiest girl in Hollywood. All she ever wanted to do was dance.

Life was so busy for Missie and Rosa it was only after supper at the end of the long day that they had time to talk to each other. About serious things, that is.

"So? What do you think Eddie is up to?" Rosa asked three months later as they sat on the porch in the gathering dusk.

Missie shrugged. "I don't know, and I wish I didn't care. What do you think he's up to, Rosa?"

"Looking for you, private detectives, costing him a fortune. He must be going crazy by now."

"He's already crazy. Obsessed." She shivered, even though the evening was a sultry one. "One day he'll find us, Rosa, I know it."

"Never." Rosa scoffed reassuringly. "He would never dream his wife would be running a boardinghouse in Hollywood." She paused and then added thoughtfully, "Unless . . ."

Missie's eyes widened with alarm. She sat up straight in her rattan chair and said nervously, "Unless . . . what?"

"Well, I was just thinking. I mean, look how easy you found me, just asking at the local schools if the kids went there. What if he were to do the same thing?"

That old familiar sinking feeling grabbed her by the stomach. "My God, how foolish I've been!" she wailed. "I thought he would try Ziegfeld, Madame Elise, the New York theater world. I never imagined he might come to Hollywood. But where else would an actress come to find work? He knows I have no money!"

"Why not just change Azaylee's name?" Rosa said, ever practical.

"Oh, no, I couldn't do that. Not again." Missie glanced at her worriedly, "The poor child will begin to wonder who she is. And besides, it's too late. Everyone knows her. No, I'll just have to take her out of school, get her a tutor." She sighed as she thought of the money it would cost. "I'll manage somehow."

The very next day Azaylee's desk was set up in the dining room and five mornings a week a young teacher, who had abandoned her profession for the riskier world of the movies, came to instruct her in arithmetic, English composition and grammar, and the rudiments of history and geography.

"But *why* can't I go to school with Hannah and Rachel?" Azaylee stormed, torrents of tears flowing down her face. *"Why* must I be taught at home, all by myself? I miss school and I miss the other kids. . . . *Why* are you doing this to me?"

"It's only temporary," Missie said, hedging, "just for a little while. I cannot tell you the reason now, but believe me it's for the best."

Azaylee stared at her mutely, her luminous pansy-gold eyes brimming, and then she turned and ran upstairs to her room. When she refused to come down for supper, Missie took her up a tray. She was lying on her bed and when she saw her she turned her head away, staring out of the window.

"Come, *milochka,*" Missie coaxed, "you must eat supper or you'll be hungry in the middle of the night."

"I'm not hungry," Azaylee said distantly.

"But you should eat something," Missie urged. "If you are to be a dancer you'll need to be strong."

"I'm not going to be a dancer," she muttered, flinging her arm across her eyes so she would not have to look at Missie.

Missie watched her uncertainly for a moment, and then she put the tray on the table and said quietly, "I'm truly sorry, Azaylee. I wish I didn't have to do this but right now I do. I know that's hard for a little girl to understand, but that's the way it is. Meanwhile, please try to eat your supper." She hesitated, her hand on the doorknob, and added, "Maybe you'll want to come downstairs afterward. Mrs. Grant has promised to play the piano and the Bathing Beauties are going to rehearse their new act for us."

Normally Azaylee would have been galvanized into activity by such information, but now she simply turned her face away again and said nothing.

Later, when Missie went in to kiss her good night, the food was still untouched and Azaylee seemed to be sleeping. She stared at her worriedly for a few moments and then carried the tray back down to the kitchen.

Azaylee appeared at breakfast the next morning looking subdued and pale. She drank a glass of milk and drifted listlessly across the lawn to Rosemont's dining room, where Miss Valerian, her tutor, was waiting.

"All the spirit has gone out of her!" Rosa cried, horrified. "What have we done, Missie?"

She shook her head, scared. Azaylee looked just the way her mother, Anouska, used to look when she retreated into that world of her own where no one could reach her, and from which each time she seemed more and more reluctant to return.

It was the boarders who finally coaxed Azaylee out of her depression, joining in her lessons and making her laugh with their silly pretend-schoolgirl errors. Millie lent her her latest copy of *Photoplay* and the Bathing Beauties showed her their new stills, taken on the beach at Santa Monica with Mack Sennett himself right in the middle between Ruth and Marie. And Lilian and Mary told her they would not go to dance class unless she went too, so of course she went. But Missie knew for certain it had been touch and go and that Azaylee was as capable of great swings in mood as Anouska.

They were sitting around the porch a few weeks later when Dick Nevern tossed aside the newspaper he was reading and said, "Imagine that, a young kid of fourteen inheriting all that money. A fortune—more than I'll ever make as a director, no matter how successful I am."

"More than Mary Pickford?" asked Millie Travers, who knew all about the stars' contracts as well as the details of their domestic lives as recounted by the movie magazines.

"Millions more than Pickford or Chaplin or any of them," Nevern retorted.

"So, who is he, this fourteen-year-old millionaire?" Rosa asked interestedly. "Maybe he'll do for my Hannah?"

Nevern picked up the newspaper again and read the headline: "Son of German Steel Baron Inherits All After Fatal Accident.

"Baron Eddie Arnhaldt was killed yesterday in an automobile accident that also took the lives of his friend, the Countess Gretel von Dussman, and another couple. The car, a new Broadman roadster, was believed to have gone out of control and struck a tree on a narrow road near Deauville. The baron and his friends were said to have died instantly. His only son, fourteen-year-old Augustus Arnhaldt, will inherit one of the world's major fortunes, including iron, steel, and armaments factories at Essen in Germany."

Rosa leapt to her feet. "Excuse me," she said faintly, "I've just thought of something very important I have to do."

Missie was sitting in the kitchen having a cup of coffee with Beulah. "What is it?" she asked, alarmed by Rosa's flushed face and glittering eyes.

"Arnhaldt is dead!" Rosa cried. "Killed in a road accident yesterday. It's all in the papers. Oh, Missie, Missie. *All your troubles are over!*"

35

New York

"King" O'Hara surveyed his crowded nightclub with a grin as big as his cigar, counting the noisy, glossy customers with a practiced eye, mentally assessing his take—and his profit. And profit was mostly what it was. King O'Hara's prices were so exorbitant, everyone knew it must be the best and they fought to get in.

Now he had opened a second club, O'Hara's Purple Orchid on West Fifty-second Street, with even higher prices and a classier image: cool gray, lilac, and gold decor, the band in dinner jackets, gold champagne coolers imported from France, crystal stemware, and hothouse flowers fresh daily, with a single exquisite, expensive purple orchid for each lady and a specially dyed purple carnation boutonnière for each man. King O'Hara's counted anybody with enough bucks and enough clout to pay for the cover and the drink as its clientele, but the Purple Orchid was high class. Its customers were the wealthy scions of high society, the leaders of café society, and the cream of the theater world. No one was ever granted membership in the Purple Orchid without O'Hara's personal say-so, and, pinned to the trailing fox furs of a beautiful, bejeweled young lady, the purple flower had become the chicest accessory in town.

The gold-studded dance floor at the Purple Orchid and the black glass dance floor at King O'Hara's were packed nightly, and even with the huge payoffs necessary to keep him from being raided, O'Hara was making a fortune—even more than the Oriconne brothers who had given him his start. And that was his one big problem. The brothers didn't like their ex-employee muscling in on their territory. They objected to him buying his bootleg liquor from another supplier, especially as he had used their contacts to get it at lower prices than they could offer. And his nightclubs were in direct competition with their own café-clubs in Manhattan, Philadelphia, Pittsburgh, and Chicago.

The nice Oriconne brothers, Giorgio and Rico, had invited him to a nice "family-style" party at Rico's mansion in New Jersey. It was Rico's daughter's sweet-sixteen birthday party. O'Hara had gone to Tiffany and asked for a suitable gift, and young Graziella Oriconne had been thrilled with the slender gold chain with sixteen exquisite pearls interspersed with angelskin coral.

"Never thought I'd see the day when I'd admit you had good taste, O'Hara," Rico had commented, smiling at his pretty dark-haired daughter's pleasure, "but I gotta hand it to you, when you adopted a new name—'King'—you bought yourself a touch of class to go with it."

"Yeah, well, about King O'Hara's, Rico." He puffed on his cigar, glancing at Rico through the smoke. "It's no skin off your nose, me running a place like that. And the Purple Orchid—well, it's just another nightspot, one among hundreds."

"Sixteen of which are the Oriconnes'," Giorgio said softly.

O'Hara watched him, waiting for what was to come next. Rico was easy to read; dark hair, soft eyes, short and plump, a real nice gentle family guy. Just look at today's party for his daughter. What real bad guy could throw a bash like this? The place was crowded with family and friends, young people and little kids—babies even —running around the sun-dappled lawns and drinking lemonade beneath the shade trees. No liquor was ever served at Oriconne's house. But Giorgio was another matter. He was of middle height with a kind of spindly thinness, slick black hair, and a whiplash mustache. His sharp dark eyes missed nothing; one penetrating glance from Giorgio's shadowed orbs and you knew he had memorized every detail—and that he would never forget.

Giorgio always seemed to O'Hara like a man waiting for the action to start. He was never still, he fidgeted silently from foot to foot, chain-smoking nervously even at a nice relaxed affair like this. And he had heard there was no woman in Giorgio's life—not since his wife died a few years back; fell off an ocean liner on her way to Italy, they had said.

Of course there had been some speculation about suicide. What need had a person like that to end her own life? Hadn't she everything a woman could ever want? Money, jewels, furs, houses? And a faithful husband? At least, no one had ever *caught* Giorgio with another woman so his innocence must be assumed. They said having no kids was the great sorrow of her life. I mean, an Italian woman with no kids is like strawberries without sugar—a little tart, a little acid—and it was known that Giorgio had envied his brother his happy family life with his half-dozen children. Still, it left Giorgio an unknown quantity and one O'Hara was careful not to rile.

"Why you do this to us, O'Hara, huh?" Giorgio said in his quiet, husky voice. "We were good to you, treated you like family. Then you try to take our business away."

O'Hara puffed on his cigar, coughing on the smoke. "Sure, and there's enough out there for us all, Giorgio," he said with a nervous grin. "Everybody in the world wants to go to a nightclub—yours, mine—what's the difference?"

"Money," Giorgio said softly, "a lot of money."

Rico's voice was suddenly cold as he said, "Me and my brother have discussed the situation, O'Hara. We have decided that in future you should buy all your liquor from us. Our rates, to an old friend, like you, will be reasonable. You know our system, how it works. Our men will contact you Monday for your first order."

"And by the way," Giorgio added, his tobacco-hoarse voice almost a growl, "there will be a premium to pay. Twenty-five percent. We reckon that's the least you owe to put matters straight between you and the family."

O'Hara's eyebrows shot up. Giorgio was talking a lot of money here: 25 percent on top of his orders meant 25 percent less in his pocket and 25 percent of his profits in the Oriconnes'. "I'll think it over," he said, grinding his cigar into the immaculate turf.

Rico raised a finger to summon a white-jacketed servant. He pointed to the cigar stub, and the man removed it immediately. "Don't think too long, O'Hara," he said, taking him by the elbow. "And now, why don't we join the party? It's almost time for Graziella to cut her cake."

Sure enough, the brothers' man had shown up the following Monday, and sure enough, O'Hara had placed his order, but it was for only half the amount he needed. The rest he got secretly from a dozen small suppliers who were happy to have his business at favorable rates, and he reckoned he had cut the Oriconnes' 25 percent down to 12½. Even though that stung him, it was a small price to pay to keep them quiet. Their liquor arrived like clockwork every Wednesday night at four and was unloaded into his cellars swiftly and silently. The Oriconnes had always run a smooth operation.

That had been six months ago and now he was thinking of opening in Chicago. He had heard of some great premises on the south side, big enough to crowd 'em in but small enough to keep it exclusive. He had learned quickly that big numbers were not important, because when you charged top dollar you could make the same profit with half the outlay. King O'Hara had earned himself the reputation of being a smart operator.

His building and contracting business in Smallwood Hills, New Jersey, was going more slowly. For some reason he was having difficulty getting the proper permits, but he knew it was all a matter of time and finding the right payola deal. He could wait.

The only bad news in his life had been Missie's running off and marrying the German baron. He still dreamed about her at nights— or rather days, for his whole life was reversed. He got up at six in the afternoon, showered, shaved, had his breakfast of corned beef hash and five cups of coffee in his smart penthouse suite atop the new Sherry Netherland Hotel. Then he might catch the latest Broadway show, always with some pretty girl on his arm—usually one from the upper social classes who adored his Irish blarney and his rugged redheaded good looks, as well as his newfound reputation as a "King" in bed. But none like Missie. She was a classier dame than even the richest and classiest of society women. Missie was a true lady, and he still loved her even though he damned her in his dreams.

After that it was dinner at a smart restaurant and on to the club, the place where he truly felt like a king. He enjoyed the turned heads as he entered his little kingdom, he enjoyed having celebrities vie to catch his eye, or his smile, or a word or two, and he enjoyed choosing whose table he should grace with his charm and jokes and presence each night. All in all, he was a very happy man. If it was not for Missie.

He wasn't a man who gave much time to reading journals, and it was a few months after the event that the headline about Arnhaldt's death caught his eye, as his cellarman unwrapped a newspaper from around the latest batch of alcohol, bought from rum runners in Bermuda.

He read and reread it, but there was only a brief mention of Arnhaldt's marriage to the Ziegfeld beauty and the fact that his son inherited everything. And where did that leave Missie? he wondered. Alone and penniless again? Anger burned in his heart as he remembered the pain and anguish of her desertion, but he knew he would still do anything for her. He guessed he was just a sucker after all. A sucker in love.

It took a team of private detectives exactly a week to uncover the fact that the young Baroness Arnhaldt had flown the coop only months after her marriage and that no one knew where she was, especially her husband, who had spent a fortune on wild goose chases, even as far as South America, trying to track her down. And also the fact that he had been living openly with the Countess Gretel von Dussman even before Missie had left him and that Eddie Arnhaldt had not left his young wife a single pfennig.

"I don't care what it costs," O'Hara told the detectives, just as Eddie must have, "find her."

"Give us a clue at least," they begged. "I mean, if Arnhaldt with all his money couldn't find her, how d'ya expect us to?"

"Try Ziegfeld," he said, "try Madame Elise, try Rivington Street." He thought for a minute and then said, "Try Rosa Perelman and Zev Abramski."

They drew blanks with Ziegfeld and Elise but found out soon enough that both Abramski and Rosa had gone to Hollywood. And it took another month of hard work to find that no one had ever heard of a Zev Abramski in Hollywood but that Rosa Perelman was running a boardinghouse on Fountain Avenue.

O'Hara immediately put on his hat, caught the Twentieth Century Limited to Chicago, where he conducted a little business and signed the lease for his new club, then took a Pullman on the next afternoon's Limited to Los Angeles.

He found his reputation had preceded him. He was welcomed personally by Mrs. Margaret Anderson, the manager of the Beverly Hills Hotel, and shown to her best pink stucco bungalow set amid lush lawns and flower beds. He showered, changed, slicked back his wet red curls, hired a chauffeured car, and set off to find Rosa.

As they drove he stared around at the roads that petered out into flat fields and citrus groves, at the palm trees and the jungly hills baking in the sunshine and the bare, glowering mountains beyond. He took in the pretty Spanish houses, the few stores, and the unfinished look of the place and knew it wasn't for him. "B'jaysus," he commented to the driver, "a man could go crazy here. What d'you do for amusement of an evening?"

"Most folks is in the movie business," the driver said glumly. "It's an early rising town and early to bed. All they do is work—

them that has work, that is. The rest of 'em sits around in casting offices—hoping."

No town for a nightclub, O'Hara thought. Or was it? Maybe everybody went to bed early because there was nowhere else to go?

"Here's Fountain, sir." The driver turned into a quiet tree-lined street. "Rosemont's 'bout the middle here." He stopped in front of a white three-storey house. The sash windows were flung open to the fresh air and clean cotton curtains blew in the faint breeze; the windowpanes sparkled and a couple of pretty blond girls sat reading on the front porch. And next to them, sprawled in the shade, was Viktor. O'Hara's heart almost burst with relief and love—if the dog was here, Azaylee was there. *And so was Missie.*

A tall, actorish-looking man strolled from the hall, surveying him as he stepped from the car and walked up the narrow path. "Sorry, old fellow," he said in a crisp English accent, "but the 'No Vacancy' sign is right there on the gate. Though I must admit, with that car and a driver, you could do a bit better for yourself than Rosemont."

"And what's wrong with Rosemont?" O'Hara demanded defensively. "If it's good enough for Rosa Perelman it's good enough for anybody."

The man nodded. "I meant that you were obviously not just anybody—like the rest of us. In other words, you look like a man in gainful employment."

"That I am," O'Hara said proudly, "as well as an old friend. King O'Hara's the name." He held out his huge fist and shook the man's hand enthusiastically.

"Marshall Makepiece," the man said, dropping his British upper-crust voice and lapsing back into everyday American.

"Are you really King O'Hara?" The twins gasped in unison.

Their voices were suitably awed and O'Hara grinned. "I sure am, and I'm delighted to meet two such beautiful girls. If you'll forgive me saying so, shouldn't you be in the movies? With eyes as innocent as yours, you'll make Mary Pickford look like a barmaid."

The girls blushed and Makepiece laughed. "Lilian and Mary are the next stars-to-be. The rest of us are just hoping."

O'Hara nodded. "And the lady proprietor? Where would she be now?"

"Who's asking for me?" Rosa appeared suddenly in the doorway, wiping her hands on a dishcloth. "Give only a look." She gasped, her eyes almost jumping from her head. "It's Shamus O'Hara from Delancey Street."

"And if ever a man was glad to see a woman it's me," he exclaimed jubilantly. "You've cost me a small fortune, Rosa, hidin' away in Hollywood like this. It took a team of detectives a month to find you."

Her shrewd eyes assessed his beaming face and she sighed. "It's not me you're searching for though, is it, O'Hara?"

He mopped his forehead with an immaculate white pocket handkerchief. "Sure, and I'll have to confess it's Missie I'm after," he said anxiously. "I'm hoping she's here with you, Rosa, and not with Zev Abramski."

She shrugged. "No one knows what's become of that mystery man. He sold his business and left for Hollywood with no forwarding address and that was that. It's a small town; I guess by now I would have heard if he was the big success." She looked O'Hara up and down again while the twins and Marshall watched interestedly. "You look like a man come into a fortune himself," she commented, inspecting his dapper tailored suit, his tan-and-white spectator brogues, his blue silk shirt with a darker blue striped tie. "What happened to the shamrock suspenders and the old tie holding up your pants?"

"I can afford better now," O'Hara said, waving his arms expansively. "Would you be stallin' me then, Rosa?" he said impatiently. "I'm a man with a mission and I need to find Missie."

"Come inside and take a seat," she said, turning away, "I'll go and get her."

O'Hara's heart was pounding. *She was going to get Missie!* He wondered suddenly if she had changed—after all, she was a married woman, a widow now . . . she had become used to money, servants, anything she wanted. . . . He sat staring at his big hands, waiting.

"O'Hara?"

He looked up and met her eyes, those same innocent, deep-violet eyes that had captured his heart an age ago.

"I can't believe it's you," she said, coming toward him smiling.

He stood up, holding out his arms, waiting for her to walk into them. And as he held her to his chest, feeling his heart beat next to hers, he knew he need not have worried. Missie hadn't changed. She would never change. She would always be the girl he loved.

36

Magic Movie Studios were located north of Hollywood Boulevard on a dirt track off Cahuenga Avenue, and though they were one of the smaller and newer outfits in town, the freshly painted studios and Spanish-style stucco offices had an air of prosperous solidity that told you they were no fly-by-night operation. The two great barnlike studios were in full production night and day now that they had the new klieg lights, and a third studio was in the process of construction. There were two street sets on the back lot, one city and one western, and Magic had three female stars: Mae French, sultry, sexy, and glamorous; Dawn Chaney, petite, girlish, and innocent; and Mitzi Harmoney, cute, curly-haired, and a comedienne. The two male stars were Ralph Lance, a sophisticated, romantic Englishman, and Tom Jacks, rough, tough, and a terrific horseman.

Magic's pictures revolved around their five stars: all the other actors were picked up as needed from the casting offices. Mostly they churned out comic one- and two-reelers and drawing-room dramas, but a new stage was being built to house their first big epic. Magic aimed to compete with Griffith with their new movie, *Scheherazade,* featuring their roster of stars and a cast of thousands. The sets were already being built, the costumes designed, the shooting script assessed and reassessed a million times; and now they had lost their director.

C. Z. Abrams—owner and president of Magic—leaned back in his large leather swivel chair and stared at his team coldly.

"So, gentlemen," he said in his low, quiet voice that had them on the edge of their seats, "which of you knew that Arnott was going to defect to Vitagraph?"

The four men shuffled the papers in their hands and stared at their feet. "It was like this, sir," the assistant director said finally. "Arnott's heart wasn't in it and . . . well, the fact is Vitagraph offered him five thousand a week. You can't blame a man for taking that kind of money."

"I can blame him for not coming to discuss it with me first," Abrams said quietly. He stared at the four young men: his assistant director, his producer and assistant, and his cameraman, all of them vital to his mammoth new production. "Do I take it then that you all agree with Arnott's decision?"

They glanced at each other and then the assistant director said, "Well, sure, Mr. Abrams, all of us reckon we would have done the same under those circumstances. And besides, the hours we're putting in we could all be earning better money."

He nodded, pushed back his chair, and stood up. "Then I suggest you follow Arnott's example and go to Vitagraph. Maybe they will pay you five thousand a week also. Gentlemen, you are all fired."

The producer leapt to his feet, red-faced and stuttering. "But, Mr. Abrams, all we said was it was understandable. . . ."

Abrams's cold eyes met his for a moment. "Not to me, it isn't," he replied. "Money can always be earned, but loyalty and integrity are beyond price." After pressing a buzzer, he told his secretary to see that they were paid off and that they left Magic's lot immediately.

He watched as the men he had worked with for over a year followed the secretary out of his office. In a way he felt sorry for them, but the rumors of discontent and impending trouble had been reported to him weeks ago. Now he wished he had acted faster. Discontent spread like gangrene in the flesh, and he knew quick amputation was the only way to stop it. It would cost him thousands more to delay the shooting of *Scheherazade* than it would to pay the men more money, but he could not bear disloyalty. He did not demand love from his employees and his stars, but he did expect honesty. He dealt fairly with them, treated them like family, ensured the happiness on the set of even the lowliest extra by paying them promptly and well. His stars were sent flowers regularly and given extra little gifts, like the brand-new low-slung scarlet Packard roadster for Mae, the floor-length ermine cape for pretty Dawn, and the biggest blue-tiled swimming pool in California for Mitzi. He even paid Tom's racehorse trainer as well as picking up the tab for Ralph's custom-made London suits and hand-crafted shoes. All he asked in return, besides good money-making pictures, was that they kept their sex lives quiet and their names out of the papers—except for the carefully posed inserts in *Picture Play, Photoplay,* and *Mo-*

tion Picture Classics. And on the rare occasions when he met his
stars socially, at a party at one of their sumptuous houses or a
formal dinner held at his own mansion next to the Burton Green
estate on Lexington Road in smart new Beverly Hills, he was cool,
charming, polite, and always remote.

And when he sat in his big office with the pictures of his stars on
the walls or strolled his fifty acres on Cahuenga, inspecting his fine
studios and his newest cameras and his revolutionary klieg lights,
he knew he was master of all he surveyed. At his fine thirty-room
mansion on Lexington he could count great paintings on his walls,
tasteful decor, and fine carpets. There were flowers in each large
sweet-smelling room, a dog sprawled on his terrace, tall cedars to
spread shade across his carefully tended lawns. He had a housekeeper and servants, a chauffeur and half a dozen automobiles, he
had accountants and lawyers and a great deal of money in the bank.
And he worked twenty-four hours a day to keep his loneliness at
bay.

He almost looked forward to the problem confronting him now.
Finding a new director for *Scheherazade* would not be easy; the best
were already working at other studios.

The intercom buzzed noisily. He pressed the switch and his secretary said, "Miss Lilian and Miss Mary Grant are here to see you,
with their mother, sir."

He sighed. Stage mothers were an eternal problem, but he always
vetted every member of the cast personally before any of his films
went into production, and his was the final yes or no. The Grant
twins were in the final round of casting for the roles of two dance
maidens, not big roles but well featured. At least they had been in
the last script he saw. Now he would have to tell them that the film
was postponed indefinitely, until he could find a new director.

He stood up as they entered, shook their hands, gave each of
them a chair, and then returned to his seat behind the desk, sitting
back with his hands folded, looking at the girls, unsmiling.

Winona Grant assessed him as he assessed her girls. She had
heard a lot about the reclusive C. Z. Abrams, how he had taken
over Schroeder's dilapidated studios and in two years made Magic a
name to be reckoned with in motion pictures. It was said he had
made a fortune turning out hundreds of cheap little comedies and
serials that fit into almost any bill at every movie theater around the
country. Magic had not made its name in big features, but now it
was on its way, after hits like *Dark Destiny* and the long-running

serial *The Adventures of Mitzi* and Tom Jacks's spectacular western
sagas. It was also said that C. Z. was about to spend a great deal of
that quickly amassed fortune on his new epic, and after the failure
of Griffith's *Intolerance,* the word around the casting offices was
that he had better know what he was doing.

However, Winona did not care about C. Z.'s great gamble. All
she wanted was featured roles for her daughters.

"Both Lilian and Mary are accomplished in all forms of dance,
Mr. Abrams," she said, gushing and smiling brightly at him. "Ballet, tap, rhythm and movement. . . ."

"I am sure they are, madam," he replied, shifting his cold stare
from the girls to her, "and may I compliment you on their beauty.
Unfortunately, we are having some problems. We are without a
director at this moment. The movie will be postponed indefinitely."

The girls' bright faces fell and they glanced at their mother appealingly. "Well, but . . ." Winona floundered, stunned by his
news. "I mean, when the movie is back on schedule, I hope my girls
will still be in running for the parts."

"Lilian and Mary will have their parts—if and when *Scehera-
zade* goes into production." A rare smile lighted his face. "I am
sorry," he said to the girls. "I know how much this meant to you. I
will tell my secretary to keep your names and photographs on file.
Thank you for taking the time to come and see me."

They gazed at him bemused as he escorted them to the door.
"Thank you, Mr. Abrams," they chorused, not knowing whether to
be disappointed about the movie or delighted by C. Z.'s attention.

"Imagine that." Winona snorted angrily as they walked across
the lot to the guarded gates. "We came all this way only to find out
he's fired the director."

"But he said he would remember us, Mother," Lilian said, her
eyes sparkling, "and you just know a man like that means it."

"There's just something about him," Mary added dreamily.
"He's so calm and controlled, an ice-man—until he smiles, and then
he lights up. And he's handsome too, in that dark, smoldering sort
of way." She shivered dramatically. "I feel he is a man of *power.*"

"Enough power to fire everybody whenever he feels like it," their
mother retorted smartly as they waited in the heat for the tramcar
to take them back to Rosemont. "A man like that has power, all
right, the power to decide over other people's lives."

C. Z. and Magic Movie Studios and the closing down of production on *Scheherazade* were discussed in depth over the supper table

at Rosemont that night. Missie was dining with O'Hara at the Beverly Hills Hotel and missed the excitement of how the twins almost got starring roles, but Dick Nevern listened thoughtfully, saying little.

The next morning he got up early, ate two helpings of ham and eggs, a plate of hash browns, and four popovers to give him energy, and then he set out for Magic.

The uniformed guard at the gate tilted back his cap and eyed him up and down unsympathetically. He saw hundreds like him every day. "What are ya? A comic?" he asked cynically when Dick said he wanted to see Mr. Abrams. "Anyways, C. Z. never sees anybody without an appointment, most of all you." He sat back and folded his arms, grinning.

Dick hesitated for a moment and he reached into his pocket, pulled out a precious five-dollar bill, and said, "Please tell him that Dick Nevern, a genius cameraman and director, is here to see him." He watched regretfully as the guard slipped the bill into his pocket, listening as he repeated his words to C. Z.'s secretary. He put down the phone and turned back to him.

"She says C. Z.'s busy all day, but if you like you can wait. Over there, third path on the right, the big office at the end," he called as Dick ran through the gate and headed excitedly toward his future.

He paused to stare at an action sequence being shot on the western street, watching the cameraman carefully, noting how he took his instructions from the director. Then he slipped quietly into the big green barn, letting his eyes get used to the darkness, staring awed at the elaborate drawing room set—why, he might have been in a real Manhattan penthouse with the light from half a dozen brilliant kliegs streaming in through the tall windows and the famous skyline behind. And there was the glamorous Miss Mae French in a long satin dress, lounging on a brocade sofa while a violin quartet played in the background to get her in the mood for her big romantic scene with Ralph Lance.

"Glamour," a quiet voice said next to him, "that's what people want. They want to forget the dark hovels they live in and for ten cents escape into a world of romance. They want to gasp at how gorgeous her clothes are and imagine themselves dining with a man like him. They want to laugh and to cry. . . ."

"They want to be entertained," Dick finished, glancing quickly at the man beside him. "Jeez, see how he's lighting her, full onto the face like that? He should shift those lamps behind her, get some shadows onto her face . . . jeez. . . ." He shifted anxiously from foot to foot, itching to get onto the set and do it his way.

"What do you think of the set?" the man asked him casually.

"Good. Too many windows though—we get the message, it's a penthouse in New York, but we could have had it all a bit grander, with paintings and drapes. More . . . more texture, I guess. Aw, jeez." He glanced at the man again. "Did you design it? I'm sorry."

The man laughed. "Tell me more."

"Well, for instance, now I think he should be approaching her from behind the sofa, kind of slip his arms around her. This way you can hardly see her face and as she's the prettiest thing around, I guess that's what the audience wants to see."

"And if they don't, you'll have one very angry Mae French," the man said feelingly. "I'm on my way over to the *Adventures* set. Why don't you come with me and take a look at that?"

"Sure thing. My name's Dick Nevern." He pumped the man's hand enthusiastically as they strode from the barn and headed for the neighboring set. Mitzi was being filmed outside, sitting on an upturned bucket, wearing frilled gingham skirts, black stockings, and black button boots, and somebody was holding an umbrella over her head to stop her makeup from melting in the sun.

They watched the action for a while, Dick passing some comments and the man asking him some questions, and then they dropped in to see a few of the fast two-reelers being made. "I know I can do better than this," Dick muttered agitatedly. "I just know I can."

"There's something I want to show you," the man said finally, "but I have to be at a meeting. Here, why don't you take this key and go and look in the big storage hangar at the back of the lot. It's a ten-minute walk, but I think you will find it interesting."

Dick hesitated. "Well, I kinda have an appointment myself. . . ." Then he remembered that C. Z. was busy all day and figured another half hour wouldn't make any difference. Besides, now he was curious. "Well, sure, why not, if it's okay, I mean, jeez, I wouldn't want to be caught trespassing where I'm not supposed to go, you know."

The man nodded. "Just drop the key off with Mr. Abrams's secretary when you're through," he said as he strode purposefully away.

The hangar was filled with monolithic sets, statues, props, and painted backdrops for *Scheherazade,* all gold and crimson and Arabian splendor. Dick guessed this was what the man had meant about giving people an escape from their drab daily lives. For ten cents they could be transported to the mysterious east via Magic's magical movie. Or they could have, if *Scheherazade* had not been canceled.

After locking the door regretfully behind him, he walked over to C. Z. Abrams's office and handed the key to his secretary.

"Oh, yes," she said, "you must be Dick Nevern. C. Z. said if you're such a big-shot genius like you say, then maybe he'd better give you a test. Be here tomorrow morning at six-thirty."

Dick let out a great whoop of excitement. After grabbing her hand and kissing it, he said, "But when do I get to meet the great man?"

"You already have," she replied. "I understand he gave you a conducted tour of the lot."

Dick told them over supper exactly how his jaw had dropped, and repeated exactly what C. Z. had said to him and what he had said to C. Z., and accepted their congratulations warily. "It's only a test," he warned.

After a sleepless night he was at the studios at six. This time the guard dropped his wisecracks and told him politely he was to go to Studio B.

Mitzi Harmoney was already there, having her makeup applied, and a couple of dozen extras were eating sandwiches and waiting around. The producer shook his hand and said, "C. Z. says you're to take over this set today. He says just to do it your way."

Dick gulped. No foolin', this was his big chance; his first day on the set and he was directing a star. Jeez, he'd just better not screw up, that's all. He glanced through the shooting script and quickly made a few amendments. Then he checked the shots with the cameraman, telling him precisely what he wanted, and then he spoke to Mitzi.

As he described what he had in mind, she nodded approvingly. At twenty she was a shrewd professional who had been working in movies since she was fourteen. She came from a family of vaudevillians and knew exactly how to construct a gag, and she knew he did too.

"Let's go," she said, sauntering outside into the sunshine.

They finished at seven that night. Though it had been a long, grueling day, Dick wasn't the least bit tired and he just hated to leave. When he was told to report again tomorrow for another test he couldn't believe his luck. He was called back the next day and the next—six in all, working on different movies or bits of movies and loving every minute of it. At the end of the week they handed him a pay packet containing a hundred dollars and told him they would let him know.

Two days went by, then three, a week . . . that weekend was the longest he had ever known. He knew he had screwed up and C. Z. wasn't interested in him anymore. Then on Sunday night Beulah called him to the phone. "Some man says he's C. Z. Abrams," she said, thrusting the receiver at him.

"Abrams!" Dick grabbed the phone to his ear. "Yes, sir?" he said, his voice suddenly squeaky with nerves.

"I have been viewing your films here at my house," Abrams said quietly. "There is something I would like to discuss with you. Please be at my office tomorrow at nine."

"Nine! Yes, sir, I'll be there!" he yelled, but Abrams had already put down the phone.

The office was cool, the white walls bare, the big solid desk immaculately tidy. And C. Z. Abrams, dark, clean-shaven, and unsmiling, in a cool gray suit and pale-blue shirt, looked tanned and rested and powerful.

"I have a deal to make with you," he said, leaning forward across the desk and clasping his hands together. "And I will tell you why. I am a man who acts on instinct, a gut reaction to circumstances and people around me. You may have heard that I fire men I cannot trust. Now my instincts tell me I can trust you. I liked what you did last week. All of it was good, some of it brilliant. I am offering you the job as director of *Scheherazade.*"

Dick gulped. "Jeez," he whispered, taking off his glasses and polishing them agitatedly, "but that's gonna be one of the most expensive movies ever made!"

"So it is," C. Z. said coolly. "And you had better do a helluva job on it because both your future and mine will rest on its outcome." He stood up and said briskly, "My lawyers will discuss the terms of the contract with you. It will be fair, you can be sure of that. I will be producing the movie myself and we will assemble the cast together. My secretary will escort you to the attorney's office. Good day, Mr. Nevern."

Dick turned at the door and said, "Why me, C. Z.? When you could have anybody you wanted?"

Abramski smiled. "When I was just beginning someone asked me how I knew I could be a moviemaker. I told him 'I just know I can.' That man believed me. You answered my question the same way, and now I believe you."

Dick walked out of the office on air, barely hearing what the lawyers said to him and caring even less. He was to direct *Scheherazade* and C. Z. was to produce. He had died and gone to heaven.

37

O'Hara bought four magnums of the best French champagne for the celebration. "A young buck like you directing a grand picture like *Scheherazade,*" he marveled, slapping Dick on his puny back with a mighty hand. "Sure and this C. Z. must be some kinda special guy, picking you off the streets like that."

"He's special all right," Dick said, edging away from him, coughing, "and you got it in one, Mr. O'Hara. He told me yesterday that he'd picked himself off the streets more than once and that's why he felt good about giving an unknown a chance."

"What is he like?" Missie asked curiously.

"Like? Oh, medium height, thick black hair, dark eyes that can be cold as ice or soft as a roe deer. Handsome, I'd say—*and* he's the best-dressed man I've ever seen. Immaculate from top to toe, even in this heat. But he's a real mystery man. No one really knows him. They say he pays fair and that he's just—and that he knows where every last buck is spent. Nothing gets past C. Z.—he even knows how much last week's postage stamps cost. And yet he sends everyone big bunches of flowers and buys his stars real big presents. Yeah, he's some kinda guy all right."

"Well, here's to C. Z. then," O'Hara said as Rosa, Missie, Beulah, and the boarders raised their glasses in a toast. "And to young Dick Nevern's grand success with *Scheherazade.*"

"I expect you'll be leaving us now you've come into money," Rosa said resignedly, thinking that would always be the way it was; as soon as the young hopefuls made some money and at last she could be sure of her rent, they would move on to a grand apartment of their own.

"The fact is I'll be working early till late and I'll have to move nearer the studio," he confessed, "but I'm keeping on my room, Rosa. Just in case."

"Oh, but you'll never come back," Azaylee wailed suddenly. "I just know you won't. It's all going to be different again."

Tears stood in her eyes and they glanced at her, alarmed.

"It won't change, Azaylee," Dick said gently, "I'll still have my room here, with my things in it. And I'll come and see you all as often as I can. You know what?" he added with a grin, "I'll even get you a little part in *Scheherazade*—if you're a good girl, that is."

"You will?" Her eyes shone with excitement, all tears forgotten. "Can I dance in it?"

"We'll see," he promised. He looked around at their beaming faces, at Marshall and Millie, Lilian and Mary, Ben and the others. "In fact, you will *all* have a role in *Scheherazade.*" His fair-skinned face was red with excitement and champagne. "The kids too. It's my thanks to Rosa and to Missie for letting me owe my rent and to all of you for putting up with my dreams."

As the cheers went up O'Hara refilled their glasses. "Hold it, hold it," he bellowed. "I have something important to say to you all. I have known Rosa Perelman and Missie O'Bryan for a long time, and for years I've been askin' one of them to be me wife. All I've ever gotten is a 'maybe' or 'ask me again in a year.' A lot of water has gone under all our bridges since then and it's just this week that I've found the woman I love again. And I love her more than anything on God's earth." Turning to Missie, he said quietly, "Missie, I'm telling all these people that I loves you, but what I really want to do is to tell the world. I'm asking you to marry me, Missie, and I'd be obliged if this time you'd give me a straight answer."

Missie's eyes linked with his and it was as if there were no one else in the room, just Missie and O'Hara. His big handsome face shone with anxiety and he looked as if he were holding his breath, waiting for her answer. He looked so rock solid and honest and was so blatantly in love with her that he was not ashamed to show his feelings in front of a roomful of people. "O'Hara," she said, "I only wish I had said yes a long time ago. . . ."

"Then you *will* marry me?" he demanded.

"Yes, I'll marry you," she whispered.

"B'jaysus," he bellowed, clasping her in his arms, laughing and crying as the others cheered. "You're mine at last, Missie!"

After planting a big kiss on her mouth, he pulled a box from his pocket. "I went to the classiest jeweler's in New York and got you this—just in case," he added with a broad wink to the others as he opened the box and showed her a large brilliant-cut diamond from Cartier. "And a matching wedding band," he said excitedly. "What d'you think of that, me darlin'?"

"Oh, they're beautiful, just beautiful," she murmured, "and far too grand for me."

"*Nothing* is too grand for the wife of King O'Hara," he exclaimed fiercely. "Why, I'd give me very life for you, Missie O'Bryan. The future Missie O'Hara!" he added with another wink. And then Winona sat down at the piano and thundered out the wedding march and he whirled her round and round in his arms. And in the flurry of excitement and congratulatory kisses no one noticed that Azaylee had disappeared.

It was dark on the porch and she lay down beside Viktor, burying her blond head in his neck so that her tears disappeared into his fur. "It's all going to change again, Viktor, *milochka*," she muttered, "I know it. They'll want to leave here and go live somewhere else." Her thin arms clutched at him and he licked her face comfortingly. "But you and I will never leave," she promised fiercely. "Never, never, never."

Golden lamplight spilled out across the grass and the music grew even gayer and the pop of champagne corks and the sound of laughter stole across the quiet street. But there was no joy for Azaylee as she sobbed herself to sleep, curled up next to her beloved dog.

The wedding was arranged for eleven-thirty the following Saturday morning at the Little Brown Church on Hollywood Boulevard, and everyone was invited. Azaylee was to be a bridesmaid and Rosa the matron of honor.

"I've never set foot in a church before," she confessed to Missie, "but since there's only one God then yours and mine must be the same."

Dresses were bought quickly, flowers ordered, and a wedding breakfast arranged at the Hotel Hollywood. When the big day dawned, calm and clear and blue as all the others, O'Hara put on his silver-gray morning suit and silk top hat. He added a large gray pearl stickpin to his cravat and a purple carnation to his lapel and departed for the church half an hour early.

The boarders dressed in their finest, borrowing hats and pinning on each other's corsages, leaving in a flurry of excitement, and taking Rosa's girls with them.

"*Nu*, Azaylee," she said, inspecting her critically, "did anybody ever tell you you are a beauty? Because it's for certain you are lovely enough to be a movie star already."

Azaylee's long golden eyes opened wide and she touched her ruffled lemon-yellow organza skirts shyly as she said, "Do you really think I could be a movie star, Rosa?"

Rosa grabbed her close and kissed her. "This very day, if Mr. C. Z. Abrams ever saw you," she replied firmly, looking relieved when the girl laughed. Azaylee had been too quiet these last few days and it worried her. The child didn't seem jealous because Missie was marrying O'Hara; she just didn't know what was the matter and Azaylee wasn't saying. Azaylee gasped and Rosa swung around and stared at Missie, framed in the doorway.

She was wearing creamy lace, tight-waisted and long-sleeved, with a fichu neckline and full skirts. A coronet of fresh orange blossom was perched on her piled silken-bronze hair and she carried a spray of tiny, perfect yellow roses. But it was her eyes that dazzled them, dark and shining with happiness.

"I love you, Missie," Azaylee exclaimed, running to her.

"And I love you too," Rosa murmured wistfully, watching as Missie kissed the child, whispering something in her ear.

"I'll never leave you," she whispered to her. "Remember, you will always be my little girl. You are more important to me than anything in this world. Please be happy, *milochka.*"

Azaylee nodded bravely. "I'll try," she promised.

Dick Nevern poked his head around the door. "Your car is waiting, Rosa," he said, and they all laughed as Azaylee darted onto the porch and came back with Viktor on the end of a length of yellow ribbon, a rose tucked into his collar.

"Viktor comes too," she said, eyeing Missie hopefully.

"Of course," she replied calmly. "Viktor always comes too."

Dick, who was to give her away, cleared his throat and said, blushing, "May I say, Missie, I have never in all my life seen any lady look so beautiful?"

She smiled. "Then you've never been in love. Just wait until you see your own bride on her wedding day. Then you'll know you've seen a beautiful woman." She remembered with a shock that she was not much older than Dick, only twenty-four, but compared with his untouched youth she felt like a woman of the world.

O'Hara's face beamed at her as she walked down the short aisle. Candles glittered on the silver and gold ornaments, heavily perfumed roses spilled from hundreds of vases, and swags of orange blossom looped every pew. The service was slow and beautiful, the choir sang, and as he took her hand in his and placed the ring on her finger, Missie felt that finally she had found true happiness with a man she loved.

The wedding breakfast at the Hotel Hollywood was so riotous with laughter and music that other guests popped their heads in to see what was going on and stayed to join in the party. O'Hara presented Azaylee with a ruby heart pendant that sent her into raptures of delight and Rosa with a diamond bracelet that stunned her into silence. He made a short speech in which he said he loved them all, and would they excuse him but he was taking his wife off to San Francisco for a week's honeymoon.

Azaylee smiled as she watched them leave in a flurry of rice and rose petals and hugs and kisses. She patted the heart pendant at her throat and held Viktor back as he lunged howling down the steps after Missie, thinking maybe it wasn't going to be so bad. Maybe O'Hara liked Hollywood so much he would decide to come and live at Rosemont. And maybe things would stay the same after all.

If Missie had any misgivings about the honeymoon after her experiences at the cruel hands of Eddie Arnhaldt, they were dispelled that first night. Big O'Hara, with his hard, strong, comforting body, his face alight with love and the wonder of her beauty, kissed her as reverently as a queen, holding her in his arms and stroking her hair, caressing her face, kissing her eyelids, her cheeks, her mouth. He told her how much he loved her, how very lovely she was, how he was the happiest man in the world. And when he made love to her he trembled with passion, crying out his love to her as she wrapped herself around him, lost in the discovery of new senses and the pleasure of being with the man she loved.

The week passed in a flash and before she knew it they were back on the Pullman heading for Los Angeles.

"You'll have to be packin' your things quickly, me girl," O'Hara said as the train slid into the station. "We'll have to be gettin' back to New York to see to me new business."

"New York?" Missie blanched. "But I thought we would be staying in Hollywood. Azaylee is so happy here. . . ." Her voice trailed off as she realized that she was being stupid. O'Hara's business was in New York and Chicago, and as his wife he would expect her to go with him.

"Don't worry yourself about Azaylee, I'll make sure she's

happy," he promised. "She'll attend the finest girls' school in New York. She'll be a real little princess now with King O'Hara as her father."

If only you knew that she is *really* a princess, Missie thought silently, but there was no way she could tell him the true story of their lives and expect him to understand. Better to keep her old secrets and fears to herself, and perhaps now, as Mr. and Mrs. O'Hara and their daughter, protected by layers of different identities, they would finally be safe from the Arnhaldts as well as the Russians.

New York

The penthouse at the Sherry Netherland proved too small for O'Hara and his new family, and he moved them atop a turret on swanky Park Avenue: four bedrooms and bathrooms, a paneled library already stocked with books, a drawing room with two marble fireplaces, and, behind the big kitchen, spacious quarters for Beulah and her two assistants.

Azaylee had refused to bring Viktor with her. "No," she had said, pale and tearless and looking very small and thin on the morning they were to leave. Even her flaxen hair had lost its luster. "Viktor will stay with Rosa. He'll be happier here on his shady porch than cooped up in some stuffy New York apartment."

Remembering Viktor sprawling on the fire escape at Rivington Street, Missie thought he could probably be happy in Manhattan again but Azaylee was firm.

"I'll come and visit you often, Viktor, *milochka,*" she whispered, kissing his soft head, and she covered her ears against his howls as they drove away.

She tried her best to be happy in the beautiful Park Avenue apartment where she had her own luxurious room. She was back once more at the Misses Beadles' School, only somehow now it didn't seem so fascinating after Rosemont and the boarders and their talk of movies and stars. It just seemed to her that every time she let herself be the least bit happy in a place, she was picked up and taken somewhere else, almost like a punishment. First there had been Rivington Street with Rosa looking after her, then the apartment on West Fifty-third, then Haus Arnhaldt, then Hollywood, and now Park Avenue. And now O'Hara was talking about going to Chicago for a few months. . . .

If she tried, she could remember all the way back to when she was very small. She knew she had lived in Russia, and some nights when she was lying in bed she tried to recall it. She remembered that the houses had felt very big and she had felt very small, and that everyone had been very beautiful. She had never talked about it with Missie but she could remember how her real Papa's bristly early-morning chin had felt next to her cheek when she had rushed in to give him a kiss, and she remembered the way her mother smelled so deliciously of flowers and how soft her skin had felt and how cool her lips as she kissed her. And she remembered Alexei's vivid face as if it were a photograph, his dark-gray eyes laughing at her as she followed him around and his young, strong legs preceding her up the tall stairs that she had labored over one at a time while he flew to the top like a pony over a jump. She remembered the way his voice had sounded and that he had spoken French to her in the mornings and English in the afternoons and that Nyanya had always sung them Russian lullabies.

These were the memories she retreated to in her dreams, her own personal, private world where she was a tiny child again and the center of everyone's love and attention, and all the world was a safe place where everyone adored her. One day she hoped to find that world again.

Meanwhile, she attended Misses Beadles' and brought home report cards that said she was a dreamer and inattentive, and she telephoned Rosa and the girls all the time to find out what was new with the boarders and if they had all played their parts in *Scheherazade* yet and if her darling Viktor was missing her too much.

And she always promised to visit them soon, but now a year had passed and they never had.

She was having supper at the kitchen table and Missie was talking to Beulah about the menus for the following week when O'Hara wandered in, a big grin on his face.

"Pack your fanciest dresses, me girls," he said, bestowing a smacking kiss on Azaylee's blond head, "we're off to Chicago tomorrow."

"Chicago?" they exclaimed.

"The Pink Orchid is just about finished," he announced proudly. "I'm planning the opening next week. I thought we'd all go along, have a little holiday together." He grabbed Missie and swung her around, laughing. "King O'Hara's third club," he boasted proudly. "How's that for an alehouse-keeper from Delancey?"

"I wish I knew," Missie replied, "but since you have never allowed me to see inside either one of your clubs, I've no way of passing an opinion."

He frowned. "Well, you know how I feel about you going to nightclubs. They are no place for a respectable woman. . . ." He blushed, embarrassed, as she burst out laughing.

"King O'Hara, do you mean to say that you run a business that's not fit for 'respectable' women?" she teased. "I wonder what our Park Avenue neighbors would say to that. And the fact that most of their sons and daughters are your customers."

"That's different," he said briskly, "that's business. B'jaysus, Missie, aren't I asking you to the opening of the Pink Orchid next week? I've hand-picked the guests meself. The cream of society will be coming to see me club and meet me wife."

"And will you be selling them bathtub gin?" she teased again.

"O'Hara's gin is niver made in a bathtub. It's genuine hooch from Bermuda."

She looked at him, surprised. "I thought you bought your liquor from your friends, the Oriconne brothers."

"The Oriconnes?" He coughed and shuffled his feet. "Yeah, well, me and the brothers had a slight disagreement about price so now I only give them half me business—for old times' sake. But what are we doing standing here talking about the Oriconnes when you should both be packing? We're catching the Twentieth Century tomorrow morning."

He glanced at Azaylee, sitting at the scrubbed kitchen table, a glass of milk beside her plate. Her eyes looked round and sad and he went and sat beside her. "And as a special surprise for me littlest love, I thought we'd go on from Chicago to Hollywood and pay a visit to your Aunt Rosa."

Azaylee's small heart-shaped face turned pink with pleasure and her pansy eyes grew rounder as she thought of seeing Viktor and Rosa and the girls again. "Oh, King O'Hara"—she laughed, throwing her arms delightedly around his big neck—"thank you, thank you."

"Just want me girls to be happy," he replied gruffly, smiling at Missie over the top of her head.

"Don't hold with a child not calling her pa 'Daddy.' " Beulah sniffed. "Same as every other child."

But Missie shook her head. She knew why Azaylee couldn't call her beloved O'Hara "daddy." It was because somewhere in the deep recesses of the past, she knew she had a real papa of her own and that one day she was hoping he would come back and find her, just the way they always did in storybooks.

Chicago

Chicago's old Palmer House Hotel featured a twenty-five-foot-high rotunda and an Egyptian Parlor as well as imported French furnishings and Italian frescoes.

"Nothing but the best for me girls," O'Hara said, puffing on his cigar and glancing at his little family as they made their way to the dining room the next evening. Enormous marble columns flanked the room and heavy crystal chandeliers hung down the center of the ornately painted ceiling. A bevy of waiters awaited their command, and O'Hara winked at Missie.

"Remember the first time I took you out to dinner in New Jersey? And you said you weren't grand enough?" She nodded. "I told you then you were grand enough for anywhere, but now you are even grander than all this." His greenish eyes shone with love as he handed her a box across the table. "And one for me littlest girl too," he said, passing an identical box to Azaylee.

Missie opened hers and said, awed, "Oh, look! A perfect orchid in pink diamonds. It's beautiful, Shamus, just beautiful."

He grinned bashfully. "Why're you callin' me Shamus, then? You've always called me O'Hara."

"Because I love you," she said softly. "Shamus *or* O'Hara, I just love you. Thank you."

Blushing, he said quickly to Azaylee, "So open it, me darlin'. Let's see what you've got."

Her golden eyes were like saucers as she opened her box and peered inside. "Mine's an orchid too," she said proudly.

"Just like your mother's, but little-girl style," he said as they exclaimed over the carved rose quartz orchid with its pink diamond center.

O'Hara beamed at them. Holding his hands out to them suddenly across the table, he said, "This may just be one of the happiest nights of me life."

The Pink Orchid was located between State Street and Calumet Avenue close by a dozen other popular speakeasies, the Sunset Café, Dreamland, the Panama, and New Orleans Babes, as well as the Big Grand Theater, the Monogram, and the Vendôme, where hot jazz bands were featured. O'Hara had chosen the location because it was more exciting than the upper-crust North Side and because he knew his classy customers would get an extra kick out of coming down to the sleazier South Side.

Searchlights raked the sky, a man with a movie camera filmed the arrival of the glamorous guests, and the French champagne was on the house. Missie looked sensational in a deep-pink chiffon dress and a corsage of pink orchids at her shoulder held by her new pink diamond brooch, and O'Hara thought he looked pretty snazzy himself in white tie and tails with his pink orchid boutonnière. And Azaylee looked so slender and vulnerable and devastatingly lovely in the palest pink organdy, her beautiful hair brushed into a shining aura of curls around her sweet young face, that O'Hara just had to hug her and tell her he was proud to be her daddy and that he would look after her forever.

She smiled, touching his face tenderly with her fingers as she said, "I'm glad you are my daddy now, O'Hara," and he roared with laughter and kissed her again.

They inspected the domed night-blue ceiling studded with shiny pink stars, the pink star-scattered dance floor, the tiers of tables with crisp pink cloths, the silver goblets and pink candelabra; the waiters in hunting-pink jackets and the cigarette girls and waitresses showing their legs and more in pink tights and brief pink net tutus. Each table had a vase with a single perfect pink orchid, and besides the resident jazz band, there was a line-up of guest celebrity stars and dancers that Azaylee was dying to see.

The South Side was jumping that night. Those who were not invited watched enviously as the guests spilled out of their smart automobiles and hurried, laughing, beneath the flashing Pink Orchid marquee into the promised land of luxury, gaiety, jazz, and hooch that was King O'Hara's special recipe for success. He introduced Missie and Azaylee to everyone and much later, when the place was crowded and the festivities in full swing, he suggested that it was time she took Azaylee home.

"See my littlest girl goes to bed as soon as she gets to the hotel," he instructed as they waited under the bright marquee for the limousine. The driver was taking his time, and O'Hara glanced impatiently up and down the street, barely noticing the closed black car driving slowly past on the opposite side. It swerved suddenly, veering fast across the empty street toward them. They stared, astonished, for a second or two as the rear window rolled down and the pink lights from the marquee glinted from the metal barrel of a snub-nosed machine gun, then with a fierce bellow O'Hara flung his big body in front of Missie and Azaylee. The hail of bullets ripped right through him, sending him spinning and leaving him a twitching, bloody heap on the sidewalk.

Azaylee knew she was screaming, just the way she remembered someone screaming in her dreams, years and years ago in the forest at Varishnya. She could hear Missie moaning and the squeal of tires as the black car pulled away and then the sound of running feet. And herself, just screaming and screaming as if all the screams had been locked inside her for years and years, and now she knew they would never stop.

=== 38 ===

Cal pressed the bell to summon Nurse Milgrim, worried by Missie's pale face and trembling voice. The clock on her table said 2 A.M., and he knew she must be exhausted as well as racked with the pain of her memories. She was staring down at the pink orchid brooch in her hands.

"I'll never part with it," she whispered. "Never."

Nurse Milgrim bustled in, crisp and alert in her starched white uniform. She looked at Missie and then at Cal and demanded, "What did I tell you? Now she's worn out and all upset. I blame you for this, young man." She poured a glass of water. "Come on now," she coaxed, "let's take our pills and then I'll get you a nice cup of tea and it's off to bed."

Missie swallowed her pills and shook her head. "Don't you understand, Nurse Milgrim?" she said. "Now I've begun, I must finish. Only then will Cal be able to help me."

Milgrim glanced at him sharply and he shrugged his shoulders. "It's important to all of us," he told her.

Her eyes widened in alarm and she said, "Well . . . in that case, maybe I'd better make some sandwiches," and departed in a rustle of white cotton.

"Azaylee couldn't go to the funeral," Missie said, "not that I would have wanted her to. They kept her in the hospital for two weeks, 'for observation,' they said, though at the end of it they were no wiser. She had just retreated into her own safe little world and no one could reach her. They said it was shock and with time she would be fine. But I knew better."

Her haunted violet eyes met his. "An enormous wreath of pink orchids was delivered to the cemetery just as O'Hara's coffin was being lowered into the grave. The delivery man handed me the card." She paused. "It was from Rico and Giorgio Oriconne."

"Then it was they who . . . ?"

She nodded. "He had underestimated their strength in Chicago. They had powerful friends and already had the place sewn up. They just let him go ahead and spend his money on his club and then . . ." She bowed her head, "No charges were ever brought, of course. It was just another seven-day wonder written off as an 'unknown gangland killing.' But that is what I have always believed."

Nurse Milgrim reappeared silently with plates of neat crustless sandwiches and a chocolate cake. "Eat a little," she urged Missie. "You'll need to keep your strength up."

Missie sipped her tea gratefully and said to Cal, "I took Azaylee out of the hospital and went back to California and Rosa. I thought being back home again would bring her out of her depression. Everyone was so sweet and kind, telling her their stories about their work in the movies, but she didn't seem to notice. All she cared about was Viktor, she wouldn't let him out of her sight. I can see them now, on the porch at Rosemont, Viktor's head on her lap as she stared across the lawn at the passersby in the street without ever seeing them. O'Hara had left me a little money, not a fortune, because he was a man who spent it as fast as it came in, but then, you see, he thought he had all the time in the world.

"A year passed and I could stand it no longer. I decided to take Azaylee to Switzerland to the eminent psychiatrist and psychoanalyst Carl Jung. I wanted to know for certain whether her problem was medical or mental." She looked at Cal again. "And I want to tell you, I prayed that it was medical because at least then we might be able to do something about it.

"Jung was very interested in her case. Of course his work was confidential and I told him, without mentioning names, how she had lost her family, of our escape and our life afterward, and that she did not know the details. I told him she had never seen a photograph of her family and didn't even know their real identities. And of course I told him about O'Hara.

"Jung said her case was one of the most interesting he had ever come across. He said Azaylee was suffering from a combination of things: depression, hysteria, and repressed emotions, locked away in her since childhood. She was in danger of losing her identity, 'a personality disorder' he called it. I told him how she had never mentioned her mama and papa and how she had just seemed to accept the fact that she lived on Rivington Street with Sofia and me. And I told him how she clung to the dog. He nodded and said she was a classic case and he would do his best to treat her.

"We lived in Zurich, off and on, for more than two years. We rented an apartment in a little hotel in the mountains; we loved the crisp clear air and the unending views, and I think somehow we both finally felt safe there. Every now and then we would journey back to California and stay for a month or two, but Azaylee was making progress and I was afraid to take her away from Dr. Jung. I knew that behind those long, lovely quiet eyes lay a mind in turmoil, and I wanted it all to be straightened out.

"Finally Jung said that for the moment he had done all he could, and we went back to Hollywood for good. Azaylee seemed happy and more outgoing than I had ever seen her. She went back to school and picked up her old friendships with Rosa's girls as if nothing had ever happened. She took up her dance lessons again and somehow they became the focus of her life. I suppose that was what she always wanted to do, really. Just dance."

She looked levelly at Cal and said, "Of course you realize I'm talking about Ava Adair."

He stared back at her, stunned. "Ava Adair? The movie star?"

"I'll tell you how it happened." She took a sip of the cold tea and pressed a hand to her brow, thinking. Then she said, "It all began with a chance meeting, and for the life of me I've never been able to decide whether it created her life or whether it ruined it. . . ."

She thought of how innocently it had all started out, telling Cal how Dick Nevern had come back to see them, flushed with success from *Scheherazade* and the three other major feature films he had completed for Magic Studios. He was an important director now but he was still the same nice, plain, bespectacled young man they had always known, and even though beautiful movie actresses threw themselves at him, he was still shy. He had never forgotten how close a shave that rocking chair on the farm porch in Oklahoma had been, and he claimed he owed it all to C. Z. Abrams, who had given him his chance.

"Abrams was reputed to be the most private person in Hollywood. No one really knew him, he had no real friends, just business acquaintances, but he really liked Dick. Dick would go to his big house on Lexington Drive several times a week to watch new movies or the day's rushes. They would have supper, always very formal with servants and all, but C. Z. never told Dick anything personal about himself. All he knew of him was that he was a devout Jew who kept the Sabbath strictly.

"Anyway, the day that Dick came round to see us Azaylee came rushing in from dance class. It was one of her really good days and she was vivacious and alive and really pleased to see him. She was fourteen years old and of course she was beautiful, in that unusual way of hers—all enormous pansy-gold eyes and a great tumble of platinum hair. She was tall for her age and still too thin, but she had beautiful legs and a sort of dancer's grace in the way she moved and walked.

"I noticed Dick looking at her interestedly and I wasn't in the least bit surprised when he said, 'You know, Missie, Azaylee is made for the movies. The cameras would just love her and so would the audiences.'

"I shook my head and smiled. I said she was way too young to think about that, and then he said something that really surprised me.

" 'I really hate to tell tales out of school,' he began, and then he grinned and said maybe he should rephrase that, because what he wanted to say was that Azaylee had been skipping high school and doing the rounds of the studios, lying about her age and looking for work as a dancer or an extra—anything, just as long as she could be part of the magical movie world.

"Of course, she had been unsuccessful because she was so obviously a child pretending to be a woman. But he said that if that was what she really wanted to do, then why didn't I let him take some tests of her and maybe get her a small role in his next movie? He would guarantee to look after her personally, guard her with his life if necessary, and he'd bet his Oklahoma boots she would be a star before too long.

"I told him again that she was too young, that I would forbid her ever to go near the studios until she was at least sixteen. This was 1928 and Hollywood had changed. It was a boom town now. Rosa and I owned five houses along Fountain Avenue. Rosemont, where we now lived ourselves instead of in the little bungalow out back, was the smallest. The studios were churning out film after film, Hollywood Boulevard was a proper thoroughfare clogged with traffic, and Beverly Hills was a proper town. A lot of the old stars were gone: Valentino dead; Mabel Normand, Fatty Arbuckle ruined by scandal, murders, drugs; it was all going on by then. Hollywood had lost its innocence, you might say, along with our own young

Bathing Beauties, who had found out that posing for nude photographs made them a great deal more money than being in Sennett's line-up. You can see why it was not a world I really wanted a vulnerable, fragile child like Azaylee exposed to. I wanted her to stay in school and life to go on just as it was, with Rosa and the girls. No ups—no downs. I had finally found anonymity and I guess I just wanted to keep it.

"The talkies were just coming in and the whole industry was in a state of flux. No one seemed to know what would happen next and soon many of the old favorites would be gone, discarded by the once-sycophantic studios because their voices were said to be unsuitable. But of course it didn't stop Azaylee haunting the studios even though I threatened her with a tutor again.

"It was when Viktor died that I changed my mind. He was the oldest dog in Hollywood, a veteran even for a borzoi, but he had been blind for years and barely moved from his favorite spot on the porch. Of course it was a tragedy because he was one of our last few links with Misha. But for Azaylee it was a disaster. We scoured the country for another borzoi and finally he arrived: six months old, a golden coat like Viktor, and ready to play. Rex was an instant hit but he wasn't Viktor, we all knew that. And when I saw that look creeping back into Azaylee's eyes, that feyness, the sliding away again, I called Dick and said that maybe he had better do those tests after all."

Hollywood

C. Z. was waiting for Dick to arrive from the studios with the day's rushes. They had got into the habit of showing them at his house late at night rather than at the studio, partly because he enjoyed Dick's company but mostly because it brought some life to his big, empty house.

It was ten o'clock and the sky outside the tall windows overlooking the perfect gardens was dark: He might have been anywhere in the world, a well-dressed anonymous person in a polished anonymous room in some anonymous city. It was eight years since he had beaten Mel Schroeder at his own game and ended up as owner of a couple of ramshackle barns on Cahuenga with a movie camera and a few reels of film, and in that time he had become the legendary C. Z. Abrams the movie mogul, up there with Goldwyn and Zukor, Fox and Warner. But in his heart he was still Zev Abramski, a lonely man. So lonely that he needed Dick Nevern's company and the pressure of a twenty-hour work day to fill his time, and then, if he was lucky, he would be so exhausted he might catch four hours of dreamless sleep before he faced another day.

He had seen from Mel Schroeder's eyes that he'd thought he had a real sucker there, sitting waiting for him on the veranda of the Hotel Hollywood sweating in his black pawnbroker suit and stiff white collar, embarrassed by his guttural English and his foreign look. But Schroeder hadn't known about the anger and despair that had kindled a fire in him, and Schroeder was only the first of a dozen men to feel the razor edge of Zev Abramski's ambitious mind cut them to the ground.

With his usual caution, learned through many hardships, Zev had done a little checking of Schroeder and discovered that he had already sold four phony "studios" to gullible men via his ads in small local journals in one-horse townships across the country. Discouraged, he had decided not to meet Schroeder after all, but then he had looked into things a little deeper and changed his mind. Schroeder's scam was to show a remote piece of land he had bought for a few dollars because there were no roads and it was virtually inaccessible. He would explain that everyone was out on location in the desert or at the beach and that he conducted all his business from his office in Hollywood, and that's why there was only one camera around and no people. He displayed the reels of film and pointed out the virtues of the tottering wooden buildings that normally housed cattle or hay that he grandiosely called studios. Next he brought out the fraudulent balance sheets for Schroeder's Movie Studios showing sales of hundreds of two-reelers to mythical distributors across the nation, with a tidy sum of one hundred thousand dollars in profit plus seventy-five thousand still owed the company. And no nasty red figures in the debits column.

"All bought and paid for by yours truly," he had told Zev, mopping his sweating brow as they strode around the hot, dusty acres, "and it's a going concern; five movies in production today and more scheduled. My trouble is I can't take the climate." He thumped his chest. "The old ticker, y'see. Doctor says I must get back East where it's cooler—and pronto. If not, I'm a dead man." He winked at Zev, pale and icy-eyed in his hot black suit. "With them odds, who am I to say no?" He stared at him silently for a moment and then he said, "I like you and I'm gonna make you an offer you can't refuse. I can see you're a decent young man and just right for this business. I'm telling you there's a fortune to be made here. It's just my tough luck that I'm struck down by illness." He sighed heavily and then added with a brave smile, "Still, God's wish is His law, and who am I to question His actions?"

Zev stared back at him without replying, and Schroeder glanced away again uncomfortably. "Tell you what I propose," he said quickly. "If I don't get back to Philadelphia by next week, you'll be following my coffin, I guarantee it. Now I'll help you, Mr. Abramski, if you'll help me. I'm offering you the whole package—the land, the studios, the five cameras, the film stock, contacts with distributors—the whole business as a going concern. And don't forget the sum of seventy-five thousand dollars still owed on the books that'll be in your pockets before the end of the year."

Zev raised his eyebrows skeptically. "How much do you want?"

"How much? I'll tell you straight, money is the last thing on my mind right now. A problem like this gets right to the guts. When it's life and death, what does money matter? For a quick sale, I'm ready to take twenty-five thousand and no questions asked. Cash on the barrel and a handshake, right here and now."

Even his bulging blue eyes seemed to be sweating as he stared eagerly at Zev. "That seems a great deal of money," Zev said, thrusting his hands into his pockets and tracing a line in the dust with the toe of his shoe.

A flicker of anxiety crossed Schroeder's face. "Well, maybe for a good man like you . . . shall we say twenty?"

"Show me again the accounts," Zev said suddenly.

Schroeder handed them to him nervously. "It's all there on paper. . . ."

Zev folded them carefully and put them in his pocket.

"Hey," Schroeder said, grinning, "you ain't bought the place yet! What about the twenty thousand?"

"I am offering you, firm, the sum of one hundred and seventy-five dollars for the ten acres you *really* own," Zev said in his low guttural voice, "and that is fifty dollars more than you paid. I'll give you seventy-five for the camera and the reels. The rest is crap. A total of two hundred and fifty dollars in all, and a fifty percent profit on your outlay. A fair deal, I think, Mr. Schroeder?"

"Pshaw, what d'you know, you little *kike*?" the man shouted angrily. "Two hundred and fifty bucks—it's probably all you've got in your pocket!"

Zev's eyes narrowed. His face was even paler than usual as he said quietly, "Two hundred more than is in your own pocket, Schroeder. Take it or leave it." He paused and then, touching the phony accounts in his pocket, added, "If it's no, then I will take these accounts to the Los Angeles Police Department and ask them to take the necessary steps to indict you for fraud. I am not the first one you have sold your studios to, Schroeder, but I am going to be the last." He smiled grimly. "All in all, two hundred and fifty dollars is a very generous offer."

Schroeder's shifty eyes shot daggers at him, but he held out his hand and said, "Okay, then, so give me the two fifty."

Zev took a piece of paper from another pocket. "This is a bill of sale drawn up by Milton Firestein, a lawyer with offices on Vine Street. I explained the circumstances to him and he said to get your signature right here." He pointed to the spot and held out a pen. "He is a well-respected member of his profession and no doubt his word would prevail against yours in court, should you ever try to claim you have not sold to me."

Schroeder glared at him and signed the paper, pocketing the bills Zev handed him without counting them. He stormed back to his flashy automobile, shouting over his shoulder, "Since you're so goddam clever, you can make your own way back to Hollywood, smart-ass!"

Zev smiled as he watched him tear away in a cloud of dust and squealing tires, then he strolled back to his ramshackle barns and gazed around. He paced out their measurements and inspected the wood for rot. He picked up his camera and stroked it wonderingly: He hadn't the faintest idea how it worked, but it fascinated him. Half an hour later he heard the *phut-phut* of the car he had ordered to pick him up as it struggled up the dirt track, and he smiled as he turned to survey his acres. Notice had been posted with the city council only last week that Universal Pictures were buying more acreage along Cahuenga, and with it would come new roads, water, power and telephone communications. He had gone out immediately and arranged to purchase thirty more acres of land surrounding Schroeder's lot, and he knew it would be relatively cheap to bring the road up here and tap into the power and water supplies.

He smiled as he drove away. He had been willing to go as high as five hundred if necessary, but it had cost Schroeder that extra two fifty for calling him a kike. And now he, Zev Abramski, was the owner of a studio.

He had done his homework and knew how the movie business

worked. He knew about the importance of distributors and how a few companies had already formed their own chains and cut out the independents, and he saw that was the future. There were just two major problems: He didn't know a single person in the business, not even an extra, and his ten thousand dollars, his savings and the money from the sale of his business, was not enough to achieve what he wanted.

The Hotel Hollywood was filled with movie folk, and there was a constant flow of gossip and rumors and inside information. Zev hung about in the dining room or on the veranda, sipping a glass of orange juice and keeping his ears open, hearing things he wished he hadn't, like which director was bedding which star and which star was bedding the waitress, as well as the price of a Sennett two-reeler and what Griffith's *Broken Blossoms* had cost. He knew the amount of Pickford's latest contract—more than a million—and that a day's pay for an extra was five bucks. He scanned the trade papers and hung around the studios, waiting in casting offices and listening to their talk. He became a professional eavesdropper, he saw every movie in town, and he heard on the grapevine that there were two bankers sympathetic to moviemakers: a young Californian by the name of Motley Flint, head of First National Security, and Amadeo Giannini, head of the Bank of Italy.

Zev chose Giannini because he was used to dealing with Italians on the Lower East Side and he liked them. And also because he had heard that Giannini's childhood had been as tragic as his own—an immigrant's son, he had seen his own father murdered by a neighbor. A successful produce broker, Giannini had retired at the age of thirty-one. He had become a banker and in 1901 he opened the Bank of Italy. Zev heard it said admiringly that Giannini always played his hunches, betting on the individual when he gave out his loans, and that "character" was his collateral.

They assessed each other silently in Giannini's office. Zev saw a shrewd, middle-aged Italian; he had known dozens like him in New York. The only difference was this Italian was a very successful man and now he held power over his life. The banker saw a slight, pale intelligent young Jew, still looking like a *landsman* in his black funeral suit.

Zev quickly explained his position and that he wanted his studios to turn out product eighteen hours a day with the actors, directors, and cameramen working on a rota basis. Cheap and cheerful, he said earnestly, the stuff to take people out of their own drab and miserable lives for five or ten minutes at a time. A volume business to finance the real core of his plan, his own distribution system and his own chain of picture palaces. And then he would make *real* movies.

"Tell me, what do you call *real* movies, Mr. Abramski?" the banker asked, smiling.

"Spectacle, glamour, history. Showing ordinary people things they could never dream of seeing in their whole lives. . . ." He looked at Giannini and said simply, "Magic."

The banker laughed. "And how much is it going to cost me to finance 'Magic'?"

Zev gulped and then said boldly, "I have ten thousand dollars of my own and I am asking you for fifty."

Giannini turned a pencil up and down in his fingers, staring at him silently. "And what makes a man like you think he can succeed in a business where so many have failed?" he asked finally.

Zev looked at him, astonished. "I just know it, that's all."

Giannini laughed and said, "Right, Abramski, the fifty thousand is yours."

Zev stared back at him, stunned. "But why are you lending me the money?"

"First, because you've got a potentially valuable piece of real estate there on Cahuenga. And second, because I like a man who believes in himself the way you do, Mr. Abramski."

He had gone back to the Hotel Hollywood with sixty thousand dollars in an account at the Bank of Italy, more elated by the fact that the banker had trusted his word than the fact that he had got the money.

Within weeks his toppling barns were rebuilt, a small set of flimsy wooden shacks added as administration offices, and cameras and film stock purchased. With the help of a casting agency he selected cameramen whom he promoted to directors, struggling walk-on artists, who he thought had something special and whose pay he jumped from thirty bucks a week to three hundred with star status, plus a changing cast of extras and assistants. He sat at his desk in the hot wooden shed, drumming up new ideas and plots based on the old popular formats he knew audiences liked, and as he wrote the cameras turned day and night.

It was a one-man operation. He controlled everything; no detail was too small to escape his nervous eagle eye. Consequently his product was good quality as well as entertaining and was soon picked up by the distributors. And when he wasn't busy at the studios, he kept an eye out for any opportunity to get Magic Distribution into the marketplace.

Hollywood was full of new moviemakers and the competition was stiff. Zev—or C. Z., as he was now known—made a point of doing the rounds of the movie houses, and when he heard that *Journey of a Lifetime* by a new young director called Francis Pearson was to be premiered at the old Woodley Theater, he made a point of going to see it. Pearson was an unknown and the movie was big-scale but made on the cheap. It showed in the rough quality of the film, but somehow the graininess just added reality to the strong saga of the immigrant nation's trek out West in covered wagons in search of a new life. It had humor, pathos, tragedy, and hope.

As the movie ended and the lights went up Zev wiped away a tear, deeply touched. As an immigrant himself he understood the dramatic life-and-death struggles of that not-too-long-ago generation and he knew instinctively that the rest of America would too.

The movie had attracted little attention, and the Woodley had been three quarters empty. He waited about in the lobby until the producer and the director emerged looking disconsolate and then he introduced himself and offered them forty thousand dollars for the distribution rights. They stared at him as if he had gone mad and then jumped at the offer.

He was in Giannini's office the next day, asking for a new loan of forty thousand to finance Magic Distribution's first venture. The banker looked at his first six months' figures and grinned. "Okay," he said, "you got it. But it's sink-or-swim time, C. Z. You'd better know what you are doing."

"I do," he promised confidently.

It was a hard sell but he got *Journey* into a major New York theater. Word of mouth soon had lines around the block, and he found himself inundated with requests for the film. He personally made more than a million from *Journey* and promptly bought up several of the small independent chains of distributors. Magic Distribution was a reality and he was a millionaire.

Francis Pearson joined Magic's roster of directors and made his next film, on a bigger budget this time and with spectacular sets and effects, and Magic Movies moved into the major leagues. Product rolled out and money rolled in; more acres were bought, the studios expanded, and new offices were built. C. Z. Abrams was a man to be reckoned with in Hollywood. He had his big house and his servants, he worked all hours that God sent, his social life was nonexistent, and his private life was his own.

As he waited for Dick Nevern to appear with the day's output of film, he ran his fingers idly over the keys of the beautiful Bechstein grand, recalling those lonesome nights in the dark back room behind the pawnshop. He rarely dreamed of the past anymore, though his mother's silver candlesticks were still displayed proudly on the dining-room sideboard. He lived for the present, each day for itself, but as he stared around at his lovely house and his tasteful possessions he would have traded it all just to feel the way he had when Missie O'Bryan first came into his life; to have his heart jump at the sight of her, to stare out of the window waiting for a glimpse of her passing by, to have the clock ticking away the hours and then the minutes on Fridays until she would fling open the door and, smiling, hand him her two dollars. And he thought he would have given ten years of his life to be sitting opposite her again at the Ukrainian café and see her smile at him with those violet eyes.

"Hi, C. Z.," Dick called, startling him from his dream. He patted the reels of film under his arm. "Just the usual. But later I've got somethin' real special to show you."

C. Z. nodded briskly. "Let's go," he said, leading the way to the basement projection room.

A table with brandy, beer, and sandwiches was set up next to the comfortable armchairs and Dick helped himself as C. Z. threaded the first reel. They watched the shorts first, commenting on the lead players and the camera angles and making notes, and then they did the same with the rushes from the two big films in production.

"Pretty good," C. Z. said in his newly acquired accentless American. "Raoul's doing a great job on *Imperfect Pair,* and as usual you've got it spot-on with *Broadway.*"

Dick wound back the reels and said eagerly, "C. Z., I reckon films are gonna have to get more realistic, now that talkies are here to stay. There's got to be a new look about them as well as a new sound, fresher, lighter, a different style of acting. We're gonna need some new faces, C. Z., and I think I may just have found us our first new star."

Zev smiled. Dick's enthusiasm was one of his greatest assets. He could carry you away with it if you weren't careful. That's why they were such a good team: one the crazy, artistic creator and the other the down-to-earth pragmatist. "So? Show me," he said, pouring himself a brandy.

Dick set up the reel and doused the lights. He took another sandwich and stood at the back, munching chicken as the magic unfolded on the screen.

There were no props, just an empty stage and a young blond girl, head bowed, her hands crossed gracefully over her chiffon skirt. Slowly she raised her head and began to dance, floating across the screen, her long hair streaming behind her as she pirouetted and turned to the faint strains of a Debussy nocturne. The music faded and she walked gracefully toward the camera. The clever backlighting created a halo from her platinum hair, casting soft shadows beneath her high cheekbones, and her light, slumbrous eyes captured all attention as she smiled nervously and said, "My name is Azaylee O'Bryan. I am fifteen years old and at Hollywood High School. All my life I have wanted to dance and most of it I've wanted to be in the movies. Thank you for giving me a test, Mr. Nevern."

As the film went blank C. Z. put down his glass with a shaking hand. His heart fluttered in his chest and he clasped a hand to it as if to stop it jumping.

"There's more," Dick said, rolling the film on. "I had her do a little scene."

"Sign her," C. Z. said abruptly. "A thousand a week. We'll sign the contracts tomorrow."

Dick stared after him, astonished, as C. Z. stood up and made for the door. He looked ashen and he seemed unsteady on his feet. "But . . . are you sure you're all right, C. Z.?" he said, striding quickly after him. "I mean, you don't look so great. . . ."

"I am sure. I meant what I said. A thousand a week and we sign tomorrow." They were in the big hall and he paused at the foot of the stairs, steadying himself with the banister. "She's underage," he said quietly. "The contract will have to be signed by her parent or guardian. Do you know her family?"

"Sure." Nevern said eagerly, "I've known her mother for years. I'll get them here tomorrow without fail."

Zev watched the hours ticking past until morning, pacing the house like a caged animal waiting for its release. At dawn he showered and dressed in a light, beautifully tailored suit and a pale shirt of the finest Sea Island cotton, knotting his French silk tie carefully in the mirror. His shoes were Italian and his thin platinum watch Swiss. He inspected his image critically, adjusting his tie yet again, adding a flowered silk handkerchief to his breast pocket, wondering what she would think of him. Then he summoned his car and drove to the studios.

Dick Nevern was on the phone to him at eight-thirty. They would be at Magic Studios at noon.

C. Z. shut his office door and paced the floor again until ten, when he called for his car and returned home. He took another shower, changed his clothes for an almost identical suit, shirt and tie, checked his appearance once more, and drove back again to Magic. It was eleven-thirty and he was ice-cold with nerves. What if Missie didn't remember him? What if she treated him coolly, an almost-stranger, just some person from a past she might not care to remember? He wondered what had happened to her husband and if she had children. And he wondered if she would still look the way he remembered.

On the stroke of noon his secretary buzzed and said Mr. Nevern was here with Azaylee O'Bryan and her mother. He told her to send them in.

He stood with one hand on his desk for support, his eyes fixed on the door as it opened.

She looked exactly as he remembered, her wide violet eyes opening even wider as she saw him. Dick hovered in the background as she stopped and said, "My God, it's Zev! *You* are C. Z. Abrams! *You* are Magic Movie Studios."

His heart flooded with the old emotion. Nothing had changed at all. He held his arms wide, his eyes fixed on her. "I did it all for you, Missie," he said quietly.

39

Azaylee was aware of the whispers that if C. Z. Abrams were not Missie's friend she would not be starring in Magic's first big talkie. She tried not to let it bother her, concentrating on each day's work in *Marietta* and staying close to her mentor, Dick. She didn't find what she was doing difficult and Dick was right, the camera loved her. Sometimes, in the evenings, she could hardly believe that the girl on the screen was really her, and the fact that she had a new name for the screen, Ava Adair, made it all the more unreal. Rosa and Missie conspired to keep her feet firmly on the ground though, insisting that no movie-star nonsense was discussed in their household and reminding her that Ava Adair was just Azaylee O'Bryan, a fifteen-year-old who still had to finish high school.

She thought it was nice coming home from the studios and becoming her old self again, a kid with a glass of milk asking what was for supper and taking the dog for a walk. But she couldn't wait to get to the studios the next morning and become Ava Adair.

She knew people were jealous because she was earning a small fortune, and that worried her because she didn't care a damn about the money. She would happily have made movies for nothing, she loved it so much. Dick had given Rachel a small role and at six-thirty every day they traveled to the studios in the big Lincoln limousine C. Z. sent for them, giggling together about Azaylee's eighteen-year-old costar Will Mexx, who had confessed he was madly in love with her.

"Love," Azaylee scoffed, laughing. "Even Dick is better-looking than him."

"Oh, I don't know," Rachel replied thoughtfully. "He's got nice teeth." And then they fell about laughing again.

Rachel was a young lady of eighteen now, small and pretty with her mother's soft features and merry dark eyes, and she was

Azaylee's best friend. They shared a joint ambition to be movie stars as well as all their secrets: like Rachel's crush on Magic's sophisticated star Ralph Lance, her blushes every time she saw him and the way the young guys stared at them now as they walked by; and Azaylee's mad passion for the boy from Santa Monica High who served behind the drugstore soda fountain on weekends.

Rosa's middle daughter, Hannah, was as pretty as her sister, but at twenty she had given up her acting ambitions in favor of a job at a casting agency, where she was constantly in trouble for allowing her sympathies to affect her judgment and sending obvious needy misfits for jobs. The eldest daughter, Sonia, was twenty-two and a teacher in San Francisco, already engaged to be married to a young man from a nice middle-class Jewish family. And Rosa had been seeing a hardware manufacturer from Pittsburgh, Sam Brockman, on a regular basis—which meant whenever he was in town—for three years now. But the romance was, as she put it, "on ice."

"Once bitten, twice shy," she quoted to Missie. "So? How do I know he's not another Meyer Perelman?" Of course, in her heart she knew he was not, but she liked her life the way it was: The boardinghouses were flourishing and romance was available on a monthly basis, with flowers and candlelit dinners and the occasional trip to Catalina Island. And she was still her own woman. No man was going to boss Rosa Perelman around again.

But it was Missie's romance with C. Z. that was riveting Hollywood. The private man's intimate life was being discussed in every studio and every restaurant in town. There were even pictures of him in movie magazines. "Magic's C. Z. Abrams with his constant companion Missie O'Hara arriving for the premiere of his latest epic," they said, or "Beautiful Missie O'Hara hosting a dinner for C. Z. at the Cocoanut Grove to celebrate the completion of *Calamity Kids.*"

Dick Nevern thought the funny thing was that C. Z. didn't seem to object. In fact, one morning he had walked into his office and caught him smiling at a picture of himself and Missie in a magazine. " 'Constant companion,' " C. Z. had said. "Half the nation must be wondering what that implies."

Dick hadn't liked to ask what he meant, but he could see that, for once, C. Z. didn't mind the attention from the press. Maybe he thought his new image as a ladies' man was good for business, some said cynically, but Dick knew better. He could see he was a happy man. And Rosa noticed the difference in Missie.

"How do you get that way?" she demanded one evening as Missie was dressing to meet C. Z. "All shining and excited because you are going to see him? You look different. With O'Hara you were soft, smiling, content. But for Zev Abramski you are a young girl again. Anyone could tell from fifty paces you're a woman in love."

"I loved O'Hara in a different way," Missie answered quietly. "He was the strong one and I was weak and wounded. Every time he took me in his arms I felt safe. O'Hara was a special man; he had a sort of joyousness about him that made life sunny. I still love him and I will never forget him. But what I feel for Zev has got nothing to do with what I felt for him." She stared at Rosa guiltily. "Is it wrong for me to love Zev the way I do, then?"

Rosa shook her head. "Only you know how you love him and that's the way it should be. And after all that's happened in your life, you should grab every chance of happiness you get."

Missie thought about Zev as she drove to his house in Beverly Hills in the new dark-blue de Courmont roadster he had given her. She had been amazed to see him behind that grand desk the morning she had gone to Magic to talk about Azaylee's contract. And even more amazed by his transformation—the frail, sallow, withdrawn young pawnbroker had been replaced by a slender, starkly handsome, well-dressed man. Only his eyes were the same, still with that lonely, yearning look she remembered. When he had held his arms wide like that and said, "I did it all for you, Missie," the eight turbulent years since she had last seen him had melted away. She was back in the dark little pawnshop on the corner of Orchard and he was sliding the fifty dollars to bury Sofia into the worn wooden groove under the brass cage.

"It's been a long time," she had said quietly, shaking his hand because she couldn't just rush over and kiss C. Z. Abrams, head of Magic Studios. "But I've never forgotten you, Zev, or your kindness. And now you are doing it again—being kind I mean, to Azaylee."

She could feel his hand tremble as it gripped hers, and he said softly, "It's been too long, Missie."

Then Azaylee rushed in exclaiming, "Zev Abramski! I remember you coming to Rivington Street on Sundays to take Missie to the Ukrainian café!" She paused and inspected him, smiling. "But you look different now you are Mr. Abrams."

"And you look different too. Quite the young lady." His somber dark eyes took her in and then he smiled. "And the camera did not lie, you are a *lovely* young lady."

She blushed and dropped her eyes. "I just hope I can be a movie actress," she told him eagerly, "especially in a movie where I can dance."

She sat next to Dick on the sofa, folding her hands in her lap and crossing her ankles neatly, the perfect little lady, listening as he talked to Missie.

"Dick showed me the test," he said abruptly. "Azaylee shone from the screen like a beacon. And something else very important now, she had a low, pretty voice with a sweet quality to it. I think she has potential. We would like to feature her in a movie called *Marietta*. With your permission, of course."

"She is only fifteen," Missie said hesitantly. "I would like her to finish high school, maybe go to college. . . ."

He nodded. "Naturally. She is still a child and would not work adult hours. We would have tutors on the set and also make sure that she took a proper rest during the day. Don't worry, Missie," he said gently. "I would look after her."

"Of course you would. . . ."

"Oh, Missie, *please, please, please!*" Azaylee flung herself on her knees at her feet. "Oh, *please* say yes."

Missie laughed, but inside she still was not sure she was doing the right thing. The doctor had warned that any stress or trauma might catapult Azaylee back into her never-never land, and it didn't seem right to subject such a vulnerable fifteen-year-old to the stresses of movie acting. Yet she wanted it so badly. She hadn't seen her so joyous and eager since O'Hara died. . . .

"I came here to refuse your offer," she said at last. "I was going to ask if you would consider seeing Azaylee again when she was a little bit older, but now that it's you, Zev, how can I say no?"

"Oh, thank you, *thank you.*" Azaylee pirouetted around the room in an ecstasy of happiness. She stopped at C. Z.'s desk and said earnestly, "I *promise* I will work hard, I'll do everything you tell me. I won't let you down."

"Of course you won't," he agreed, laughing, and Dick Nevern thought, surprised, that he rarely remembered him laughing, not even at Magic's own comedies. Even a smile was rare praise from C. Z.

C. Z. suggested Dick show Azaylee around the studios and afterward take her home while he took Missie to lunch and talked business.

Missie remembered that first lunch now as she drove to his house. He had called for his car and taken her to his home as if he couldn't wait to show her he was no longer a poor pawnbroker but a man of taste and refinement. But his quiet, grand house with its silken carpets and fine paintings had felt as unlived in as a museum.

A manservant served them an exquisite lunch as they sat stiffly opposite each other at a beautiful antique walnut table, making conversation about the weather and his lovely gardens until suddenly he took her hand across the table and said, "Tell me what happened to make you so sad."

She looked at him, startled. "I didn't know it still showed."

"Oh, yes," he replied quietly, "the scar is still there, in your expression and your quietness, and in your eyes."

She told him everything, just the way she had before, holding nothing back, not even how she had felt about Eddie on their wedding night or about finding the Ivanoff brooch or about Azaylee, and her own love for O'Hara. She cried when she told him about O'Hara's murder, but he made no attempt to comfort her, merely passing her a handkerchief, letting her cry it out.

"And what now?" he asked at last. "You have put Azaylee back together, but what about yourself? Maybe you should have talked to Dr. Jung too?"

She shook her head. "I'm the strong one," she said with an attempt at a jaunty smile. "Besides, I had Rosa to talk to, I didn't keep it all locked up inside the way Azaylee does. That's why I hesitated about letting her become a movie actress. What if she is no good? I've seen the hatchet jobs critics can do, and I don't know if she's strong enough to take that sort of rejection."

"And how will she ever know if you don't let her try? She may be a great success. You can't go on protecting her from life, Missie. You have to let her live it."

"I suppose you are right." She sighed. Nevertheless, always wary of discovery, she insisted that Azaylee use a screen name, and after a lot of thought the studios decided on "Ava Adair."

They wandered into the big drawing room with its view through the avenue of palms leading to a midnight-blue swimming pool, and Zev ran his fingers over the keys of the ebony grand.

"I used to play this piece every time I saw you," he confessed as the soft crystal notes of a Chopin étude filled the room. "I would go home after those evenings in the Ukrainian café and dream about you. My whole life changed when I met you, Missie." He stared down at the ivory keys. "I meant it when I said I did it all for you. I was in love with you in New York but I asked myself, What could I offer a girl of such refinement, a *baryshnya,* a lady? Two rooms behind a pawnshop and a husband who lent quarters on other men's Sunday shirts? When I sold my business and came out here to Hollywood, I was determined to become a success, to be someone who counted, someone you could look up to. Then I would return and ask you to marry me. When I read about your marriage to Arnhaldt, I wanted to kill him." He laughed mockingly. "Instead I took that anger out on a man who thought I was a sucker and tried to fleece me. Of course I beat him, and that was the beginning of Magic Studios."

"And now you are C. Z. Abrams, one of Hollywood's most important men," she said, coming to stand beside him. "But it makes no difference to me. I always respected you, Zev. You were always my equal."

She had stayed for a long time as afternoon drifted into evening and evening into dusk while they sipped champagne and poured out their hearts to each other like old, intimate friends, the way they used to over a bottle of rough red wine in the Ukrainian café.

That had been eight months ago and their courtship had progressed slowly, along with the making of *Marietta.* Now the movie was finished and tonight he was to give her a private showing. Not even Dick was to be there.

The house smelled divinely of beeswax and roses, not the stiff formal arrangements from before, but big silver bowls of garden roses spilling their petals onto polished surfaces in a last tender gasp of fading beauty. His borzoi, Juliet, sprawled on a sofa in the hall, and the doors and windows were flung open to catch the evening sunshine. The heavy brocade curtains were gone and simple cream silk ones hung in their place; the formal dark furniture had been banished and now comfortable sofas and chairs were grouped cozily. Books and magazines were scattered around and a dog-chewed leather slipper lay unnoticed under the table. Under Missie's influence the house had changed its personality and so had Zev. He looked different: relaxed, smiling, and casual.

"It's all set up," he said excitedly, "and I think I can promise you a surprise."

"Good or bad?" she asked, kissing him.

He grinned. "I'll leave that for you to decide." After taking her hand, he led her onto the terrace, where supper was set on a white table beneath a blue awning. There was nothing he did not know about her, nothing that she did not know about him, and now their lives had become intertwined. As they sat at the table talking of the wine, the strawberries, the movie, they had the intimate easiness of a couple who had been married for years. And yet they were not even lovers.

She thought Zev looked particularly handsome tonight. He caught her hand and said at last, "It's the moment of truth. Are you ready for it?"

He set up the reel, turned out the lights, and came to sit beside her. The story of Marietta was a simple one of an orphaned girl who makes good. It had both pathos and humor and a great director in Dick Nevern. The images flickered and the credits rolled and suddenly there was Azaylee staring at her from the screen, her eyes wide and frightened as she asked where her mother and father had gone. There was a low urgency in her voice that gripped the heart immediately, and for the rest of the movie it was impossible to take your eyes off her.

Missie was silent while he changed the reels, watching without comment until the end, and then she burst into tears. "I didn't know she could be like that, Zev." She sniffed. "I didn't know she could break hearts."

"But I did," he said softly. "I knew it the minute I saw her."

A month later *Marietta* premiered simultaneously in New York, Philadelphia, and San Francisco to rave reviews. The critics showered young Ava Adair with praise, hailing her as "a find," "a star in bud," and best of all, "an accomplished young actress." She was just sixteen and it seemed silly to suggest she go to college with such a glittering career in front of her. So Missie took her and Rachel for a holiday.

"Take her down to Mexico, to Agua Caliente," Zev suggested. "Magic will pick up the tab."

Unlike nearby honky-tonk Tijuana, Agua Caliente was a high-class spa resort featuring hot springs and mud baths, a golf course, tennis courts, and a huge marble swimming pool, said to have cost $750,000. The hotel boasted fifty luxurious bungalows with pink bathrooms and tortoiseshell fittings, and the dining room featured gold flatware with European food and the finest French wines. Zev wanted nothing but the best for his future star and his future wife, even though he had not yet asked her to marry him because he wanted to give her time to forget the tragedy of O'Hara.

Agua Caliente was also famous for its horse racing and dog track, and the hotel attracted a varied clientele of gamblers, celebrities, and socialites taking a rest in the sun. Rachel and Azaylee spent most of the day dipping in and out of the immense pool, sipping iced lemonade from tall glasses, and giving the silent treatment to any boy who tried to flirt with them, collapsing in a heap of giggles when he retreated, baffled by the silent amusement of two pairs of beautiful, challenging eyes. There was one man they both rather fancied, a rakish-looking Mexican by the name of Carlos del Villaloso. He was older, at least thirty they guessed, and after a single lingering glance that had made their toes curl up, he never looked at them. To their chagrin, he seemed to pay attention to every other woman in the hotel except them—even Missie.

She was taking a stroll through the gardens in the cool of the evening when she was aware of a long stride matching her own and glanced up to see him walking beside her.

"Such a beautiful evening, señora," he said with a dazzling smile. "I see that, like myself, you are a lover of nature. Beautiful gardens are one of the world's great joys. France, Italy, England, of course they are perfection, their climates guarantee it. But today I believe my native Mexico does not fare too badly. It is most disturbing. I always believe my own estate is the most lovely until I see somewhere else."

She paused under an arbor of bougainvillea. "It would be difficult to choose which is best," she replied with a cool smile. "I have decided that the happiest policy is to love the garden you are standing in best."

He clicked his heels together in a formal bow. "*Con su permisión, señora.* Carlos del Villaloso."

He was tall, slender, and elegant in a white dinner jacket, and his olive skin was so smooth it looked polished. He had intense brown eyes, a thin mustache, and very white, even teeth. His black hair was oiled into sleekness, and he wore a large diamond on his left pinkie.

"Mrs. O'Hara," she said, offering her hand.

"O'Hara?" he said, his brow furrowing, "I seem to know that name. . . ."

She turned away hastily. "I'm afraid I must get back. My daughter will be anxious to go in to dinner by now."

He laughed and said, "Ah, young girls are always hungry. We can only watch them in amazement and wonder where they put it all." He strode along the path beside her. "A pleasure to meet you, señora," he said with another courtly little bow as she hurried back into the hotel.

Later, in the dining room, he bowed and smiled as he strolled past on his way to his table and the girls stared after him in amazement.

"You mean you've actually met him?" they chorused excitedly.

Missie nodded. "We discussed gardens."

"Imagine discussing gardens with a man like that," Rachel said, rolling her eyes. "Why, he's the most *wicked*-looking man I've ever seen."

They stared at him across the room, lowering their eyes, blushing as he caught their glance and smiled at them.

"He's interesting," Azaylee breathed, "not like these silly boys who've been pestering us all week long."

"Interestingly wicked," Rachel added, and Missie sighed as they collapsed into giggles again.

Nevertheless, she made a few discreet inquiries at the hotel about Señor del Villaloso and discovered that he was a regular customer, well known as a heavy bettor at the racetrack and also as a ladies' man. He was rarely around during the day, but in future she merely nodded politely when she saw him and went out of her way to avoid being alone in the garden.

"You know what," Azaylee said to Rachel one evening after dinner. "I'm bored." She was sprawled across a sofa, her long slender legs flung over the back. "Unless you're mad about racing or booze, there's really not much to do around here. Not even *sex.*"

"And what do you know about *sex*?" Rachel scoffed.

Azaylee swung her legs back over the sofa and sat up. "Not much," she admitted, "but I'm willing to learn. Tijuana's just up the road, Rache. What do you say we pay it a little visit?"

Her eyes lighted up with excitement and Rachel stared at her doubtfully. "What do you mean?"

"Let's just dress up older and go see what it's like there. We can stroll around, peek through a few doors . . . just do *something.*" She giggled. "Come on, admit it, Rache, you're just the teeniest bit curious?"

"Not as curious as you," she admitted, grinning, "but I'm game if you are."

Azaylee ran to the closet. "We'll put on our slinkiest dresses. You'll look okay because your hair is bobbed, but I'll just have to pin mine up and put on a hat."

Dressed in their raciest attire, which was pretty sedate, they sneaked out of the hotel and asked for a taxi. The driver stared at them in astonishment when they demanded to be taken to Tijuana and then he asked double the usual price.

"*A dónde ahora?*" he asked as they cruised slowly down the narrow, crowded main street, lined with bars and honky-tonk joints.

"Right here will do." Azaylee leapt out, thrusting half his fare into his outstretched hand. "Kindly wait. We shall be back in one hour."

He shrugged indifferently, watching as they walked off, arms linked, clutching each other nervously as if they expected someone to leap from an alley and kidnap them to be sold into white slavery. Loud music spilled from a hundred bars and touts, pimps, whores, and drunks hung around the doorways.

Azaylee stopped to stare at the pictures outside the notorious Venus and the sign that said "Anything Goes." She peered interestedly at the louvered door, drawing back with a gasp as it swung open to eject yet another drunk. Her eyes widened as she caught a glimpse of a naked woman on stage with two men.

With a gasp, she grabbed Rachel's arm and hurried on. "Did you see that?" she muttered. "Did you see what they were doing, Rache?"

"No." Azaylee's startled eyes stared into hers, and she said, "*What*, Azaylee? Come on, tell me!"

Azaylee gulped and whispered, "Rache, there were three of them . . . naked and . . ."

She shivered and Rachel wailed nervously, "I knew we shouldn't have come here!"

"Oh, but, Rache, I am sure we should!" Azaylee was gripped by a strange, nervous excitement. She could *never* tell anyone exactly what she had seen, not even Rachel. After crossing the road, she stopped outside the Commerciale.

"Maybe we should just go home," Rachel said, hanging back reluctantly.

Carlos del Villaloso spotted them as he strolled down the street having just lost five grand at the Foreigners' Club. He had exactly three hundred dollars left in his pocket, not even enough to pay his hotel bill, let alone finance his gambling fever. The two young girls dithering on the sidewalk outside the Commerciale stood out from the crowd like virgins at the gates of hell, and he grinned as he watched them clutching each other's arms and daring each other on. So, they had escaped from the beautiful dragon lady and come to find a bit of excitement. Then who better than he to show them the ropes? Straightening his tie, he strolled across the road to the Commerciale.

"Buenas noches, señoritas." He smiled disarmingly at them as they swung round, startled. "I recognized you from the hotel and wondered if you realized it is not exactly *comme il faut* for well brought up girls to wander around Tijuana?"

They blushed, lowering their eyes, embarrassed, and he added, "It would be better if you allowed me to escort you. The Commerciale is a rough place for women alone."

He held open the door and they filed through, smiling shyly at him and murmuring their thanks. He found them seats at the three-hundred-foot-long bar and, after grabbing one of the fifteen bartenders, asked what they would like to drink, flinching when they asked for lemonade. With a wink at the barman he added in a low voice, "With a touch of gin."

Azaylee leaned her elbows on the counter, sipping her lemonade and staring wide-eyed at the raffish crowd of drinkers, punters, pimps, and hookers who streamed nightly across the border in search of pleasures forbidden in their native America. Pretty dark-eyed girls paraded their wares, for which there were plenty of takers; alcohol flowed like an endless river and music blared deafeningly. Her nerve ends tingled: It was the most exciting place she had ever been to.

Carlos decided that the dark one was obviously very frightened but the blonde was interesting, with her pale, tumbling hair and those strange, dazzling eyes reflecting her excitement. She couldn't keep still. She was wriggling on her barstool and nervously knocking back her "lemonade" as if she expected any minute to be arrested. Of course they were too young and innocent to warrant his attentions. He needed someone like their mother, a woman in charge of substantial purse strings, not juveniles out for a thrill. Still, innocence had its own charm, and it might be fun to give the blonde her first taste of corruption. Giving the barman a wink, he ordered two more "lemonades."

"You must be on vacation from college?" he asked as the barman placed the fresh drinks in front of them.

Azaylee's face was flushed from the gin and her eyes sparkled as she replied, "Oh, no. We are in the movies."

"Movies, eh?" He thought of Mrs. O'Hara, the dragon lady who was too beautiful for her own good—or his. She hadn't looked like his idea of a stage mother; she was far too grand and dignified. A lady, he would have guessed, with a background of solid family wealth and education. She had put him off so obviously, he had not bothered to find out more about her, but now he was intrigued.

"And your father?" he asked, leaning closer to Azaylee. "Where is he?"

She hiccupped loudly, putting a hand to her mouth and blushing. "Papa is . . . Papa is dead," she finished. Her lips trembled, and he quickly took her hand and squeezed it.

"I understand," he said gently, "and I am sorry I asked such a personal question. It was unforgivable."

Rachel stared into her lemonade, her eyelids drooping as she yawned and said, "It's okay. Missie's going to marry C. Z. now."

"C. Z. Abrams?" His eyebrows lifted in surprise. Now he remembered, he had seen it often enough in the newspapers. She was King O'Hara's widow—and the blonde must be his daughter.

Azaylee glanced at his hand still clutching hers on her lap. She stared up at him, her mouth slack, and then she licked her lips. He felt a tingle of desire for her, though virgins were not his usual territory. He preferred a woman with experience as well as money, and preferably one who enjoyed sex as much as he did. But she had potential, this little one. . . .

"This lemonade tastes funny," Rachel said sleepily. Her face was pale and she added suddenly, "I don't think it agrees with my stomach."

Carlos groaned. All he needed was her to throw up. "Come on," he ordered briskly. "It's time all good girls were in bed."

Azaylee shot him a flirtatious glance from under her lashes and murmured, "I thought that's where all the bad girls went."

He laughed, putting his arm casually across her slender shoulders as he guided her from the bar. "And sometimes good ones too," he whispered in her ear.

He sat between the two girls in the taxi, opening Rachel's window in case she felt ill, but she promptly fell asleep. Azaylee leaned her head against his shoulder, her eyes closed, and he put his arm around her.

"I'm so sleepy." She yawned, snuggling against his chest.

He stroked her face with his finger, tracing her eyelids, her cheek-bones, and her mouth, which trembled under his touch. Her eyes closed but he could tell she was not sleeping, and he let his fingers drift slowly down her neck until his hand rested against her small, soft breast. He could feel her heart pounding, and she breathed quicker as his fingers wandered across the soft flesh exposed by the low neckline of her pink silk dress. She gasped as he slid his hand inside. He could feel the heat coming from her as he twisted her face toward him and he put his mouth over hers, drawing her into him in a kiss that lasted forever.

She clung to him, dazed with passion. He took her hand and guided it to his bulging crotch. "There," he whispered. "See what girls like you do to a man? You get them all hot and ready, leading them on, and then you cast them aside. You don't know the pain you leave a man in. *The agony!*" He pressed her hand harder into his throbbing groin and she struggled feebly. "I just wanted you to feel what it was like so you would remember what you have done to me, you cruel, cold-hearted little virgin."

Azaylee twisted away from him and sat up. Her face was flushed and her eyes glittered as she began to cry, the tears trickling down her cheeks and dripping unheeded onto her pink dress. "I didn't mean to do it. I don't want to hurt you. I just didn't know. . . ." She hiccuped again and he sighed as he passed her his handkerchief.

"So now you do," he said brusquely as the cab drew up in front of the hotel. "And a word of warning, young Miss O'Hara. You are playing with fire."

The driver grinned knowingly as Carlos helped the girls from the cab and sent them hurrying into the hotel. Carlos watched them spin through the revolving door and lurch unsteadily across the hall. That was just a beginning, he thought. Just wait, little Miss Azaylee. Then he lighted a cigarillo and took a stroll around the grounds, thinking about Missie O'Hara.

The next morning over a subdued and silent breakfast, Azaylee was shocked to see him approaching. Kicking Rachel under the table, she kept her eyes on her plate, blushing furiously. Rachel glanced apprehensively at Missie and then at Carlos as he nodded to them, smiling.

Azaylee felt as if she were melting inside at the sound of his voice and his nearness as he said, *"Buenos días, Señora* O'Hara, *señoritas.* Forgive me for interrupting your breakfast, but it is such a lovely day and"—he hesitated—"I was wondering if you would do me the honor of lunching with me. I thought a little picnic, and then maybe you might like to visit the racetrack. After all, sometimes it gets boring here for the young people."

"It's very kind of you, Señor del Villaloso," Missie said briskly, "but we have already made plans for today."

Azaylee's head shot up. "Oh, Missie," she said, glancing imploringly at her, and Missie stared back at her, surprised.

"I understand," Villaloso replied coolly. "Another day perhaps?"

Azaylee stared after him as he walked away without even a glance in her direction. After all that had happened between them last night. . . .

"Whatever's the matter with you?" Missie grumbled. "You would think I had refused to let you be Queen of the Rose Bowl Parade instead of sending that nasty man on his way. He's a gambler and a womanizer and I'm certainly not going on any picnic with him, let alone to a racetrack."

"How can you say that?" Azaylee muttered angrily. "You barely know him."

Missie's eyebrows rose in a question. "And I suppose you know him better? Now let's finish breakfast. I've arranged for the pro to give you both a tennis lesson. You look as if you could use a good run around the court to put some life back into you." She inspected their faces critically. "Goodness, we come here for a rest and a holiday and you both look like ghosts."

Rachel sighed, remembering the night spent throwing up, and said feelingly, "I guess it was the lemonade. . . ." She put her hand to her mouth with a little gasp. "I mean, maybe we've been drinking too much lemonade."

"Too much food and not enough exercise," Missie agreed, sweeping them quickly from the dining room before Villaloso could speak to them again.

Missie kept the two of them busy for the next few days, sending them to tennis lessons morning and afternoon, organizing times for proper swimming, not just playing about in the water, with twenty laps to be completed each time, taking them for long walks and sending them to bed early. But when the end of the holiday came and they were driving back to Los Angeles, she wondered worriedly if she had overdone it. Azaylee looked so pale and tired and Rachel was so quiet. She watched her, puzzled, as the miles sped by, because whenever Azaylee's eye caught hers she could swear she looked frightened. She shrugged away the idea as ridiculous. After all, what could the girl possibly be frightened of? She was just returning from a lovely holiday.

40

Missie had been thinking of Zev a lot while she was away and she had come to a decision. If Zev Abramski was not going to ask her to marry him, then she would ask him.

She dressed simply the night they got back, in a plain blue skirt and white blouse. She brushed her softly waved cap of short bronze hair, wishing she hadn't cut it—Zev had loved her long hair so much. She sprayed on her old favorite lily perfume from Elise and inspected herself critically in the mirror, wondering how different this twice-married, twice-widowed twenty-nine-year-old woman looked to him from the eighteen-year-old naïve girl he had first met. Rosa said she still walked like a young deer, and despite all her sorrows and struggles her face looked the same. Just the eyes were warier now.

On an impulse, she tugged the old cardboard valise from beneath the bed and tipped its contents onto the pink coverlet. The diamonds in the tiara glittered and the huge emerald looked the color of the sea off Constantinople, shot with sunlight. Russia and the past had never seemed farther away, and she realized that since she had been with Zev she had barely thought of the Cheka and the Arnhaldts, except in her dreams. They were buried in the past along with the Ivanoff treasure.

She picked up Misha's photograph and gazed at it tenderly, and then she took Azaylee's picture from her dresser and compared the two. There was no resemblance; the girl was just like her mother. She held his picture to her breast wondering whether after all these years she should show it to Azaylee and tell her the truth; but the doctor had warned her that she was not strong enough mentally to cope with the double shock of finding her real parents only to lose them to a cruel death.

"I'll always love you, Misha," she whispered, pressing him

against her heart, "but you understand, now I have found a man I truly love and who loves me."

After replacing the photograph in the valise, she took out the Ivanoff brooch, turning it this way and that in the sunlight so that it glittered with a thousand points of light. She hesitated a moment, and then, returning to the mirror, she pinned it at the neck of her blouse. It was far too grand for her simple outfit, but wearing it somehow made her feel she had Misha's approval for what she was going to do.

She replaced the valise and hurried downstairs to the kitchen, where Rosa and her beau, the hardware merchant from Pittsburgh, were sitting over a glass of lemon tea. Rosa's eyes widened as they fastened on the brooch. She said, "You look as if one half of you decided to go to a ball and the other thought she would just stay home."

Missie snatched a cookie from the batch cooling under the open window, laughing as Beulah scowled at her. "Wrong on both counts. I'm going to ask the man I love if he will marry me."

"I wish my woman was as smart as that," Sam Brockman said gloomily.

"You sure you know what you're doing this time?" Rosa asked.

Missie nodded. "Certain sure." After snatching another cookie, she headed gaily for the door. "After all, how else is a girl to get what she wants if she doesn't ask for it?"

"It's not correct!" Rosa yelled after her. "The man should be asking. . . ."

Missie stuck her head back around the door and said, "Then if he says no, I shall run home and cry on your shoulder and you can say 'I told you so.' "

"Crazy woman, crazy," Rosa murmured as she departed.

"You should be so crazy," Sam said firmly. "If you asked, I'd say yes in a minute."

"I'm not asking," Rosa retorted with a sniff, "*and* I'm not saying yes until I'm good and ready."

"One day, maybe," he said, and they smiled at each other contentedly.

Zev had been waiting for this moment all day—more, he had been waiting two long weeks for her to walk up the steps and back into his life again. He hurried to meet her, opening his arms wide, and she walked right into them just as if she belonged. "God, I missed you," he murmured, burying his face in her sweet-smelling hair.

They walked out onto the terrace and leaned on the stone balustrade, listening to the cicadas and the bird calls and the cool little cataract that tumbled past on its way to the pool. His narrow, handsome face looked stern with tension.

"Don't ever leave me again, Missie," he said tightly, staring straight ahead. "Stay here. Marry me, please."

She turned to look at him, astonished, but he was still leaning against the balustrade, still staring straight ahead. She laughed. "Zev Abramski, I thought you would never ask."

He turned slowly to look at her, hope in his eyes. "Then you will?"

She nodded. "Yes, I will marry you. I love you more than I've loved any man." She touched her hand to Misha's brooch and added, "In a different sort of way."

He shook his head. "I don't care about such different ways. All I know is you love me." He scooped her joyously into his arms. "What I want to know is, when?"

"Give me a month," she said, thinking of O'Hara and their whirlwind marriage. "But just a small wedding, Zev. Just family."

Zev got through the next four weeks in a state of nervous tension, half afraid she would change her mind. He buried himself in his work, refusing to allow his thoughts to stray to her, but secretly he was living for those precious evening hours when they were together.

Only Rosa, Rachel, Hannah, and Sonia were invited to the wedding, and Azaylee was to be bridesmaid. Dick Nevern, as Zev's closest associate and friend, would give the bride away. The wedding was to be at Beverly Hills City Hall on Canon Drive with a reception afterward at Zev's house.

Magic was in the middle of filming *Marietta in the Mountains,* starring Azaylee, a sequel to the successful *Marietta,* and Zev was loath to leave final approval in anyone's hands but his own, so the honeymoon was postponed until it was finished. Meanwhile Azaylee would stay with Rosa.

But Missie realized something was wrong. Azaylee would set off for the studios each morning full of laughter and girlish chatter and return each evening limp and exhausted. She would eat her supper silently and, after complaining she was tired, go immediately to bed.

A week before the wedding, Missie decided she could stand it no longer and followed her up the stairs. Azaylee was lying fully dressed on the bed, clutching her favorite little French doll O'Hara had given her all those years ago on the trip to New Jersey. She thought guiltily, That's what's wrong. She loved O'Hara. He was her papa.

"Don't you want me to marry Zev?" she asked, sitting on the bed and stroking Azaylee's hair back from her hot forehead. "I thought you liked him."

"But I do, and of course I want you to marry him. I want you to be happy, Missie, truly I do."

Missie could tell she meant it, but there was that old fey look in her eyes that put her warning signals up. "Then tell me what is wrong, *milochka*," she said softly. "You know I'll understand."

"It's nothing . . . except . . ." Azaylee sat up, her pansy eyes wide and staring. "Everyone has different names here. No one is who they really are. Isn't that true, Missie? Even C. Z. is really Zev. And I'm Marietta as well as Ava Adair and Azaylee, and before that I was some other girl. . . ."

"That's the way it is in Hollywood," Missie replied quickly. "Actors like to choose prettier names than the ones they were born with, and immigrants like Zev change their names to make them sound more American. It's just easier, that's all."

"That's not what I mean," she cried despairingly, sinking back into the pillows and clutching her doll. "Sometimes it just makes me wonder who I am, Missie, as if there were two of me—a bad girl and a good girl—"

"A bad girl," Missie echoed, shocked. "Why, Azaylee, you were always the most angelic child, everybody said so. And look at you now, working hard and behaving like a perfect lady on the set. You never give anybody the slightest trouble."

Azaylee turned her face away again, staring out of the window vacantly. "I remember Papa," she said in a faraway voice. "His chin was rough when he kissed me and he was very tall with a quiet voice. And I remember my big brother . . . so much bigger than me . . . but that was when I was someone else, wasn't it, Missie?"

Missie hesitated and then she took her hand and said, "We changed your name to save you from being killed. Your real name was Xenia."

"Xenia Ivanoff," she said slowly, "now I remember. She was a fairy-tale child in a storybook land where everybody loved her, especially her papa. He's not dead," she added, looking at Missie strangely. "Truly he's not. I know because I have seen him."

"In your dreams, Azaylee. Only in your dreams," Missie murmured unhappily. "Your papa is with your mother and grandmother Sofia in heaven."

Azaylee gave Missie a wistful little smile and said, "I guess I'm just tired, that's all."

"You'll need another little holiday after *Marietta in the Mountains,*" Missie said, wanting to please her. "Maybe we all could go back to Agua Caliente. You liked it there."

"No!" Azaylee shot up in bed, panicked. "I never want to go back there again," she exclaimed passionately.

"Very well," Missie agreed, surprised. "Now, why don't you take your bath and I'll bring you a glass of hot milk with cinnamon, the way Grandmother Sofia used to make it. You know you always like that."

Azaylee took her bath and drank her milk obediently. When Missie tucked the girl in bed and kissed her good night, she thought that in her white cotton nightdress with her hair pulled back into a braid she looked like a sleepy, innocent child.

The wedding day was cloudy with a promise of rain, but that did not affect the radiance of the bride or the happiness of the groom as they stood before the judge and promised to love and care for each other forever. Missie looked lovely and elegant in an expensive aquamarine silk dress with a small matching hat and a corsage of lilies, and Zev Abramski looked a man of the world in a light-gray custom-tailored suit. A delicious wedding lunch was served by smiling servants to the strains of a string quartet playing Mozart and the champagne flowed.

When the guests finally left Missie kissed Azaylee good-bye but her eyes were anxious as she watched the girl go.

"You wish she were here with us?" Zev said.

She shook her head, smiling ruefully. "Oh, no, I don't, Zev Abramski. I want you all to myself."

He played the piano for her and she listened for a while, hearing the emotion he usually kept locked behind his cool, reserved façade. Later she prepared herself for bed, anointing herself with perfume and brushing her smooth seal-brown hair until it shone like silk. After walking to the mirror she stared at her slender naked body, seeing it as he might, her small high breasts, the subtle curve of her hips, and her long shapely legs—and she wished she were eighteen again and inexperienced, young and unscarred by life so she might give herself to him wholly.

She slipped the soft lace-trimmed nightdress over her head, smoothed its cool satin folds against her body, and, after switching off the dressing-room lamp, walked barefoot across the soft carpet to the door. When she turned for one last glimpse in the mirror, she saw only a pale shadowy figure. In the half-light she might have been a young girl again, a bride going to her marriage bed.

A single lamp was lighted in the bedroom, and Zev was standing by the window, staring out into the night. He was wearing a claret silk robe. As he turned to smile at her, she thought how handsome he looked.

"Missie," he said, holding out his arms as he came toward her, "do you know how beautiful you are?"

Flushed with happiness, she lay beside him on the bed. "I want to tell you how *much* I love you, how I've *always* loved you, but there are only these inadequate words," he murmured, kissing her gently.

He knelt to kiss her feet, telling her how he had never felt worthy of more, and she took him in her arms and said he was worthy of better than her. They embraced passionately.

All their façades and defenses were down. They were two people deeply in love; they wanted to touch, to feel, to explore, to possess each other's bodies. And when Zev Abramski finally entered her and they were one, all memories of Arnhaldt and O'Hara were expelled from Missie's mind, and even Misha became just a dream. Zev made her his woman that night—as if her other loves had never existed. And much later, when she fell asleep in his arms, it was as if it was the one place in the world she was meant to be.

Maryland

The first faint hint of dawn touched the sky with opal as Missie said wearily to Cal, "What happened next was my fault and I will never forgive myself. But you see, I was young too, and in love. I was selfish and all I wanted was to be with Zev. I thought that Magic was not just the name of his studio but something of which he was capable. He was thirty-five years old and he had transformed himself from an uneducated immigrant into a Hollywood legend. He had taken Magic from a quick one- and two-reeler operation into a powerful studio with a glittering roster of stars and directors, and he had done it because he knew instinctively what the public wanted.

"But it was more than just his business that made him a legend. He was a mystery man with a reputation for aloofness and for avoiding the splashy Hollywood life-style and its gaudy publicity. There was something about him that sent hotel managers and head-waiters running to offer him their grandest suites or their best tables. He was Hollywood royalty and now I was his queen, and we were so wrapped up in each other we barely had time for anyone else.

"When *Marietta in the Mountains* was finished, he had planned a sequel, *Marietta in Malibu.* It was scheduled for production a month later, so Zev and I decided to fit our belated honeymoon into the gap. We didn't go far, just to Catalina Island. The Hotel St. Catherine was quiet, a retreat for movie people who wanted to escape from the glare of publicity for a while. And that's just what we did.

"We were like teenagers, doing all the simple touristy things, taking the glass-bottomed boat, dancing at the casino to one of the great bands, strolling back to the hotel around Avalon Bay. I remember the moon making a path across the water, silhouetting the palm trees and the music drifting across the bay from the pillared white casino on the point. It was all so beautiful and romantic. We had been there a week and I can't tell you how happy we were—and then the telephone call came from Rosa. Azaylee had disappeared and she didn't know what to do.

"Zev chartered a little plane and we flew back right away. Rosa was distraught and Rachel was in tears. Apparently Azaylee had just packed a few things and disappeared in the middle of the night. When she didn't appear for breakfast Rosa thought she was sleeping late, and it wasn't until hours later that she realized she was missing.

"Zev guessed that Rachel knew something, and he took her outside and asked her what was going on."

Missie hesitated and Cal noticed how tightly her hands were gripped together, but he knew she was determined to tell her story so he didn't interrupt her.

"She told him that Carlos del Villaloso had raped Azaylee, that she was pregnant and had gone to Agua Caliente to find him so they could get married. Of course I refused to believe it. I ranted up and down screaming it could not be true, that she was just an innocent child. . . .

"Zev knew he couldn't call in the police. The story would be sure to get out and the publicity would kill her. He called Burbank again and chartered another plane, only this time he wouldn't let me go with him. Instead he took a couple of bodyguards they used at the studio to keep away the cranks and riffraff who always haunted the stars. They were big, brutal-looking men, and up until then I'd always thought they had been chosen because they looked the role. Now I knew different.

"We all spent a sleepless night. You'll never know how many times I asked myself, 'After all I had gone through to protect her, how could this have happened? What had I done that left her so weak and vulnerable to a heel like Carlos del Villaloso?'

"Zev found Villaloso at his usual place, the racetrack. He didn't want a public scene so he told him he wanted to speak to him outside. Zev could tell from Villaloso's face that he knew he was in trouble, but at first he just shrugged off his accusations. He said he barely knew Azaylee and that he had never seen her alone. Then Zev let the bodyguards loose on him, and after a few minutes he changed his tune. He said she had come to him with some ridiculous story about him being the father of her child, wanting him to marry her. He said she had thrown herself at him, that she had followed him to Tijuana, and that she was nothing but a little tramp.

"That was when Zev took over, knocking out a few of Villaloso's precious white teeth in the process.

" 'Where is she?' Zev demanded, so filled with rage that he didn't even feel the pain from his bruised fists. 'Tell me what has happened to her, or I'll kill you with my own hands.'

"Villaloso's face was part of his stock-in-trade. Now it was a mess and he decided he didn't want to die too. 'I gave her some money,' he said, gasping, spitting out blood and some more teeth. 'She went to Tijuana. . . .'

"Zev knew what he meant. Cheap abortions were available in every back street of Tijuana. He groaned and put his hands to his face as he thought of Azaylee in the hands of some butcher. He knew he had better move fast before they could touch her. Leaving Villaloso in care of one of the guards, he and the other took off for Tijuana.

"They started with the 'clinics,' but she wasn't there. Villaloso hadn't given her enough money for that. Someone suggested they try 'Doc' Miller, usually known as 'Doc Loco' because he was always 'loco' from tequila. He was an American who had migrated south to Mexico after being struck off the medical register years before for almost killing a patient with an ovedose while under the influence of drink.

"They found him, all right, propping up his usual sleazy bar, dead drunk of course and with money in his pocket—the money Villaloso had given Azaylee. Zev just left him there and went to find her.

"The room was filthy with cockroaches the size of silver dollars all over the place and the stink of raw sewage from the open drain outside the tiny window that let in just enough light for him to see her. She was lying on a sagging iron cot, covered with a dirty, bloodstained sheet. Her eyes were closed and her breathing shallow and beads of sweat stood out on her forehead.

"Her face was as gray as the sheet, and Zev groaned as he felt her head: She was burning with fever. He pulled back the sheet and stared at the bloody mess, then he closed his eyes, tilting back his head and praying out loud for God to help her, for he had no doubt Azaylee was mortally ill.

"She opened her eyes suddenly and looked at him, puzzled. 'Zev?' she whispered. 'Am I alive?'

"He could hardly speak he was so choked with emotion. 'Yes, milochka,' he replied, 'you are alive.'

" 'Good,' she murmured, 'I wouldn't want to let you down with Marietta.'

"He took her to the hospital, where they cleaned her up and gave her blood transfusions and told him there was no hope. He stayed by her bedside all night, holding her hand, praying for her, and wondering how he was going to break the news to me, but early in the morning—the crisis time when the doctors told him people usually die or else they rally and live—a little color crept into her face. She began to breathe more quietly, and by nine o'clock she was resting peacefully and they knew she would pull through. And then Zev went to find Doc Loco.

"The 'doctor' was picked up later by the police, his face beaten to a pulp. He was taken to jail and never heard from again. The police also arrested Villaloso and charged him with racetrack fraud, and by noon that day he was on his way to Mexico City to await trial. Eventually, after months of delay, he was sentenced to ten years, but he was lucky to be alive—if you can call a Mexican jail 'lucky.' C. Z. Abrams was a powerful man, and he had used that power the way he thought best.

"Azaylee was like a broken doll, completely bewildered by what had happened to her. She kept insisting that it wasn't true, that she had done nothing, and we were afraid to argue with her in case we upset her.

"She was weak and subdued, but when she was finally strong enough I tried to talk to her. She acted vague and strange and I knew at once we were in trouble. Zev called in a famous New York doctor who said she was lost under layers of different identities and suffering from a disassociation of personality. A person suffering from this psychosis is not a real character at all. She is not an individual but a 'collective.' It is impossible to know which is the true personality. Azaylee was not 'a bad girl,' she was a confused being who did not really know who she was. In her normal surroundings she would behave the 'normal' way we expected; in strange circumstances she would behave like another person and therefore do whatever was expected of that person. The doctor said she would need treatment for at least three years, maybe longer.

"So Azaylee began her new treatment and life went back to normal, although, of course, now we were never sure what 'normal' was.

"Zev shelved the Marietta movie she had made and canceled production of the next, and we concentrated on giving her a stable home life and just getting her well again. The final blow was that the doctors said she had been so badly damaged in the abortion that she would never be able to bear children. And afterward I thought maybe that wasn't such a bad thing after all. You see, this was only the first of her troubles with men."

Missie sighed as she glanced helplessly at Cal. "The years passed, we had tutors and she finished her high school education, but we dared not let her go away to college. Instead, she concentrated on her dancing. The psychiatrist said that Azaylee understood that what had happened was because of her mother and her confused childhood and she also understood now that it had happened to her and not 'another girl.' But he warned us he could never guarantee her stability, and all we could do was continue the therapy and hope one day she would be well enough to cope with normal life again.

"When she was eighteen we gave a little birthday party for her, just Rosa and Sam, Rachel, Dick, and Hannah. We went to the

Cocoanut Grove and there was a cake with candles and she blushed when the band played 'Happy Birthday.' She was just the most sweet, naïve, innocent girl you could ever imagine, and she looked so lovely in a pale-green dress and the ruby heart pendant O'Hara had given her when she was our bridesmaid. The table was full of little presents from everyone, especially Zev, who believed presents should come in multiples of at least a dozen. But his biggest present was the news that he had commissioned a script especially for her, a musical to be called *Flying High.*"

"I remember it," Cal exclaimed, smiling, "from too many sleepless nights in college watching the *Late Late Show.* She was wonderful."

"Wasn't she? And she enjoyed it so much. The doctor had given permission, and we all kept a careful eye on her, vetting everyone from her costar to the lowliest gofer on the set. Zev produced and Dick Nevern directed, and her sheer youth and exuberance came through.

"It was 1932 and Magic, like most of the big Hollywood studios, had weathered the depression. Zev put a lot of money into promoting the movie but interviews with her were kept to the minimum, just the top Hollywood and New York reporters. Still, her photograph was in all the fan magazines and suddenly she was a star.

"It didn't go to her head. She just accepted it and carried on as usual, taking Rex, her dog, to the studios every day along with Baby, the puppy. By this time Rex had had his way with Zev's bitch, Juliet, and we now had a household of *six* borzois. Azaylee loved them all so we kept them. She was busy learning her new dance routines for the next movie and at last she seemed completely happy, though of course her life was still very protected. Rachel was her only close friend. Rachel practically lived with us, and she also had a role in all the movies. By now she was dating Dick Nevern seriously and they were in love.

"The first signs of trouble came when Azaylee was twenty-one. She announced she had rented an apartment in Hollywood and was moving out. Soon after she met the man who was to become her dance partner, Milos Zoran, the son of a Polish immigrant farmworker who looked like everybody's idea of a blond Greek god. She met him at dance class and saw immediately he was good, but of course it was when they danced together that the magic happened. They looked so perfect, both so blond and beautiful, he in white tie and tails and she in those soft, clinging chiffon gowns, dancing to Cole Porter and Jerome Kern. All those old standards were new to us then.

"The first movie was an instant success. The pair were 'an item' in the gossip columns, and of course we realized what must be going on. We tried, but there was no way to stop her, and when Zev threatened to fire Zoran she said if he did she would go too. Azaylee was on her own and living the life *she* wanted. Or was she?" Missie shook her head helplessly. "We never really knew."

"Zoran's influence grew stronger; soon he was choreographing their routines so *he* became the important figure and Azaylee told Zev that she wanted all billing to be changed to 'Zoran and Adair,' with his name in front and hers second, and that he should get top billing over title in the next movie. Zev said sure he would do it, but of course he didn't, and when Zoran strutted in to complain, he grabbed him by the lapels of his fancy new suit and told him that he had already put one guy behind bars who had tried to exploit Azaylee and he was not averse to putting another there. Zoran backed down but he walked out in the middle of the next movie. It almost destroyed Azaylee and we were right back to square one: the therapy, the protected private life—and no more movies until she was better.

"This became the pattern. As you probably know, she had several dance partners, but her most famous was Teddy Adams. 'Adair and Adams' is what she will be remembered for. She was the epitome of thirties glamour: She sang, she danced, she was beautiful and young, and the fact that her turbulent private life often hit the headlines only made her more fascinating. Zev always said later that you could bet any woman you met called Ava who had been born in the thirties had been named after Ava Adair.

"She would seem quite normal and happy for long periods of time, and then there would be another crisis. Zev masterminded her career and she was an enormous star, and as long as he was in charge she never made a bad movie. But then the final disaster happened. She met Jakey Jerome—and Grigori Solovsky."

41

"On screen Azaylee was always the open, sunny girl everyone adored, but in private life she seemed to have a penchant for bad characters—good-looking, pimplike men who exploited her. Jakey Jerome seemed different.

"He was short and ugly but with a kind of charm. He had a ready smile and was an easy conversationalist, and he worked at Magic as a scriptwriter. Not a great one, just a regular hack turning out reissues of other people's ideas, but he was good at that. He worked hard and, unlike a lot of the other writers, he didn't drink too much. Zev liked him well enough. It was he who introduced them, and he thought no more about it until he heard they had been seen together in a corner booth at the Brown Derby. But he still wasn't really worried about Jakey. He knew he wasn't Azaylee's type.

"Their friendship progressed and she began to bring him to the house to visit us. We saw he treated her gently, not bullying her like the others, and he didn't seem to want to use her. He hadn't moved in with her as her boyfriends usually did. By this time Rachel was married to Dick Nevern and they had two children—boys. I often caught Azaylee looking at them longingly, and I felt so sorry for her because she knew she would always be childless. We began to wonder if this was serious, if she was really in love at last.

"Zev gave Jakey a new position as a script supervisor with a raise in salary, and the first thing he did was spend his entire month's paycheck on a pair of antique Venetian mirrors Azaylee had admired in a store. She was so thrilled that he had bought her such a wonderful gift that she decided to have her sitting room redesigned around them. When it was finished she invited us to dinner, just Azaylee, Jakey, Zev, and myself.

"He was casual, easy, relaxed, and so was she. I thought I had never seen her look so well and I was grateful to him for being so good to her, helping her. It was 1937 and Azaylee was still only twenty-four years old, but of course she had been a star since she was sixteen. Jakey was twenty-nine and an unknown quantity. He never talked about his family except to say they were Jewish, that he was from Philadelphia, and that most of his family still lived in Poland.

"We admired the new all-white and crystal sitting room and the beautiful mirrors, and then Azaylee announced that Jakey wanted to say something. He stood up, cleared his throat, and then asked Zev formally for Azaylee's hand in marriage—though of course he only knew her as 'Ava.' He was the perfect gentleman, deferential, even shy, though if you ever knew Jakey Jerome you would never believe that. Azaylee looked imploringly at me and said, 'Oh, please, *please,* Missie, *say yes* . . .' just the way she had when she had wanted to be in the movies. So of course we laughed and said yes and champagne was drunk and a wedding planned for October. A big one with all the trimmings. Azaylee seemed happy and completely rational, and we thought if Jakey could do that for her, then he would make her a good husband.

"After supper he said he had come across a script—a play, which he thought had the makings of a great musical. 'How about letting Ava do it on Broadway first?' he asked Zev. 'And maybe do the movie later. That way you would have a double-header success. Besides, Ava says she would enjoy playing theater for a change.'

"Zev was surprised, but he agreed to read it. It wasn't wonderful, just a vehicle for her to dance and sing some pretty songs—Jakey had Irving Berlin in mind or Cole Porter, nothing but the best. He had bought the play for a few thousand dollars and he said he wanted to give it to Azaylee as an engagement present. How could Zev refuse to back it?

"Jakey did the rewrite and produced. Azaylee asked Dick to direct—his first stage job, as it was hers, but she trusted him. A theater was found for a March opening and Jakey set up an office on Broadway and found a costar, Will Hunter, good-looking and talented enough to support Azaylee without stealing her thunder. When she was working she was always absolutely professional, but now she was devoted to her task and to Jakey. She put all her faith in him and I have to say that he did not let her down. After six turbulent weeks out of town, *Hollywood Girl* opened on Broadway on an icy March night. The audience didn't seem to mind the cold. They applauded every number and at the end they gave Ava a standing ovation. I couldn't help remembering my own little success in the Follies, though poor Ziegfeld was long since dead, and I knew how she must feel. I just sat there with tears streaming down my face. I was so proud of her. And of how far she had come—not only in her career, but in struggling back from never-never land. Tonight she was a whole person, Ava Adair, and she was beautiful and a success.

"We went on to Sardi's for the party afterward, waiting nervously for the first editions of the newspapers. When they came we all cheered—they were unanimous in their praise—for Ava, Dick, and the music, that is. They didn't think much of the story. But it didn't matter. The crowds flocked to the theater, and *Hollywood Girl* made a fortune. Zev owned sixty percent and Jakey twenty. For the first time in his life Jakey was rich and he spent money like water, treating everyone to lunches at Twenty-One and presiding over *his* table at the Stork Club every night after the show. He gave Azaylee a large diamond engagement ring to replace the tiny one that was all he had been able to afford before. And he moved from the small Broadway apartment over his office into a suite at the Plaza, opposite her hotel, the Sherry Netherland.

"There was nothing sexual going on between them, and we thought Jakey was just being an old-fashioned gentleman about it. Azaylee had set her heart on a big October wedding at Lexington Drive with a marquee on the lawn and her family and her show-business friends, but with the show such a hit, the wedding was rearranged for the following April to give them enough time to find a replacement to take over her role.

"I often visited her in New York, taking the train because I've always mistrusted airplanes. I stayed with her at the Sherry Netherland, but the days were my own to fill in as I liked because she kept such late hours, partying every night after the show, and she slept most of the day. Jakey would come around at about four and order room service for her—he kept an eye on her diet and made sure she ate properly. He fussed over her a lot and she seemed to like it. Like a little girl with a father, I thought, only he wasn't that much older than she.

"By now it was impossible for her to walk down the street without being mobbed. She went everywhere by limousine and it was getting on her nerves, so on Sundays he would take her out to friends' places on Long Island, and she would swim and race around playing tennis. She had such phenomenal energy then.

"The World's Fair was to open soon and New York was filled with international visitors. She was constantly entertaining important foreign delegations backstage after the show. She was always charming, sparkling, and laughing, just the way they expected a star to be. Everyone adored her. She had known Jakey almost two years and in all that time, she had never once been 'ill.' I thought she had forgotten all about it, forgotten the doctors in their white coats and the sanatorium and the long leaden days when all she had wanted to do was sleep because being awake and trying to cope was just too painful.

"I was backstage one night after the show—in October, I think it was—when the manager said there were some important Russian visitors out front who would very much like to meet Miss Adair. I felt myself going pale and my voice shook as I inquired exactly who they were. Top political men, he said, here for the conferences. Their leader was a man by the name of General Grigori Solovsky.

"In a second I was catapulted back in time to that crowded train crawling its way through the frozen countryside as Captain Grigori Solovsky asked Azaylee her name. I held my breath, just as I had done then, waiting agonizedly for her reply. 'Azaylee,' she had said, laughing, 'Azaylee O'Bryan. . . .'" And then even farther back to the night in the forest when Solovsky had taken Alexei away for ever. I still relived it in my dreams. And now what I had feared had finally happened. He had found us.

"I heard Azaylee saying 'Of course I'll see them. How interesting Missie, they are Russian.'

" 'Maybe you shouldn't . . .' I began, and then suddenly there he was in the doorway. The same dark-haired, stocky little peasant of twenty years ago. Only then he had been young and still unsure enough of himself to accept my story, even though he hadn't really believed it. And now he was a man of power, resplendent in a general's uniform. My heart was in my mouth as I searched behind him, half expecting to see Alexei.

"I was standing out of the circle of light by the dressing table but anyway their eyes were focused on Ava Adair. I watched, trembling, as Solovsky took her hand and bowed. 'We enjoyed the show so much,' he said in heavily accented English, 'that we felt we must tell you personally. It is not often that we Russians have such a treat. My compliments, Miss Adair, on your wonderful talent.'

"Solovsky chatted for a few minutes and then he said, 'I cannot help feeling we have met before, Miss Adair. Your face is familiar to me.'

"She said eagerly, 'Do you think it's possible?'

"I knew what she was going to say next and I rushed to interrupt her. 'I don't mean to appear rude,' I said quickly, 'but Jakey wants you to hurry over to the Stork Club as quickly as possible. Cole is there and Dick. . . .'

"Solovsky's eyes met mine and I knew he recognized me. 'This is my mother, Mrs. Abrams.' Azaylee introduced me. 'I'm so sorry, General Solovsky, but I really must hurry. Maybe we could talk about this some other time. . . .'

"He bowed to her again and said, 'I would be delighted,' but he was looking at me. He came over and shook my hand and he said quietly so the others wouldn't hear, 'We know each other, do we not, Mrs. O'Bryan?'

"I didn't know what to say, I was so frightened I thought my heart was about to stop. 'We must talk,' he murmured.

"I wondered if the Cheka were waiting outside to arrest us, and he read my mind easily and smiled. 'Just you and I,' he said quietly. I nodded, and agreed to meet him in my hotel suite in half an hour."

New York

Grigori would have picked Missie's face out from a thousand others because he had never forgotten the day on the train. It had been one of the few times he had allowed himself to slip back into the old ingrained peasant subservience, allowing her to spin him a story he suspected was not true and then letting her get away with it because he was afraid of looking a fool. The memory had rankled but it was when he reached St. Petersburg and had investigated the Ivanoff deaths that he had put two and two together, and by then it was too late. They had disappeared and even the Cheka's desperate searches had not come up with a single clue. His growing love for Alexei/ Sergei had overcome his duty to his country, and even though Russia was desperate to get her hands on the Ivanoff billions, he had never wavered. Lenin would have not approved but for him, his "son" came first.

He had thought Ava Adair's face was familiar, but it was only when he had seen Missie that he realized he was looking at Alexei's sister. Xenia Ivanoff—alive and well and as beautiful as her famous mother.

Now, as he stepped into the elevator and was wafted slowly up to Missie's hotel suite, he knew that this woman was the only person in the world who knew that he had taken Alexei. And if he was clever there would finally be a way to get Russia the money she wanted.

She was waiting for him beside a tray of silver jugs and china cups. Though she looked as calm as if she were about to preside over a ladies' tea party, his experienced glance noted her dark eyes with the dilated pupils. She was afraid.

"So we meet again," he said, speaking to her in Russian.

She shook her head. "It has been too many years since I spoke your language, Captain—*General* Solovsky."

He sat opposite her in the expensive rose-pink and gilt room with its opulent swagged drapes and carved mirrors. "I think you will find my English has improved. It would not be easy to fool me a second time."

"And nor would it be easy for you to fool me."

Their glances met. "Then we are equal," he said softly. "You have one Ivanoff child. I have the other."

She said nothing, pouring tea with a steady hand, and he smiled. She was a fighter and he respected that.

She placed the cup in front of him, offering lemon and sugar. "Please, tell me about Alexei."

"It seemed I had two choices as far as the boy," he said abruptly. "I could have killed him and left him for the wolves along with the rest. Or I could take him with me, a prisoner of the new Russia. But there was a third option, a private one. I could reverse the roles and bring up the prince as a common man."

He told her about his own upbringing in Siberia, about his meeting with Lenin, his *klassnaya dama* and his education and how he had dragged himself up by his peasant bootstraps via the army to become a man of importance in the new regime of the Socialist Republics.

"I already had a son," he said, his deep voice booming through the pretty room, "and now I would have two.

"Sergei, as I called him, followed me around like a puppy. His gratitude was overwhelming, not for saving his life but for avenging his mother. He never spoke of his family and tried his best to fit into our simple life. My plan was working well—he was clever at sports as well as book learning. He quickly won a scholarship to a good school and left our home in Byelorussia to come and live with me in Moscow. It was years before I let him set foot in Leningrad—St. Petersburg as he had known it. I was afraid to trigger old memories and disturb our relationship.

"Sergei went on to Moscow University and then did his army training. He proved a capable officer and now, at twenty-seven, he is a dedicated Party member with his feet on the first rungs of the ladder to high political position. He never talks to me about the past. It is forgotten."

He said calmly, "I am proud of the success of my experiment. And proud of my son Sergei. So you can imagine my surprise when tonight I stumbled over you and realized that I had found what Russia had been searching for for years. Except, of course, they never had any real proof that the Ivanoffs did escape. Only you and I know that. They searched the world for them and they have not given up that search. It is important to Russia that if the Ivanoffs are alive, they be found. And you know why."

Gripping her hands tightly together to stop them trembling, Missie asked, "Are you going to tell them?"

It was the question that had been burning in her brain since she met him and he knew it. He smiled at her pleasantly. "May I have another cup of tea? It's very cozy here by the fire. Almost like being back in a Russian *dacha* in the old days."

He studied her face as she poured the tea. Her downcast eyes hid her expression, but he knew he had her exactly where he wanted her.

"You and I have done our duty by our 'children,'" he said. "Now our work for them is done. Ava and Sergei have found the kind of personal success they could never have dreamed of as the son and daughter of Prince and Princess Ivanoff. Sergei is his own man. He can be proud of his achievements because they were not bought for him. Can you say that my experiment was wrong then, Missie? Any more than yours was, in bringing up Xenia as your own daughter?"

He folded his hands together, propping his chin on them, staring at her with his piercing dark eyes.

"You are a clever woman, Missie," he said softly. "I need not explain to you what could happen if I were just to pick up this telephone, right here, and call the Cheka. They are always with me, even here in New York, always around. . . ."

If her face could have turned paler it would have. He smiled with satisfaction. He was about to drive a hard bargain. "I could take Ava away from you forever," he said. "I could turn her over to my government to do with as they will because she is the key to the fortune that Russia so badly needs." He paused for a second or two, watching her like a hawk hovering over the sparrow before it drops for the kill. "But I see that you love her like your own child. I am a compassionate man. I am going to make a bargain with you. I want to give something to Sergei to reward him for the happiness he has brought me. I can think of no greater gift than reuniting him with his sister. The Ivanoff affair will remain a secret between us if you will agree to let Ava come to Russia for a few weeks. I will arrange a 'cultural visit,' a few concerts. I will take care of her and see she comes to no harm."

Missie's scalp prickled as she sensed danger. The pretty room was heavy with the scent of it, just the way it had been in the train. Through the fog of fear clouding her brain she saw through his plan. He would take Azaylee back to Russia and hand her over to the Cheka so that they could get their hands on the fortune. Alexei would never see her or even know about her. And Solovsky would still have his son. But she knew there was just one trump card left to play in this game—and it was hers.

"I understand your 'compassionate' motive exactly," she replied, "but what you suggest is impossible. And so, General Solovsky, is your threat of the Cheka."

"And why is that?" He stood up and began to pace the room, his hands clasped behind his back.

"Because America is a democratic nation where intimidation is not a way of life. Ava Adair is a famous woman. There would be an international incident. A scandal against Russia."

He shrugged. "Russia has a strong back. She has weathered many scandals."

"The other reason," she said, sitting ramrod straight on the pink sofa and meeting his eye, "is that I know what happened to Alexei Ivanoff. I intend to make a statement in front of witnesses to this effect. Copies of that statement will be placed in a safe deposit box at my bank with my lawyers. If you ever attempt to touch Ava Adair, General Solovsky, you will hang yourself. And also your 'son.' "

He stared at her angrily. He knew he was beaten. She had found the only loophole and she had used it.

He sighed and sat down again opposite her. "You and I are cursed by a crippling disease—*love*. You know I would die rather than hurt Sergei. The brother and sister will never meet. Alexei Ivanoff will lead his new life and Xenia Ivanoff hers. There is no more to be said."

"And the fortune that Russia wants so badly?" she asked, the old fear of the Cheka lurking at the back of her mind.

"You must maintain your silence and your anonymity. I can promise nothing."

He stood up, looking at her with a faint amused smile. "I knew when I met you on the train that you were a tough adversary."

"Only in love," she said quietly. "Not in war." There was just one more question she had to ask, something she needed to know finally. "Please tell me what happened to the prince."

"Misha Ivanoff was shot by the peasant rebels at Varishnya. His body was burned when they dynamited the house."

The door separating her sitting room from Azaylee's suite crashed back against the wall and they swung around, startled. It was Azaylee, her face ghostlike against her blond hair. She was wringing her hands together. "I'm sorry if I interrupted," she said in a small voice. "I came home early . . . I had a headache."

"Then I will leave you in peace." Solovsky bowed to her and Missie. "I will not forget," he added as he strode through the door, and Missie had no doubt he would not.

She turned to look at Azaylee, still standing there twisting her hands together and staring at her, and she knew she had heard. And then she saw the look in her eyes, the same look she had had when O'Hara had been mown down by the machine-gun bullets, when she had screamed and screamed as if she would never stop. Only this time she knew Azaylee was screaming inside, and this time she did not know how they were going to bring her back.

══ 42 ══

The carefully tended gardens of the big house on Lexington Drive looked peaceful under the golden summer sunshine: Birds sang, cicadas fretted, and the pool glittered invitingly, but somehow, no one had the heart to accept its invitation.

From his vantage point at the end of the terrace with the dogs sprawled beside him in the shade, Zev watched Missie serving iced tea, wishing he could turn the clock back a year and that Grigori Solovsky had never been to New York. They had just returned from visiting Azaylee at the Rancho Velo Clinic, up the coast a way in Ventura County. It was the first time in a month that the doctor had permitted them to see her. She had walked slowly toward them clinging to the nurse's arm and they stared at her, horrified.

They had cut her lovely blond hair to facilitate the use of electrodes on her head in some new form of treatment they swore by, and it stood out like an angel's halo. Her face was so shrunken and pinched all that seemed left were the eyes, as velvety golden and inhuman as the pansy flowers they had always been compared with. Her scrawny body and rake-thin limbs looked barely capable of supporting her.

"She won't eat," the doctor told Missie. "There's no reason for it. She is not physically ill. But she just refuses nourishment."

"She wants to die," Missie said flatly. "She wants to be with her father."

"We are drip-feeding her, of course. It will keep her alive, but if she doesn't start to eat soon. . . ." He shrugged graphically, and they all knew what he meant.

Azaylee glanced distantly at them and their false eager smiles faded as they realized she didn't recognize them. Suddenly she clutched Missie's hand and said, "Have you brought him, like I asked you? Have you brought Alexei to see me?" Tears stood in her beautiful eyes. *"Milochka,"* she whispered, "tell me that Papa is safe after all. Tell me he will come for me soon."

And then she retreated again into a no-man's-land of dark despair, locked behind her blank gaze with the tears still streaming down her cheeks—and theirs.

Zev stared down the terrace, troubled, as Missie suddenly put her head in her hands and began to weep. He could think of nothing to say that would comfort her. Not for the first time, he wished they had children of their own, but it seemed it was not to be.

"I can't stand it any longer," Rosa exploded, leaping to her feet and stalking the terrace angrily. "Every time you see her, she's worse. They are killing her with their treatments in that fancy clinic. Bring her home, Missie. If she's going to die crazy at least let her do it here, where we love her."

Of course, Zev thought with a faint smile, Rosa, with her practical mind, had got right to the heart of the matter. After picking up the intercom, he told his chauffeur to have the car ready in five minutes.

"But where are you going?" Missie asked tearfully.

He kissed her and said, "I'm going to bring her home, of course."

Ignoring the doctor's warnings, he wrapped Azaylee in a shawl and held her in his arms all the way back. But in his heart he thought he was bringing her home to die. Her room had been prepared but he refused to let them shut her away. "Let her stay here with us," he ordered. "Let her be aware that life is continuing normally around her. She will sit at the table with us even though she may not eat. She will rest on the terrace, walk in the gardens. Rosa is right, she must be with her family."

Her borzois, Rex and Baby, leapt around barking excitedly, and she patted their heads absently. Whimpering with delight, Rex rolled at her feet and she sighed and suddenly said, "Hello, Rex."

Then she looked at Rosa and said, "Am I going to bed now?"

"So? Why are you going to bed?" Rosa demanded. "You are not sick."

"Am I not?" She looked at them, bewildered.

"Sit here by me," Missie coaxed as Zev helped her into a long comfortable chair. The dogs flopped at her feet and Missie held out a glass of cinnamon milk. "Grandmother Sofia's special," she said with a smile. "You know how you always like it."

"Thank you." Azaylee held it absently, gazing around her at the beautiful flower-laden terrace and the gardens under the serene evening sky, then she sighed. "How lovely," she said, closing her eyes.

They clustered around her silently, all except Jakey, who was leaning against the stone balustrade, drinking scotch. Zev said sympathetically, "I know how hard this is on you, Jakey. I want you to know that we would not blame you if you just left and never came back. No one would hold you to an offer of marriage to a girl who is . . . a girl as unstable as Ava."

Jakey shrugged and drained his glass. "I'll do my best to help her, C. Z., but it's kinda tough when she doesn't even know I'm around. If only I could forget it for a while, maybe if I had a project at the studio I could bury myself in, something really meaty that took up all my time. I've been thinking, after the success of *Hollywood Girl* I'd kinda like to have a shot at producing a movie."

He glanced sideways at Zev as he poured himself another scotch. "I've come across a script I think you might find interesting, C. Z. Maybe you'd like to see it?"

"Send it to my office first thing Monday." Zev threw a friendly arm across Jakey's shoulders. "I'll see what I can do to help."

The next day they began to ease Azaylee back into a normal way of life. She was woken in the morning at the same time as they and sat with them at the breakfast table. Her blank stare swept over them unnervingly, but they kept up a normal conversation as they forced down their food while her plate was removed, untouched. Afterward Missie and Rosa walked up and down the terrace, supporting her between them until she seemed so fatigued that they were forced to stop. Lunch was served and again she ignored it, staring into space. Another little stroll, and at dinner the same blank silent routine. Even Rex seemed depressed, lying limply at her feet, never moving until she did.

After three days they felt they were going crazy too, and at another silent dinner Rosa exploded. "So," she exclaimed with an angry snarl, "are you just gonna sit there and not eat? You don't remember the days when Missie worked her hands to the bone to buy food for you? Are you too grand a movie star now?"

Azaylee's shocked eyes met hers and Rosa stared at her nervously, afraid she had gone too far in her anger and frustration.

"I'm sorry," Azaylee said meekly, picking up her spoon and tasting the soup. "I know how hard Missie works." She patted Rex at her feet and added, "She always makes sure Viktor gets his food too." She smiled at Missie and said, "Thank you, *matiushka.*"

They realized Azaylee thought she was a child again, but at least it was contact. She was talking and she was eating.

Zev approved Jake's script and made him a producer with a big budget, a hefty salary, and the rare freedom to choose his own cast and director. The studio was flourishing but Zev had another interest. For the past few years he had been doing what he could to help refugees fleeing from Nazi Germany, Hungary, Czechoslovakia, and Poland, sending large sums of money through various organizations.

He followed the political events in Europe with dread in his heart. When on September 1, 1939, Germany invaded Poland and two days later Britain and France declared war on Germany, he bowed his head and wept.

Missie was absorbed in helping Azaylee on her slow return to reality, and for the first time in years he felt that deep sense of helplessness. To forget he threw himself into his work. In the next eighteen months Magic's production increased by 30 percent and their profits by 50 percent. Jakey's film scored a small success and made enough to ensure him another, and Azaylee had lost that terrifying blank stare and looked like her old self again. She smiled and chatted to Rachel and her boys and she lighted up whenever Jakey came to see her.

On December 7, 1941, when the Japanese bombed Pearl Harbor, precipitating America into the war, Dick Nevern was one of the first to enlist. "They say I'm too old at forty-one," he said proudly, "but I talked 'em out of it."

"Then you'd better talk them out of the desk job they'll give you too." Jakey laughed. But he didn't follow Dick's example even though he was only thirty-three. Instead he got exemption on the grounds that he had important work making propaganda movies about the war effort. And he asked Azaylee to marry him again.

It was as if someone had turned on the klieg lights and suddenly she became Ava Adair. She grew beautiful again before their eyes, she talked, she laughed, she sparkled. She acted like a woman in love—or rather, Ava Adair in love. Missie and Zev stared worriedly at each other as she said one more time, "Oh, please, *please*, Missie, *say yes*. . . ." She was a grown woman. How could they say no, even though they were worried?

The wedding was the grand affair she had always wanted. The bride was breathtaking in a silvery sheath of heavy white satin. There was a big marquee on the lawn and the guests, many of them in uniform, drank vintage champagne from Zev's private stock and devoured lobster and caviar as if there were no tomorrow. When the bride and groom left for their honeymoon, Zev thought what a contrast they made, Jakey so swarthy, almost as wide as he was tall, his ugly face fixed in a grin; his bride so slender and frail and so blond and beautiful.

"Don't worry. You are not losing me," Azaylee whispered as she hugged Missie and Zev good-bye. "Soon I'll have a baby and you can become doting grandparents."

They stared at each other helplessly as they waved good-bye to the happy pair, knowing it was impossible. "Let's just allow her her dreams," Zev said, "as long as it makes her happy."

As soon as they returned from the honeymoon, Jakey announced his plans to star his wife in a new movie, *Sweetheart of the Forces,* an all-singing, all-dancing, big-band blockbuster featuring battleships, aircraft carriers, and airplane wings as backgrounds for dance routines. The movie was a success and Azaylee plunged right into the next one, working long days at the studio and rushing to help at the Hollywood Canteen at night as well as making time to sell War Bonds and help scrap metal drives. And as Jakey went from success to success, Zev gave him more and more freedom.

Dick had beaten the age ban and had been sent to Britain as a special movie correspondent. He expected to be sent to join Montgomery's forces in the desert at Alamein and was whiling away his time impatiently in London awaiting news of a plane on which he could hitch a ride. He was at a bar with some other American news correspondents when it received a direct hit; they were all killed instantly.

Azaylee forgot about everything, including her own problems, in her attempts to console her friend Rachel, a widow at thirty-two with three young boys aged between ten and five. Then Sam Brockman died suddenly of a heart attack, and Zev insisted that Rosa and Rachel and the children all come and live with them for as long as they wanted.

"It will fill up this big house," he said with a smile, but inside he was devastated by Dick's death. Dick was his friend and ally, and he had planned that Dick should be heir to the studio he had helped make such a phenomenal success. Without him Magic seemed to lose its point, and Zev realized that he had fallen out of love with the movie business just as quickly as he had fallen in love with it. He was fifty years old and he was tired of movies, tired of wars and troubles. All he really wanted to do was be with Missie.

=== 43 ===

"So, there we were," Missie said to Cal, "living in the big house on Lexington with Rosa, Rachel, and the children, and instead of masterminding the studios Zev was acting like a father to them, taking Dick's place. He went to their school meetings and inspected their report cards, got them tennis and swimming coaches and took them to baseball games. And more and more, he let Jakey Jerome take over Magic. At first Jakey used to make a great show of consulting him, but it soon became apparent that it didn't matter what Zev said: He was running it his own way. Zev would go there two or three days a week to check production and sit in on the meetings they told him about, but he knew nothing about the other meetings —the secret ones.

"Since she had left the clinic after the incident with Solovsky, Azaylee had never answered to that name again. She really became 'Ava Adair,' and it seemed she had left all her problems behind with her old name. She was making film after film and Zev warned Jakey he was squeezing her dry, putting her into the same thing over and over again; only the titles and the leading men ever really changed. 'She needs a new style, a new look,' he told him after viewing the rushes of her latest epic. 'She's got more to offer than just her beauty.'

"But Jakey just shrugged. 'That's what the public wants,' he said. 'They're lapping it up.'

"When Zev mentioned it to Azaylee she just gave him that vague smile and said Jakey must know what he was doing, and then she rushed off again to rehearse for some charity concert she had promised to take part in.

"After the war was over movies seemed to change, even the musicals were different, there was a harder edge to them. Her latest movie was a flop and lost Magic some phenomenal sum. Zev was really angry and called Jakey into his office to explain, but he just blamed it on her. He said she had refused to change with the times and insisted on playing it her way.

"They had a wonderful house on Crescent Drive and Jakey loved to give parties. We would put in an occasional appearance at their Sunday poolside brunches, and I couldn't help noticing how things had changed. When they first met, Azaylee had been unattainable for a man like Jakey. She was the beautiful star—and the stepdaughter of C. Z. Abrams—while he was the unattractive, untalented, broke young scriptwriter with his feet on the shaky first rung of the Hollywood ladder. Now he was the Hollywood movie mogul, squat, loud, and flashy in his Italian silk suits and his big cigar. And she had become the movie actress with the reputation of being unstable, eclipsed by a new generation of beautiful starlets who would stop at nothing on their climb to success. And there were always plenty of those around at Jakey's parties.

"He treated her more brusquely, cutting her off in the middle of sentences, turning away from her as if she weren't there. Or he would ignore her all afternoon, chatting to everyone else, the jolly host full of bonhomie. And Zev heard stories that he was out most nights at 'poker games,' or at least that's where he told her he was.

"Life jogged along for a few more years. Zev and I were still as happy as the day we had married, and because of the war I thought that finally the threat from the Cheka had ended, that by now they must have forgotten all about the Ivanoffs. I pushed it to the back of my mind and tried to forget.

"In the spring of 1950 Zev and I decided to take a trip to Europe. It was the holiday of a lifetime: London, Paris, Rome. My early memories of Oxford clashed with 1950s reality and I barely recognized it, only the colleges were the same. But I found our old house, and the professor who lived there kindly allowed me to look around. At least that hadn't changed much—even Papa's worn old chair was still there. When I told him how I remembered climbing on to my father's knee on that very chair, the professor kindly gave it to me and I had it shipped back to California. My father was buried in Russia so there was no grave or other memory there for me. It was just another ghost laid to rest from the past.

"We arrived back in California feeling wonderful. Zev was rested and completely revitalized. After the war when the full horrors of the concentration camps were revealed, he had donated large sums of money to international charities and had given most of his time to supporting them. Now he said he was going to get back into the business again. He was going to take back control of Magic and run it his way.

"The telephone rang as we walked through the door and I picked it up and said hello.

" '*Matiushka,*' she said, 'it's Azaylee.' It was the first time she had called herself that in twelve years, and I knew it meant trouble.

"We went over to see her right away. She was sitting on a sofa with her legs tucked under her, twisting a handkerchief in her hands, and she looked pale and shrunken and afraid.

"She stared at Zev as if he were a ghost. 'You don't look ill!' she exclaimed.

" 'Of course I'm not ill,' he said with a laugh. 'I've never felt better in my life.'

" 'Oh, thank God!' A look of relief replaced the tension on her face and she smiled. 'After what Jakey was saying I thought you were dying. . . .'

"He sat beside her and took her hand. 'And what is Jakey saying?'

" 'That you are getting old, that your era has come and gone, that it's time for new blood in Magic's veins. He said you've slowed down, that you have some mysterious illness no one wants to talk about. I overheard it at a poker game he held here a few weeks ago. It wasn't the usual sort of poker game. There were important men there, money men. . . .' She looked at him, as clear-eyed and alert as I'd ever seen her, and said, 'Oh, my God, Zev, now I see what he's doing, now I see why he's telling everyone you are sick. . . . He wants Magic!'

"Word flew around Hollywood that C. Z. Abrams was ill. He hadn't gotten where he was in the business without making enemies, and now they were snapping at his heels like a pack of wolves eager to snatch the prey from their rival. Jakey had played a dirty maneuvering game. Magic was a corporation with millions in assets, mostly their lot on Cahuenga, but as their movies—and the business —got bigger, so did their borrowings. Jakey had been in control for the past few years, and he had been switching the company's business to new banks he told Zev were eager to finance the big productions he had in mind. He had become very friendly with a particular young banker, Alan Rackman, who was always there with the big loan when he needed it.

"Jakey told Zev that Magic was in trouble. Their year's profits had fallen by sixty percent but not only that, the accountants said that large sums of money were unaccounted for: They had 'gone missing.' He said it was a good thing Zev was back because they needed to talk to him urgently. When Zev asked about the stories that he was 'ill,' he said he'd just been repeating what he'd heard around town—he'd even read it in *Daily Variety.* And there it was: 'C. Z. Abrams dashes to Europe for treatment for a mystery "illness." Worries about brain tumor said to be affecting his business decisions.'

"It went on to say how Magic's performance had been declining since the long absence of its chairman, along with the death of Dick Nevern, but that despite rumors of hefty financial trouble, its president, Jakey Jerome, was going ahead with production of three major movies that season as planned.

"Everything happened quickly after that. Jakey's friend Rackman, the banker, accused Zev of diverting large sums of company money to his 'charities,' insinuating that they were not charities at all but had simply ended up in Zev's foreign bank accounts. He produced 'doctored' checks on Magic's accounts to prove it. It was what they used to call in gangster movies a 'frame-up,' but they were piling up the evidence against him as well as citing loss of competence and accusing him of being responsible for the company's financial disasters, even though Jakey had been running the company for the past few years. They even threatened to cite senility as a cause of his supposed 'actions.'

" 'It would be a hell of a scandal, C. Z.,' Jakey said smoothly. 'The headlines alone would kill you, even if you spent ten years trying to prove none of it was true. And it would kill Magic. Why don't you just give in gracefully and let us run the company? You've had your day—now it's mine.'

"Zev stared at his grinning face and he wanted to punch his teeth right down his throat, but he knew it wasn't worth it. He suddenly realized that Jakey had never loved Azaylee, it had all been an act. 'That's what you wanted right from the beginning, wasn't it?' he said.

"Jakey stared back at him with that cocky grin. 'You betcha!' he replied.

"The next day Zev announced his resignation as chairman of Magic. Filmmaking was not the way it used to be in the beginning, now it was all big corporations, television, takeovers, and money men. He wanted no part of it. He had bought a winery years ago and now he decided to take an interest in that.

"Nothing was ever heard about any enormous sums of money supposedly 'missing' from Magic's accounts, and Alan Rackman was appointed as the new president with Jakey as chairman. Suddenly Magic had all the money it needed and Jakey had exactly what he wanted."

Missie smiled sadly as she looked at Cal and said, "That's why C. Z. Abrams died a forgotten man. And Jakey Jerome became a legend in his own time."

"Azaylee walked out on him. She stayed at the Lexington Drive house alone except for her dogs and the servants. Jakey barred her from Magic's lot and sued for divorce, claiming she was mentally unstable. It was the cruelest thing he could have done and he knew it, but he didn't want any counterclaim and he also knew she could not contest it.

"The divorce went through quickly but it certainly hit the headlines, and there were those awful pictures of her hiding behind dark glasses and a big hat, looking as if she were playing a role in a bad movie. Of course she cracked under the strain and ended up in another clinic, and once again we had to try to put her back together. Eventually, when she was allowed home, she went to live with Rachel and her boys at their new house in Beverly Hills. Rosa had finally married again, a builder by trade, and had gone to live in San Diego. And Zev and I were at the winery in northern California.

"He had bought it years before as an 'investment' but it had never made a penny, and we used to laugh about how bad the wine was. Now, with Magic gone and nothing to occupy his mind, he decided to take it up again. But being Zev he was going to do it properly, just the way he had with the movies. He wanted to learn everything about making wine so of course that meant another trip to France to see how it was done there.

"We went to all the big châteaux, and I was thrilled to see how quickly he put his mind away from Hollywood and concentrated on his new business. Without Magic and Zev's enormous salary we were no longer as rich as we had been, and we decided to sell Lexington Drive and build ourselves a new house on a hill overlooking our five hundred acres of vineyards. While work was going on we lived in a little ranch house and Zev went to work every day with his estate manager to watch the planting of his new French vines. He had a ten-year plan and then he said the world would really start to hear about California wines, especially 'C. Z. Vineyards.'

"He liked to drive over there in the evenings to show me how his new little vines were growing. He was so proud of them, I swear he knew every single one. The climate is different in northern California, especially in those long valleys where you get a chill wind, like the French mistral, blowing in from the northwest. Zev still behaved as if he were living in the south and rarely wore a jacket or a sweater. One night when we went to the vineyards and strolled around as we usually did, chatting about the crop and the type of wine he wanted to produce, I saw him shiver in the wind. It was October and really quite raw, and I wanted to leave. But there was just one more thing he wanted to show me and then another and another. The next day he came down with a bad cold, shivering and coughing, and that evening his temperature shot up. I called the doctor and he said it was bronchitis and it looked bad, and then it turned to pneumonia.

"They took him to hospital and shot him full of the new wonder drug—penicillin—but he didn't improve. I sat by his bedside holding his hand and I knew he was dying. We had known each other for thirty-four years and had been married for twenty-three of them. The happiest years of my life, even with all their problems.

"They put tubes in his throat to help him breathe but they could not cure him, and it only made him more distressed because now he couldn't speak. I knew what he wanted to say and I said it for him. 'I love you too, Zev,' I told him. 'We will always love each other.'

"I took his body back to Hollywood and buried him there, the place where he had found himself as a man. It was where he belonged. His death rated a headline in *Variety* and a long obituary listing his achievements, and they were charitable enough to say that he had retired from his role as Magic's Chairman for 'health reasons' and not mention Jakey's takeover. But he had always been a man who shied away from publicity, and his death didn't merit more than an odd column in the international press. I thought the ceremony would be a small one but I was astonished how many people showed up. Zev was well respected and liked, and he had more friends in the business than he knew. I still think if he had fought Jakey his friends would have supported him and he would have won. But Jakey Jerome was a street fighter and he knew exactly how to kick a man where it hurt him most psychologically.

"I was left a fairly rich widow, and I sold the vineyard and bought a small, rambling ranch-style house in the suburb of Encino in the San Fernando Valley. I bred borzois and played bridge and involved myself in charity work. And I tried to keep Azaylee out of trouble.

"She had always been so professional and the rumors were cruel, they said that without C. Z. and Magic behind her she was no good. They said she was drinking—but it wasn't true, she was just Azaylee again, instead of Ava Adair. She drifted between her two personas, and the studios never knew what to expect from her. One day she would be fine, the next she couldn't even remember what she was supposed to be doing. But she was still very beautiful and there were always men. And in bad times, the clinic.

"She was in the Valley Loma Clinic when I went to see her one day in 1959. She had not worked for several years, and I always took care of her medical expenses. I didn't want Azaylee to be burdened with money worries on top of everything else. She had been in and out of the clinic on an almost monthly basis that year, fluctuating between bouts of riotous living and deep depression.

"She was sitting in a wicker chair on the porch and I sat beside her. She smiled at me as I gave her the roses I had brought and said, 'Hello, *matiushka*. Guess what? I'm pregnant.'

"I thought: Oh, my God, now she has really gone mad, now she thinks she's pregnant. At forty-four years old when she knows she can never have children.

" 'Of course you are not pregnant, Azaylee,' I said as calmly as I could. 'You know the doctors said it was just not possible.'

"She grinned at me, her face full of mischief. 'They were wrong,' she said triumphantly. 'The test was confirmed today. You are to be a grandmother, *matiushka*. At last.'

"The clinic confirmed it and said they must keep an eye on her; she would either have to stay there or come and live with me. I took her home right away and she was happier than I have ever seen her. She was determined to do everything right: She ate the right foods, gained weight, took all her vitamins, exercised, walked, and swam. Her baby was going to be the best baby in the whole world. But if she knew the identity of the father, she wasn't telling me. She just shrugged and said it could be one of half a dozen but I needn't worry, they were all nice, good-looking young men. 'Younger than me. Maybe that's how I got pregnant,' she said wonderingly. But it wasn't, it was just a billion-to-one chance that came off.

"She was physically fit so the birth wasn't too difficult, and I'll never forget the love on her face as she held the baby toward me. 'There, *matiushka*,' she said proudly. 'She is just as beautiful as Anouska.'

"Of course she wasn't. She was a funny-looking little thing, almost bald, and her nose looked too big for her tiny face, but to her she was a miracle of beauty. She gave the child the Russian family names and her stage name, Adair. Anna Adair.

"With Anna's birth she seemed to come to life again. Six months later she began looking for work and I was left to bring up the child. There were just two things I wished: that Misha could have seen his granddaughter and that Zev could have been there to share her with me.

"Sometimes Azaylee worked, sometimes she didn't, but she was always involved with some man or other, usually bad ones, and she was still in and out of the sanatorium. Until one day when Anna was six, she just went into the clinic and never came out. Her mind had finally cracked under a depression so acute that she became a virtual zombie, not even able to recognize us or communicate. At first I used to take Anna there to visit, but it was no good for her and finally I stopped. That's when I met Tariq Kazahn again, in Paris, and Anna's whole life changed. At last she had a real family.

"At this point too I discovered that most of Azaylee's money had been squandered by her lovers and that she was virtually penniless. My own money was being eaten up on her clinic and doctors' bills. They told me it would make no difference to her if I put her in a state institution because she didn't even know where she was, but I would never do that.

"Azaylee died tragically in a fire at the clinic in 1972. Despite my sadness I was glad she had finally escaped from her years of torture and glad that Anna would no longer have the burden of knowing her mother was insane. Ava Adair was a middle-aged woman but all anyone talked about in the newspapers and magazines was how beautiful she had been, and how talented. They said there would never be anyone like her and that she and her movies would be remembered forever. And I was left alone to bring up twelve-year-old Anna.

"There was not a great deal of money left," she said quietly to Cal. "Most of what I had had gone on Azaylee, and now I was left with a mountain of debts for her medical care and the house. I would have to live carefully if I was going to see young Anna through college and into a career and a life of her own. I only hoped I would be spared long enough to accomplish my task." She laughed. "I didn't realize then that maybe I would be spared too long. Because you see, Cal, if I had died earlier, none of this would have happened. Anna knows only part of the story. She sold those jewels innocently in order to keep me here in luxury. It's her way of saying thank you for all I did for her mother."

It was seven in the morning and the sun was shining brightly as Nurse Milgrim rustled through the door. "It will take days to get over this," she whispered angrily to Missie. "A whole night's sleep lost."

"Oh, Nurse Milgrim, this has been much better than sleep: a catharsis, a relief. And now Cal can take over."

She looked at him appealingly and he knew how lovely she must have been. "Two questions," he said quickly. "Do you know where she has gone?"

"Why, to Istanbul. To the Kazahns, of course," she said as if it were the most logical place in the world.

He nodded. "And do you know if she has any papers, any legal documents . . . ?"

"The lease to the mines, you mean? Oh, yes, Anna had everything. She took the lot when I came in here." She laughed. "You can hardly keep an old cardboard valise full of priceless jewels under a bed at Fairlawns. They would sweep it out with the cobwebs." She looked at him and said, "There is something else I have to explain. When I saw the young Russian diplomat, Valentin Solovsky, on television, I knew him at once. He is Alexei's son, Anna's cousin."

She handed Cal a small photograph of a pretty blond girl and said, "Please, find Anna for me. *Help her.*"

Cal stared in stunned silence at the mystery girl everyone was searching for. The Ivanoff heiress. *He was looking at a picture of Genie Reese.*

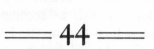

44

Istanbul

Istanbul tumbled and crumbled under the hot spring sun, blistering and peeling, layered with dust and grime, clogged with traffic and clapped-out taxis, carpet sellers and cats. The domes of its tarnished jewels, Topkapi, Ayasofya, and the Blue Mosque glittered in the sun, the famous minarets needled the blue sky, and here and there, like an oasis of calm in the constant growl of the city, lay broad peaceful squares where people took their ease with a glass of *cai* at café tables under the trees. Below snaked the Bosphorus—the route to Russia, one shore Asia, the other Europe, abuzz with fishing boats and ferries and big gray ships, the verdant hills on either side dotted with new villas and the palaces and wooden summer houses of a past century.

Boris Solovsky scarcely noticed that the spring afternoon was blue and cloudless, nor that he was in a city of breathtaking antiquity. He cared nothing for the gentle, smiling people crowding the sidewalks, nor the dark-eyed red-lipped women, chic in couture suits, being transported to smart lunches in smart limousines, and he had only a passing glance for the soldiers outside the Dolmabahçe Palace.

He had flown from Moscow to Ankara yesterday, ostensibly on a diplomatic mission to Turkey's capital, but later that night he had taken a private jet to Istanbul and his target. Genie Reese had escaped his agents in Washington; she had been on a flight to Heathrow while they were still tying up the guards at her house. In London she had taken a connecting British Airways flight to Istanbul, but this time the KGB had been waiting for her. As she walked from the airport terminal they had surrounded her, jostling her into a waiting car so fast she had no time even to cry out. A quick injection and she had slumped in the seat incapable of any further protest. Now Genie Reese, alias Anna Ivanoff, awaited his pleasure.

Boris permitted himself a smile of satisfaction. It was going to be the greatest act of pleasure in a life devoted to satisfying his baser instincts. She was the key to the final destruction of Alexei and Valentin Ivanoff.

Valentin focused his powerful binoculars, scouring the buildings opposite his room in a small, rundown hotel in the Istanbul suburb of Emirgan. He saw nothing untoward; no marksmen waiting on the roofs or lurking behind open windows. The street below was busy, jammed with buses spitting diesel fumes and ancient Chevrolets with stuttering exhausts. An old-fashioned tea seller, his silver urn strapped over his shoulders, padded down the sidewalk in pointed Turkish slippers; a street vendor was doing a roaring trade with peeled and salted cucumbers to cool throats parched from the city's dust; and at a café terrace a group of gnarled fishermen smoked hubble-bubble pipes and drank coffee that was stiff with grounds and sugar, gossiping about the old days.

It was a normal everyday Istanbul scene, far removed from the menace he knew lay in wait for him. But at least it told him he had a few hours' grace before the KGB heard he was here. His father, Sergei, had telephoned Washington last night and greatly daring, had said urgently, "Valentin, they picked Genie Reese up at Istanbul Airport. As you have worked so hard on this case, I am sure Boris would appreciate your help."

His heart sank as he thought about Genie and her announcement on TV. He knew she had as good as signed her own death warrant. He had gone straight to her apartment, cursing the rush-hour traffic that delayed him ten precious minutes, only to find the guards bound, gagged, and unconscious and no sign of Genie. The KGB had gotten there before him. He was certain they had not killed her yet because she had the information they needed. A discreet check with the airlines revealed she had taken a flight to London, then onward to Istanbul. She was somewhere in this city and he meant to find her. He knew that Boris would try to get her to Russia, and the easiest, most direct way was on one of the many Soviet ships that traversed the Bosphorus every day. She might be on any one of a dozen in the harbor. He decided to go take a look at them for any telltale signs of unusual activity.

An hour later he hailed a taxi and rode unhappily back to Emirgan. The Russian freighters in the harbor had been going about their business as usual with no extra guards or special precautions.

He sighed as he passed a restaurant, realizing he had not eaten in twenty-four hours. After telling the driver to take the route along the coast, he looked for a waterfront café. As they rounded the bend at Istinye, the great rust-red hull of the freighter the *Leonid Brezhnev* loomed in front of him. *And at the top of the gangway were two heavily armed* Spetsnaz *troopers.*

Valentin turned to stare at the big silent ship as the taxi drove on. He had stumbled across the very thing he was searching for. He was sure the special soldiers were there to guard a prisoner—Genie was on board the *Brezhnev* and if Boris was not already there, then he soon would be. Somehow he had to get her off. She would tell him who the "Lady" was—and he would do what he must do.

Ferdie Arnhaldt sat at a table by the large stone fountain in the courtyard of the Yesil Ev Hotel, sipping dry white Kavaklidere wine and waiting nervously for his contact. The man's lateness grated like sandpaper on his raw nerve ends, and his foot twitched in an unstoppable nervous rhythm as he glared yet again toward the arched entrance.

He looked as if he were about to explode, and the waiter standing on the steps leading into the pistachio-colored clapboard hotel watched him anxiously. Arnhaldt drained his glass and the waiter hurried to refill it, but he shook his head, flapping his hand at the man, waving him away like an irritating fly. The boy shrugged as he walked, puzzled, back to his post by the kitchen. His customer had been there for three quarters of an hour, staring at the entrance to the courtyard as if expecting a miracle to happen. He guessed he was waiting for a woman, and he thought she must really be something to cause such tension.

But ten minutes later when the customer's companion finally arrived it wasn't a woman, it was a squat, overweight Turk with a large mustache and a cigarette dangling from the corner of his mouth. The Turk glanced at him coldly and demanded a *raki.*

"Well?" Arnhaldt asked, his face a mask of anger.

The Turk shrugged. "In Istanbul the traffic is always hell. It is impossible to be anywhere on time."

He swallowed the *raki* in two gulps and nodded to the waiter to bring another. "This little exercise is costing you a fortune," he added truculently. "I have a dozen men watching the airport, the Kazahn villas, and the *yali*. A day-and-night watch."

"Get on with it," Arnhaldt hissed. "And if it's costing me a fortune you had better have results."

"You can be sure I do." He lighted another cigarette, enjoying his moment of power over this wealthy, important man. "Mr. Steel," he called himself. He was sure that was not his proper name but he was not interested enough to find out his real one. He was paying good money and that was all he cared about. He intended to take him for every Deutschmark, especially now he could deliver the goods.

Arnhaldt's foot beat its nervous rhythm again as the Turk sipped his *raki* and said, "The KGB agents were at Ataturk Airport yesterday, a dozen of them—a very large number, I thought, for such a small operation."

Arnhaldt's fist banged on the table, upsetting his glass, and the young waiter came running. "*What* operation?"

"Why, just to pick up one girl—a blond, pretty American."

Arnhaldt frowned. He was in Istanbul to follow up the Kazahn connection, but now it looked like the KGB had beaten him to it.

"There were a couple of CIA guys there too," the Turk said, blowing smoke rings into the air, "but they were too late. The Russians hustled her into a car before they could even turn around. They followed her. And we followed them."

"Where to?"

"The boatyard at Istinye—or what's left of it. There's a Russian freighter. The *Leonid Brezhnev*. A big bastard. Anyway, that's where she is. She never did reach the Kazahns so you can bet your ass that soon they will be looking for her too."

"She is on board the vessel?"

The Turk nodded and said with a grin, "There are soldiers on the decks and guarding the gangways. It would take an armored attack to get her off that boat, Mr. Steel. My guess is the captain will wait for nightfall and slip away under cover of darkness. Head back to Russia—it's an easy trip." He glanced curiously at his employer. He was staring silently into space, his foot still swinging its nervous rhythm.

"Looks like they've got you beat," the Turk offered, tossing back his third *raki*. But the German still stared silently ahead.

"I have found out something else that will interest you," he added, "something important. More important than the price you paid me."

Arnhaldt's eyes were murderous as they met the Turk's, and the man felt a prickle of danger up his scalp. The German's hand slid inside his jacket as if reaching for a gun, but it was a fistful of Deutschmarks he took out and thrust across the table.

"That should be enough for any man's greed," Arnhaldt said coldly. "But I warn you, it had better be worth it."

Pocketing the money, the Turk leaned closer and whispered, "The Kazahn connection you mentioned. I looked into it. There is only one daughter, Ahmet Kazahn's girl, Leyla. The other cousins are all older and married and live in Turkey. But there was another girl that old Tariq Kazahn always used to call his daughter—a young American girl who lived most of the year in Los Angeles and spent every summer with them. Her name was Anna Adair."

The name meant nothing and Arnhaldt stared at him impatiently.

"I called a contact in L.A. and had him do some research. He called me back an hour ago. Anna Adair is the step-granddaughter of the old-time movie tycoon C. Z. Abrams. Her mother was the actress Ava Adair. She works as a television reporter in Washington, D.C. He faxed a photo of her—and one of Ava Adair."

He put the faxes on the tablecloth and Arnhaldt stared at them. "She changed her name," the Turk said. "Now she's called—" "Genie Reese."

"Got it in one, as the Americans say." The Turk grinned. "What next, Mr. Steel?"

Arnhaldt's mind clicked everything into place as smoothly as the bolts of a safe into their electronic locks. His only hope lay in the Kazahns. They were a proud, loyal family, and once they knew she had been abducted and was in danger, they would act. "Keep watch on the freighter," he told the Turk quickly, "and double the watch on the Kazahns. Contact me here *immediately* if there is any action. And I mean *immediately*—not an hour later."

"Yes, sir!" He stood up. "You know it'll cost you," he said cockily.

Arnhaldt eyed him coldly. "And it will cost you—dearly—if you let me down."

The Turk eyed him uneasily as he left. There was something unpredictable about the German, a brooding violence that he suspected could erupt at any moment.

Arnhaldt watched him go and then he went to his room and looked up the telephone number of Michael Kazahn. He wrote it down on a slip of paper, then walked fifty yards from the hotel to the café square in front of the Blue Mosque.

As usual it was crowded with touts selling carpets and leather jackets to the tourists and small dark-eyed urchins trying to make a quick profit selling postcards no one wanted. After ordering a glass of *cai,* Arnhaldt inspected the scene, searching the crowd until his glance fastened on a young boy, maybe eight years old, a string of postcards dangling from his hand and an anxious look on his face. Raising his hand, he called him over and bought the cards for the six hundred lire the boy asked, even though he knew he would have taken less.

"You like leather jacket?" the kid asked eagerly. "I know best place for buy."

Arnhaldt shook his head. "You speak English?"

"Sure I spik. All Turkish boys spik Engleesh, French, Italian." He grinned and added, "*Some* words I spik."

His eyes widened as Arnhaldt placed a ten-thousand-lire note on the table. He backed off a step or two, afraid of what he wanted, but his eyes were still fastened on it.

"I need to make a telephone call," Arnhaldt said slowly, "but I do not speak Turkish. I would like you to make the call for me. To this number." He showed the boy the paper. The child looked at it and nodded. "You ask for Mr. Michael Kazahn. All you say is 'Anna is on the *Leonid Brezhnev* at Istinye.' You repeat this message twice and then put down the telephone." He looked anxiously at the boy. "You understand?"

"Sure." His head nodded up and down like an overeager puppet, his eyes still on the big-lire note that was more than he could ever hope to make in six months, even if he worked at the carpet factory.

"Repeat it," Arnhaldt commanded.

"I ask for Mr. Michael Kazahn. I tell him Anna is on the *Leonid Brezhnev* at Istinye." His hand hovered over the note.

Arnhaldt's fist closed over it first. "*After* the telephone call," he said.

The first telephone booth was out of order, and the second. "I know a shop," the kid said, heading back up the street and into a small grocery. A tiny goat nibbled at Arnhaldt's heels as the boy ran in, handed over his token, and asked to use the phone. Arnhaldt kicked away the goat, watching as he dialed the number and asked for Michael Kazahn. There was a wait and then the boy said his message excitedly in Turkish, repeated it quickly, and slammed down the telephone. He emerged from the shop, holding out his hand, and Arnhaldt slid the note into his sticky palm.

"Thank you, thank you, sir. You very good," the boy called after him as Arnhaldt strode quickly away.

All he could do for the moment was wait.

Refika Kazahn noticed that her husband's hand trembled as he put down the phone. He walked to the window of their big modern hilltop villa and stared down at the Bosphorus, bustling with ferries and the day-to-day business of European and Russian shipping.

Refika watched him, a little frown of anxiety creasing her brow. She knew Michael Kazahn's every mood: Earlier he had been angry, excited, full of nervous energy, but now, after that telephone call, he looked a deeply troubled man. More than that—he looked like an *old* man. Age was something he never acknowledged, but it was a fact. They had grown old together, and their long marriage had been one of two strong individuals bonded by a deep love and respect for each other. In all those years she had never once referred to the fact that he had a crippled leg; he had always ignored his disability and therefore so had she. It had never mattered. Like his father, Michael was dynamic, larger than life, and his strange swinging walk only added to his vivid character. She watched him pityingly as he searched for his cane and then limped back across the room and sat down heavily beside her.

He said quietly, "The telephone call was from a boy. He said Anna is on the *Leonid Brezhnev* at Istinye. Obviously someone paid him to give me the message."

Refika stared at him anxiously. "But *who*? And *why*?"

"I wish I knew. They must have abducted her from the airport as she arrived." He groaned. "Why didn't she telephone and tell us she was coming? How the hell am I going to get her out of this one?"

"You cannot do it alone," Refika said quickly. "You need help. Call the foreign minister. Call the police. Call the *Americans.* Get her off that boat, Michael, or for certain they will sail to Russia with her tonight."

Michael stared at the portrait of his father and mother on the opposite wall. Tariq looked fierce and proud in his naval uniform and the diminutive Han-Su as fragile as a Chinese sparrow in her *cheongsam.*

"What would you have done, eh, Father?" he bellowed. Then he laughed. "You would have listened to your wife, Han-Su," he answered, "just as you always did." He smiled at Refika. "And I should always listen to mine."

He telephoned Ahmet, told him quickly what had happened, and asked him to come over right away. Then he made three other rapid calls. Within half an hour four men arrived for a meeting at the Villa Kazahn: the foreign minister, Malik Gulsen; the chief of police, Mehmet Keliç; the American consul, Jim Herbert; and Ahmet Kazahn.

Refika sat quietly by the window overlooking the Bosphorus, listening to their conversation. Her face was calm but inside she was in a turmoil. Anna was like one of her own children, and if anything happened to her she would die too. If only the foolish girl had come to them they would willingly have given her the money for Missie and none of this would have happened. But Anna had always been a stubborn child, proud of her independence and the career she was carving out for herself. She glanced anxiously at Michael, noticing the change in him. He was no longer the broken old man of an hour ago. He was upright, charged with the old electric energy that had carried him through a lifetime of crises. If anyone could get Anna back, Michael could.

Gulsen, the foreign minister, said worriedly, "It is true the Russian freighter is in Turkish waters and subject to Turkish maritime laws, but if we are to confront them and insist on a search as you wish, Michael, we must be very sure the girl is on board. If we are wrong this could cause a major international incident—one that Turkey does not need."

"I have had the ship checked. There are armed guards at the top of both gangplanks and they are wearing Russian army uniforms. *Spetsnaz* uniforms." Michael's voice rang out with confidence. *"I am sure."*

The American consul, Jim Herbert, sighed. "The girl is an American citizen. Something must be done to find her. But as Gulsen pointed out, none of us needs an international incident. If those are *Spetsnaz* troopers then they are obviously there to guard something —or someone—very important. Either way, I think Turkey has a right to ask a few questions. I'll speak to Washington and take instructions."

Michael pointed to the telephone. "Call now, Mr. Herbert. There is no time to be lost."

"Anna arrived on a British Airways flight from Heathrow," Ahmet said. "She passed through immigration and spoke to one of the customs officers who knows her. He watched her leave but lost sight of her in a crowd of men. They seemed to be jostling her. He walked across to see what was going on but by the time he got to the doors, she had gone. He just assumed she had taken a taxi and left." He added quietly, "There is no doubt the Russians abducted Anna from the airport. You all know the reasons why. The next logical thing for them to do would be to take her back to Russia. What easier way than by freighter? They travel up the Bosphorus to Russia every day of the week. No one thinks twice about it. It's obvious they will wait for nightfall and then try to slip away unnoticed."

They glared at Jim Herbert, who had returned from his phone call subdued. He looked grave as he told them of the events in Washington and that Cal Warrender of the State Department was already on his way there and should arrive late that night. He hesitated—he wasn't about to disclose the presence of American CIA agents on Turkish soil—and said only, "Washington agrees that the girl must be on board the *Brezhnev*. They offer full support in any action Turkey wishes to take, though naturally they will respect your feelings in the matter."

"It seems to me that if we are to stay away from an international incident, it would be better to let the police deal with this matter," Chief Keliç said crisply.

Gulsen nodded thoughtfully. "Maybe we could give the Russians an out by saying we think one of the sailors has smuggled a girl on board. If they return her, nothing more will be said about the matter."

"And if they don't?" Michael asked.

He shrugged. "Then we must insist on a search." He sighed. "We will try the civilized approach first and pray we do not have to go further."

Gulsen was a tall man but, even so, Michael towered over him. "I am giving you warning," he said tersely, "that if you fail I shall take matters into my own hands. Anna must be found *before it is too late.*"

The four men stared at him in silence. They knew what he really meant was *"before she is killed."*

Gulsen glanced inquiringly at the police chief. He nodded and said quietly, "You have my permission to do whatever is necessary."

Michael and Refika watched as the men filed from the room and then they looked at each other. "Well?" he asked.

She nodded, "It is as you said. If their plan does not work you must take matters into your own hands."

Genie opened her eyes. At least she thought she had opened them, but it was just as dark as when they were shut. She blinked but it made no difference. She twisted from side to side searching for light, but there was nothing. Pain rippled through her head and she groaned, struggling through the layers of fog swirling in her brain to understand why she could not put her hands up to touch it. But it was no good, her brain just didn't seem to be working.

It was hot and airless and the darkness pressed against her eyeballs. Her spine crawled as she remembered all the old horror stories about nuns buried alive behind stone convent walls and of people suffering from a rare form of paralysis, unable to scream as they were placed in their coffins and the lids nailed down. . . .

Her screams sounded small in the blackness, thin with terror, but no one came running to help her. There was no one to hear her. Sobbing with fear, she tried to sit up, but her hands were stuck behind her and her feet joined at the ankles in a most peculiar way. . . . And then it dawned on her: *She was tied up.*

She lay back exhausted, searching for a breath of fresh air in the fetid darkness, but it was like breathing cotton. Tears pricked her eyes as she struggled to remember what had happened. At first all she could recall was getting off the British Airways flight from Heathrow; then, as her head began to clear a little, she slowly unscrambled the sequence of events.

She had arrived at her decision to tell the truth about the "Lady" on television because she knew it had all gone too far. People were being killed, and she was afraid not only for her own life but for Missie. She also desperately wanted to keep her promise to Cal, her promise to help her country. But before she did anything she needed to see the Kazahns personally to warn them what to expect and also to ask Michael's advice about the little matter of the several billion dollars inheritance in the Swiss banks. She had thought about the money a lot since she discovered its existence. She knew what she wanted to do with it, and Michael would know how to go about it. And besides, she had known she would be safe with them.

Her family would look after her. But her plan had gone all wrong and now she was a prisoner.

She still didn't know how it had happened. She thought she had thrown everyone off the scent by skipping onto the London flight instead of going back to her apartment, but somehow they had caught up with her. All she remembered was the men in dark glasses crowding her at the airport and then nothing else until she woke up here. Wherever *here* was.

She frowned, puzzled. Something strange seemed to be happening to the floor—it was rocking slightly, a familiar movement, something she remembered from holidays on the Kazahns' yacht and in sailboats off Rhode Island. . . . Of course, she wasn't buried alive —she was on board a ship! She strained her ears into the silence, listening for the sound of engines, but there was nothing—not even the slap of waves against the hull, and she guessed they were at anchor. But where? Was she in Istanbul? Or Russia?

She concentrated on her surroundings, feeling the floor with her hands and discovering bare wooden boards. She rolled over, biting her lip as the ropes cut painfully into her flesh, coming to a stop against a wall. It felt cold under her touch, like metal . . . steel. . . .

She jumped as a footstep sounded close by. *Someone was coming down a ladder.* Frozen with fear, she stared into the pitch darkness.

A key rasped in the lock and the room was suddenly filled with light so bright it burned her eyes. She squeezed them shut as pain zigzagged through her head.

"So?" a harsh voice said in heavily accented English. "You are awake at last, Anna Adair."

Anna Adair. . . . She hadn't used that name in years. She hadn't wanted her mother's notoriety to tarnish her own young life any longer. She was eighteen, just starting college, and she had wanted to start her new grown-up life as her own person, not as her scandalous mother's daughter. Besides, there was always the lurking fear that she might turn out just like her. Missie had told her she was being silly, that she wasn't a bit like Ava Adair, but the fear had still been there and changing her name seemed to put it all a little farther away. She had chosen the name "Reese" from the first college textbook she had bought. And that's who she was, Genie Reese. Her own name and nobody's heiress—not even to their dread diseases of the mind. None of her friends at college ever knew she was Ava Adair's daughter, and she had remained Anna only to Missie and the Kazahns.

The man with the harsh voice hauled her onto a chair, forcing a glass against her lips. "Drink," he said coldly.

She peered at him through slitted eyes.

"It's only water," he said contemptuously. "Drink it, so we can talk."

He tilted the glass and cool water ran down her face. With a sudden terrible thirst she began to drink, but after a few sips he removed it, laughing mockingly.

"Sit up," he commanded. "Let me look at the face of Prince Misha Ivanoff's granddaughter." His eyes devoured her in the long silence. Then he laughed suddenly. "A pity you did not inherit your grandmother's beauty—nor your mother's. But they tell me you are clever, with a keen mind, so I suppose it is some compensation not to have inherited their insanity."

His heels rang on the wooden floorboards as he began to pace the small room, and she blinked her eyes, trying to adjust to the light.

"Who are you?" she asked, her voice a hoarse whisper. "Why am I here?"

"Do you not know?" He perched on the edge of a small table opposite her and she could make out his bulk, his bald head, his arrogant posture, the folded arms. And then quite suddenly, as if surfacing from a pool, her vision cleared and she could see the flat face, the small eyes under the lowering brow, the jutting jaw and cruel mouth twisted into a smile.

"Surely you must know who I am?" he said. "Or who I represent?"

She nodded. "Russia."

His snatch of laughter was mocking. "I am Marshal Boris Solovsky, head of the KGB."

"Solovsky?" She stared at him, puzzled.

"Ah, the name rings a bell! Yes. . . . I am uncle to the handsome Valentin, the famous diplomat." She trembled as he leaned forward and took her by the shoulder, thrusting his face next to hers until she breathed his stale breath, saw the open pores, the scar beside his mouth, and the insane gleam in his eyes. Then he reached out quickly and gripped her right breast, squeezing hard. She screamed but he only twisted harder.

"Good," he said, satisfied. "Now we can begin."

Valentin parked the perky black Ford Scorpio in the lot at Yildiz Park and walked through the woods to a vantage point overlooking the Bosphorus. Massed banks of bright spring tulips striped the grass with color and the sun dipped in a glowing orange ball over the water. As he watched he thought about Genie.

The sun soon disappeared leaving a grayish light and he turned and made his way back to the car. It was only a few minutes' drive to Istinye, but by the time he got there it was almost dark. He parked behind a crane at the far end of the small dock and checked the Luger in the holster under his armpit. Then he took the compact Micro-Uzi submachine gun from his briefcase and examined that. It was lightweight and small; with its butt folded it measured only 250 millimeters and was compact enough to fit into his jacket pocket. And it could fire 1,250 rounds of lethal 9-mm cartridges a minute. Pocket death. After leaving the car unlocked, he walked the 150 yards to the *Leonid Brezhnev.*

There were two gangplanks, one amidships leading to the holds and one at the stern leading to the bridge and the crew's quarters, and there were two guards on each. As he walked to the stern the soldiers stepped forward, their carbines pointing at him.

He saluted and said in Russian, *"Spetsnaz* Major Valentin Solovsky, here to see the captain." The men relaxed their trigger fingers, saluting back, but they looked at each other uncertainly and he knew they were under orders to admit no one. Taking a chance, he called out that his uncle, Major-General Solovsky, was on board, and this time one soldier came down the gangplank and asked to see his identification. He inspected it carefully, then quickly saluted. Valentin stared coldly at him. He knew his commanding attitude and his superior rank had done the trick. They were going to let him on board.

"I will escort you to the captain, sir," the soldier said respectfully.

He told them not to bother, they should stay on guard, he would find his own way.

He could feel their eyes on his back as he strode along the deck and prayed they would not get nervous and change their minds. Still, if he were their commanding officer he would have had them court-martialed. It was more than a *Spetsnaz* soldier's life was worth to disobey an order.

He found the captain alone in his quarters, eating his evening meal and drinking Turkish beer from the bottle. He was a heavy-built, rough-looking man, whose normal job—plying his freighter between Russia and Libya—was a matter of routine, requiring little brainpower, and he was already out of his depth with his important visitor, Major-General Solovsky of the KGB. He stared at Valentin, his mouth open in astonishment.

"Who the hell are you?" he demanded, slamming down his beer.

Valentin's lip curled. "On your feet," he commanded. *"Spetsnaz* Major Valentin Solovsky."

The captain lumbered quickly to his feet, wiping his mouth with his hand. "Sorry, sir," he mumbled. "I was not expecting anyone. . . . The orders were that no one was to be allowed. . . ."

"Except me," Valentin said angrily. "When will you people ever get things right? I am here to see my uncle, Major-General Solovsky."

The captain's eyes widened as he caught the connection. "Yes, sir, of course, sir," he said fawningly. "I will take you to him myself."

"No need." Valentin glanced at the enormous steaming plate of brownish stew. "Finish your meal. Just direct me to him."

As he walked quickly through the ship he heard the crew talking and knew they must have been confined to quarters so they would not glimpse the important Russian they had on board. But there were no KGB agents or guards around, and he guessed that Boris had decided the fewer people who knew he was there the better. He wanted his visit kept top secret.

He made his way down a spiral staircase into the bowels of the ship. It sat high in the water, rocking gently under his feet, and a single electric bulb showed that the holds were empty. To the left of the stairs was a small office with the door firmly shut. As he had guessed, there were no guards, and from inside he could hear Boris talking.

The door was unlocked. He strode in and came face-to-face with his uncle. Behind him, sitting on a wooden chair, her hands and feet bound, was Genie.

"Valentin!" Boris's expression flickered rapidly from amazement to fury to satisfaction as he stared at him. "I won't ask how you got here. But I suppose you might call this a *family* occasion, so come on in." He laughed harshly. "This is a moment I have been waiting for. *A moment to treasure.*"

Valentin closed the door behind him. Genie's desperate eyes stared at him, but she said nothing and he ignored her. Leaning against the wall, he folded his arms and said, "Well, Uncle Boris, it looks as if you beat me to it."

"What did you expect?" he replied, his lip curling disdainfully. "Did you think you could outwit the KGB? *And* me? You forget, Valentin, who you are dealing with. You forget my power. *You forget I know everything.*"

Boris took a step toward him. His piggy eyes were murderous, and Valentin felt the thrill of fear a prisoner must feel waiting to have Boris Solovsky practice his polished little games of torture on him, but with a contemptuous shrug he strode past Boris to Genie. She was wearing jeans and a black T-shirt and she looked very pale except for a red handprint on her cheek where Boris had slapped her. She stared at him mutely. "Are you afraid she will run away, Boris?" he asked, "Or do you always tie your women this way?"

"Do not imagine you can rile me, Valentin," Boris replied coldly. "The girl is tied because she is my prisoner."

"Not for much longer." Valentin made himself comfortable in Boris's chair, his feet arrogantly on the table. "I telephoned the authorities, anonymously of course, and I think the Turkish police are about to pay you a visit. And that's only a preliminary. Next comes the American government, then the Turkish government, the FBI, Interpol, the CIA. . . ." He stared mockingly at Boris, whose face had turned to stone. "This little escapade has all the makings of an international incident, Uncle. And I'm just wondering how you are going to feel when they discover that the head of the KGB is aboard a Russian freighter moored in Turkish waters. *And* that he has the missing American girl tied up on board. It will make headlines in every newspaper! 'The Shame of the Russian KGB—Major-General Solovsky, Caught in the Act of International Kidnapping.' Apart from the trouble to our family, I am just wondering how our president will react. What do you think, Uncle Boris? Is he going to forgive you for the disgrace you have brought on Russia?"

"You are lying. No one else knows she is here."

"Of course they do. Do you take them for fools? Do you imagine they wouldn't figure out that the easiest thing is to smuggle her onto a ship and take her back to Russia? So? What is your next move?"

Genie stared at Valentin, lazing back in his chair, then her eyes swiveled nervously to Boris, standing by the door. His bald head shone under the naked light bulb and his heavy frowning face was set in angry lines.

"We shall sail at once," Boris decided.

Valentin shook his head. "Go on deck, Uncle. Take a look. There is already a cordon around this ship."

"Do you really expect me to believe all this?" Boris laughed contemptuously.

"You should, Uncle. It is the truth. But I have a suggestion to save you. You and I could walk off this ship together. I will get you on a private jet to Ankara. You can be out of this mess in less than an hour, if you wish."

"And I suppose I just give you the girl?" He laughed mockingly. "How can you take me for such a fool? Surely you know your 'uncle' better than that." He prowled the tiny cabin, his hands behind his back, chuckling mirthlessly. "Your trouble is that you are an idealist, Valentin, and idealists always want to keep their cake and eat it too." He glanced shrewdly at Valentin. "But not quite idealistic enough to think of *Russia* first. All you really want is to save your own skin—and your father's."

"And what do you want, Uncle?"

"Me?" He walked over to Genie and stood in front of her, his hands behind his back, swaying up and down on his built-up heels the way he always did when he wore his jackboots. "I want to achieve my life's ambition. To destroy you both. *At last.*" Throwing back his head, he began to laugh, insane, uncontrollable laughter. Tears squeezed from his eyes and he coughed, turning purple as he began to choke.

Genie glanced, terrified, at Valentin as he eased the Luger from the holster and slid on the silencer, and her eyes and mouth rounded in alarm. He shook his head, putting his finger to his lips.

Boris heard the familiar *click* of a safety catch and spun around. He stared contemptuously at the Luger. "You would never get away with it," he said with another snort of defiant laughter. "On a *Russian* ship? If you kill me you'll never get off here alive—nor will she." He grabbed Genie and held her in front of him. "You will have to kill her first," he added with a triumphant smile.

Valentin shrugged indifferently and took aim, "It would probably make things easier if I did just that," he said thoughtfully. "In fact, I could probably take you both with a single shot."

Genie slumped forward, half fainting with terror, and Boris tugged her angrily upright again. She stared at Valentin in horror. She had thought he had come to her rescue and now he was going to kill her as well. Her head swam and she trembled as Boris tightened his grip.

"There is a way out of this," Valentin said quietly. "You can walk off this ship with me now. We take the girl with us. I guarantee I will get you to the airport and onto that private jet back to Ankara. It is waiting on the runway now. You will be out of this international mess and no one will be any the wiser. Of course, if you choose not to . . ." His finger tightened on the trigger and Genie suddenly began to scream.

Boris thrust her back into her chair. Perspiration was trickling down his forehead. He licked his lips nervously, his small, treacherous eyes flickering around the cabin, searching for a way out.

"You have five seconds," Valentin said coldly. "One . . . two . . . three . . ."

"Very well, I agree." Boris's voice was pitched high with fear as he held up a hand, palm outward, to stop the deadly count. "I will do as you say. But how do I know you will keep your word?"

Valentin shrugged. "Trust me," he said coldly. "Untie the girl's bonds."

As Boris's hand went to his pocket, Valentin jammed the revolver into his ribs. "I need my knife!" Boris shouted. The jackknife blade flashed under the harsh light of the electric bulb and the gun pressed against his temple as Valentin said quietly, "Just the rope, Uncle. . . ."

Sighing, he slit the thin rope at Genie's wrists and ankles. She moaned as the blood pumped painfully back into her hands and feet.

"Give me the knife, then put up your hands," Valentin commanded. Boris did as he was told, standing stiffly while Valentin frisked him, removing the heavy Colt that was his favorite weapon.

"Rub your feet, Genie," Valentin ordered. "You must get the circulation going quickly. You will have to walk by yourself."

She rubbed her raw ankles, searching the floor for her sneakers and forcing them onto her swollen feet, that were still burning with pins and needles. Valentin kept the gun trained on Boris, who was staring at it with the fascination of a cobra at a mongoose.

"You will go in front of me with Genie," Valentin told him. "You will tell the guards that we are leaving. We will walk down the gangplank together and at the bottom we will walk toward the crane a hundred fifty yards on the left. Make no mistake, I will be right behind you. I will not take my eyes off you. And at a distance of two feet, I cannot miss."

Boris's mouth tightened but he made no reply, smoothing his

bald head in a nervous gesture. His eyes darted from side to side as they stepped into the hold, searching for a sailor or a guard, anyone who could raise the alarm, cursing as he remembered that he had confined the crew to quarters until they sailed. He climbed the spiral steel ladders, glancing behind him once and meeting Valentin's stare. Hate burned his guts. Valentin was just like his father. *He finally had both Ivanoff children together and he would see them in hell before he would let them get away.* He would bide his time, take care, be alert for an opportunity. . . .

The troopers at the gangplank snapped to attention as they appeared. Boris spoke to them quickly and they saluted and stepped aside. Valentin was two steps behind them as they filed down the gangplank, his hand on the Luger in his pocket. The area around the ship was shrouded in darkness, and as they walked away Boris felt the thrust of the gun in his ribs. He could hear Genie moaning as she stumbled along behind him.

After ordering Boris into the backseat, Valentin gave Genie the gun. "Sit next to him. If he makes a single move, pull the trigger. You can't miss."

Boris smiled confidently as he saw how her hand shook. Now he knew he had his chance. "I didn't know you two knew each other," he said silkily. "It just goes to show what a small world it is."

As Valentin switched on the engine Boris said, "Don't you think it's odd, Valentin, that you knew her? That the answer was right there in Washington all this time?"

Their eyes met in the mirror and he gave a snort of laughter as he realized Valentin didn't know what he was talking about. "You didn't know," he marveled. "You *still* don't know, you *still* don't understand. . . ."

The Luger thudded against his ribs and Genie said, "Shut up, you bastard, or I'll kill you right now."

"Are you all right?" Valentin asked.

She turned to look at him and in that split second Boris thrust downward on her hand. There was a dull *plop* as her finger slid nervously on the trigger but the bullet passed harmlessly through the floor of the car, and then the Luger was in Boris's hands. He held it to Valentin's neck, the sweat trickling down his bald head into his collar, one eye on Genie shrinking back in the corner, ready to kill her if she moved. "Get out of the car," he ordered. "Start walking back to the ship. If you try to run away, I'll shoot."

She hesitated. She knew it would take Boris only a second to switch the gun from Valentin to her if she tried to run. A second was all she had to save herself and Valentin.

"*Hurry!*" he screamed. "*Move!*"

She half turned as if to open the door and then flung herself recklessly on the hand holding the gun. The Luger dropped to the floor again. Shouting a string of curses, Boris pushed her away and bent to pick it up. His fingers had just closed around the gun when Genie stamped on them as hard as she could.

Valentin was out of the car and hauling Boris out by his collar. He pinned him against the door, lashing a sideways chop to the carotid artery at the left of his neck. Boris's eyes spat hatred for a moment before they glazed and then he slumped silently to the ground.

Genie limped around the car and stared down at him. She licked her lips nervously. "Is he . . . ?" she asked in a small, frightened voice.

Valentin nodded. "It was the only way," he said tiredly. "Me or him. That's the way it has always been. Now it's over."

She looked about to faint and he put his arm protectively around her shoulders. "I'm sorry."

"That's okay. It's just shock, I guess. And my foot. I thought it was going to explode when I stamped on him."

"Sit in the car," he said quietly. "I have to take care of him."

She climbed into the passenger seat, watching numbly as Valentin slung Boris over his shoulder and disappeared into the darkness. A few moments later she heard a faint splash, then the sound of his hurrying footsteps as he returned to her.

The Scorpio's engine was still running. He slid it into gear and swung around, heading in the direction of the city. As they joined the evening traffic four police cars sped past them, blue lights flashing and sirens blaring, heading toward Istinye. She turned to watch them. "Are they really going to the freighter?" she asked.

He smiled wryly. "I concocted the story for Boris's benefit, but it turned out to be true."

He cut across the hills, past the smart hotels, and down through Taksim Square. Genie was trembling with shock. It all looked so familiar, so normal. If it were not for Valentin she would still be on the freighter, still at the mercy of that evil man. . . .

Valentin fought his way through the traffic jam at the Galata Bridge, heading for Eminonu; he cut through the back streets behind the Spice Market and stopped outside a sleazy hotel with a green neon sign proclaiming it the Hotel Tourist. The sign had all the *T*'s missing and it was the kind of cheap rooming place where there was no desk clerk after seven in the evening and guests were expected to let themselves in and out. It suited Valentin's purpose better than his earlier room at Emirgan.

He put a helping arm under Genie's shoulders as she limped across the pavement. "Two flights of stairs," he said, picking her up. "You'll never make it."

She clung to him like a frightened child, burying her face in his neck. Valentin had saved her. He loved her. He would call Michael and soon she would be back home and she would never do anything as stupid as this again. She just wished Cal were there too so she could confess what a fool she had been and ask him to forgive her for causing so much trouble.

45

The American air force C21A, a six-seater twin-turbo fan jet, dropped from an altitude of 41,000 feet through the clouds clustered over Turkey and landed at a small airfield north of Istanbul. It had been a long flight from Washington's Andrews Air Base with only half an hour on the ground for refueling at Gander, Newfoundland, and again at Upper Heyford in England. The pilot turned and grinned at Cal. "Feel any better?"

"Sure. Now we're on the ground." He unbuckled his seat belt, sighing with relief as they taxied toward a concrete apron to the left of the runway. "I feel like I left my breakfast back in Washington just a couple of hours ago."

"You'll wish you did when you get a loada that Turkish food," the pilot commented. "Tripe soup. Yuk. Watch out for the eyeballs."

"I thought they only served that stuff in Arabia." Cal laughed as he shook hands.

"Y'never know." The pilot gave him the thumbs-up sign, grinning.

"Thanks for the ride," Cal called as he turned away.

Men in greenish uniforms were running toward him waving guns and he decided he'd better stay where he was.

"Identification?" The officer in charge held out his hand while his sidekick covered Cal with a rifle.

He handed over his diplomatic passport and a copy of his special briefing from the White House, waiting quietly while the officer inspected them.

"Very good, Mr. Warrender," the Turk said in perfect English. "We have a helicopter waiting to take you to Istanbul."

He could see the C21A refueling for his return trip to Washington as he walked across to the helicopter. It was a small camouflage-green bubble with open sides and Cal groaned. The aerobatic rapid-transit flight in the air force jet had been more than enough for his vertigo. Somebody should have told them he hated heights.

The baby-faced pilot saluted and he groaned again, closing his eyes as the rotors began to whine: The Turks had *kids* flying these things, for God's sake. . . .

He didn't open them again until fifteen minutes later when the pilot said, "Sir, we are coming in to land." Istanbul lay below him, lighted by a full moon and strung with a million sparkling lights, and he heaved a sigh of relief; getting to grips with the KGB would be nothing compared with this trip.

A long black Mercedes limo was waiting on the tarmac and inside it were the American consul, the Turkish foreign minister, and Ahmet Kazahn.

"It's not looking good, Cal," Jim Herbert said after the introductions were completed. "The chief of police searched the freighter and found only half a dozen Russian troops. Of course that is a grave offense—foreign soldiers on a cargo ship in Turkish waters—but it didn't further our cause any."

Cal's heart sank; he had been *sure* she was on the ship.

"But we *know* she was on there," he said angrily.

The foreign minister nodded. "Pretty sure. The captain claims he knew nothing, just that they were to expect an important visitor—maybe an admiral—hence the troops." He sighed. "I ask you, a Russian admiral visiting a rusting old freighter, what excuse will they think of next? But the police did find some pieces of rope in a small cabin in the hold. They had obviously been used to tie someone up and then cut off."

"Then how did they get her off the ship?"

He shrugged. "We had a flotilla of powerful speedboats surrounding Istinye, so it could not have been by sea. The police were delayed by a bus that got stuck trying to turn a tight corner, blocking the only through road. They must have arrived just minutes too late."

The telephone buzzed and he picked it up. "Gulsen," he said, nodding as he listened. "You are sure?" he asked in Turkish. "There was identification? I understand. Thank you."

He turned to the others and said quietly, "The police have fished a man's body from the water near Istinye. He was wearing a dark suit and all his personal effects—wallet, wristwatch, et cetera—had been removed before he was put into the water. But he has been positively identified from photographs as Major-General Boris Solovsky."

"Jesus H. Christ," Herbert said into the silence.

"That's probably who he thought he was," Cal commented gloomily, "or some sort of self-made god."

"You can only imagine the problem this presents for Turkey," Gulsen said angrily. "The head of the KGB murdered in Istanbul."

"It seems to me," Ahmet said quickly, "that the first problem is to find Anna. Someone killed Solovsky and helped her to escape. It must be someone she trusts."

Cal's eyes met his as the Mercedes swung into the courtyard of the Villa Kazahn.

Cal nodded. "Of course," he said. "I know who she is with. Valentin Solovsky."

Michael Kazahn scanned the group of men standing around drinking whiskey and filling his beautiful room with cigarette smoke, listening gloomily while Cal explained what had happened. He was sitting beside Refika on the long divan under the window, and she put her hand over his as Cal told them they believed Anna—or Genie, as they all called her—was with Valentin Solovsky.

"Missie never told Genie the full story," Cal said. "She never knew about the money in the Swiss banks. She didn't even know about the jewels until Missie was forced to hand them over to her when she went into Fairlawns, and she *still* doesn't know about the mines. Missie always downplayed the Russian background. She never showed her the old photos or talked about it much at all. She wanted it all forgotten so that when she died, the story—and the threat—would die with her. She was keeping her promise to Misha right to the end.

"Valentin is as dangerous as his uncle Boris," he concluded quietly. "He is a career diplomat with his eyes on Russia's highest position, and so far he has let nothing stand in his way. There is no reason to believe he will now. The last thing he can allow is for Genie to go on TV and tell the truth. He is looking to kill Anna Adair and he believes Genie will lead him to her. All we can do now is pray that in some misguided moment, believing he is her rescuer, she does not confess everything to him and tell him who she really is. Because there is only one ending to that scenario."

"And what do you propose we do now?" Michael demanded, limping over to the police chief. "After you have bungled the raid on the ship and lost her? Are we supposed to wait around while your men get stuck in traffic again? Or do you have some master plan you haven't told us?"

"It was not our fault." Keliç blustered, red-faced. "Istanbul's traffic is notorious. Even our own prime minister's motorcade gets delayed. . . ."

"Bah!" Michael limped back to Cal. He leaned heavily on his ebony cane, staring hard at him, assessing him. "You know her," he said finally. "What do you think she is likely to do?"

Cal hesitated. He was thinking of Genie's meeting with Valentin in Geneva and her odd behavior afterward. He was finally forced to face the painful truth. "Valentin is a handsome, charming man," he said quietly. "Genie is . . . attracted . . . to him and I believe he is to her, but that would not be enough to stop him killing her if he knew who she really was. I think all we can do now is wait and let the police try to trace them. And we must pray that she telephones you."

Refika met her husband's eyes across the room and she knew what he was thinking. *He was thinking of Tariq's pledge of loyalty to the Ivanoffs—and that he had let his father down.*

Ferdie Arnhaldt's face was a mask of fury as he slammed down the telephone in his room at the Yesil Ev Hotel. Genie Reese had escaped and the Turk had lost them in a traffic jam at the Galata Bridge. If he had the bastard here now, he would strangle him. He would enjoy watching his eyes pop out of his stupid, mercenary face. . . .

He flung back the fringed velvet curtains with shaking hands and peered into the busy nighttime street. She could be anywhere out there, anywhere at all, with the man who had rescued her. "A young man," the Turk had said, "foreign. Maybe American."

He prowled the room, irritated by its smallness and the pretty Victorian decor. He needed the vastness of Haus Arnhaldt to contain his rages. He wanted to get out of there, to stalk the streets looking for his prey as he had Markheim and Abyss—but he had been stymied by the Turk's incompetence.

The telephone jangled again and he leapt to pick it up. *"Ja?"* he said quickly.

"A limo arrived ten minutes ago at the Villa Kazahn," the Turk said. "We have identified three of the men in it as Ahmet Kazahn, the Turkish foreign minister, and the American consul. The fourth is unknown but I'd guess he was American too. He arrived at the airport by army helicopter. The chief of police got here five minutes later."

"Watch the house," Arnhaldt said icily, "and next time do not wait ten minutes to tell me. I want to know *immediately* they leave —and where they go. If you let me down again, you idiot, there will be no more money."

He slammed down the phone, pacing the room again, trying to figure out who Genie was with if it wasn't Boris Solovsky. After ten minutes he could stand it no longer. He left the hotel and walked quickly to his rented car parked a block away. He was taking no more chances with the Turk: He was going to watch the Kazahns himself.

=== 46 ===

Genie lay on the bed watching as Valentin took off his jacket, then washed his hands in the tiny washbasin in the corner of the room.

" 'Will these hands ne'er be clean,' " she quoted softly.

He grimaced. "Lady Macbeth, washing off the blood after the murder." Their eyes met and he added, "It's not difficult to kill, Genie. I was trained for it. But it is not something I enjoy. With Boris Solovsky I had no choice. My father is a man of integrity and honor and Boris was out to ruin him and to glorify himself in Russia's eyes. I love my country and all she stands for, but I also love my father."

She made no reply, her eyes following him as he picked up his jacket, took the Uzi from the pocket, and placed it on the table. It gleamed under the light like a small, malevolent creature, and a shiver ran down her spine.

After flinging down his jacket, he sat next to her. "Do you feel better now?" he asked, putting his hand under her chin and tilting her face toward him. "Are you in pain still?"

He looked at her raw, bleeding ankles and swollen feet. "Poor Genie," he murmured tenderly. "You just didn't know what you were getting yourself into, did you?"

He went to the sink, filled a bowl with water, and, kneeling in front of her, began to bathe her wounds. "I must go to the pharmacy," he said worriedly, "you need antiseptics and pain-killers." He sat on the bed again and put his arms around her. "I've never felt like this about anyone else," he said softly.

She shook her head. "Nor I, Valentin. What would I have done without you?"

He was kissing her eyes, her ears, her hair, her mouth. She was filled with tenderness for him, he was her savior, her ally, her lover.

It was so easy, so natural, so real that he should make love to her. . . .

She had no idea how much time had passed when she awoke: an hour, two, maybe more. Valentin was sitting at the table cleaning the gun. The light shone on his blond hair and he looked like a beautiful child absorbed in a toy. A lethal toy.

He lifted his head and smiled. "You must be hungry." He slotted the metal stock onto the Uzi and put it back on the table.

She shook her head. "I think I'm beyond hunger. I don't remember when I last ate, maybe on the plane . . . I don't even know how long ago that was." She felt light-headed, disoriented. "Valentin, what do we do next?"

He pulled over an upright wooden chair and sat in front of her, his eyes fixed on hers.

"This time I need *your* help, Genie," he said quietly. "I have to find the 'Lady' before the KGB or the CIA."

She looked at him, puzzled. "But I thought you knew."

"*You* are the only one who knows."

It suddenly dawned on her. *Valentin did not know who she was. He still thought she was just Genie Reese, the hot-headed TV reporter who had gotten herself in too deep on the trail of a career coup.* Her heart sank and she said flatly, "Is that why you rescued me from Boris? So I would lead you to the 'Lady'?"

"I admit it was one of the reasons," he said carefully, "but you know it was not the only one."

She looked at the gleaming gun, just lying there waiting for this man to turn it into an instrument of death, and her mouth went dry with fear. *She suddenly knew beyond any doubt that when Valentin found out he would kill her.*

"Time has run out for me," he was saying quietly. "Remember the saying, Genie, a life for a life? I saved yours—and now I'm asking you to save mine. *I must know.*"

She closed her eyes, shutting out the evil shape of the gun, but it was still there under the blackness of her closed lids. "I . . . I don't really know who she is," she said quickly, "I . . . well, I was supposed to call a certain number when I got here. Someone who knows her. . . ."

"*Who?*" he demanded eagerly. He leaned closer, grasping her hands tightly. "*Who knows?*"

She took a deep breath and looked him in the eye. "*Michael Kazahn,*" she said shakily.

He nodded. "That makes sense. The emerald was sold by one of the Kazahn companies. I investigated their background; the family is originally Russian and worked for the Ivanoffs."

"They have been protecting her all these years," she said, hurriedly embroidering her story. "Michael Kazahn contacted me because he thought things had gone too far. He wanted to put a stop to the international speculation. He said it was safer if her identity was known . . . before someone found her and—" She bit her lip, praying he would believe her. "She is at their villa."

He lifted her hands to his lips. "Thank you, Genie."

His eyes were full of tenderness and she thought he didn't look like a murderer. He looked like Valentin, the man she loved . . . but in the back of her mind she could hear Cal Warrender telling her, *"Valentin is a Russian first, and a man second. Never forget that."*

She bowed her head, tears trickling down her cheeks, and he said, "I'm sorry, Genie, really I am."

He rearranged her pillows and kissed her gently, then he walked to the table and picked up the Uzi. She stared at him, eyes dark with terror. She didn't want to scream, she didn't even want to run. He was going to kill her, after all. It was inevitable.

Valentin folded the metal stock, fitted the compact little submachine gun into his pocket, and put on his jacket.

"Get some sleep," he said quietly. "I'll be back as soon as I can." A smile lighted his handsome boyish face. "And then life can get back to normal." He strode casually to the door as if he were going on a hunting trip. "Just you and me."

The door closed behind him and she heard the key turn in the lock. Then she heard his footsteps disappearing along the corridor, and she turned her face into her pillow and sobbed. But she wasn't crying in relief, she was crying because she was in love with a man who wanted to kill her.

After a while she sat up and mopped her eyes on the worn sheet. She got out of bed, walked to the window, and looked out. It was dawn. The black Ford Scorpio was gone and the hotel sign blinked above the empty street. Turning back into the room, she thought about Missie's warnings and how, through not heeding them, she had brought about their destruction. Because she knew with a terrible certainty that once Valentin found out the truth he would kill Missie too. And she had to get out of there! She had to get help!

She remembered all the clever tricks with locks and credit cards she had heard about, but her purse had been lost when she was abducted. She had nothing, not even a hairpin. She prowled the room, searching for some kind of tool to open the door, and in a frenzy of despair she grabbed the handle, shaking it angrily, wailing like a madwoman. With a crack like a pistol shot the handle came off in her hand and the door suddenly sprang open.

For a moment she was too stunned to move. Then, pulling her wits together, she stepped cautiously into the corridor. It was as empty and silent as if she were the only guest. She ran to the stairs and stopped to listen. Everything was quiet. She hurried down the first flight, listening for footsteps again before fleeing down the remaining stairs and letting herself out onto the street.

There was still no sign of the Scorpio and she breathed a small sigh of relief as she hobbled in the direction of the Hippodrome, keeping an eye open for a passing taxi. But the big square, usually packed with tourists, was deserted this early. She glanced around uncertainly at the shadows. She had no idea where the nearest police station might be and she thought wistfully of Cal, wishing he were there to help her. Why, oh, why had she not told him the truth earlier? She had always known she could trust him. She wondered whether if she was lucky enough to survive, Cal would ever trust *her* again. The only thing to do now was call Michael. Michael would come for her. Michael would save her.

Valentin watched her from across the square. He had tried to get to the Kazahn villa but the road leading to it was blocked by police cars and he had been forced to make a quick turn before they stopped him. He was driving back up the side street to the hotel when he spotted Genie in his mirror. He parked the car half a block away and followed her. He had not expected her to try to escape. He had thought she trusted him and he watched her sadly, trying to decide whether to grab her now or wait to see where she led him. She was jiggling the phone up and down but it was obviously out of order and she hobbled to the next one, but that too was out of order. She put her head in her hands, her body drooped in an attitude of defeat, and he thought how sad it was she had deceived him. Poor Genie. Poor, reckless, lovely girl.

Genie looked desperately around for help but there was no one, and she hobbled north through Sultanhamet Square, searching for an early café where she could make a call, praying for a taxi . . . anything . . . anyone. . . . She passed the old water tower at the top of deserted Yerebatan Street and paused outside the Sunken

Palace. Through the glass entry doors she could see an office—*and a telephone.* After picking up an empty beer bottle from the gutter, she hurled it through the glass, watching numbly as it shattered into a thousand fragments at her feet. Then she ducked quickly inside, grabbed the telephone, and dialed Michael's number. "Pick up, oh, please, Michael, pick up," she begged, sobbing with fear, sagging with relief as he answered on the fourth ring. "Michael, oh, Michael," she cried, "it's Anna!"

He said quickly, "Don't try to explain. Just tell me where you are."

"The *Yerebatan Sarayi.* I broke the glass door to get to the phone—"

"Wait right there. I'll come and get you. Are you all right, Anna? Were you followed?"

"Yes . . . no . . ." she answered wildly. "Oh, Michael, I'm just so scared."

"I'm coming to get you right now. Hide in the cisterns where no one can see you. I will be there as soon as I can."

There was a *click* as he put down the receiver. Glancing nervously over her shoulder, she did as he had told her. But as she pushed through the turnstile and walked down the steps to the Sunken Palace, she felt as if she had just cut off her lifeline.

Outside, Valentin leaned against the wall, his arms folded and a look of pain on his face. She had spoken in English to Michael Kazahn; he had heard every word she said. Genie was Anna. She was his cousin. *Genie* was the "Lady" he was looking for.

"It was her," Michael said to Refika. "She has escaped her captors. She is waiting for me at the *Yerebatan Sarayi.*"

A look of relief crossed her face and then she said anxiously, "You must call the police. There is no time to be lost."

He shook his head. "No more police. This time Michael Kazahn is in charge." He limped across the room to the display cabinet by Tariq's portrait, unlocked it, and took out the ancient Tartar sword.

Refika stared at him, aghast. "What are you doing?" she demanded. "You are dealing with murderers, men with powerful guns, and you buckle on an antique sword as if you were going into battle with Genghis Khan."

"I am a man of peace," Michael said quietly. "There are no modern weapons in my house. This sword saw my father through many a battle with the Russians and now it will do the same for me." After picking up his cane, he limped to the door. He stopped and gave her one last long look. "I will return," he said, "with Anna."

Refika heard the front door slam behind him and then the sound of the car's engine. She ran to the window, watching as the taillights disappeared down the driveway, then with a little moan she covered her face with her hands. She felt like a wife sending her husband off to war. After a moment she ran to the phone and called Ahmet and told him what had happened.

"I am leaving now," he said quietly. "I will be there with the police. Mother, I want you to call Cal Warrender and Malik Gulsen and tell them what's happening. Do you know their numbers?"

She nodded. "Yes," she whispered, tears raining down her face. "Please, Ahmet, hurry."

Michael waved away the police blockade impatiently. "Out of my way," he roared. "I have important business."

They stepped back respectfully as the big silver Bentley Turbo roared down the hill, then the officer in charge hurried back to his car to report to headquarters that Kazahn Pasha had left in a hurry.

Ferdie caught the Bentley in his powerful binoculars as it wound its way down the hill. He was in the empty gas station forecourt across the main road, and he switched on the ignition, gunning his engine, waiting for the Bentley to reach the coast road. He smiled with satisfaction as the car skidded to a half stop at the intersection and then swung quickly right toward Istanbul. Michael Kazahn was in a hurry, and he bet he knew why. As he pulled out onto the coast road after him, he thought that the long wait had been worth it.

There was a single light over the stair leading down to the old cistern, and beyond it lay inky blackness. Genie closed the door behind her and walked slowly down the stone steps. Her feet throbbed painfully and the cuts on her ankles were bleeding again. She hesitated at the edge of the tiny pool of light, peering into the blackness before taking a tentative step forward. It was almost as bad as the cabin on the ship, only here the air felt moist and she could hear water dripping.

Istanbul was riddled with underground cisterns. The Basilica was one of the oldest, built by the emperor Constantine to store water brought in by aqueduct from the forests of Belgrade and kept here for emergencies like siege or drought. The monolithic Byzantine and Corinthian columns supported a vaulted brick roof, and the cistern was so grand it had become known as the *Yerebatan Sarayi*, the Sunken Palace. In the old days men had explored it by boat, but now the constantly seeping water was kept to a depth of less than a yard and wooden walkways had been built to make exploration by tourists easier.

Genie remembered visiting it when spotlights had illuminated the eerie columned aisles and grottos, and the solemn music of Bach played over loudspeakers had made the old legends of men lost in endless underground tunnels and carried away by mysterious currents seem just what they were—legends. But now, as she stood in the dark on the concrete platform leading to the walkways, she could believe them. She thought of Cal, thousands of miles away, probably wondering what had happened to her, and she was swept by a sudden longing for his reassuring presence. She would give anything to see his steady red-setter eyes smiling into hers, to hear him telling her everything would be fine, there was no danger. And she would believe him, because this was not his doing, it was hers. It was she who had played a dangerous game, she who was responsible for her own fate. And now she was all alone.

She took a cautious step forward, her hands held out searching for a wall, testing the ground in front of her so as not to take a tumble into the murky water three feet below. Her fingers connected with a guide rail and she felt the wooden planks of the walkway. Keeping one hand on the rail, she stepped bravely forward into the dark, slowly following the path over the water until at last she came to a dead end. With a sigh of relief she sank to the floor, legs crossed, hugging her arms around her for warmth. The blackness pressed against her eyelids and the silence clamored against her straining ears as she began silently counting off the seconds, waiting for Michael to come and save her.

She had almost reached three minutes when she heard the sound. She stiffened, straining her eyes vainly into the darkness. It had been less than ten minutes since she had called Michael, and that was not enough time for him to get from his villa to the center of Istanbul. The patch of light near the steps was out of her vision around a corner, and from where she sat all was in darkness. She listened again but there was only the constant sound of dripping water, and she relaxed a little. She must have been mistaken. Her head drooped with weariness as she began counting—ten, twenty, thirty, forty seconds—and then she heard it again. Only this time she knew it was a footstep. And she knew it was not Michael's—he would surely have called out to her.

Panic flooded through her. She pressed her hands against her mouth to stop herself from screaming.

"Genie?" a man's voice called. "I know you are in here. Tell me where you are. I need to speak to you."

It was Valentin. She hid her head in her arms, thinking of how their bodies had entwined as they made love only hours ago, of how happy she had been in his arms, how safe she had felt, and she shook her head disbelievingly. Valentin had found her—he was going to kill her. And now even Michael Kazahn could not stop him.

"Genie, answer me," he pleaded. "I must talk to you before it's too late. We must stop before this whole thing blows up into a big international disaster. Answer me, Genie, please. I'm *begging* you."

He sounded so concerned, so desperate, so *tender,* she could almost believe him, and she quickly reminded herself of who he was:

Valentin Solovsky, a Russian, nephew of the head of the KGB whom she had just seen him murder. A trained killer who "did not enjoy it" but murdered when he must.

Genie hid her face in her hands and wept silently. It was only a matter of minutes before he found her—and then it would be all over.

Valentin picked his way by the beam of a tiny flashlight, cursing himself for not having a stronger one. It would be a slow job to find her like this, and the one thing he did not have was time. He guessed Kazahn would be there with the police within the next five minutes.

He swung the tiny beam around, illuminating snatches of dank vaulted walls and massive half-submerged columns. "Genie," he called, his voice echoing eerily through the cavern, "please talk to me. There's something you must know." He waited for a moment and then said, "Very well then, just *listen* to me. I know now it was you I was looking for. But what you don't know is *why* I was looking for you."

Genie hugged her knees tightly, hiding her face as the silence fell again. "Genie, my father's name was once Alexei Ivanoff. He is your mother's brother. I am your cousin, your blood.—"

She buried her face in her arms. She wanted to shut her ears against his lies, to scream at him to stop it.

"My father was saved from the forest at Varishyna by Grigori Solovsky. He brought him up alongside his own son, Boris. Boris hated him. He knew who he really was and he wanted to destroy him, but to carry out his plan he needed proof of Alexei's identity. *You* were to be his proof, and that is why I had to kill Boris Solovsky. I am telling you the truth. Please believe me, Genie. I did it for you." He waited for a long moment and then said with a sigh, "I cannot tell you how sorry I am about this. I just wish it had never happened."

She jumped as the door at the top of the steps suddenly crashed open and Michael's voice called, "Anna? Are you there?"

She heard his uneven step on the stairs and thought of Valentin, waiting in the darkness to kill him.

"Michael," she screamed. "He's here, waiting for you, he'll kill both of us!"

Valentin sighed as he took the Uzi from his pocket and unfolded the stock. Kazahn had stepped into the pool of light and was glaring contemptuously into the dark void in front of him. Valentin shook his head sadly. He was just a white-haired old man. Life was so unfair. As he clicked the cartridge into position, he spotted a shadow. Someone else was coming down the stairs, a man holding an automatic pistol. His eyes narrowed as he recognized Ferdie Arnhaldt.

Ferdie paused halfway down the stairs, his gun trained on Kazahn. He had no compunction about what he was going to do. He had already killed Markheim and Abyss, and he would kill anyone else who stood in the way of his plan. He intended that the Arnhaldt companies would control world armaments. Governments would fawn for his favors. They would all fear him. He, Ferdie Arnhaldt, would control world power.

Michael spun around as Ferdie called his name. "I suggest you tell Anna to come out here," the German said. "Tell her she has exactly one minute to make her whereabouts known or I will shoot you."

"You stupid bastard," Michael bellowed, unsheathing his sword, "do you think I am just going to stand here and let you kill her? The police are already outside. You are as good as a dead man."

Arnhaldt began counting.

"Stop it! Stop it!" Genie screamed, stumbling back along the walkway. "Please stop, I'm coming."

Ferdie's head swung in her direction and, with a warrior's cry, Michael rushed at him.

The Uzi spat sudden fire, shattering the silence. With a look of surprise on his face, Ferdie Arnhaldt turned to see his assassin. And then he fell dead at Michael's feet.

Valentin ran toward them, the compact submachine gun at his shoulder, just as Genie appeared around the corner. "It's Solovsky," she screamed, warning her uncle. "He'll kill you!"

And then Michael raised his sword above his head and smote Valentin, just the way his ancestors had done in battle.

Valentin fell like a stone at his feet. Genie ran and knelt beside him. She stroked his blond hair back from his brow and put her hand over the gaping wound in his neck, trying to stanch the blood that was pumping away his life. "Why, Valentin? Oh, why?" she whispered, agonized, as her tears fell onto his cold hands.

His gray eyes were calm as he looked at her. "It was all true," he murmured, "I could never have killed you, Genie." A faint smile curled the corners of his mouth and his breath rattled in his throat.

And then the light went out from his eyes and she was looking at a dead man.

Cal was first down the steps in front of the police. The columned cisterns were now bathed in white halogen light. Some fool had pressed the wrong switch and the sounds of a Bach cantata echoed over the dark water. He looked at Arnhaldt's body and then at Kazahn with the sword in his hands and the Russian dead at his feet. It was like a scene of vengeance from the Bible. He stared at Genie weeping over the body of Valentin Solovsky and he shook his head. In a black-and-white world, the good guys were alive and the bad guys were dead. And that was the way it should be. Putting his arm comfortingly around her, he led her back up the stairs to safety.

=== 48 ===

It was a week later that Cal went to see Missie again. She knew what had happened but there was something else he had to tell her. And besides, he wanted to be with her when Genie went on television at six o'clock.

She was wearing a violet dress that matched her eyes. Her beautiful silver hair was immaculately upswept, and on the table beside her was the photograph of Misha Ivanoff.

She held out her hand to him and he brushed it with his lips as Nurse Milgrim bustled in with the Earl Grey tea.

"I hope you're not going to be upsetting her any more," the nurse said, standing by Missie's chair ready to protect her if he said one word out of line.

"It's all been said, Milgrim," she replied calmly. "It's all over now."

"Just one more thing," Cal said. "We picked up a report from the TASS news agency. It said that the wreckage of a small plane had been found off the Crimean coast. Moscow claims that the bodies of the two people on board have been identified as Major-General Boris Solovsky and his nephew Valentin. Their plane had been lost on a return flight from Ankara, where they had been on a diplomatic mission."

Missie nodded sadly. "Why must they lie?"

"It was agreed that it was the most diplomatic ending to the episode. Russia is embarrassed and has apologized to the Turkish government."

"Poor Alexei," she said, tears shining in her eyes. "He has lost his only son."

"TASS also reported that Sergei Solovsky has resigned from his position in the Politburo and has retired with his wife to his country *dacha.* The Soviet people mourn for him in his sorrow." He hesitated and added, "They are known to be a devoted couple, and we can only hope that they find comfort in each other."

"I should have told Anna," she said tiredly. "Maybe then none of this would have happened. Valentin would still be alive and Anna would not have suffered these terrible events." She shook her head slowly. "I thought I was doing the best for her. I didn't want to burden her with an old woman's fears."

"If it were not for you, Missie, America would have been on the losing scale in the balance of power."

"It's strange how the gypsy prophecy came true after all," she said, half to herself. "She told me a great responsibility would fall on my shoulders, but I never knew quite how great until now." She sighed. "And what about Ferdie Arnhaldt?"

"He was a megalomaniac, born into a family obsessed with their own power. First Eddie Arnhaldt wanted the mines because he was sick of paying Russia what he considered a ransom for the rights to them. I think he intended Azaylee to marry his son Augie as soon as she was old enough, and then no one could have disputed the Arnhaldts' claim. But Ferdie went a step further in his madness. He was prepared to kill anyone who stood in his way. Including Genie."

"Michael Kazahn saved her," she said. "He is a reckless and very brave man—just like his father."

"Genie tells me that the Kazahns want you to go and live with them in Turkey."

She nodded. "Michael telephoned. He wants to send his plane to fetch me; he has prepared a suite at his house, or I could have the *yali* and just sit and dream my days away on the terrace overlooking the Bosphorus. I can even take Nurse Milgrim if I want."

"And?"

She laughed. "I'm too old now for such changes. I am happy here with the lawns and the trees and the mallards outside my window. And besides, I have Anna."

Nurse Milgrim put her head around the door and said, "It's almost six, Missie. Time for the program."

Missie reached for the remote and switched on the television. There was an announcement and then the cameras switched to Genie, looking pale but attractive in a black dress and pearls, her blond hair pulled back into a velvet bow. Cal thought she still looked like a girl who would smell deliciously of Chanel No. 5, but she wasn't the same person he had watched on TV last time. She was no longer the jaunty upwardly mobile girl reporter on her way to a great career and what she was saying bore no resemblance to the snappy "journalese" of her previous reports. There was a sad look in her blue eyes and a faint tremor in her voice as she began to speak, and it was obvious she cared deeply about what she was saying.

"This story began long ago," she said quietly, "in a fairy-tale house called Varishnya, lived in by a fairy-tale family. The father was a handsome prince and the mother the most beautiful of all princesses, and they adored their two small children, Alexei and Xenia. And with them in this wonderful house lived their friend, a young English girl. . . ."

America watched, spellbound, as she plotted the story, showing photographs of the beautiful Ivanoffs, careful to say how everyone, including the son, Alexei, had been murdered and the only ones to escape were Xenia and the grandmother with their friend, the young English girl.

Tears stood in Missie's eyes as she heard Genie explaining her own long, turbulent life and her efforts to protect their identity.

"And she succeeded," Genie said, "until one foolhardy act brought the Ivanoffs back into the limelight. Suddenly everyone wanted to know who the 'Lady' selling the Ivanoff emerald was, and everyone wanted to find her. Because it seems those stories about the billions in the Swiss banks waiting to be claimed by the rightful heir were true. And there was one more thing the big nations wanted—the right to certain mines in Rajasthan that had been found to contain valuable deposits of strategic minerals."

She paused, shuffling her notes, and then she looked directly into the camera and said, "*I* am the 'Lady' they were looking for. My real name is Anna Sofia Yevgenia Adair. My mother was the Xenia Ivanoff who escaped from the forest at Varishnya all those years ago."

Cal glanced anxiously at Missie. She was leaning forward, chin in hand, listening intently as Genie told the story of Ava Adair and their lives. She went on to say that she had handed over the rights to the mines to the U.S. government and that with her billion-dollar inheritance she intended to set up a foundation to help the needy of the world, the refugees, the homeless, the starving children, as well as for education, and that she would be giving up her career in television to run it.

Missie gasped as Genie held up a photograph of her and said,

"But it is not me to whom America owes a debt of gratitude. It is Missie O'Bryan, because if it were not for her, none of this would belong to our country. Missie O'Bryan Abrams is the true 'Lady' America should honor."

The picture faded and the announcer thanked Genie and said there would be a discussion on the situation later that evening.

"So," Cal said, switching off the set, "everything worked out all right, after all." But Missie was staring silently at the black screen, lost in her own dreams. He added cheerily, "Genie will be here soon. Why don't we ask Nurse Milgrim for some tea while we wait?"

He pressed the bell and a few minutes later Nurse Milgrim appeared with a tray. She glanced doubtfully at Missie and then back to Cal.

"There's no need to be angry with Cal," Missie said quietly. "I'm just thinking about the past. . . ."

He watched her silently as the minutes ticked by on her little mantel clock, so many minutes, such a long, eventful life. He knew now where Genie got her spirit. Missie O'Bryan, one of life's great survivors, had taught her to meet the world head on and to follow her heart as well as her head.

He glanced up as the door opened and Genie's sad eyes met his. His heart lurched as she smiled gamely at him, tilting her chin at the old arrogant angle.

"Okay?" she asked quietly.

"You were great," he replied simply.

She walked over to Missie, and sinking to her knees, took her hand. They gazed at each other in silence and though neither one spoke, for a few moments Cal felt as if he were eavesdropping on their silent conversation. He knew they had no need for words.

Genie sighed as she rested her head on her "grandmother's" knee, and Missie stroked her soft blond hair lovingly.

She looked at Genie and then at Cal, and then she picked up Misha's photograph and looked at it for a long time.

"You know, Misha," she said softly at last, "sometimes I wonder whether it was all true. Did I *really* love you, and did you *really* love me?"

She replaced the photograph with a sigh. "And sometimes I ask myself whether I based my whole life on the romantic dreams of a young girl."

She sat back in her chair, her eyes closed, and Genie stroked her hand gently. She knew what Missie was telling her. That the past was the past. And life was for living. Her glance locked with Cal's —those lovely red-setter brown eyes—and she smiled.